Riddle of the Red Bible

A Riddle in Time

K.T. Jae

British Library Cataloguing in Publication Data: a catalogue record
for this book is available from the British Library.

ISBN: 10: 1478326867
ISBN-13: 978-1478326861

DEDICATION

To Cassandra and Caitlyn; without whom there would be no
heroine to make this story possible.
To Cris for everything.
To Chessie (the dog) for reminding me regularly that I need
to take a break and play.
To Mum.
To Dad

~ PROLOGUE ~

I love this house
(November; Eighteen years ago)

Many long nights of late had been occupied decorating the small box room of Mr and Mrs Nivots's newly acquired Victorian cottage; a dream first home positioned atop a hill within a leafy Hertfordshire suburb just outside London. They were a pretty ordinary couple who would spend their time (like most) doing pretty ordinary things. Cliff Nivots, a young English man in his mid-twenties, was perhaps the perfect specimen of normal; quite tall and slim with straight mid-length hair that swept fashionably across his forehead; although any fashion sense he had was definitely more of an accident. Bordering on that age where he would soon be a parent, his fashion choices would shortly be severely questioned by the next generation, but the more appropriate reasoning behind his hair style wasn't so that he could be 'down' with the latest trend. He was actually hiding his Vitiligo; a hereditary skin whitening condition that caused blotches to appear over most of his face. That affliction was perhaps the most unique thing about him, but to further disguise the ailment he would always sport some form of stubble on his face.

The married couple had not long exchanged vows, but soon they would both experience yet another normal occurrence and the very reason for their late nights and messed up body clocks. Like a sacred central possession in a highly revered shrine, the pride of place in their newly decorated room would soon be taken by their very first child. Yet as the subsequent years would prove, their only child was set to become anything but ordinary.

To pass the time while they prepared the new nursery, they had been disagreeing about something mankind has quibbled about for centuries.

'The bible is the most important book ever written,' said Mazel, a Filipino lady with a near perfect English accent having acquired the skill after many years spent in London performing as a teenager in various West End shows. Although she was slightly older than Cliff by a few years, she had always been a very fashionable lady, and to Cliff's annoyance, the age difference was never acknowledged because of her ever youthful and exotic complexion. If anything, he would often be declared as the older of the two.

'Well ... that may be true in terms of the bible's influence, but that certainly doesn't prove it was ever written by anyone other than a bunch of people who just wanted to control mankind, does it?'

Mazel looked at Cliff with a very familiar look of disdain which clearly revealed that she had obviously been through similar discussions with him many times before. 'Sometimes I wonder how we ever managed to get married, you atheist moron.' Mazel lifted her arm, and with her very large paint brush, she playfully painted his face a pale baby blue colour.

Cliff stood in disbelief with his eyes wide. 'Well I obviously was not attracted to your sense of humour that's for sure.' Although England was to some extent still very Christian, Cliff had never been christened nor baptised. 'You are very lucky to be with child right now or that would require serious punishment and repentance.'

'Ooh, I better hurry up and get this baby out then,' she said giving him a wink as she turned to resume painting the last wall.

'That almost sounds like you don't have an actual baby in there but some *other* type of weird creature.'

'Maybe it is - you never know. After all you are the father,' she said teasing him. 'Now let's get this baby decorated.'

Cliff shook his head disparagingly at her effort to be humorous and continued to place some decorative luminous stickers and stencils all over the walls and ceiling. The couple weren't sure of the gender of the impending birth, so they were trying to make it as neutral as possible. The ceiling was now covered with glow-in-the-dark stickers of stars and planets and the walls had rockets and spacemen. However, in the event it turned out to be a girl, the spacemen were coloured pink and purple.

'I know one thing,' said Cliff.

Mazel interrupted, 'That you have a baby blue face which makes you look like a ridiculous children's T.V. character.'

Cliff pulled her towards him and imprinted his painted face onto her t-shirt. 'Err ... that would be a noooo.'

Mazel giggled as she felt his face press against her large tummy.

'That this child, assuming it is human of course, be it catholic or atheist; boy or girl, will grow up to be a wonderful human being with the most rounded and grounded view of the world.'

Mazel smiled at his tender words.

'Oh, and if it takes after you, be the trickiest child the world has ever known ... and also become an astronaut ... or maybe a purple spaceman-'

'Ok I get it.' As Mazel playfully stopped him from overdoing the moment, the room lit up from an explosion of lightning. Mazel shuddered in shock and seconds later there was a tremendous crack of thunder. Squeezing Cliff tight she said, 'I love this house; I do. But being alone up on this hill can be a bit eerie at night. Promise me you'll never ever make me stay here alone.'

'I'll do my best, but at least you've got your cross to protect you,' he said with a smile.

Just as he finished his sentence there was a loud bang from downstairs.

Mazel edged closer and whispered, 'What the hell was

3

that?'

'It sounded like a door slamming. Did you leave anything open?

'No, I haven't opened anything today. It's been too cold. Go check it out,' she demanded with a forceful but nervous tone.

'But why would a burglar slam doors?'

'Maybe it's not a burglar,' she muttered with a deadpan expression. 'Maybe it's something else.'

Cliff grinned at her dubiously.

The sound of rain suddenly hammered against the window, as if a dam in the sky had just been opened. Almost immediately generating a raucous noise as it pelted against the glass. Mazel gasped and grabbed hold of Cliff's hand. 'I'm not staying alone.'

'Come on then. You've got your cross on though right?'

'Oh I get it; now you want to use my religion as a crutch for your fear,' she asserted sarcastically.

'I was asking for your benefit you fool.'

'Fool huh? Ok, well when I'm banishing the devil's creatures with it, you better not come running to me asking to borrow it,' she said with her eyes furrowed as they both exited the room.

Outside, the thunder continued with an ominous and foreboding energy; cracking with such a force that it even made the glass windows on the house shudder with fear. Thunder like that had rarely been experienced in England before and gave an undeniable sign to anyone with any kind of faith in a deity that something was coming.

Some ten minutes or so had passed before Mazel returned to the small bedroom having been temporarily assured of their safety after they both had a good look around and found nothing at all suspicious.

Cliff was still downstairs and with the first sign that everything was ok, he shouted, 'Do you want a cuppa tea?' Tea being the standard response in England after experiencing any form of stress, as it is believed that everything seems better after a nice hot brew.

'Sure, perfect,' she shouted as she entered the room. After living in Britain for such a long time, she had come to realise that there just may be something in that philosophy. However, as she finished responding, she was immediately taken aback by something that she hadn't noticed in the room before.

Over on the window ledge was a small porcelain figurine of Jesus Christ on a round base attached to a young girl with her back to him. Jesus was wearing a robe and was looking down at the girl who had her hands clasped in prayer. She was dressed in a pretty first communion dress; a flower garland was in her hair, and she had a soft and gentle expression on her face.

In a playful tone Mazel shouted, 'What the ... Hey, what is this for? Did you leave this here?' There was no reply from downstairs, so she walked inquisitively over to the window and picked up the figurine. Turning it upside down, she noticed a beautifully written inscription on the bottom that read:

Search and you shall find.
Together forever,
your father.

A tiny smirk appeared on her face. 'He's such a fool.'

At that moment Cliff walked into the room holding two mugs of tea.

Mazel held the mystery figurine out in front of her. 'What is this all about?'

Cliff looked dubiously at the figurine and said, 'I don't know. What is it all about?'

'Like you don't know.'

'I really don't ... I didn't put it there,' he insisted.

'You can't really hide it after what you wrote. You don't need to pretend. It's a lovely thought you know. You do realise this is for a first communion though not a birth, right?'

'I honestly wouldn't know coz it didn't come from me. I've been with you the whole time remember?'

Mazel walked towards him, grabbed her tea with the other hand and pointed at him with the hand that was holding the figurine. 'You ... are such a tricky man, but I guess that's what I love about you. Just don't be embarrassed. I'm sure the little one will love it.' She took a sip of her tea and then exited the room.

Cliff stood alone and remained still for a brief moment. He then pursed his lips; furrowed his brow; shrugged his shoulders and said, 'Crazy woman.' Nonchalantly, he took a sip of his tea and resumed his stencilling.

~ CHAPTER ONE ~

Mr Time
(September; Thirteen years ago)

Time was ebbing away, hour by hour, minute by minute and second by second. The hands of the clock on the wall seemed like they were moving at a snail's pace.

Courtney Nivots, a very cute, half English-half Filipino five year old girl, was lying alone in her small but cosy bedroom. She had long dark brown hair; a small button nose that turned up slightly at the end and unusually for an oriental she had huge dark brown eyes. Her skin was naturally tanned and to set the whole image off, she was dressed in her favourite red Japanese style set of pyjamas. A white trim went all the way around and there was a dragon stitched on to the breast pocket. If someone was to draw a picture of her, she would not look out of place in a Japanese comic book. However, with her strong and distinctive London accent, she could not be mistaken for anything but English.

Feeling very restless and fidgety, she lay on her bed looking up at the stars and planets on the ceiling whilst contemplating something that she had been thinking about for a long time; something that was clearly bothering her and obviously had been for a while.

Her ceiling really was a spectacle for any young mind to ponder; a wonderful sight. It was a sort of homemade planetarium that had clearly been created lovingly for her by someone special.

The door to her bedroom opened and Mazel walked in. Courtney quickly turned over and grabbed her duvet to pretend she was asleep.

'You're not quick enough,' snapped Mazel. 'I saw that, and I know you're still awake.'

'But I can't sleep mummy,' whined Courtney in her delicate soft voice as she spun around to face Mazel.

'I don't care, this has to stop. You need to get to sleep. You can't continue to stay up like this or you will not grow tall and beautiful, remember?' She leaned over the bed and stroked Courtney's hair gently, before giving her a kiss on the forehead.

'I'll try mummy, I promise.'

'Thank you sweetheart, your dad would be proud. You don't think he would want you up all hours of the night do you?'

The expression on Courtney's face dropped upon hearing the mention of her dad.

'Ok, now get to sleep. Now pray to your father, I know he's watching over you, and I'm sure he'll help you close your eyes.' She pulled Courtney's duvet up tighter and then walked towards the door.

'Mummy?'

Mazel stopped and turned to face Courtney. 'Yes?'

'Will he ever come back so I can meet him?'

'He's watching over you my darling, and he always will be. He loves you very much, and one day I'm positive that you will see him again.'

'Why did he have to die then?'

'We all die at some point I'm afraid, but we go to a better place, so there is nothing to worry about. He may not have ever met you, but he spent many nights talking to you in my tummy, so there'll always be a part of him embedded inside you.' She blew Courtney a kiss and then closed the bedroom door.

Courtney knew however, that as comforting as her mum's words were, she couldn't sleep just yet. Something else in her room had emerged as the thing that kept her mind on overdrive each night, and it was not what anyone would have expected a child of her age to be fixated with. Hung on the wall at the end of her bed was a rather large clock that had been specially designed to help young children learn to tell the time. Everything needed for the task was labelled largely and clearly. Hours, minutes and even seconds as well as indicators for half past, quarter past and quarter to. Ever since it was placed there it had become her friend, and she had been totally mesmerized by it over the years. Whispering to the clock she said, 'You're such a good friend to me do you know that? In fact, you're my only friend. Just make sure you never stop. Can I count on you to do that?' She paused for a while. 'Shall I tell you a secret, hmmm? Your heart ticking all the time is the only thing that *does* help me to sleep.' She pondered more as she cuddled her only other friend; a stuffed cuddly toy tiger.

The ticking was relatively loud, so she constantly heard it, whether she was awake or asleep; mainly due to the fact that it had been there right from the day she was born. The sound had been permanently embedded into her brain and had become such a part of her that even if it were to stop it would relentlessly continue in her mind as an imprinted memory. She would even sometimes put her tap shoes on and dance merrily to its rhythm. However, that night she had a different agenda

'We've got big plans tonight you know,' she said decidedly. 'I hope you're ready. I've been racking my brain about this moment for a long time. Do you want to know what I've come up with?' She looked at the face of the clock as she would whenever she spoke to it and would see shapes in the position of the hands that would give her different facial expressions that answered her questions. Night after night for months on end, she had racked her young but imaginative brain in preparation. 'Right, now listen up ok. This is going to be quite monumental, and not just for us, potentially, for the whole world. You do know what monumental means don't you?'

Courtney's mind was particularly advanced for her age. People would often comment on her vocabulary and understanding of things, and tonight was no different as she lay scrutinising and pondering whether she had figured out one of mankind's biggest questions; how do you turn time backwards? It was a notion she had been fascinated by since she was told that her father passed away just before she was born due to his *ticker* suddenly stopping.

'We're going to go back and meet my father.' She scrunched up her face in anger. 'Don't look at me like that. I've been dreaming about this forever. I want to know what it will be like to travel back and meet with him and maybe ... have a conversation. I'm convinced I've gotten to the bottom of this. Something big is about to happen, so make sure you're ready. I don't want you stopping in the middle of it all.' The expression on her face was that of wonderment, excitement and confusion, all rolled into one; with a little bit of panic thrown in for good measure.

She only had a lamp on for light, and it was very dark outside her window; way past her bedtime. She sat watching the seconds hand as it passed around the clock, edging closer and closer to midnight. *Thirty – thirty one – thirty two – thirty three.* She continued to stare as if she was waiting for something to happen. 'Fifty five – fifty six – fifty seven,' she whispered in unison with the seconds hand that was constantly ticking like a time bomb. She was anticipating the moment everything would change until - that moment arrived.

When the hands finally positioned themselves at twelve o'clock, she stood up. Her whole body was drenched in sweat, anxiousness and excitement as she walked to the end of her bed to the piece of silver plastic and mechanics that had transfixed her for so long. Outstretching her index finger, she jammed the hands of the clock, stopping them from proceeding any further. 'Don't worry, this shouldn't hurt.' Closing her eyes tight in preparation for the big moment, she slowly pushed the hands backwards around the face of the timepiece and simultaneously began to swing her head around in a pendulum motion with each full circle of the clock, building up a unity between her and the timepiece. The harder she concentrated, the more intense the speed became as she moved the hands and her head faster and faster.

At the point where she could not go much quicker, she raised her head toward the ceiling and squeezed her eyes tight in concentration, but all the while she continued to swing her head around and around; relentlessly pushing the hands of the clock backwards to build up the specific speed she needed. 'Don't give up on me – we're nearly there.' She had somehow come to the conclusion that if she managed to reach eighty eight revolutions per minute, it would happen. She could not remember how she came up with that number, but she was convinced it was important somehow.

However, all the spinning and concentrated energy, along with her constantly swinging head, had suddenly made her very dizzy. 'This is it,' she whispered. 'This is the moment.'

The rush of blood and chemicals to her brain caused her to topple backwards onto her mattress, almost hitting her head on the wooden frame that surrounded the bed.

As she lay flat on the mattress, eyes closed and attempting to regain her composure, she very slowly and tentatively opened her eyes to see when exactly she was. As her vision adjusted after the rush of blood to the head, she was faced with a very disappointing and familiar sight. Above her was the same ceiling full of stars and planets that had been there when she started. 'Hang on,' she said in realisation. 'Of course, I *would* be in the same room. But maybe I've gone back a few days, or even a few hours; that would be a start,' she exclaimed excitedly and hopefully to herself.

Slowly, she leant over toward the digital alarm clock that was on top of her chest of drawers. Her eyes were wide in anticipation of the pivotal turning point in her life. 'Six minutes past twelve. September the seventh,' she remarked with a disappointed tone. 'Oh dear, another attempt bites the dust.'

Although it was hard to accept, she took it in her stride and rolled onto her back, giggling to herself. It wasn't her first rudimentary attempt at being the first to time travel. 'I know we've tried on numerous occasions Mister but don't worry, keep your chin up, and we'll get there. I promise.'

As much as she undoubtedly had an unusually large intelligence and comprehension of things for her age, she knew she was ultimately still a child and was not quite ready to start a new epoch just yet. She may know more than her mother on most academic subjects but innocence dictated that despite these advantages, she still needed help with the simple things like washing her hair and making a sandwich. So for the moment, time travel was a little out of her reach; still something only possible in the movies. Deep down Courtney was well aware of that having seen every single one of them on the subject; she just desperately needed something that would mean she could avoid having to sleep, and what better way than coming up with a new time travel theory each night; her favourite fantasy but one that was now over, for that night anyway.

Right on cue, and with a melancholy smile, she once again realised that she had no choice but to try to get some rest. 'Ok, Mister Time ...,' she whispered as she lay looking at the ceiling. '... I may be too young for you right now, and you may have beaten me once again, but I promise I'll figure you out one day my everlasting friend and companion.'

~ CHAPTER TWO ~

Search and you shall find

After cosily lying on her bed for a while trying to get to sleep, Courtney suddenly remembered she had forgotten something. So she quickly sat up, knelt at the edge of her bed, raised her arms and clenched her hands together. Before starting her prayer though, she reached down and grabbed hold of a very familiar item, the small porcelain figurine of Jesus Christ that resided upon her window ledge. Although the whole figurine was only about the size of Courtney's hand, it meant more to her emotionally than any other possession in her life.

The funny story of how it had mysteriously appeared in her nursery a few days before she was born and with a heartfelt message inscribed onto the bottom, had always been relayed to her by Mazel. Courtney had always assumed that the inscription was written with some kind of knowledge by her father that he knew he was going to die. She never thought that he killed himself, and nobody ever implied that either; she just thought he somehow instinctively knew, and just before his time came he must have had a panic attack that maybe heaven is real and so quickly had to do something to make sure he would be let in. Mazel told Courtney that she had mocked him for such a sentimental and slushy gesture but that he had denied it using his most innocent voice. Even with that glimmer of doubt, it still meant more to her than anything. Life had dealt her such a cruel and early blow;

taking away the treasured and precious moment of being held in your father's arms for the first time. As a result the figurine was now clung to with great devotion, since she carried with her the knowledge that her father had once held it in his hands. So whenever she touched it, she believed she was touching a part of him and didn't want to think about the idea of anything ever happening to such a precious token.

Clasping the figurine tightly she closed her eyes to pray. Afterwards, she opened her eyes and leaned over to carefully place it back on the desk, but as she did, the worst possible thing happened as her hand knocked against the side of the bed, causing the figurine to fall perilously towards the wooden floor. Her eyes widened in panic, but she was too scared to look over the edge of the bed to see if it had broken. Instead, she collapsed onto her mattress, pulled the duvet closer to her and huddled up tight. All of it was done in a split second, only giving her time to scrunch up her face and wait for the inevitable crash. Yet that moment never arrived, and her pained expression turned into a look of confusion. *How could that be?* Almost immediately her expression turned to fear, and for a girl of darker complexion, her skin turned unusually pale. *Oh no*, she whined in her head. *What's going on? Surely that should have smashed, why didn't that smash?*

Although she should have been relieved, she was too scared to look over the bed to check what had cushioned its fall, as she was actually panicked by the idea that something more unnatural could be happening in her room. So she closed her eyes and began to speak the words that had been repeated to her by her mother since the day she was born. Mazel believed it helped keep bad dreams and spirits at bay, but her beloved figurine was missing to aide in the prayer now. She never prayed without it and was very scared that Mummy would severely scold her if it was broken. Yet what was worse than the idea of her mum scolding her was the thought that evil spirits could enter her room now that the figurine was no longer in her hand to protect her. 'Angel of God, my guardian dear, to whom God's love commits me here. Ever this day be at my side, to light and guard, to rule and guide. Amen.' She rushed through the protective prayer so she could quickly go to sleep and not have to think about what might lay ahead.

However, Courtney was unknowingly about to experience just what she had been praying to banish – a truly frightening phenomenon, and something that would alter her life forever.

~ CHAPTER THREE ~

Thrust into hell Satan and all the evil spirits

Quickly reaching up, Courtney flicked the switch on the lamp above her bed. As expected, the light went out, but it was instantly replaced with a strange blinding white glow by the window; roughly shaped like a human but with blurred edges. No face or definition could be seen, and its gender was not distinguishable either.

Courtney jolted up and sat hunched in the top corner of her bed; panicking that she was going to die. Her face turned ever more pale, and her expression was nothing short of petrified. She was breathing deep and heavy, and tears were trickling uncontrollably down her face. 'Mum,' she tried calling out. However, only a whispered cry came from her mouth. Like a giant cloud only allowing glimmers of the sun's rays to shine through, the fear had forced her voice into a constrained and whispered state as her larynx tightened. All but minimal sound had metaphorically been forced into submission by the dark cloud that had appeared in her room.

The figure stood silently, not moving at all. The sight of something so alien in her presence made Courtney react as any child would - with fear. However, it also had an angel-like quality and seemed as though it was possibly studying Courtney. The silent and gentle appearance soon diminished though when Courtney reacted in fear. Almost as if in response, its mood suddenly became disturbed and irritated, and it jerked around with agitated movements.

Courtney was literally scared stiff as she stared at it with her eyes wide open. Her fear increased even further, as the figure then moved about the room; passing through furniture and anything else in its way. No longer appearing in any way angel-like, Courtney was now convinced that it was very angry about something as she could see it constantly reaching out, trying to grab hold of things in her room, but it just kept passing right through them; unable for some reason to make any contact.

Courtney was completely frozen, except for the tears that were swelling up like a turbulent ocean under her eyes. She tried to speak her prayers again, but hardly a sound came out, although she persisted nonetheless as it was the only defence she had. 'Oh Prince of the heavenly host, by the power of God, thrust into hell Satan and all the evil spirits who wander through the world for ruin of souls. Amen.'

Over and over again, she could not stop frantically repeating the prayer. Suddenly and very quickly, the ghostly figure came and stood right beside her bed, and though no face was visible, Courtney could tell it was staring right into her eyes.

'Huh,' she gasped and pushed back against the wall, shaking with fear.

The unwelcome visitor made a faint but disturbing scream as it became considerably brighter. Not loud enough to alert anyone outside the bedroom, but the silence within the room made it seem excruciatingly loud to Courtney, so she placed her hands over her ears in the hope of blocking it out.

She wanted to get out of there so badly, but to get to the door, she would have to literally walk right past the spooky and disturbing apparition, and she knew there was no way she would have the courage to do that.

The visitor shook uncontrollably, but it was hard for Courtney to tell anything through the tears that had swamped her eyes; after all, it was not like ghosts were something that little girls witnessed every day. Increasingly, it was becoming more difficult for her to determine anything, but she could see that something had definitely affected the visitor's mood.

Without warning it disappeared through the wall over by the window causing the room to fall eerily silent. Courtney sat in shock at what had just happened in her room; far too scared to move in case it was not yet over.

'Move faster, c'mon. Go faster, faster,' she said desperately to her mechanical friend on the wall through gritted teeth. 'Get us out of here, you can do it. Please, make it morning already.'

Her worst nightmare was then confirmed as she spotted the figure floating around outside the window. For a split second her mood calmed as it descended from above. Once again she thought that it seemed spiritual. *A visiting angel from the heavens perhaps?* As soon as it re-entered the room, any thoughts of it being friendly were quickly dispersed as it scoured around the room violently. In appearance it seemed to be searching desperately for something, but just like before it passed right through things. This time however at a more frenzied speed and with more strange and eerie sounds emanating from it.

Courtney suddenly decided she had seen enough and something inside her snapped. She wasn't prepared to die before seeing out her dreams and ambitions, so she managed to muster up enough courage to reach across her bed and scream at it whilst tears were streaming down her face. 'Shut up, just shut up.' Her face turned crimson red from the pressure of shouting at the top of her voice.

She knew that now she had found her vocal chords, her mother would surely hear her and come to her rescue. However, before that could happen, the figure turned to her in response to her outburst, as if it had heard her and did not like what she had to say. It swept its arm across her dressing table, passing through everything until it seemed to spot what it would have appeared to have been looking for; her Jesus figurine that sat upon the tabletop.

Courtney noticed the ornament just as the visitor came close to it. *How did that get there? At least it wasn't bro—*

Before she could finish her thought something dreadful

happened; the white ghostly figure hit the figurine, and the treasured item leapt off the table and into the air. Courtney's eyes widened as she watched it fly at incredible force and speed. Her ultimate nightmare was suddenly coming true in front of her very eyes. The figurine flew into the wall so hard that Jesus smashed into a thousand pieces, scattering all over the floor and making it impossible to ever piece back together.

She let out a distressed cry, and in response, the seemingly violent ghostly figure turned and again stared at her for a moment. All Courtney could do was stare straight back in shock and disbelief.

The figure left hurriedly. As quickly as it came, it was gone, but it left behind a million questions; as well as a young heart that was now permanently shattered along with the figurine.

From the shock of everything that had just occurred, Courtney remained still for some moments. Then, as if she had just realised what her life was created for, her facial expression changed. 'Right,' she uttered as she turned to look at the clock. 'That's it; we're going to do this. We're going to figure it out. I'm going to come back to this day. I promise you. And you're going to help me.'

Time travel had begun as a fun hobby, and a distraction from having to go to sleep, but from that moment on, Courtney turned it into a serious and dedicated obsession.

'Trust me when I tell you this,' she spouted in her most adult and articulate manner. 'I will one day figure out how to travel back in time; just like they do in the movies.'

With it no longer being a playful intention, she decided in that moment that she would spend as long as it took researching the dead (as well as time) so that she could one day come back and discover who destroyed her most cherished item and most importantly, why? Inquisitively, but trying desperately to hold back her tears she said, 'Who would want to destroy my only connection with my dad?' There must be a reason, or was this something to do with mum's God? Maybe it didn't like my prayers and crucifixes, and my figure of Jesus.'

All the prayers and teachings she had been given by her devout Catholic mother, were supposed to stop that night's event ever occurring, but on the night of September 17th they had failed miserably, and Courtney needed to know why.

~ CHAPTER FOUR ~

It doesn't scare me any more
(Ten years later)

November had just arrived, and a very nearly full moon was shining as bright as a light bulb; as though it had its own tungsten filament inside and someone had pulled on the power cord. Not a single leaf remained on the trees, and as the winter progressed, they had become an ominous presence in the neighbourhood with their bare and spindly branches jutting out into the air. They were like ghoulish arms protruding from huge scarecrows along the roads; except it wasn't crows the branches were scaring.

Ice sheets had formed on the tarmac as the temperature plummeted below zero; a treacherous night for anyone foolish enough to get behind the wheel of a vehicle. Some had no alternative; in particular the massive Gritters that spewed sand and salt on the icy roads ready for the morning traffic. One such lorry was travelling down the major A10 highway that connects Hertfordshire to London, spewing grit like a fan out of the huge, dangerous-looking impeller on its rear.

Speeding up behind the truck was a brand new blue people carrier. Mazel was sitting behind the steering wheel, wearing a smart business outfit and speaking loudly into an expensive looking Bluetooth headset. 'I'm actually on my way to her now, but I'm running late. She's going to kill me.'

As she approached the Gritter, she heard the sound of small, rock-hard pieces of salt combined with little stones and sand, hitting the paintwork of her new car.

'Ayy, Diyos ko naman,' she exclaimed, reverting to her Filipino dialect for a moment. 'Now I've got a stupid truck spraying salt all over my brand new car, and he's moving at the speed of a hearse.'

She put her foot down on the accelerator, and the car sped around the side, overtaking the lorry. The wheels spun on the slush and ice that had yet to be gritted. 'Yes, I know they're there for a reason, and of course I'm being careful, but it'll be me in a hearse if I leave her stranded at the doc's one more time. She resents me enough as it is.'

Sat on a shiny leather sofa, in the living room of a large Victorian house in North London, was Courtney. Now fifteen years old, she had grown into a very attractive teenager; most likely the result of the mixed blood in her family. Mazel's Filipino side had Spanish and Oriental history, and combining that with her father's English heritage created a mix of genes that made for a unique and striking look. Even with her subtle Oriental traits though, perhaps her most prominent feature alongside her naturally tanned complexion, were her very large, round, dark and piercing eyes. The older she became, the more they were proving to be able to convince anyone of anything. So far in her life, many had struggled to pin down her origins. Most opted for one of the Mediterranean countries, with some even suggesting the Middle East, but whatever they went for, the reason they talked about her in the first place was always because of her wonderfully intense eyes. That was until she opened her mouth and her distinctive English accent became patently evident.

As she sat in the rather bland and clinical looking house, she glanced up at the clock on the wall and wondered whether her mum would be on time (for once) to pick her up that day.

Seated at a desk by the bay fronted window and directly opposite Courtney, was Dr Flux; a psychiatrist in his late forties. He was short and slim with a strong North Belfast accent. His dark brown but slightly greying hair had receded quite considerably, leaving just a tuft front and centre that gave him an air of aged authority. However, his manner was very kind and caring and was coupled with a soft and gentle tone in his voice. 'Well?'

Courtney looked at him with a confused expression on her face. 'Hmm?'

'That just says it all really, doesn't it? Look, you really need to pay attention. I'm not here to be your enemy or to be the pain in your backside that keeps you from being with your friends on a Friday night.'

'Friends?' She frowned and looked at him with a disdainful look on her face.

'I'm here, or I'm supposed to be here, to make sure you've come to terms with what you think occurred when you were five.'

'There you go with that word 'think' again.'

Dr Flux raised his hands in a silent apology before continuing. 'You were saying something earlier about why you used to stay up late.'

She looked at him sceptically. 'Yeah, well. I knew I shouldn't, because if mum knew she would tell me off for staying up past my bedtime. She would say she could always tell because of the bags under my eyes, but I used to tell her I was a vampire and sleeping upside down caused the weight of my big eyes to pull on my skin.' She widened her eyes at him and smiled gleefully at her own wisecrack.

'Making up stories doesn't help your case when you're trying to convince people you had an experience with a ghost.'

She looked down in silent acknowledgement of his observation.

'This is quite serious. You need to start taking responsibility, or nobody will believe anything you say ... ever again.'

She looked at him and remained silent for a moment before sighing.

'So c'mon, tell me. What was the real reason you stayed up so late?'

Only Courtney knew the answer to that question. She had always worried about telling anyone in case it became another reason for the bullies to get on her case. She never wanted the possibility of her secret getting out and making her situation in school any worse than it already was.

Although very pretty, she had found that being incredibly smart, cancelled out the fact that she was attractive and left her open to ridicule by the class bully. She also stood out like a sore thumb amongst her predominantly white peers in the playground, because although living in Hertfordshire was very picturesque, it was quite different to multicultural London; having very few ethnic minorities around. Courtney was convinced she looked very English, and she definitely felt very English, but amongst a load of pale English countryside children, she appeared distinctly foreign. She was like Wasabi and they were English Mustard; two very different colours but the end result being almost the same. On top of that, once word got out that she had been visited by spirits, the taunts escalated. Not everyone bullied her but like she had found out over the years, it only takes one to make you unhappy.

One of the bullies in question, a girl called Alexandra, could not have been more different in the popularity stakes, but ironically, she was quite plain looking with pale skin and short blonde hair. However, the boys in their year seemed to be mysteriously drawn to her. The most noticeable difference was in their academic intelligence. Courtney had found that being 'pretty but dumb' was becoming the way to get popular.

The doctor prompted her and said, 'Well?'

She sighed again. 'I stayed up late each night, because if I kept the light on and was awake ... evil spirits couldn't visit me. Plus, I would get so tired, that when I finally did fall asleep, nothing could wake me; not even a poltergeist. I guess it turns out that on that night, I must've stayed up five minutes too long, as it didn't *need* to wake me.'

'It?' He knew what she meant but wanted her to say it, though she seemed more interested in staring at the clock.

'Can't you speed this up?'

'Excuse me.'

Courtney looked at Dr Flux. 'Oh sorry; I wasn't talking to you.'

'Well then who were you talking to?'

'My only friend Mr Time ... of course.'

'You need to focus my dear. You stayed up late so you'd fall asleep and never have to deal with ...?'

'Ok, I stayed up late, because I was scared of ghosts. There, I said it.'

'And you're still convinced that being so tired had absolutely nothing to do with the visions–'

'What visions? I was tired, but I didn't imagine my figurine flying across the room and smashing into a thousand pieces.'

'Perhaps not ... after all, we do know the figurine was definitely broken don't we? So maybe the question really ... is who broke it?'

'Exactly,' she said excitedly. 'And why?'

'Why indeed. Tell me; have you ever felt angry with your father for passing away before you were even born?'

'Excuse me?' She was a little shocked by his insinuation. 'I'm sorry; I can't do this anymore. I know what you're saying makes sense in your head, but if you honestly think I smashed it myself, you're crazier than everyone assumes I am.'

'Courtney.'

'I'm sorry; it's just ...' she turned her head and looked up at the clock. 'Ah, thank you.' She then turned back to Dr Flux. 'Actually, I think our time is up now, so maybe I should be going anyway. I don't want to hold up your next patient.' She was trying to avoid any further probing; something she had gotten better at the older she became. She had even been thinking recently that now she was fifteen, it may be time to stop seeing Dr Flux altogether.

She had been forced to come to his appointments once a week, for the past ten years; ever since her incident with the 'violent spirit' as she called it; in her bedroom. Coming to see him each week had become such a regular occurrence, but even if she felt she had been able to put it all behind her, stopping the visits would probably feel a little like her mother telling her she need not shower anymore. On the one hand a relief, as she could get a little bit of time back each week to trawl across the internet researching all the theories behind time travel or evil spirits, but on the other hand, she had grown so accustomed to coming that stopping now would leave her with a huge, empty gap in her life; as well as a twisted sense of guilt that she had not managed to deal with her issues; even if she knew she did not really have any. Her mother had put so much weight on them being dealt with and for so long, her issues almost felt normal to her now.

In a strange way, there would also be a feeling that she would be saying goodbye to an old friend, as although she could sometimes get a little bored, she would also often cherish her conversations with the doctor as she felt she could go into a bit more detail on certain subjects with *him* than she ever could with her mother; even if she was not convinced that he totally believed anything she said. Mazel did love talking with her daughter, but she could not quite cope with her level of conversation when it veered onto either ghosts or time travel; the two subjects she loved the most; more than boys, more than clothes; much to her mother's amazement.

Dr Flux was also the only real male influence in Courtney's life, so he had a huge responsibility to be a positive male role model and ultimately a very good listener and friend.

He stared at Courtney and gave her a look that stated he knew she was just trying to get out of there.

'You know, my mum has never believed what happened to me, but of course that's why I'm here, isn't it? It annoys me that no matter what I say, she just won't accept that it could have been true. Plus, anyone at school who has found out also thinks I'm crazy, and as much as I kind of like talking with you, I know you don't really believe me either. I believe you believe that I believe.' She smiled, but his expression remained staid. 'Look, do you know how much fun it is growing up when everyone thinks you're a Reese's Peanut Cup?' She used the joke to try and keep the obvious serious comment on her childhood from becoming another endless topic to keep her in therapy. 'The answer is not a lot, but the thing is, I know it happened, and whether I come to these sessions or not, I'm going to find out why it happened. That thing came to me for a reason, and in doing so destroyed the only real connection I had with my father.' Her expression turned serious. 'So the most real solution I've found to one day getting my figurine back and at the same time finding out why it was destroyed in the first place, is not sitting here asking myself if I resent not having a dad; it's figuring out and understanding what happens when we die and ... studying the science of time travel.'

Dr Flux raised an eyebrow of dubious intent.

'Yeah I know ... 'Peanut Cup'. But one way or another I have to find out. You haven't really given me any answers. I mean why? Why me? The only thing it did before it disappeared was destroy my figurine which destroyed the link to my dad. I'm convinced it somehow knew it was my most precious item.'

Dr Flux sat back in his chair and crossed his legs, giving Courtney a sign that he had perhaps finally accepted that she was old enough to decide what she believed in.

'So, maybe if I can go back to the day it happened. See it from the eyes of an adult. Perhaps I can stop it or even just communicate with it and find out why it wanted to sever the connection with my father.'

'Or maybe you'll find out that it was you who smashed the figurine all along and you invented this story of a ghost to alleviate the guilt of blaming your father for not being there. It's not unusual for people to blame others for dying and leaving them alone; even when it's not their fault. Do you really want to put yourself through that? Think what it will do to your mother.'

Courtney exhaled disappointedly. 'How could I blame my dad for dying? It's not like he killed himself.'

'If you want to stop the name calling and having to come to these sessions–'

'I know, I know; I've got to stop with the crazy talk. But why is a fifteen year old told to shut the hell up, yet Stephen Hawking is a genius? He was fifteen once you know.'

'Well ...'

She jumped in before he had a chance to speak. Animated and a little frustrated she said, 'It's just circumstance. You have to understand that travelling through time is a real possibility for the future – I've explained this to you before. I may just be a fifteen year old kid but one day, I promise you; I will be a world-renowned scientist and one of, if not the first to travel through time.'

'Courtney, I don't want to put a dampener–'

'My point is that I am totally over the shock of it all happening. It was a long time ago. It doesn't scare me anymore. However, one thing that does scare me a little is losing my mother because of all this. There is a part of me that wants to just tell you I'm over everything, and that I'll pursue a normal life so I can get some kind of relationship back with her. Coz I've already lost my dad; I really don't want to lose my mum too.'

They both fell silent for a moment, as what she had just said hit the pair of them hard.

'I truly believe that the day the spirit came to my bedroom was the day my future was written for me. I really don't think anything said here will alter that.' She was desperately trying to convince herself that she was doing the right thing. 'We are our experiences Dr Flux, and nothing is going to change that.'

Mazel's was speeding down an unlit portion of the A10 highway inside her blue people carrier desperately trying to make up for lost time. She knew she was driving too fast for the icy and dark conditions of the road, but she also knew that she was now running very late.

She was struggling to keep her eyes focused on the road, as the lack of streetlamps, the icy roads, as well as the speed she was travelling at were all playing havoc with her imagination; fooling her into thinking she was seeing things in front of her. She felt very tense, and as a result she kept jerking her foot towards the brake pedal when she thought she saw something in front of her, but each time she neared, she realised it was just bushes and the scarecrow trees jutting out on both sides of the road. Her perception of things was all over the place, and she would dangerously swerve when she mistook foliage for vehicles edging out of lay-bys. She was doing seventy five miles an hour, and although five miles an hour over the speed limit would not normally be seen by most (including Mazel) as much of a problem, in these dark, perilous and icy conditions, she felt like she was on a hazardous race track with no appropriate skill, and in a very unsuitable vehicle.

She clasped her hands tightly on the steering wheel, knowing that if she was to slam her foot on the brake for any reason, the car would almost certainly skid, and at that speed the result would be devastating. The easiest thing would be to slow down, but something was telling her there was not much farther to go, and stupidly, she would rather put herself at risk, than have another night of silence from Courtney for being late. After all, it wasn't Courtney's idea to be sent to a psychiatrist.

The thing that kept her going was not having had an experience to compare to the carnage that would occur, if something tragic was to happen. Even though she would not like to admit it out loud, somewhere deep inside the recesses of Mazel's mind were the thoughts, *I've seen it on the news a hundred times, but it won't happen to me. How could it? I know what I'm doing.*

Famous last words, as at that moment, the unfathomable did happen; the car skidded. At first, it happened as if in slow motion, as the back end spun out until the car was almost parallel with the road. Then, all of a sudden, real time kicked in when the car began to barrel-roll down the road at a terrific speed; performing a sequence of spins that most have only witnessed in the movies. The outer shell of the car crumbled in on itself, like a fizzy drink's can being crushed by someone's hand in an exhibition of machismo.

Inside the vehicle, both passenger and driver airbags were released, as shards of glass pierced the air with huge ferocity, as if they were being grated onto a dish of carnage. The driver's airbag was stained with the blood from Mazel's injuries, and her limbs were being flung around as if her bones were made of jelly. All of the devastation was encapsulated in a spinning wheel that was only just beginning to slow down.

In a moment of devastating brutality, as nature collided with technology, the car folded in half with a massive jolt as it hit a large oak tree on a bend in the road. The wreck flew a few metres upwards into the air, before it came crashing down at the base of the tree. All went completely silent, as the car finally laid peacefully in a tangled and horrific mess.

~ *CHAPTER FIVE* ~

I love her very much

Fifteen minutes had passed since Mazel's horrific accident. Police, ambulance and fire crews were dotted all around the scene. Emergency sirens echoed in the previously silent night air. Traffic cones had been placed all over the road, sectioning off the busy area. A number of cars had built up in a queue due to the police stopping any traffic from coming through. A medical helicopter lowered itself onto the road, and its powerful spinning blades blew leaves and dirt around like an ensuing hurricane.

A team of fireman worked hard to get through the wreckage with their hydraulic spreaders and cutters, attempting to reach Mazel who was trapped inside the mangled car. Paramedics used towels and blankets to shield her from the sparks that flew out from the tools that the fire crew were using to cut through the metal. Other members of the fire crew were trying to stop the vehicle's leaking petrol from catching fire, because inside the car, Mazel was miraculously still alive.

'Push those vehicles back further in case the fuel tank blows,' screamed one of the firemen to the police blockade. To the outside eyes of the waiting drivers and passengers it seemed like chaos all around, although clearly by their actions, the emergency services knew exactly what they were doing.

The cutting stopped momentarily, and Dave, a tall, well-built firemen said, 'How are you doing, Madam?' He was in his mid-thirties; his hair was jet black, and he had a round, friendly face.

'Really ... not good. I can't breathe,' she cried. 'It hurts to talk.'

'We'll try to make this as painless as possible.'

'Please, do me a favour ... before I go—'

'You're not going anywhere. We're gonna get you out of here.'

'Please ... just listen, before it's too late.' Mazel was agitated and in pain. Her breathing was putting more pressure on her chest, which was already being crushed by the steering wheel. 'Tell my daughter ... tell her ... tell her I love her very much.' She paused and took a gulp, trying to catch some breath before it was too late. 'But most importantly, tell her I—'

The yelling from the other firemen suddenly became louder and fiercer. The petrol had caught fire and very quickly became out of control. Another fireman ran over to Dave who was still talking to a clearly very frightened Mazel and with no regard for his own safety. 'Dave, get out of here.' The fireman grabbed Dave and dragged him away from the burning vehicle. 'It's gonna blow. There's nothing we can do,' he yelled, continuing to drag him to safety.

As he was being hauled backwards, Dave dropped his cutting equipment and stared back at Mazel. She mouthed something to him, but he couldn't work out what it was. Desperation was written all over her face, like what she was saying was the most important thing in the world, but unfortunately, there was too much noise all around for Dave to hear her. As flames suddenly engulfed the car, something came over Dave as he realised by the look on Mazel's face, that she was really desperate to say something. Having been moved by her drastic situation, he became determined that the woman would have her last words heard. He vigorously shrugged off his colleague and ran back to the car.

'Dave, don't be stupid! You're going to get yourself killed.

It's not worth it.'

As he reached Mazel, the flames had become stronger, and he could feel the intense heat burning into his skin. He wasn't even inside the car, so could only imagine what Mazel must be feeling within. The thought that the poor, helpless and damned woman was about to be swallowed up by the flames and that there was nothing he could do was killing him inside. He leaned forward as close as he could get and without seriously burning himself, so he could at least hear the last words she was so desperate to speak. Mazel whispered something, not because she did not want to be heard, but simply because she even found talking so excruciatingly painful now. Dave struggled to hear but did just about manage to catch the strange and desperate message she had demanded must be heard. He looked a little bewildered by it as he suddenly pulled back his head.

'Dave!' shouted his colleague.

He quickly snapped back into reality and once more felt the heat from the flames that raged from the back of the car. He looked straight into Mazel's eyes intently and began to sympathetically feel her pain.

'Ok,' he said with a little trepidation but mixed with a certain amount of determination. 'I promise.' After a moment's contemplation, he hesitantly turned and ran back to safety, but he carried with him a remorseful conscience that would stay with him for a long time.

The fire crew could no longer bear to watch, as the whole car was quickly eaten up by the monster flames. They turned their heads away as their greatest enemy took yet another victim. The burning car lit up the dark, unlit road like a medieval torch. At the last moment, the flames enveloped the car so quickly it was reminiscent of someone squirting a bottle of lighter fluid onto the dying flames of a barbecue. Everyone closed their eyes and took a step back to shield them from the searing heat of the fire. Any meat left stuck to the rack would not only have a stench of petroleum, but it would be unrecognisable from its original form. Similarly, anything left inside the car that night, suffered the same fate, but even if the fire was treating Mazel like a piece of meat, to everyone else watching she was a person, and as Dave had just discovered, she was also someone's mother.

~ CHAPTER SIX ~

A light – can't – walk

To most, graveyards will always be a spooky place once night draws in; not really welcoming to those still alive as the daylight slips creepily away. The local crematorium situated off the main road in Courtney's childhood town, was certainly no exception.

Winter had truly set in and the wind rustled through any remaining leaves on the trees; relentlessly pushing with all its might, to fell the ones which were still clinging to their branches with any ounce of life they had left in them. All varying colours they once wore as a symbol of how alive they were, had almost totally been sucked from them. Soon, the leaves that once flourished in the summer air, would lay dead on the damp winter floor; left to decompose into the soil below. With an uncanny similarity, the bodies in the graveyard beneath the trees had been going through a comparable process of decomposition.

Standing, introspectively by her mother's grave was Courtney. She had been staring at the freshly covered plot for a few hours.

Earlier, a crowd of mourners had thrown handfuls of dirt onto the wooden box below, but darkness had since swept across the land, turning the place of respectful mourning, into a place of eerie death.

Courtney had been standing in a stunned silence, brought

on by the day's solemn proceedings, as if she was frozen in time due to the sudden loss of her only living parent. Lost, hurt and confused, were only some of the emotions she had experienced in the apparent hell she had recently been forced into. Unsurprisingly, she was not aware of any sombre change of mood from the sun having set on the cemetery, as all she could focus on was her mother, who lay silently beneath the earth in a box six feet below her. She found it tough to come to terms with the fact that she would never get to see or touch her ever again. At the same time, she was punishing herself for not being able to get the resentment she felt toward her mum, out of her head. She found it incredibly difficult to let go of all the resentment from the years she had spent as a figure of fun and intrigue amongst her peers, as well as all the wasted hours in Dr Flux's office trying to determine why she had made up stories about ghosts. 'All this could have been avoided if you had just believed me,' she said with massive disappointment, as she struggled to fight back tears.

She had wrestled with the thought that it was all her fault for so long, that she had not even paid much attention to the fact that the crowds had left and she was standing all alone in the darkness; amongst a very different crowd of people; the deceased.

As she took one last look down at the soft earth that covered her mother's coffin, a strong cold wind blew across the cemetery. For the first time she felt the reality of the situation and realised she was standing in the dark, amongst a set of individuals that she, of all people, should be anxious about being around.

Suddenly, a car horn pierced the silence that permeated the cemetery and instantly broke Courtney's concentration, causing her to jut off the ground in surprise. In the distance, by the huge iron gates at the entrance to the cemetery, a lone car was parked with its engine and lights off. Inside, she could just make out a figure sat behind the wheel. 'No ... I'm not ready yet,' she mumbled to herself.

She turned back to her mother's grave, and a single tear

emerged from one eye and fell to the earth. The lone tear was immediately sucked up by the dry, freshly dug soil; just like the first drop of rain that hits the ground after a drought, right before a million more follow on its tail.

She dropped to her knees, and right on cue the ground was bombarded with the posthumous downfall that poured from her eyes. At that precise moment, the heavens above her also opened up to join in with her mourning; a possible message from nature that she was not alone in her moment of grief. As the downpour heavily fell upon the cemetery, Courtney's hands, which she had rested on the soil by her mother's grave, sank into the fresh mud. She lifted herself up to stop them from submerging into the soft, newly laid soil, and even though she was fully aware that her hands were covered in mud, she placed them on her face in despair.

'Why is this happening? Who's next huh, me? Is this my fault for seeing a ghost in the first place? If seeing them causes this much pain, then tell me why do they exist? What's the point?' She looked down at her mother's coffin. 'Or is it your fault for making such a fuss about it? Why couldn't you just believe me and drop it. If only you had some faith in me, and not just in your God; if you trusted me a bit more. Was that too much to ask from my mother?' She had started to shout as the rain became heavier. 'You should have just let it go, why did you have to push it? Dad would've believed me.'

As she knelt with her muddy hands on her face, experiencing a confused combination of sorrow over her mother's death and distress over her troubled upbringing, she suddenly got a worrying feeling that she was being watched.

Spreading her fingers open across her face, she peeked through the cracks at the car over by the gates. Then she slowly turned her head toward the small brick chapel in the centre of the cemetery grounds. 'No ... not here. Not now.'

A faint white light emanated from the side of the building. She rubbed her eyes and unintentionally plastered even more mud all over her face. The rain that continuously pelted down did not help her visibility, but she could definitely see there was something there.

Is it a night light on the building? In that moment, the worst possible thing she could imagine happened, as the light slowly moved towards her and away from the building.

'A light – can't – walk,' she whispered to herself with a panic-stricken tone.

What she saw suddenly became very reminiscent of the memory that resided in the recesses of her mind; the fateful night in her bedroom ten years ago. Of course she was not able to forget it, as she had been reminded of it every week in her sessions with Dr Flux, but the actual real physical memory of what everything looked like on that night, the finer details, had faded into her memory long ago. She even subconsciously wondered if everyone was right, and that she had imagined her ghostly encounter; though she would never admit to anyone that a thought like that had entered her head, even for a second.

What she could see before her through the tears, the rain and the darkness, was quickly jogging her memory though. *Could it really be happening all over again?* Courtney wondered as panic permeated her thoughts.

As the light moved forward, the answer to her question was confirmed right in front of her. 'What does it want now?' She couldn't help but wonder if she had some kind of gift for seeing spirits? *What are the odds of having another encounter when most haven't had a single experience in their whole lifetime?* She then spoke to the apparition and quietly said, 'Who are you? Are you someone different ... or are you back for unfinished business?'

Her breathing was deep and frantic, and her face fell instantly pale like a boiled chicken, until something totally unexpected happened causing the colour in her face to permeate her skin, like blood seeping into a shirt after a bullet wound. All the built-up angst and emotion from the last ten years, which had culminated in the burial of her last remaining parent that very afternoon, came flooding out in a ferocious burst of anger. Any fear, she converted into pure aggression which she directed straight at the figure that had re-appeared in front of her after ten long years.

In a split second, she rationalised something in her head.

'My mother wouldn't even be dead were it not for you. She wouldn't have been coming to collect me if I weren't in therapy because of my 'disturbing experience' as they called it'. Consequently, her expression changed to pure anger. 'This is all, your fault,' she said accusingly. She lifted one foot off the ground and then another, until she found herself running with a fierce determination towards the glowing figure in the distance. She had no idea what she was going to do when she reached it, but her anger and frustration was now in control of the legs that were stomping through the mud and water beneath her feet.

One of the car doors of the vehicle parked by the gate opened, and a black lady called Claudette urgently stepped out. Claudette was a slightly plump social worker in her mid thirties, with shoulder length, black hair. 'Courtney,' she yelled with a concerned tone.

Courtney continued to run, edging closer to something she had been indirectly suffering at the hands of for years but never expected to actually see again. 'Where are you now mum, just when I need you? If you can see this, I hope you're happy. You made me suffer for years with people thinking I'm crazy. Do I look crazy now, huh? I told you I wasn't,' she screamed, as she charged forward through the graveyard and the pounding rain in total darkness, towards a glowing white light in the distance.

The glowing figure jerked forward, almost as if it was taken aback by Courtney's show of aggression, and within moments it was also moving at a similar speed towards Courtney. Although it was not distinguishable as a human figure, much like the one she had witnessed in her bedroom, its size and shape indicated once again that a human was the most likely explanation, especially given the seemingly appropriate and clichéd location of its appearance.

As Courtney ran, she had to negotiate the various gravestones and low metal fences that had been erected around some of them. The glowing figure on the other hand, passed straight through anything that was in its path.

With the two destined figures about to meet and only a metre at most away from each other, Courtney slipped in the mud and fell directly on to one of the spiked metal fences, slicing one of her palms open and spurting blood all over a nearby gravestone. She quickly looked up and was instantaneously faced with the speeding figure that was now only a few feet away. Exhausted and in pain, she quickly cowered, ready for whatever was about to befall her, but as quick as they both came face to face, it disappeared again.

She looked up to where there should be an ominous figure glaring down at her, but all that was left from their near meeting was some blood dripping from a nearby headstone and a serious wound to her hand; a wound that was ultimately self-inflicted. Blood oozed from the gash, mud was covering her innocent face and her hair looked like she had been made up for Halloween.

She lay on the floor by the poor soul's gravestone that she had defaced with her blood and let out the most horrifying scream that contained a mixture of anger, frustration and sadness.

Claudette approached from behind, carrying an umbrella. 'I suppose I'm going to have to let this one go, aren't I, because it's your mother's funeral? But this behaviour really can't go on.'

'She let me down again,' said Courtney, with tears in her eyes. 'She should have been here to see it.' Even after death, she could not stop being angry at her mother.

'Courtney, darling ... you can't blame your mother for not attending her own funeral. That's a little unfair by anyone's standards, don't you think?'

Courtney looked up and realised it would be another futile exercise to try and explain what had just happened.

Claudette then noticed the blood that had soaked into Courtney's top as she held it against her with the other hand. 'Oh God, what have you done? C'mon, let's get you to casualty before that gets infected.' She offered her hand to Courtney. 'Then, we'll look at getting the remainder of your stuff from the house and see if we can get you a family that can help you forget your past. How does that sound?'

Courtney looked at Claudette through the blood, sweat and tears. 'Are you mad? I don't wanna forget the past. It's what determines my future,' she blasted. Her eyes flickered from the build up of pressure as more tears uncontrollably began to pour from her eyes. 'I'm not crazy you know.'

Claudette looked at Courtney slumped on the ground in complete darkness, soaking wet and bleeding over some anonymous, poor soul's grave. 'No, sweetheart, of course you're not.'

~ CHAPTER SEVEN ~

Mercury, flanked by Hercules and Minerva

Since Courtney had reluctantly laid her mother to rest, Christmas and New Year had come and gone, and for a fifteen year old girl that could only mean one thing; a new school term.

A few months had passed since her mother's funeral, and things had not been easy for her during that time. She tried desperately hard to get used to being in a care home with other children, an experience that had so far been very unsettling. Although the staff tried to make everyone feel like a family, Courtney was all too aware that if you were in there in the first place, it was because you had no family.

She was not one to wonder what could have been though, even as she lay alone each night in a cold, soulless room, in a government-run children's care home. She firmly believed that everything she had experienced happened for a reason, although she was still to figure out what that reason was. Money from the forced sale of her mother's house, along with her father's life insurance, had been placed in a trust fund for when she reached the age of eighteen, but financial security was a somewhat reluctant prize for losing both her parents, even if some other less fortunate children in the home thought otherwise. Everywhere she went, no matter how tragic her life became, it seemed there was always someone ready to criticise her. However, she had convinced herself that if there was some kind of higher power out there, it wouldn't make money the grand purpose and design for both of her parents passing away so young.

So the one thing that was actually keeping her focused and sane through all the depression was her stoic belief in the prospect of time travel. Although it was a little ironic, as many had told her that entertaining the idea of travelling through time was anything but sane, yet it was something she would always have more belief in than the traditional faith her mother had tried to instil into her.

The first day of the new school term had arrived and Courtney could not have been happier. Anything that got her out of the care home and got her mind working on something other than the supposed mental problems she was perceived to have was welcomed with enthusiasm.

'C'mon then young lady,' asserted Claudette, as she poked her head into Courtney's bedroom. 'Let's get you to school, so you can unleash that superior mind onto more unwilling victims.'

'You can mock all you want, but you and I both know I should be going somewhere that can actually keep up with me.'

'Well, I'm afraid we all have to deal with the cards we are dealt, and you're certainly not the first to feel that way, but unless you have a stack of cash hidden under your bed then you're just going to have to make the most of it, and be thankful you live in a country that even offers free education. Anyway, it's a good school. I went there.' Claudette smiled.

'Blah blah blah isn't life grand. Sorry if I don't share your enthusiasm, but it's not exactly the most challenging school in the country. It's just a basic mixed comprehensive with no special rules for attending other than the distance pupils live from it. It just caters to the average child's intellect and no time is dedicated to the gifted. Excuse me for recognising myself as being gifted, but if I don't, who will? So I'm sure you did very well there but I'm looking at slightly more challenging goals here.'

'I could be offended by that, but as I know you're talking

about time travel I'm going to let that one slide. Now get your stuff together, and let's go, or the only 'time' you'll be concerned with is more detention time.'

Most of the advanced level Courtney had already attained in school was achieved by using her own initiative, and she had to put up with the fact that most of the teachers were considerably less intelligent than her; a very hard thing for a child to truthfully realise when they're always being told that children always think they are smarter than the adults. Actually, the only thing they did have over her was *life* experience. However, lately she had been fast catching up with them in that area too.

On arrival at school she entered the large concrete playground. Surrounding it was a brick wall with metal railings running around the entire perimeter. At one end, the rundown Victorian structure that was the main school building loomed over the whole landscape. Most knew it couldn't continue into the modern age without serious change. Perhaps a great location for a movie about an old Victorian school, but a place of education it was not. Jokes of an impending arson attack were not sounding so funny lately; something the school may need just to get the historic pale blue paint off the walls. Courtney made her way over to a huge looming brick wall over at the back where a long row of wooden benches ran along the length of it. She sat down in her regular spot and took out some books to while away some time before the bell rang. Etched across the wall behind her were various differently coloured circles. The shape and design were reminiscent of something you would use for target practise, although they were more commonly used for ball games during break times. An altogether different use for them however had been found by Courtney.

One summer morning, she had arrived at school earlier than all the others for the specific task of going on a rare journey into the art of graffiti. With a pack of coloured chalk she had bought especially for the purpose, she proceeded to draw the sun in the centre of the circles. Then on each outer line in relevant sizes and colours, she drew the succession of planets by their distance to the giant star; Mercury, Venus, Earth, Mars, Jupiter, Saturn, Uranus and Neptune. She also had Pluto on there but she had put an asterisk next to it with the following description: *On August 24th 2006, Pluto's planetary status was revoked.* The whole thing was reminiscent of her old bedroom ceiling and was perhaps an attempt to hold on to something from her past.

Since its appearance, the other kids in the playground had become fascinated by it. Much to her surprise, they would often stand and point while discussing their own versions of what the universe consisted of. Ironically, as much as it ignited a spark in a number of children's minds about what the universe around them was really all about, she was reprimanded for 'defacing and vandalising school property'.

Six months later there she sat, underneath her apparent act of rebellion. Other students had now entered the playground, boys with their various mobile phones that doubled as game devices and girls in groups discussed their hair whilst simultaneously listening to the latest downloads on their various coloured iPod and MP3 players.

Courtney on the other hand remained alone with just her books and her imagination. Although pretty and clearly maturing in all the right places, boys did not seem to know a good thing when it was staring them right in the face. She had been branded the weird brainy one while other not so attractive girls were the ones that got the attention, as they were the ones forcing the issue with all the make-up and hair styling.

Courtney busied herself writing all her current thoughts down in her 'Time Journal' as she called it. She needed a book with many blank pages to be able to contain all her ideas. In one form or another, it had stayed with her throughout the years, since she had first become fascinated with time and all its possibilities. Inside the book was a mixture of drawings, thoughts and stories that she would jot down, imagining what she would do if she could one day use time to her advantage.

The current incarnation was an A4 drawing pad with a black and white picture of the sculpture that sits atop Grand Central Station in New York; a stone sculpture of Mercury, flanked by Hercules and Minerva, surrounding a beautiful Roman numeric clock. Given a choice between that and a cover containing Hannah Montana, the world famous New York clock would win every time. If they had one with Big Ben and the Clock Tower, she would have bought that too; as long as it reflected her ambitions somehow, she was happy. The paper inside the pad was actually more like thick card, similar to what you would use for drawing, but Courtney loved the feel of freshly sharpened pencils leaving their mark on its thickness and felt it gave what she wrote a real sense of credence. She felt that plain old flimsy paper was just not worthy of her intellect, yet lately she had been thinking that perhaps an upcoming school event was.

That very afternoon in school was the annual literacy competition where all students are given the opportunity to enter a piece of writing that consists of no more than eight hundred words on that year's chosen subject.

In previous years, Courtney did not have any inclination to enter. The topics had not been anything that she had felt she had any wisdom on. Also, to make it open to all and to try and get everyone's creative instincts to flow, the headmistress would set topics of a 'relevant' nature. Last year they were asked to write a piece on what makes people attractive. How that was in any way interesting, Courtney could never work out? She also noted that previous winners would often be students who would not usually be expected to make the effort. This was something she always took a grievance to and that she suspected was the only reason for the whole competition in the first place. She always felt they should award the best writing, plain and simple, not who they felt sorry for. That year though, the subject was left more open for interpretation and ideas. She wasn't sure what had changed the school's outlook. 'Maybe its just destiny,' she said to herself. The posters all over the school had the statement:

'Things that make us think – in 800 words or less. Put an idea to the school that will make us all question what we know to be true.'

Perhaps a little deep for the school, but at least now she could finally let her thoughts loose on everyone. For the last few weeks she had been busy collating her theories and ideas together, trying to get them to make sense to other people. She knew that it would have to be good. 'So good that perhaps I can convince the doubters that time travel is actually possible and even stop someone taking the prize for writing something like, 'How do you get the hottest boy in school to like you?' There was an uncomfortable sense of dread in her stomach that indicated to her that she would be humiliated for evermore and laughed out of the hall in front of the whole school, for not writing about exactly that subject.

As the playground filled, ready for the school bell, she was busy writing the finishing touches in her journal. The more she focused on the ideas, the closer she felt she was getting to achieving something remarkable.

A group of three girls were standing nearby talking to two boys and by the look of them, were possibly the authors of, 'How do you get the hottest boy in school to like you?'

The girls were done up as if they were purely in school to impress the male population. They poked fun at Courtney, who was sitting, totally unaware and with her head in her journal.

'Hey Witch,' said Alexandra, the leader of the posse and Courtney's childhood bully from primary school. 'You can't just read out all your spells today you know. Unless you were thinking of using one of them on us so you'd win.' She smiled with glee, as if she had just said the smartest and funniest thing in the world. Her group of friends laughed with her.

'What are you talking about? Clearly, having a brain is no longer a prerequisite for coming to school,' responded Courtney. 'So ... do you actually have a brain or is that thing on top of your shoulders just there for hair styling and make-up sessions?'

Alexandra's smile dropped.

'You're like a real life Bratz doll aren't you? Always have been as well. I bet your friends have such a blast playing around with your head.'

The two boys next to Alexandra laughed involuntarily at the way their friend had been put down. Alexandra turned and poured heated scorn on both of them. Clearly intimidated and not wanting to upset her, they tried very hard to stop laughing.

'That's right, boys,' said Courtney. 'You better shut up or she definitely won't be playing with your heads later.'

Alexandra stared at her. 'Why don't you just shut up?'

'Wow,' said Courtney. 'That was an amazingly, awesome comeback. You know, you really are priceless. Oh hang on, or is it worthless? I'm not quite sure. I get confused between the two. Hey, maybe I can place an ad on eBay for you and we'll find out which it is,' she said, excitedly.

'Are you calling me stupid?'

'Not at all, you have lots of redeeming features.' She then described her with a home-shopping channel style to her voice. 'Let's see ... no reserve on this real life hair-styling and make-up doll that comes with all the original accessories, including earrings, bracelets, glitter and lip gloss (slightly used) and a brush. With this doll you can style and brush her hair, do her make-up, paint her nails and decorate her top, belt, arms and tummy. This doll is in ok condition and the hair has no knots or tangles. It looks brand new, although it has been used and played with a little and is a little worn around the edges.' She raised her eyebrows. 'Oh, and it comes from a smoke and pet free home ... actually, that last bit I'm jumping to conclusions about – do your parents smoke?'

Everybody laughed. Alexandra had no smart comments to come back with, so she did the next best thing and lunged directly at her. She pulled her off the bench by her hair and tried to pin her down to the wet concrete floor. Courtney's journal fell to the ground and landed in a puddle. A boy who was standing nearby chanted the most recognisable sound in the school playground, beckoning the rest of the school populace to form a circle around the female gladiators. 'Fight – fight – fight.'

~ CHAPTER EIGHT ~

The glory

On hearing the school's unofficial anthem, everybody in the playground made a stampede over to see the ensuing battle. Before long a huge crowd had gathered, all chanting in unison, 'Fight, fight, fight.'

Courtney and Alexandra violently tussled with each other. Hair was being pulled; some of Alexandra's extensions were torn from her head and there was lots of screaming from both girls. Courtney's blouse was ripped open, exposing her bra for all to see. Privileged boys, who were fortunate enough to have ringside viewing, howled with joy.

At that precise moment, like the parting of the waves, the crowd split in two, and through the middle stalked an ominous looking male teacher. Mr Adams was in his mid-forties, wore a blue sports tracksuit and was very large. His build was sort of a cross between the world's strongest man and a local pub darts player. In other words, it was hard to tell if he was actually rather fit due to being a PE teacher, or if he was just fat from eating too many pies. At least that's how the students liked to put it.

On seeing him, the chants stopped and the crowd dispersed. Everyone was clearly intimidated by him. He reached the two girls, who now had each other in head locks, and for a brief moment just stared, letting them continue to see who would eventually relinquish their hold on the other.

Alexandra's grip slightly loosened, and her face was a tad more purple than Courtney's.

'Oi,' he boomed with an authoritative tone on noticing the slight advantage. 'Pack it in before I knock your heads together.' He had a very distinctive London cockney accent with a distinguishing colloquial use of the English language.

His technique was reminiscent of a drill sergeant; a quality that was dying out as relics like him, were replaced with more politically correct mentors. But everybody seemed to respond positively to him and nobody could deny he had control of the large urban crowd. However, he still had a glint in his eye and unless things got too out of control, he treated everything with a little tongue in cheek. Something the majority of children in school had come to respect.

Nevertheless, the two girls did not let go of each other, as neither wanted to be seen as the weaker one. Mr Adams grabbed them both by the scruff of the neck. 'Come here, the pair of you.' He pulled them apart with ease and held them, one in each hand. 'Now get inside the sports hall and start putting all the footballs in the net. I'll be there in five minutes. Touch each other again and you'll be scrubbing the crapper instead, and you'll be pleased to know I had a curry for lunch and just finished a session in there. Is that understood?'

The crowd all winced and laughed at his gross comment.

'Yes, Mr Adams,' said the two girls in unison.

'Courtney, this is really disappointing. You just can't stay out of trouble can you?' He then turned and walked away, leaving Courtney stood open-mouthed from the nature of his comment.

'Oh my God, I am so not a bad kid. I spend my life defending myself and get in trouble for it. What's going on?'

'Yeah I know, it's funny isn't it,' said Alexandra as she giggled. She then grabbed her bag and walked slowly towards the sports hall.

Courtney did the same, but after a few steps she remembered her Journal was still in a puddle getting wetter by the second. She picked it up, shook the dirty water off and opened it to check inside. 'Now that's the reason you pay a little extra for quality,' she said to herself with a smile. She picked up her bag and ran to catch up with Alexandra. As they walked over to the huge grey metal building, there was an uncomfortable silence between them. Courtney, not being particularly spiteful, had always found it hard to hold a grudge, so as they walked she wondered if she could redeem anything from the situation or whether she should just shut up and keep quiet. Against her better judgement, she decided to make an effort and see what could happen if she tried to communicate. 'Did he really just say touch each other?'

Alexandra turned to her with a blank expression on her face. Courtney looked at her equally dead-pan and wondered if she had made the right decision. She had tried to think of the wittiest thing at short notice that may just be on Alexandra's level, but now she was stood uncomfortably waiting for a response, she wasn't so sure it was the best thing to have done. As she waited for what seemed like a lifetime for a hint of reaction, she was unaware that Alexandra was actually fighting the urge to respond, and in a moment that would change their friendship forever, she could no longer resist and burst into laughter.

Courtney was taken aback but knew she had to join in if she was to maintain the mood. So a split second later she joined in with the laughter, attempting to hide the fact that she had planned the comment all along. She knew that to succeed she would have to convince Alexandra that it was spontaneous.

'You so know he wants to watch us touch each other,' remarked Alexandra in a remarkable show of affiliation.

'That's probably why he teaches sports.'

'Eeewww.'

Both grossed out by their comments, they smiled at each other in unity.

'Listen ... I'm sorry about the witch thing,' said Alexandra.

'Don't worry about it. I guess I'm not exactly normal, and I probably went overboard with the Bratz comments anyway. It is a sort of backhanded compliment in a way though, coz those things are pretty, right? It's not like I said you are one of them little trolls that sit at the end of a pencil.' Courtney jolted her head wondering if she actually let those words come out of her mouth, but she had sensed an interesting change in mood.

There was a moment's pause before Alexandra raised a small smile and said, 'I love those trolls.' Then out of the blue she said, 'I'm sorry about your mum by the way.' Alexandra seemed to be a very different girl from ten minutes earlier; a result of being separated from her friends, as well as falling victim to Courtney's humour.

Courtney did not respond. Instead, she looked down to the ground, as Alexandra's last comment really struck deep.

They reached the double doors of the sports hall, and Alexandra pulled them open to let Courtney through. 'Hey,' she said, as she stood holding one of the doors open. 'I hope you win today – but don't you dare tell anyone I said that.'

Courtney looked at her for a second and wondered where the friendship had suddenly come from. She presumed it must be the classic scenario of school bravado, but once the group of friends are gone, the bravado turns out to be a front. *Perhaps she doesn't really like her friends. Maybe she just fell into it and then had to keep up the act for the sake of her image. On the other hand, it could just be for that brief moment, and I'll end up fighting her again because her reputation is more important than a real friend. Well at least for now someone's talking to me like I actually exist.* 'Thank you,' she said. 'Although I can't imagine I will win. That's not really why I'm doing it. I'm doing it for myself. I've been working out what I'm going to say today since I was five years old, but I don't suppose anyone else will even understand what I'm talking about.'

'Well you've definitely got a chance. After all ... I'm not entering this year.'

They stared at each other and for the first time, burst into genuine unified laughter.

'So what is it about anyway?'

'Well ...' Courtney thought hard before answering and then decided to test the water first with a question. 'What's your opinion on time travel?'

'Oh my God, I looove time travel,' said Alexandra, bursting with excitement on hearing the phrase, time travel. 'I'd change so much if I could go back.'

'Oh really? Then you'd better hold on tight when I speak today,' said Courtney, slightly taken aback by the genuine interest. 'I plan to take the school on a wild journey through my mind on that very subject.' She had built up a little confidence and was attempting to deliver her lines in an exaggerated Hollywood, movie-trailer type of voice.

'Oh – my – God, you've so figured out how to time travel, haven't you?'

'Err ... no,' said Courtney very matter of fact. 'Not quite. Not yet anyway.' She spoke with a slightly mocking tone and a giggle.

'I didn't realise you were into all this time travel stuff, I really thought you were into witches and evil stuff.'

'Why on earth would you think that?'

'Because you like ... ghosts and things'

'I don't *like* ghosts. I was traumatised by one when I was five, but there was nothing to like about it.'

Alexandra thought for a moment before changing her tone back to wonderment. 'But time travel though ... so cool. I am so gonna stick with you from now on.' She turned and walked through into the sports hall.

Courtney stood alone for a moment and raised her eyebrows in surprise at what had just occurred. Maybe she should go around challenging everyone to a fight if that's how you are supposed to make friends these days. She watched Alexandra disappear through the next set of doors at the other end of the foyer. 'Or perhaps you're smarter than I give you credit for, and you actually just want to stick with me for the glory,' she whispered. 'Hmm, we'll see ... only my other friend Time will tell that.'

~ CHAPTER NINE ~

How can you change what already exists?

The balls had been packed away, a new and unlikely friendship had been made, and the school hall was now full of students sitting on rows of plastic chairs. Down each side, all the teachers were standing like guards, trying to keep an authoritative eye over them. A raised stage was at one end with awful green curtains hung on either side. Sections of the curtains had been torn in the past, usually from someone swinging on them during a PE or drama lesson and had been repaired with strips of silver duct tape. Rather than getting out a needle and thread, or heaven forbid some new curtains, the school just kept adding more silver tape.

Down one side there were eight huge, floor-to-ceiling windows that looked out over the playground. All of them had the same awful curtains hung either side, and at the centre of the stage was a lectern that had a microphone rigged up to the top. Lined up across the back wall, and sitting on slightly nicer wooden chairs, were this year's participants in the literary competition and just to the side of the stage was a school photographer taking snapshots for the school's website.

First prize was to have the winning piece entered onto the school's website, as well as into a book that contained examples of children's work from around the country. Published yearly, it was intended as an incentive to get more children writing their ideas down.

The competition was already underway, and currently at the lectern was a boy reading his piece on recycling and how the government deceive us on what they actually do with all our recyclable materials. Courtney was sitting at the back, waiting patiently for her turn. *This is just the sort of thing the school wants to hear.* With every second that passed, she kept wondering if she had made a huge mistake. She realised that on some level, every preceding speech was to a large degree based in reality and aimed at making the planet a better place; something that people could understand and relate to. Hers on the other hand was going to be seen as pure fantasy and possibly a bit selfish; even though she absolutely believed every word of it. Her doubts changed slightly when she looked nervously out into the baying audience and caught many of the students with their eyes closed and yawning. Perhaps recycling wasn't as entertaining as she feared it may be. On the other hand, the students weren't going to be the ones judging.

To take her mind off being the next one up, she began to analyse the room. In particular, she stared at the wallpaper around the hall. *How anyone expects children to be inspired in such dated and drab surroundings is a mystery still waiting to be answered.*

She looked at the huge windows that looked out onto the playground, partly wishing that she was out there and not in the stuffy hall. She then noticed something familiar at the farthest end. She could not quite make it out, but what she thought she saw was some kind of white light coming from the other side of the glass. It was hard for her to tell if it was simply the sun shining through, but something told her it was more than that. 'It can't be what I think it is, can it?' She could not make out a figure, just a distinctive glow – a glow that she had now seen twice before.

She panicked deep within but continued to stare, wondering if she was possibly some kind of a psychic vessel for the dead. *What else could it be?*

Glaring at the visitor, she suddenly heard a voice calling her.

'Courtney ... Courtney.' It repeated her name, again and again, growing louder with each repetition.

She closed her eyes in the hope of it all being in her mind. 'This is not happening; this is not happening. Angel of God, my guardian dear, to whom – no, shut up. I don't even believe in that stuff anymore,' she whispered to herself.

The voice in her head had become louder and with each recurrence had a sterner tone to it. She raised her hands to cover her ears, but just before she could cover them completely, she was broken out of her petrified state.

'COURTNEY.'

She looked up toward the lectern and realised her name was bellowing from the loudspeakers in the hall. The voice was that of the head teacher, Mrs Landor, who was calling her to approach the front of the stage.

Mrs Landor was a rather tall woman in her late fifties. She wore a grey trouser suit (she never wore skirts) and had shoulder length brown hair that was obviously dyed to cover the grey, which was forcing its way through regardless. Her speaking voice was incredibly proper and stern but still somehow managed to remain very soft and gentle. 'Courtney,' she said for the fifth time with her pleasant yet clearly agitated manner. 'You're up now, my dear. Could you please pay attention?'

Courtney realised the crowd were giggling and must have seen her whispering to herself. She looked directly at Mrs Landor, then at the window to where the glowing figure was, but it had gone. The audience stared at her like a mob of meerkats in anticipation of the unintentional piece of entertainment that was set to come.

She began to really question if she was indeed a little kooky as that type of thing always seems to happen when she's anxious and agitated. She turned to Mrs Landor. 'It's ok,' she whispered. 'You can move on, my piece isn't really ready anyway.' She was trying to get out of the embarrassing situation she had developed for herself, which she was convinced could now only get worse by reading her most personal thoughts out loud to the whole school.

'Hey Courtney,' shouted a female voice from the audience. 'I'm holding on girl, just like you said.'

Courtney heard the voice of encouragement and instantly recognised that it came unexpectedly from her new found friend, Alexandra. She looked at the floor toward her journal that was resting by her chair and thought hard about whether it was the right time to let it be heard by anyone other than herself. *Are you just encouraging me to walk straight through a land mine?* With the little amount of time she had left to decide, she picked up her journal and opened the first page. Inside, there was a quote that she had written shortly after her mother died that suddenly seemed very relevant now. It read, 'Life's too short for regrets. Always remember – everything happens for a reason.' She originally wrote it so that she would always stay focused on the idea that her mum and dad didn't die for nothing.

With that, she came to a decision. She gulped in apprehension, carefully closed the journal and walked tentatively to the lectern. She placed the book open in front of her like she was about to deliver a sermon to the congregation, adjusted the microphone to suit her height, took a deep breath and began her speech. 'You know,' she said nervously, attempting to get comfortable with hearing her own voice come out of the speakers. She mumbled to herself in shock and said, 'Whoa ... is that what I sound like?' What she further failed to realise was that whether you mumble or not, if you're near a microphone, you will still be heard.

A boy who was sitting in front of Alexandra shouted, 'You mean like a total bore?' A number of other students giggled at the comment. Alexandra clenched her fist and rammed it into the shoulder of the boy, who screeched in agony.

Courtney looked over at Alexandra and chuckled. 'Sorry, I'm just nervous.' She took a deep breath and slowly but bravely began her speech. 'You see, many things have happened to me - horrible things that I wouldn't wish on anyone. Things that at first glance, would appear to have had a negative effect on the rest of my life – things that in my estimation were terrible injustices, so much so that I find myself constantly asking, why me? Why did I lose my dad before I even met him? Why ten years later, did I lose my mum in a horrific car accident? Why was I visited by ...' she paused and looked out at the audience where twelve hundred eyes were boring into her. She looked over at the window where she had seen the glow, but all she could see now were those dreadful curtains. She turned back to the crowd, and with an apologetic tone as if she was looking for acceptance, she nervously said, '... an evil spirit?'

Some of the students in the audience looked at each other and smiled.

'No,' said Courtney very loudly and assertively. 'An evil spirit.' This time it was said as a definite statement of fact, with an air of confidence and certainty. She realised that it was time she stopped hiding from what she knew had happened in her own past. 'Just for everyone to think that I must have serious problems. Why do I find myself being bullied for being intelligent?'

Alexandra, who was seated toward the back, bowed her head on hearing Courtney's sadness at being bullied, before punching the boy in front of her again.

'And why oh why, can I not get my hair to do what I want in the morning?' Some of the crowd thankfully giggled at her one attempt at humour. 'Of course, there will always be others all over the world who would consider themselves to be in a far worse position than your own, and there is absolutely no doubt that is true. So if we could travel back in time, back to our past and change things to work more in our favour, would we? Would you?'

On hearing her questions, the students noticeably sat up and started listening with interest. The words time travel evoked everyone's fantasies about what it would mean to change their past or see the future.

'If time travel is possible, then I believe that the future must already have happened in the same way that the past has. It's just that memories don't exist on a forward plane.

59

But basically every moment in time, be it past, present or future, has already taken place.

The whole crowd, including the teachers, were now all listening intently with curious frowns on their faces.

'Let me try to explain. With the past, we know it exists because we have been there, as well as seen documentation, photographs and even some videos. With the present, we know it exists because we are in it right now. However, as far as the future is concerned, there's currently no way of seeing or experiencing it. So if we hypothetically say that time travel is possible, most likely via a black hole, well then if we were to travel back to the past, our present would suddenly become our past self's future. Because our past self is living in what they can only determine to be their present, but because we have come back from their future, we know that it exists already – that it's already happened. Therefore, if we take that theory forward, our present – i.e. right now – must be our future self's past. What will you all be doing one year from now? Well in one year's time, we'll all catch up with our future self and find out the answer. Then you'll realise that this moment; today; the present, is now the past. What we just don't realise is that our future self is there right now, already looking back at today as one of those memories I talked about; perhaps by looking at one of those photographs that he just took.' She pointed at the photographer who wasn't keen on all the eyes suddenly averting their gaze toward him.

Alexandra scratched her head, as did many of the others in the hall, but as confused as some of them were, they seemed strangely interested in listening further.

'The present is the only real time we know. The past is a memory existing only in our minds. The future is a dream that we are not quite sure of yet, in a similar way that we are not sure about the past as our memories start to fade.

'Now if I can one day create a black hole that will bend time to my advantage, then I will be able to travel both forward and back, but if as many think, our futures haven't happened yet, then no black hole could take us there as it would have no destination that currently exists to go to; therefore implying that the black hole is not only taking us to the future but is also creating the future in order for it to be able to get us there in the first place.' She paused and took a breath. 'Now I don't know about you, but in my estimation, that just sounds crazy. Now, as we have known for some years that time travel to the future is theoretically possible – just search time travel on Google to see the current theories – it begs the question, how can it be unless the future has already happened? I can't travel in a rocket to the second sun that sits directly next to our sun can I? But why?'

The crowd had been taken in so much by everything she had said, that as they looked quizzically at her for an answer, they had forgotten obvious facts that they already knew, even with their limited education.

'Because quite clearly a second sun does not exist.'

The crowd all nodded at each other as they realised the obviousness of the statement.

Courtney smiled as she grew in confidence.

The young crowd, as well as the teachers, were all sitting open-mouthed at the scope of everything she had said. She could almost hear all their combined brains ticking as they tried to comprehend everything she had verbally thrown at them.

'You see, there must be a destination in order to take the journey to it. However, what my theory ultimately means is that our whole existence must be pre-destined. It cannot be changed or altered because it has already happened. The universe knows exactly what we are going to do next. How can we change what already exists? Well I promise you; if it's possible, I'm gonna find out. As I for one would ...' she paused for a moment as she suddenly felt her eyes being weighted down with water. 'I would like ... my mum and dad back.' She continued to get more emotional as she spoke. A couple of tears rolled down her cheek and her voice quivered. 'I'd like to be part of a normal family. I'd also like to change what turned me into a school freak and most definitely, take away all those years of psychiatrist's visits but I doubt very much if any of that is possible so if it's not ...' She suddenly became more assertive but was still clearly very emotional. 'We are all just going to have to come to the realisation that certain things in our lives will always suck, and there is nothing we can do about it.'

She stood and faced the crowd, who were now in a sort of stunned silence and with her sleeve she wiped the tears from her face. She reached for her journal and took it off the lectern before walking back to her seat, fearing she had just made the biggest mistake of her life. She knew that letting everybody in on her most personal thoughts may have just resulted in her making a total fool of herself in front of the whole school.

Then a single clap echoed from the back of the hall. To Courtney, the sound was like a surgeon who has been waiting for that first beat of the heart after performing a risky surgery. Gradually, a few more started until the heart was beating once more. Then the hall erupted in raucous applause. Some of the boys whistled. Loud cheers came from every section of the hall, and the ground shook as they all began to stamp their feet.

Courtney sat on her chair, a little intimidated by all the commotion. She sheepishly raised a smile and stared out at the huge crowd. As good as it felt, there was one thing that she had not quite realised. As she looked over at Alexandra who was standing atop her chair, waving her fist in the air, she was totally oblivious to the fact that today was the day that she quite possibly just gave the most important speech of her life - a speech that would undoubtedly change her life forever. However, if her theory was actually correct, it would not have changed anything. Instead, she would be about to step down an undoubtedly huge but inevitable path of discovery.

When the applause eventually died down, Courtney and the other contestants were told they could leave the hall to go on their lunch break while the winning piece was deliberated amongst the teachers. The select group of literary students were signalled out first in early celebration of their achievements. The early departure would give them a chance to gain the most sought after prize in the school playground; first place in the queue for the ice cream van. Soon after, the hoards of remaining students who had been sitting patiently listening to their fellow students would also be released. However, although Courtney was still riding emotionally high from being treated like a rock star as she exited the school hall, there was something else that still bothered her. So she allowed her coveted place in the junk food line to be potentially lost and strolled cautiously over to the other side of the window where she thought she saw another spirit ten minutes previously. As she approached, she was somewhat relieved to find that there was nothing noticeably out of sorts. She stood underneath the huge tall window and took a deep sigh of double intention. She was relieved to discover there was nothing untoward, but at the same time, she was contented that her moment in the spotlight went totally in the opposite direction to how she originally thought it might. Just as she took a step back to go and grab some kind of semi-decent place in the ice cream queue before the throng of students were let out, she spotted something in the gravel that surrounded the perimeter of the school building. She looked down to see what it could be and was surprised to find what looked like an exact same copy of her notebook that she had just read from. *That's weird. What are the chances of that?* She purchased the book from a speciality art shop in town. Bending over to pick it up, she immediately noticed that not only were all of its pages missing, but the cover looked like it had been very wet at some stage in its existence. 'How odd,' she muttered to herself and curiously opened it up to find that there was actually one page left inside, and as she stared at it, she could not believe what she saw written in front of her. Her expression turned to a deep shock, but just at that moment, she was broken out of her state by a familiar lone voice.

'Court,' shouted Alexandra as she ran over to her.

The rest of the school students were now pouring out the doors of the hall towards the ice cream van. Courtney quickly closed the book and shoved it hurriedly in her bag just as Alexandra arrived in front of her.

'What was that you just shoved in there?'

'Oh ... nothing. It's not important, don't worry.' Courtney had a slightly unreadable expression on her face, but it quickly changed to a happier demeanour as she grabbed hold of Alexandra's hand. 'But what is important, is that we go grab our place in the ice cream queue so I can buy you a huge double cone with sprinkles, two flakes and a squirt of raspberry sauce; my way of saying a big fat thank you.'

As they both hastily walked towards the ice cream van with each other's arms linked together, Courtney's expression suddenly changed from the happy appearance she had just shown Alexandra, to a concerned and worried look. Was it a result of the inevitable wait to find out if she had won the competition, or was it something far more concerning? One thing Courtney knew was that nothing in her life ever seemed to be straightforward and her friendship with Alexandra was already proving to be anything but.

~ CHAPTER TEN ~

Pik Thistle

Two years had passed since Courtney's inaugural speech and she was back in the same school hall, except she was now trying to finish the last question on one of her exam papers. She was having trouble concentrating though as other things preyed heavily on her mind. Having chosen to stay on at sixth form to gain the qualifications she needed to attend university and study physics, she found there was someone else missing from the hall that had not chosen to remain. Soon after Courtney's winning performance on time travel, and shortly after she turned sixteen, Alexandra left school for good, as she was convinced she had 'done her time,' as she crudely put it.

Courtney couldn't help but wonder what trouble Alexandra may have gotten herself into since leaving school. She could only imagine the nuisance she must be making of herself. She and her family had moved out of the area due to some family issues and they hadn't seen each other since. Courtney had plenty of time to think about it as she was trying to pace herself so she didn't finish her exam too quickly again, only to be accused of cheating.

'The one and only time I make any kind of friend and she vanishes, leaving me all alone again. Just my luck,' she whispered to her watch, the one friend she knew could never leave her.

Courtney's eighteenth birthday was coming up in May and she had been thinking lately that it would be great to celebrate it with Alexandra. She was the only person who ever resembled a friend in her life, even if it had just been for a short period, and even if she wasn't totally sure if Alexandra ever considered her to really be a true friend in the first place.

'Maybe she really was a bully, just giving me fake respect. As if she was choosing not to fight me because she really had a soft spot for me, but in truth, she was never actually sure if she would win,' she continued to whisper. 'Well maybe one day I'll find out, if I ever see her again.'

'Shhhh,' said one of the teachers.

Courtney quickly averted her attention back to the test paper to finish the last question. The paper was for her mathematics exam and it had pictures of balloons as an aid to work out the puzzle. She didn't find the brainteaser particularly problematic. In fact, it was the exact opposite. She found the question so easy that the balloons distracted her, and so she began to daydream about happier times when she was younger.

She remembered how much she used to love releasing helium balloons into the air with different messages on them. How she would grab them from birthday parties, shopping centres and fun fairs, take them to her garden to release into the wind, and watch them soar into the sky. For days, weeks and sometimes months, she was left wondering where they could be and who could have found them, but much to her dismay, she never ever heard anything back, not once.

This year however, she got a response from a very different kind of balloon message that she did not even realise she had sent.

Once she had regained her concentration and placed the last digit down on her paper, she put all her pencils and rulers into her bag and stood up to walk out of the hall. Just before she was about to walk, she noticed Mrs Landor who came through the main doorway and whispered something into the ear of the teacher who was on guard by the door. She then pointed directly in Courtney's direction.

Delicately under her breath Courtney mumbled, 'Surely they don't think I've cheated again? This is a perfectly reasonable amount of time to have finished an exam.'

Mrs Landor raised a smile and beckoned her to hurry up and approach her.

'Perhaps not then.' Courtney was struggling to imagine what it could be about, so she tentatively walked towards them. As her worry increased Mrs Landor smiled once again. Ok, somewhat odd, thought Courtney as she raised her eyebrows.

'Courtney my dear, would you please come with me, I have a message for you.'

Courtney found Mrs Landor's expression very hard to read because she'd always had a hard time differentiating between her good and bad demeanour. 'You mean just me? What kind of message, Miss?'

'Indeed, my dear; just you. All I will say is that this message has travelled a long way to reach you.'

'What ... like a message balloon?' Courtney smiled at her own comment, as she thought about her earlier recollection.

'Yes, I suppose so. And that balloon has landed ... in a manner of speaking, and written all over it was your winning piece of writing on time travel.'

'Huh?'

'Don't panic my dear. I may have just confused you unnecessarily. Why don't you come to my office and I'll explain everything.' She smiled at her reassuringly.

'Ok,' replied Courtney with an uneasy delivery. She had only previously been to the headmistress's office to be reprimanded, so she found the situation a little unsettling.

Mrs Landor walked down the hallway and Courtney followed close behind in complete silence. To Courtney, the walk seemed like the length of a marathon, because as much as she did not have a problem with Mrs Landor; she also did not have much to say to her either.

They reached the office and Courtney was beckoned inside. 'Come in my dear, sit down.'

She tentatively entered as she couldn't help but feel like Red Riding Hood being summoned inside by the wolf. She walked over to the centre of the room and sat on a seat in front of the large desk by the window. Mrs Landor sat on the seat opposite. The room was a bog standard head teacher's office, not much to shout about, just a desk with some chairs and a few dull pictures on the wall of totally random landscapes.

'You're probably wondering what this is all about.'

Courtney raised her eyebrows, as she found it even more difficult to respond vocally now that she was alone with the head of the school.

'I received a phone call today; a phone call which in of itself will certainly leave me happy for a very long time, because of the simple fact that I got to speak with this gentleman. However, more importantly, he was enquiring about you dear.' She spoke with an unmistakable tone of excitement in her voice.

'Who was, Miss?'

'A gentleman with the rather unique name of Professor Pinakin Thistle, MA, PhD and some other qualifications. I Googled him after I hung up the phone and he has about fifteen letters after—'

'Professor Pik Thistle?'

'Yes … indeed, but it gets better. Let me explain.' She turned to her computer screen. 'Professor Pik Thistle is an American theoretical physicist, known for his prolific contributions in gravitational physics and astrophysics and for having trained a generation of scientists.'

Courtney listened, as Mrs Landor (who was clearly reading off the internet) spoke with the excitement of a child reading their first letter from Father Christmas.

'He has had many books published on the subject of time travel and space and is widely regarded as one of the best theoretical physicists of the modern age. His recent work has covered wormholes and black hole cosmology and most recently, gravitational waves … whatever they are.' Mrs Landor chuckled at her own bemusement. 'He is currently one of the leading professors at America's most prolific scientific institute in Los Angeles; LosTech.'

'Miss, I know who he is. He's my idol.'

'Oh, yes of course he would be. How stupid of me. Well Courtney, how would you feel ... about moving to America?' She stared at Courtney with a huge grin on her face.

Courtney stared back at her in total shock.

'To study at LosTech?'

All of a sudden, as if she had been holding her breath while trying to comprehend the situation, Courtney couldn't help but spit out her next words. 'This is clearly a joke, but why would the head of the school play this kind of joke on me. What date is it? It's not Comic Relief or April Fool's Day, is it?'

'It's no joke, my dear. It is absolutely possible. All you have to do ... is say yes.'

The seriousness of what had just been said suddenly hit Courtney, and heavy emotion quickly took over her body. Her eyes swelled up as she began to cry from the gravity of what it all could mean.

'Somehow, your theories, and in particular that piece you did on time travel a couple of years ago, landed on the desk of Professor Thistle. He said something about reading it on MySpace.'

'I put it on MySpace after it won,' she said in surprise as if she never expected anyone to ever see that page. '... oh my God.'

'Yes, well, he also said, and I quote, 'Any fifteen year old who can theorise like that, deserves to explore those theories in the best possible surroundings. I'd like to offer her a place at LosTech in California this coming academic year'. All you have to do dear, is sign the paperwork he's e-mailed over and send it back.'

'This is ridiculous. This is just crazy. I don't even have my results yet. Why would he do this? I need to go and think somewhere.' Courtney had become a little tongue-tied due to the shock. Nothing that positive had ever even remotely happened to her before. Yet there she was, in complete shock, having just won her equivalent of the lottery and unsurprisingly, totally lost for words.

'This is it, Courtney. The moment you've been waiting

for. I'm so proud of you. It's time for you to go and do something amazing. Just promise me you'll leave your troublemaking side behind.'

Courtney looked at her, eyes and mouth wide open. The thought that the school was only supporting her now that something good had happened, did run through her mind. *In future years they'll say they taught the girl that went to LosTech.* Too excited to worry about any false credit the school would take, she accepted Mrs Landor's words as genuine.

Mrs Landor leant forward and in her proudest voice said, 'Go on Courtney, go and change the world. I know you can.'

~ CHAPTER ELEVEN ~

What not to do with your life

Hunched up inside the large recessed doorway of an electrical store on London's busy Oxford Street on a wet morning in May, was Alexandra. She was filthy dirty, hungry and wearing ragged jeans and a t-shirt that looked like it had not been washed for months. There were various boxes and dirty blankets over her that she was using in an attempt to keep warm and her hair had been crudely cut short to make it easier to look after but ironically, it had ended up not being looked after at all, causing her to look quite the opposite of the girl Courtney had once described as a 'real life, hair-styling and make-up doll.'

She had been living on the streets for about a year, ever since her parents got divorced when her mum found out her dad had regularly visited escorts. She felt that she'd had enough of her mum's hypocrisy – as *she'd* met Alexandra's father when she was an escort herself.

After a blazing row, she left for a life on the streets and had become more and more used to it by the day. Whenever she had a notion to try to do something positive, she just couldn't get Courtney's damning statement out of her head, *'We are all just going to have to come to the realisation that certain things in our lives will always suck, and there is nothing we can do about it.'*

Over the last two years, the poignant quote from Courtney's speech had become lodged in her head like a splinter; painful and very hard to get out. The most ambitious decision she had made lately, was to make a home for herself on Oxford Street; the busiest street for shopping in the whole of London. She had been told you could make more there from passers-by, than anywhere else in the city. As it turned out, it was very true, as that's where all the tourists came in their thousands to spend their money.

However, the double-edged sword was that she knew it was also the place you were most often moved on by the police and most likely to meet undesirables. If she slept in too long, she would often get a rude awakening from the shop owner when they opened up in the morning. Being a young, attractive female, she was also often approached by unsavoury men wanting to take her somewhere private. None of which was how she thought her life would turn out and certainly not what Courtney always imagined she'd be doing, but she was also short-sighted of the possibility of anything coming around the corner to change it.

At that same moment, somewhere close by, Courtney and Claudette had in fact just walked around a corner together, looking for a particular London address.

Throughout the years, Courtney had progressively found her own style and now that she was eighteen, she had definitely decided on what made her comfortable. Always influenced by her oriental bloodline, whilst still retaining her Hertfordshire roots, she had become more and more individual and now sported a very eclectic sense of fashion. Items would vary day to day, but her favourites were scruffy black Doc Martin boots, between five and ten bracelets on each wrist and some form of waistcoat that could be anything from denim to woollen. She also wore lots of different clips in her long hair to keep most of it up in a quirky and funky style, leaving sections of it to hang down and a fringe that sat just over her eyebrows. Today, for her eighteenth birthday, she had chosen to wear a long and loose chiffon floral blouse consisting of pinks, greens and yellows, with a brown skirt underneath that fell just below her knees. To finish the look, she wore a black, heavy metal style hipster belt with metal studs. The whole getup was young, fresh, and modern, but at the same time, she managed to retain an intellectual and expressive look.

'Do you have any idea what you'll do with the money?'

'I'm not gonna throw it all away, if that's what you're asking,' said Courtney

'I just need to make sure you're looking at it with the eyes of a responsible adult. Girls your age don't often get two hundred and ten thousand pounds handed to them.'

'It's going to help me find out why certain things in my life have happened to me. I know everyone thinks I'm crazy, but it's what I have to do. Where that will take me, I don't know. We all take journeys in our lives. Some get us to our destinations, some don't, but now I'm eighteen, I'm just glad I can make these decisions on my own without being held back and forced to find out if I'm crazy or not first.'

'You know, I think I've learnt after the last few years of knowing you, that you'll do exactly what you want once you've made your mind up on something. So I guess the time for lectures is over. Like you said, you're eighteen now, so it's time for you to make your own decisions. Just be careful, that's all. Oh, and by the way, happy birthday. I don't think I said it yet, did I?'

'No, you didn't, but I forgive you,' she said smiling. 'I don't suppose I'll have much of a celebration though. To be honest, getting this money officially signed over to me is all the celebration I need today. This money is basically my father's life, so it's not only my birthday, but more importantly, it's a celebration of him.'

'That's lovely, Courtney. I'm sure he's watching over you right now, and I'm sure he's very proud.'

'You're such a sucker. I'm gonna go and spend it all on drugs.'

'No, Courtney, you can't. You need to–'

'Oh dear, suckered again. You need to be wiser to the youth or someone less trustworthy will be able to convince you of anything.'

'You are a nightmare,' she said smiling. 'Please reassure

me the thing about your dad was genuine.'

'Do I really need to? What time do the solicitors open anyway?'

'Nine.' Claudette looked at her watch. 'It's only half past eight now, so don't worry.'

'What was the address again? What number are we looking for?'

'First we have to get to Oxford Street, but we're nearly there. It's so annoying you can't park closer these days. When I was a kid—'

'Yes, I know. When you were a kid, life was so much easier. You could park where you wanted; you were a name not a number and you actually talked to people with your voice instead of texting or Facebooking.'

'Yes, alright, Miss Sarcasm, so I've said that once or twice before. Well anyway, once we're on Oxford Street, we're looking for two hundred and ninety two. I've been there before so don't worry, I know where it is.'

The doorway Alexandra was in was large and deep, which made her feel, even if only to a tiny degree, like she was not actually sleeping directly on the street. This was a small comfort in her dreadful world.

'Excuse me, love,' said a man dressed in an expensive looking suit. 'You wouldn't know where three hundred and sixty five is would you? I've already walked up here twice and I can't find it.'

Alexandra looked at the man whilst still trying to adjust her eyes to the morning sunlight. In the past, that moment was reserved for just herself and her teddies. Now, strangers on the street could just walk straight into her bedroom and ask for directions. *How would he like it if I just walked into his bedroom? On the other hand, maybe he would.* 'Idiot,' she mumbled.

The man didn't clearly hear what she said. 'Excuse me?' As he spoke he looked at her, and suddenly huge compassion reigned over him. In the space of ten seconds, he had looked into her eyes and saw all the sadness within. 'I'm sorry; you've obviously just woken up.' He reached in his pocket and took out his wallet. 'Here, take this.' He handed her a twenty pound note. 'Don't worry, I won't bother you anymore. I'll ask someone else. Just try and spend it on something positive.'

Alexandra had experienced that kind of thing from men many times. She thought she recognised the pattern now and had realised that amazingly, even though she looked as rough as hell, men could be suckers for a young girl in need of help. This was how she made most of her money, from men who thought that a twenty pound note was some form of chat up line to the homeless. She also quickly realised that to a lot of men, she was a fantasy, a challenge or possibly worse. As if once they hand her the money, they expect an offer to go somewhere and earn it in return. She stared at the man for a split second, reached out and took his money. 'Thanks.' She did not mind taking someone's money if they were stupid enough to offer it.

The man grinned, thinking he had done his good deed for the day, and they both stood for a moment staring in silence.

Alexandra was convinced he was waiting for her to say something provocative, even if he did not even realise it himself.

The man seemed confused and just continued to stare at her. He then turned and walked away.

∞

'It's just down there,' said Claudette as she and Courtney finally turned into Oxford Street. 'You see where that electrical store sign is sticking out?'

'How far down are you looking?'

'You see where that homeless lad is just packing his stuff up? It's right there.'

'Oh right, yeah. I see now. I was looking way off down the road.' Courtney smiled. 'That's not a guy though, that's a girl. Age really is creeping up on you – perhaps you should take things easy.'

Claudette stared at her with squinted eyes and then

simultaneously, they both giggled. They crossed a junction and carried on walking.

They arrived at the solicitor's office, and it turned out to be a glass door directly to the side of the electrical store where Alexandra had made her home minutes before. Except Alexandra was now gone. Courtney was desperate to see Alexandra on her birthday and without realising, for a brief moment, her wish had just come true. Claudette rang the solicitor's office buzzer, but as they were early; nobody answered, and they were left to stand outside in the cold.

'I could really use a coffee,' said Claudette.

'Told you.'

'What? No you didn't. Don't try and tell me I'm going deaf as well.'

'No, look,' said Courtney as she gestured her head down the street, trying very hard to be discreet.

'What the hell are you talking about?'

'The girl – I told you it was a girl.'

Claudette looked down the street and saw the same homeless person, now minus her home of boxes and blankets, walking back up the road towards them. 'Well done. You have perfect vision. Just wait till you get to my age. The future comes to us all one day.'

Alexandra was now in striking distance and as Courtney caught a glimpse, her expression changed. Alexandra had her head slightly down and so didn't notice Courtney.

Courtney tentatively spoke, 'Alexandra?' She was completely stunned by the sight of her friend. 'Alexandra,' she screamed excitedly once she was one hundred percent sure it was her. 'Oh my God.'

Alexandra looked up at Courtney and noticed how beautiful she was. She began to feel a little ashamed of her own appearance. 'Court ... wow. Look at you.'

Suddenly, the reality of seeing Alexandra there like that hit Courtney like a thundering train. 'How ... why? What's going on?' She was confused as to how it could have happened, knowing how clued up and street smart Alexandra was back in school and how she had always kept herself well groomed and presentable.

'It's a long story, but I guess you wouldn't get much on eBay for me now, huh? It's all good though; don't worry about me. I've been here a while. This is me now.'

'Oh it so isn't.'

A middle aged man in a suit approached the solicitor's door.

'Oh God, another one,' said Alexandra. 'I can see I'll be busy today.'

'Courtney?'

Courtney nodded but still couldn't take her gaze off Alexandra.

'Come on up then and we'll get this sorted. Big day for you huh?' He turned his key in the door and walked inside the building.

'In more ways than you could imagine.'

The man turned and looked at her. He then glanced at Alexandra and sighed. 'Don't tell me you've just been sold a sob story and now you're thinking maybe you don't deserve this or something?'

'Deserve what? What's he on about?' Alexandra was slightly bemused by the question.

'No, no, I deserve it alright, but once it's mine, I can do what I want with it. So please, keep your opinions to yourself.' Courtney turned to Alexandra although she continued to speak to the solicitor. 'You've just made a very big decision very easy.'

'You mean what not to do with your life? You're welcome. No need to thank me.'

'Alex, will you do me a favour and wait for me across the road in McDonalds? There's something I have to sort out here first, but then I'd like to speak with you, if that's ok?' Courtney turned to Claudette. 'Could you do me a favour, and give her some money for a coffee?'

'Hey don't worry,' said Alexandra, raising the twenty pound note in the air. 'Work started early for me today. I don't know if I can hang around though. I'm really quite busy.'

Courtney sighed, misreading where the money had come from. 'Please, there's something I really need to ask you.'

Alexandra stared at her thinking she could feel the world's largest pep talk coming.

'Alright,' said Courtney. 'At the very least, have a birthday coffee with me.'

'It's your birthday?'

She nodded.

'Well,' sighed Alexandra. 'Why didn't you say? I guess one coffee wouldn't hurt then.'

'Thank you, but please do wait for me. I had this idea, something I should do, and you've just cemented it for me. I promise it will be worth your while.'

'Alright, I promise. I'll be waiting.' Alexandra could not hide the fact that she was a little intrigued by what her friend could possibly be proposing and also figured that Courtney probably owed her a little something in life anyway, as she was convinced that her lack of motivation was somehow down to Courtney's prediction of everyone's future.

'Maybe I do deserve a little payback ... I mean payment,' she said, correcting her Freudian slip, as she carefully negotiated the traffic to make her way across the road to McDonald's.

~ CHAPTER TWELVE ~

I think I hate time

Three years had passed since Courtney's fateful altercation in the school playground with Alexandra, but something about her current environment seemed strangely reminiscent of that time, as she sat on yet another long wooden bench that spanned the length of a wall. Although, there were no hand drawn star charts behind her now. There were however some items in exactly the same vein, but instead of being drawn with chalk; they were now high quality photos of different planetary systems, along with other phenomena of the universe.

She was definitely nowhere near the John Twaddle School. Instead, she sat in a waiting room, somewhere on the campus of LosTech University. However, it wasn't so much a room; it was more like a long and very wide hallway, with unusually tall wooden doors at both ends and a desk in the far corner where it looked like a receptionist should be sat.

There were no windows, just a couple of fans on the ceiling and a water dispenser at one end that created an overall dark and stuffy atmosphere.

The school building had originally been built sometime in the nineteen thirties, and consequently had a very distinct Art Deco style. Beginning its life as a large mansion, it had once been the home of a respected and important scientist. Over the years, the structure had been extended as more and more students flocked to LosTech, flawlessly mixing new architecture with the old. The magnificent combination was reflected in the university's mission statement that was inscribed into a large wooden plaque positioned above the main entrance to the school that read, 'LosTech is a highly regarded, very successful and historic school, founded for the purpose of studying what the future may hold by embracing the discoveries of the past and cultivating all which is scientific, making sure no theory is an impossibility, just a breakthrough yet to be discovered.'

Courtney was sitting uncomfortably in one of the oldest sections of the school. Her hair gently blew in the wind that was being generated by the fans that were spinning slowly on the ceiling above her. Yet these very basic contraptions barely made any difference to the lack of air conditioning in the room.

'No wonder there's no receptionist,' muttered Courtney to herself. 'She probably melted and is now stuck to the floor.' She looked incredibly hot and weary, a definite result of the lack of ventilation in the room, as well as the constant Californian heat she was experiencing for the first time.

The jet lag she was suffering from was not helping either. After travelling long haul for the first time in her life, she was finding the adjustment quite difficult. Her mother had promised to take her to the Philippines one day to meet the rest of her family, but the trip never materialised. So she now sat, struggling to get to grips with the time difference and fighting a heat of which she rarely experienced for more than one day per year back home.

'I think I hate time,' she whispered as she waited patiently, sweat pouring from her forehead. Deep within she was panicking – for the man awaiting her on the other side of the large ominous wooden door that was positioned at one end of the long room, was none other than the world famous, Professor Pinakin Thistle.

Inside, the professor's office was very large but full of all manner of things, giving it a cluttered lived-in look. There was a distinct smell of old books circulating in the warm air, largely due to the fact that on two of the walls on either side, were shelves that stretched from the floor to the ceiling that were filled with said books on every aspect of space and time, as well as all manner of other loosely related subjects. Further books that would not fit on the shelves were piled up waist height on the floor behind his desk. The only thing even remotely modern in there was to the left of the desk, where there was a huge glass aquarium that had been built into a pillar and housed a large amount of amazingly coloured marine fish of all different shapes and sizes; something he had demanded from the school funds to help him focus his thoughts. The room was extremely bright, a noticeable contrast from the dingy waiting room outside. Four slim but very tall ceiling-high windows at the farthest end of the room looked out over a large Creek that had a huge stone sculpture sundial at its centre; a symbol of what the university stood for – natural physics embodied by time and space.

Professor Pik Thistle was a relatively short man. He was in his mid-sixties with rather large ears that protruded from his shaven head. He had a full beard that was totally black, apart from an inch and a half wide white strip on his chin that gave him a look reminiscent of a skunk, a nickname he was also given by some of the students due to his constant sweating whenever he gave one of his very animated lectures. He had huge bags under his eyes from the years of staying up until the early hours waiting for a life-changing breakthrough in the physics of space and time.

Professor Thistle closed the file he had been reading on Courtney and pushed a telecom button on his desk. 'Miss Nivots,' he said in his strong southern Californian accent. 'Would you like to come through?'

~ CHAPTER THIRTEEN ~

I'm definitely not Doc Emmett Brown

Courtney's eyes opened as soon as she heard her name being spoken by the deep resonant voice that was projecting through a loudspeaker on the wall. After a split second of contemplation, she realised that she was finally about to meet the man whose images she had seen in books and on the internet since she was a very young girl.

With her eyelids feeling like a pair of blinds which were being pulled down for the night, she hastily filled a plastic cup from the water dispenser next to her. After taking a few large gulps, she poured the last little bit over her hot and sweaty face and then wiped the excess off with her hands, gave a quick shake of her head to wake herself up and while brimming with fake confidence, she opened the door to the office.

Californian sunlight flooded out, enveloping her like a blanket. The contrast in brightness from where she had been waiting was almost blinding.

'Good afternoon Professor,' she said, with possibly a tad too much excitement in her voice. 'Can I just say before it's too late, I'm really sorry if ... whoa, nice fish,' she said noticing the large tropical fish tank embedded into the pillar. 'I always wanted fish like that, but I never seemed to even be able to look after a goldfish without killing it, let alone anything like–' She stopped talking when she realised she had let her nerves take off on a tangent and that Professor Thistle was staring at her with a bemused and stern expression on his face. 'As I was saying, I apologise now if I act like an idiot, or if I already have acted like an idiot,' she said. 'I knew I probably would. It's just that I can't believe I'm actually here.'

'Come Courtney, sit down over here.' He beckoned her to a chair opposite him. 'It's great to finally meet you.' He stood up and offered his hand.

Courtney looked at him in disbelief and said, 'Meet me?' She thought the reverse would have been more apt.

'I've been waiting a long time. Sit, please, let's chat.'

She sat down opposite him on a large ornate chair that looked like it belonged in a throne room rather than a head teacher's office. She was still a little staggered that she was even in America, as well as being invited there personally to study at the foremost university of science by one of the pioneers of current time and space theories. Differences between the two countries were already patently clear, and she was still suffering from the nine-hour flight. As the sunshine poured through the glass windows, she found herself massively struggling to keep her eyes open.

'So time — a funny thing, huh? But I could tell right away after reading your paper, that you just love it.'

'Uh huh.' She nodded her head in agreement. 'Struggling with it a little right now though,' she said, letting him know of her fatigue with a little humour.

'Before you start here at this school, I just wanted to make sure you understand a few things.'

'Yes, I do,' she responded instantly, only having heard the word 'understand'.

'You do what?'

She froze, realising that within just a few seconds of meeting him, she may have already made a terrible first impression. 'Un-der-stand,' she answered carefully, trying to think what he may want to hear.

'Understand what?'

She stared at him in silence and panicked internally as she realised she had no idea what he was talking about. 'I ... don't know,' she admitted embarrassingly, before continuing to speak at the speed of a train, in an attempt to ease the awkwardness she had created. 'I'm really sorry, I really am. I'm just so tired.'

'Look.' Professor Thistle's response was noticeably agitated. 'This is not a game. It's not a movie, and I'm definitely not Doc Emmett Brown, as some students like to joke. This is science at its most interesting, but it also happens to be one of the few examples of science that strikes a massive chord with the general populace. So because you're still young, I need to know that you understand this and are not just here because you saw *Back to the Future* when you were a child.'

Courtney stared at him, half listening but half panicking that she was already being told off on her first day as well as thinking about how much she loved *Back to the Future*.

'If you are serious,' he continued. 'This will engulf your whole life. Nothing else will matter. It will be extremely hard work. Although don't misunderstand, it can also be tons of fun as we discover new possibilities together.' His demeanour changed as he became even more serious. He focused hard on Courtney's eyes. 'But know this ...'

Her eyes quickly widened at the sudden assertion from him after they had slowly almost closed once again.

'And let me make one thing very clear. As human beings, we are hundreds, if not thousands of years away, from being capable of travelling through time. Hopefully, we'll discover the principles behind it and prove it's theoretically possible very soon, but to actually accomplish it, to get to see another time outside of your own ... is way beyond all of our lifetimes. If you have any other notion in your head than that, then you can just fly back ... right now.'

Courtney stared into Professor Thistle's eyes for what seemed like a lifetime, though in reality it was just a few seconds. She was frozen, trying to work out the smartest thing she could say without totally destroying her chances of making a good first impression on her initial day. She finally opened her mouth but as soon as she spoke, she realised her tiredness was more in control than her intelligence. 'Back ... to the future,' she said flippantly, with a smile and in the style of Doc Emmett Brown. From Professor Thistle's expression, she realised it was not the moment for poorly timed jokes.

'Are you mocking me?'

'No, not at all sir but with all due respect,' she said, knowing she was about to run the risk of putting her opinion out there a little too early. 'Surely we can never assume to know what is waiting for us around the corner.' Although it was not a question, she phrased it slightly like one on purpose so as not to offend him with her youthful positivism. 'Where I come from, everyone would've said I would never be sat here in front of you. You're like the Simon Cowell of science.' Her smile beamed wide once again in the hope of easing the tense atmosphere in the room.

Professor Thistle stared at her. His lack of expression suggested to Courtney she may have been treading on dangerous ground with her attempt at lightening the mood.

'But here I am ...' her smile transformed into a healthy slab of cheese. '... ready to be told to shut up and stop digging great big holes for myself to fall into.'

Professor Thistle remained silent for a moment as he contemplated what he had let himself in for. 'School term begins first thing Monday morning,' he said with a serious tone. 'I look forward to seeing what ... insights you can offer this place once you've had time to rest. It would appear that you may have a little tenacity. So relax over the weekend and get yourself acclimatised. I'm very interested to see just what you're capable of Miss Nivots.'

~ CHAPTER FOURTEEN ~

A tale of horror

A slightly cooler air was now circulating inside Professor Thistle's office and Courtney noticed the light had dimmed a little outside. She wasn't yet clear how she was going to get to her accommodation, as she had literally come straight from the airport to the school. Feeling a little concerned about time she had asked the professor if he could give her directions. She knew it was very close but didn't want to spend hours on a journey that should only take minutes, especially on her own.

The professor said, 'Where exactly are you staying while you're here then?'

'Oh,' replied Courtney. 'Just five minutes from here apparently; isn't that great? It's an amazing, typically American-looking place. I feel like I've seen it in the movies my whole life, but it's so cheap.' Professor Thistle's decision to not kick her out on the spot was helping her relax a little as she began to chit chat with him. 'I'm sharing with four others that study here.'

'You're speaking of Creekside House?'

'Yes, that's it. Isn't that a great name as well? Although you're probably used to it, being American. We would never get a house in England with a name like that. It'd be something more like, Horsemuck Cottage, and you may think that's an exaggeration, but do you know I've actually seen a place-'

'It's haunted,' asserted the professor, cutting her off from her ramble.

'Huh?'

'Apparently ... I just thought you should know. I know exactly where it is, because it actually belongs to the university as nobody else would buy it. There's an old creek that runs past the house, hence the name. It's actually connected to the large Creek out front here, but it's blocked off by bollards so the tourists don't row their boats right onto campus.' Professor Thistle grinned before immediately replacing the smile with a more serious expression. 'But both the creek and the house hold a real tale of horror.'

'What like, spooky stuff?'

'That's what they say. Nothing we would put any weight on of course though, being scientists.'

Courtney felt herself being drawn into the story as she stared at the professor in anticipation of him continuing to tell her the details of what happened there. 'So what occurred there?'

'One of the previous inhabitants drowned her two children in the creek a hundred years or so ago. She tied rocks to their feet and threw them both in. Then apparently stood and watched as they struggled, grabbing at anything around them to stay afloat. As the story goes, her husband cheated on her and she couldn't bear the idea of anyone else having him. After she murdered the two little ones, she went upstairs where her husband was bathing and shot him between the eyes. She then dragged him naked to the creek, tied herself to him and pulled the two of them into the water. They say she wanted the family to be together forever. Apparently, the water ran red for weeks from all the blood. This place wasn't even built yet. So who knows? Maybe their bodies are still at the bottom of the Creek out there. Still think it's a great deal?' Professor Thistle had managed to create an eerie silence between them.

Courtney couldn't help but wonder if it was a test to gauge what her reaction to such a revelation would be. 'That's not nice,' she said slowly, breaking the silence whilst at the same time trying to figure out why he had just told her all that.

'That's why it's cheap you see. So every year, it's now filled with students from this school. Because of course, with you all being budding scientists, the idea of ghosts is quite laughable, right? Besides, since it started being let out to our students, there's been no report of any sightings. So fortunately for you, you get a great deal on the rent without having to worry about spooky spirits visiting you in the night.'

Courtney smiled back at him, but she was hiding a little unease behind her facade. She wondered if he had forgotten or indeed remembered what she had written in her school project and whether it was some kind of assessment. She decided to let it go for now and just head on to the house to find out if the story he had told her was actually true. She did her best not to show the professor the trepidation she now felt at the prospect of staying in a genuine haunted house. She really thought she had gotten away from all that, at least for the time being anyway. However, if Professor Thistle was right, they would seem to be following her everywhere she went. 'I suppose I better get going then. You know, get some rest.'

'Sure thing, I'll see you Monday, bright and early.'

She got up, directions in hand and walked towards the door.

'Miss Nivots?'

Courtney stopped and turned back to face Professor Thistle again. 'Yes Sir?'

'I have high hopes for you. I get the feeling you'll end up playing a big part in the research of time. But I warn you now – don't ever cross me - keep your smart remarks in line. We're a team here, with one goal. I won't tolerate anyone working alone for selfish reasons. If we can all stick to those core principles, everything will be fine. Are we clear?' He stared at her with piercing eyes.

She looked at him, a little taken aback. She had never been spoken to in that way by a teacher, but more importantly; she was thinking that it was definitely not clear, so of course with confidence she replied, 'Yes sir ... as crystal.'

~ CHAPTER FIFTEEN ~

Simply haunt us

Creekside House was a very large detached building in a very unique setting. The house was positioned relatively alone in front of a long, wide river that was used throughout the year by tourists for fishing, boating or somewhere peaceful to walk; amazing anyone who passed, as they couldn't help but be impressed with its aged beauty and quaint character. Unusually for California, the house used the Venetian influenced Palladian style quite heavily (not too dissimilar from The White House in Washington D.C.) but on a much smaller scale. Four white stone pillars stretched across the front of a large porch that you reached by climbing several red stone steps in the centre. On both sides of the large blue wooden door, were two large windows, each with wooden shutters on the inside and iron cages securing them from intruders on the outside; perhaps the only Spanish influence that was adopted. There were another six windows running across the top, with the middle four encompassed by a red, rickety looking iron balcony and all of which were minus the crude security measures. One solitary attic window was positioned in the centre of the pitched red roof.

Built well over one hundred years ago, when the rough gravel path alongside the river would have been used as an access road for the occupant's horses and carriages, it has remained architecturally unchanged to that day, but the peeling paint, water stained walls and wild green creeping fig that covered the walls, steps and railings, made a once beautiful home look a tad creepy now. The records detailing the building's exact construction date had strangely been lost over time. As well as why the distinctive Palladian style, had been used that far west where colonial Spanish homes were far more prominent.

The people living along the river still used the stony dirt track for access, be it by car, or on foot. Being the first of only a few houses, you could initially be fooled into thinking you were walking along a tourist riverside footpath, as opposed to a residential road.

Many years ago the house stood totally alone, isolated; a remote residence for notable members of the community who would enter through the huge, double door in the centre. Today however, it was a very different story. Various ice cream stalls, booths for hiring rowboats and huts selling fishing tackle lined the route. However, the mood changed very quickly and ever more dramatically, once night fell upon the area. All the tourists and pleasure seekers would disappear and the residents who now occupied the unusual neighbourhood were all that would remain. If you were to believe the locals, you could also bump into some unsavoury residents from times past too. As Courtney walked along the uneven path she couldn't help but be reminded of being back at home in Hertfordshire, walking peacefully home along the river. Yet the searing sun made it abundantly clear she was no longer in England. As she squinted her eyes, wondering why it seemed so much larger in the Californian sky, Creekside House suddenly appeared in front of her, as if out of nowhere. As she looked up at the striking residence, she gulped in trepidation as she felt its eerie aura engulf her; a feeling that was trebled as she noticed a solemn looking male figure staring down at her from the attic window.

'Huh,' she said as her body involuntarily jolted with dread.

'She's here,' shouted the person with a nondescript tone; their voice echoing through the trees.

Courtney took a deep breath and using the extractable handle, she began to drag her suitcase behind her across the pebbles and towards the steps of her new home.

∞

Some of the current occupants of Creekside House had now gathered in the living room to welcome their new addition.

'So what happens if you need something in the night?' Courtney was concerned about the isolated location and colourful history of the house.

'Well just make sure you don't need anything in the night,' answered Becky, a very cute but also slightly geeky looking, half black, half Caucasian girl with short, brown curly hair. 'It's a long walk back to the main road, especially in darkness.' She had a very genuine and friendly manner that Courtney had already warmed to, although she did speak extremely quickly, as if she had too much in her head and didn't have enough time in the day to get it all out.

'Isn't it safe here then?'

'It doesn't matter how safe the area is; once darkness falls and it gets as dark as it does outside here, your own footsteps can give you heart failure. If you don't believe me, just go ahead and try it. Go on, I guarantee you won't get more than five feet before you think you hear something being tossed into the water, or you hear children crying, or footsteps dragging something across the pebbles.'

Becky had managed to silence the room with her creepy comments.

'But we're all scientists with logical minds and answers for everything, right? I mean, I thought you were gonna warn me about getting mugged or something, not ghosts.'

'You've been talking to the skunk, haven't you?'

Courtney looked at Becky with a puzzled expression. 'I don't think so.'

'She means the professor,' said Nathan, a tall skinny boy who was sitting cross-legged on a footstool. 'But whatever he says, we're all human, and he's not the one who has to live here.' Nathan wore dark rimmed round glasses that Courtney instantly decided made him look like a particular twenty-something wizard.

91

'So you all believe in ghosts?' She half wanted them to say 'no' to make her feel safer in the house but also wanted them to say yes in the hope she was finally amongst like-minded people.

'I never used to, but you kinda can't help but start to after you've lived here for a while,' said a boy called Wazer in a rather nervous manner. He was a very overweight young man with thinning hair, even though he was only twenty years old. His face was greasy and pale, except for the red blotches where he had been burnt by the sun. 'Wazer' was actually an abbreviation that he had been called since he was small with his full name being Zak Wazerton. 'This house has really bad memories,' he said with a worried tone.

'So why do you all stay here? Why don't you just go somewhere else? Anyway, you haven't actually seen anything have you, because the professor said there had been no sightings?'

'Of course, he would say that,' said Nathan, who was sipping a glass of red wine. He didn't particularly like alcohol, but he always drank wine to help convince others he was more intellectual. 'If we left this house, we would likely be thrown out of school, or at the very least, become the butt of jokes and get terrible grades. I'm afraid once you are here, you can't leave. It would be a sign of weakness, a sign that we can't be great scientists, and in answer to your question ... yes, I have seen something, but nobody outside this house must know ... especially the professor.' He widened his eyes to emphasise the seriousness of his point. 'What I'd love to do one day is actually use science to find out exactly what ghosts are. Not only to prove their existence to the professor but also find out their true purpose. I mean, they must have one; other than to simply haunt us. I just wish I didn't have to live with them at the same time.'

'Well at least you don't sleep in the same room where the bitch shot her husband,' said a girl called Ellie as she came walking into the room. She was twenty two years old, tall and very attractive, with long, dark hair similar to Courtney's, except she had lightened hers with blond streaks. She came in with a slight swagger and attitude and stared the new girl up and down. She took a seat over by the bay-fronted window. 'Although sorry honey that room is now yours; consequence of being the new geek.'

'That's fine,' replied Courtney confidently. 'You'd have to be really gullible to think that a ghost would only haunt the room they died in. If there are ghosts here, I'm sure they won't discriminate.' She smiled back at Ellie and then turned again to face everyone else. 'So guys, this story of the wife that killed her husband and kids – did it really happen the way the professor told me, or is it just an exaggerated Chinese whisper?'

'Well, when all is said and done, at the end of the day, it's a case by where–' said Wazer before being cut short by Ellie.

'Why is it you can say so much but so very little at the same time?' Her tone was sarcastic and had an attacking quality. Ellie and the others had heard his trio of sayings preceding anything Wazer said a hundred times before. Becky giggled at Ellie's bluntness.

Wazer stared at Ellie with a serious squint before looking back at Courtney. 'Yes, it really happened,' he said with an exaggerated serious tone. 'It's in all the history books of the area but the strange thing was they never pulled any bodies out of the creek. To this day they remain unfound. That's why we think maybe she's the one wandering around the house, searching for any family that move in so she can drag them into the creek as well.'

'That makes no sense,' retorted Courtney. 'That's just your horror movie mind putting that spin on it.'

The others all looked surprised by her seemingly dismissive attitude toward ghosts.

'If anything, it would be the husband and children wanting revenge,' she countered with confidence.

'Don't say that,' said Nathan in a panicked, croaky and high pitched voice. 'I'm sure I've already seen something wandering around here at night, when I've been up getting a glass of milk.'

'That was definitely more Ron Weasley than Harry

Potter,' said Courtney under her breath as she smiled at Nathan.

Everyone in the room laughed at the apparent obvious observation she had just made.

'Why are you all laughing? I don't look like Harry Potter.'

'It's either him or Buzz Lightyear's pal Woody, but at least Harry wouldn't be scared of ghosts. So take your pick,' said Ellie. The others in the room continued to erupt with laughter, causing Nathan's face to turn bright red from humiliation.

'I'm sorry. I really didn't mean to offend you,' said Courtney, with a genuine inflection. 'I didn't realise it was a common observation or even a sore subject.'

The laughter quietened down as Nathan looked at his shoes despondently.

Ellie then said, 'So what do you make of the skunk now you've met him?'

'Well, the professor is my idol,' replied Courtney a little hesitantly.

'Yeah, yeah, but what do you really think of him now you've met him?' She knowingly repeated herself to really punctuate the question.

'I suppose, I thought he isn't like any teacher I ever had in school but then this isn't any old school is it? So that's probably why, right?'

Everyone in the room fell silent at the prospect of anyone answering her question.

'Just ignore her,' said Wazer. 'He's fine, just a little eccentric but then aren't all geniuses?' He turned to Ellie. 'You're just jealous because he's found a new prodigy to mould. You're worried you'll be tossed to the kerb now.' Wazer took on a mock horror voice. 'Or maybe into the riverrrr, oooohhhh.' He laughed hysterically at his own joke before snorting uncontrollably.

'You're fat and nearly bald. I think I'll always be above you in the pecking order. Besides, I never welcomed his obsession with me. It's creepy.' Ellie turned to Courtney. 'As you'll find out soon enough.'

'What are you talking about? What's the deal with him? Is he a pervert or something?'

'Wow, so many questions,' said Ellie, who had become the group's unofficial spokesperson. 'Well where to begin? Is he a pervert? You know I think it would be a lot simpler if he was. Maybe I'd give him a quick grope to get it out of his system and then maybe we could get on with what we're here for.'

The group all stared at Ellie with disgust.

'What? Hey, sometimes you gotta get ya tits out for the lads.'

'You're so wrong,' said Nathan shaking his head.

'Not at all. What is wrong is that you're a guy and you're saying that. Every guy deserves an eye full of boobs. If either of you guys just had the guts to ask, you may well find that I'd oblige,' she said with a smile.

'I think I just got who you are,' said Courtney with a contemplative look on her face. Ellie looked at her and widened her eyes. 'You're so trying to cover up your intelligence, which you obviously have or you wouldn't be here, with what you believe guys think is cool.'

Ellie raised her eyebrows at her analysis, silently asking what that would be.

'A girl who loves sex and loves to talk about it.'

'Honey,' said Ellie, with confidence and determination in her voice. 'You don't know me.' Her tone then changed to a playful one as she realised that she had gotten to her. 'But if you want, maybe a bit later you and I can get to know each other better in my room, if you get what I'm saying. I don't limit myself, what a waste of this ...' She gestured at her body. '... that would be.' She turned to look at Nathan, then turned again and winked at Courtney. 'Hey, you may enjoy it,' she said in an attempt to remain solid and collected in front of the others.

'Maybe some other time,' said Courtney. She recognized meeting that kind of girl before and so knew exactly how to deal with her. 'I'm a bit tired after my journey.' She then winked back at her.

Ellie lightly smiled to herself as she realised she may have found someone on her level who was not intimidated by her overbearing personality. She turned to Nathan and Wazer. 'Guys, close your mouths. I know I've given you some images that will be burned into your minds forever, but when you're lying alone tonight, try to keep your noises to a minimum, ok?' Wazer and Nathan were trying hard to lift their jaws off the floor. 'You see Courtney, sex or even talk of sex, is an easy weapon when dealing with guys. It's very easy to get what you want from them, if you know how to use it. I think I could probably teach you a thing or two. I'd hate to see your beauty go to waste just because you've chosen to be a scientist. You can actually have both brains and sex appeal. It's the perfect combination. But unfortunately, it's not that simple with Mr Prick Thistle. He has a whole other agenda.'

'And what would that be?'

Ellie leaned in close to Courtney's face with a knowing and assured demeanour. She stared into her eyes and was so close she left her breath straddling Courtney's lips. She smiled furtively and said, 'To find a replacement daughter of course.'

~ CHAPTER SIXTEEN ~

People from different times

After a long and confused silence following Ellie's bombshell statement, Courtney uneasily looked to Becky for confirmation of what she had just heard. Becky nodded her head in reluctant agreement. Courtney then looked back at Ellie in readiness for more detail.

'Why do you think your presence was requested here rather than having to apply?'

'But that's ridiculous.'

'He lost his only daughter when she was seventeen. Apparently she was a chip off the old block; a genius of science. He didn't take her death too well and has been scouring the world since, looking for someone to mould. You're just the latest.' There wasn't anyone in the room who didn't hear the hint of jealousy in her delivery.

'Don't take it personally,' said Becky. 'You also have to be very smart to fit the bill. It's not like you're only here because of the way you look, it just helped a little. I had to apply in the normal way, just like these guys.' Becky nodded at Nathan and Wazer.

'Well at least you did it with just your mind. That's something to be proud about. All that talk of being a team; I thought it was a personal attack, but he was basically grooming me?'

Nathan looked at her dubiously and said, 'Why would it be personal?' The others all looked at Courtney, thinking the same thing.

'Oh ...' she said, trying to decide whether to tell them

about her ghostly past. 'Well ... basically-'

They all stared at her. She stared back at them and began to reel off her reply very fast and very matter of fact. 'Ok look, I've already lost both my parents and I sort of vowed to one day use time travel to go back and meet them again, or in my dad's case, for the first time. Then, maybe even stop it from happening.' She knew that her statement clashed with her own theories on time travel, but hoped and assumed that none of them would have read her work and know that.

'Oh wow, sorry to hear that,' said Wazer. 'But hey, maybe if you manage it, you can stop his daughter from dying; then maybe he'll stop chasing young girls.'

'But I still don't get it – what would he gain from this? It's not like one of us will actually become his daughter. Surely he must know that?'

'Of course he does,' said Ellie. 'It's very simple though. You see, one part of him is a little crazy and genuinely wants someone around him who reminds him of his daughter. But the real reason is more cynical than that. There's another side to him, the side with the real motivation.'

'What are you talking about?'

Ellie looked to Becky to do the long explanation. Becky reluctantly sighed in acceptance of the task. 'Well,' she said begrudgingly. 'Everyone knows that his worst nightmare would be for someone other than himself to discover time travel. For him it's like the space race where he's the American, and anybody not working alongside him must be the Soviets, but he's realistic enough to know that it's likely not to be discovered in his lifetime. So he wants to make sure that whoever does discover it and whenever they discover it, that they will ultimately be linked back to him. He has no bloodline left and time, ironically is running away from him. So he's looking to find a new adopted daughter to take on; someone who can continue his work. Bad news for you is that you seem to fit the bill more perfectly than anyone so far; particularly with no father of your own alive.'

Courtney sat still in her chair, stunned by what she had heard. 'This is awful. I can't believe I've been manipulated like this. Now I'm not even sure I want to stay here.'

'What? You would sacrifice your place here because of that? You'd be throwing away any chance of a decent career,' said Becky. She then changed her tone mid sentence as she became a little intrigued by the notion of somebody standing up to Professor Thistle. 'Wouldn't you?'

'I didn't come here to get a career or a qualification. I came because I thought studying here was the next step on my journey, my destiny. But maybe it's not. Maybe the universe has other plans and that's why it made sure you told me this stuff on my first day here. Maybe I was supposed to meet you guys, and that's why I was offered a place to study here. Life has always taught me that you should take whatever you can from any given situation, but it won't always be what seems obvious.'

The others in the room all stared at each other; almost as if they had been waiting for someone like Courtney to come along and say something like that for a long time.

'Don't tell me,' said Wazer. 'You're about to tell us that we are destined for something great.' He spoke with a sarcastic tone in his voice.

'Shut up, Wazer,' said Becky. She turned back to Courtney. 'What exactly are you saying?' She was buying more into Courtney's beliefs by the second. She had been studying at LosTech for two years but had become fed up with being constantly ignored by Professor Thistle. She knew it was probably because she did not fit the physical criteria that he seemed to have set out. As well as the fact that her father, a successful businessman, was quite vocal about Professor Thistle's questionable methods and had rationalised that he was only interested in his own progression and only taught at LosTech for the money.

Professor Thistle was without a doubt a very important figure, not only at the university, but also in the field of science around the world. Unfortunately for his students, he knew that fact only too well and had developed a bit of a God complex, walking around the university like he owned the place; sometimes he had even been heard referring to it as his university.

Becky had previously discussed her ideas with the rest of the guys in the house and with Courtney being yet another student admitted under dubious criteria, she was now very much drawn into her anger.

Ellie, on the other hand, was someone who would simply latch on to any idea that might cause the professor some annoyance, as she had lately begun to resent him due to his drop in interest toward her. 'Yeah, what are you saying? You've suddenly become a little more interesting than I first realised.'

'I don't know, maybe you shouldn't listen to me. I'm just angry and feel manipulated by this whole situation.'

'Oh great,' said Nathan. 'Get our hopes up of something interesting happening around here and then just backtrack.' He had studied at the school the longest and was close to graduating that coming summer. His grades however had been suffering and he was not predicted to graduate with any kind of decent grades. He had been interested in time since he first saw the TV show 'Quantum Leap' when he was five, but the realities of the science behind it differed hugely from the fun that movies and television shows created in his mind. That combined with Professor Thistle's fixation on particular students.

'Ok, look,' said Courtney, sensing they seemed interested in what she had to say. 'I believe everything happens for a reason; ultimately because we're all destined for something, large or small. Our future is already written and there is nothing we can do. So you shouldn't worry too much about how you are going to get there because regardless of how, you will. I have slightly lied to you though, so I think I should come clean. What I know about my life is this - I'm here because I was visited by an evil spirit when I was five. It took something from me and I want it back. So in order to get what I want ... I need to believe it's my destiny.'

Everyone in the room looked at each other, wondering whether or not she was serious, but by the tone of her voice, they quickly realised she obviously believed everything she had said.

'Most would say it's just one of those things,' she continued. 'Or that I'm crazy. But there has to be more to it than that. The spirit destroyed my childhood. It knew what would hurt me the most and I want to know how, and why. So I'm gonna use time travel to go back and see it with fresh eyes so I can figure it all out. I don't care what the professor says. I don't care what you or anyone else says. I will use time travel in my lifetime, and I will find out why that thing specifically chose to hurt me.'

Everyone in the room fell silent after listening intently to what she had said. For Courtney, it was like being back on stage at The John Twaddle School; further evidence that she was discovering a talent for getting people to listen to what she had to say.

'I mean why are some of us visited by ghosts while others never experience a single encounter in their entire lifetime?' She looked at Nathan, who had also started to buy into everything she had said. 'Ultimately, they're people from different times, so time must know the answer, right? Spending the next three years waiting for someone to decide if I'm good enough to be called their daughter is not my idea of progression.'

Everyone was a little stunned by her honesty. They had not experienced anyone in the school before having that much confidence in their future and more ironically, the whole concept of time travel. They all simultaneously thought about what it would mean to think independently again and follow the dreams they had before coming under the influence of the school and Professor Thistle.

'This is like all my dreams rolled into one,' said Nathan, shocking even himself at what he had said. 'I'll help you.'

Wazer looked at him stunned and said, 'Are you crazy?' He was worried about how it would all affect him. 'She's nuts. She's going to get us all in the crap, man.' He looked around at the others for confirmation of his analysis but found nothing coming back from them. 'Guys?'

'I'm not sure I'm ready to quit school just yet ...' said Ellie, lacking complete confidence in what Courtney had just said but liking the idea enough to contemplate a bit of rebellion. 'But I like your attitude, so I'll try to do whatever I can to help you from the inside, how's that?'

'I know the pass code to the lock on the professor's office,' blurted out Becky.

Everyone turned and looked at her with some surprise.

'I sort of know the guy who comes to clean and fix up his computer,' she continued, a little embarrassed. 'He's very ... how shall I say ... friendly.'

'Oooo ... k,' said Ellie with a smirk on her face. 'But what about getting in to the actual building?'

'Well you know how the professor's office is near the back door? My guy told me that the code for that door is the same as his office. He was laughing about it one day because he couldn't believe such a renowned scientist didn't want to have to remember two codes. He put it down to his age. That's why he's the only one that comes and goes via that back door.'

Ellie placed her hand on Becky's shoulder. 'You did good my child. I taught you well.'

'Guys, I really appreciate your support, but I don't exactly know what we're saying here. You've all taken me by surprise. I don't exactly have a plan.'

'Well I do,' said Ellie, who was relishing the idea of causing some trouble in the school. 'We go get all the research we can find from Mr Prick's office–'

'And then we work out how we can send you back. Back ... to the future,' said Nathan in his best impression of his favourite movie character.

'Yeah, something like that,' said Ellie, rather dryly.

'That's not even the right context you fool,' said Wazer, with contempt. 'She wants to go back, not forward. Besides, she's not even serious.' He turned to Courtney. 'Please, tell them you're not serious.'

There was a brief silence in the room as they all waited for her response. She looked at them, knowing she really did mean everything she had said. She did not actually care about the school and the grades, or the qualifications she could get. She was only interested in her goal and without the pressures of parents that want her to do well in school; she could just follow her instincts. Over the last few years she had found that there was just one plus side to not having her parents around; it had made it easier for her to make brave decisions. As harsh as that sounded, she no longer had to worry about anyone saying 'What would people think?' or 'How would this reflect on your mother?' There was nobody she had to please, except herself.

So she lifted her head and addressed them all. 'Firstly, I don't want to put anyone's career in jeopardy just because of me, so I'm not gonna try and convince you either way. This is your decision and your decision only. However, I was definitely brought here for a reason. Now I know what I know, maybe that reason wasn't to study. Of course I have no evidence to back that up, and you would be perfectly justified to think I'm crazy as well, but at the end of the day, as Dr. Pepper says, what's the worst that could happen? We have a bit of an adventure? Isn't that what you're all really here for?'

'Er, it may sound crazy to you all, but I'm actually here to pass this course and become a scientist,' said Wazer, as if he was intentionally stating the most obvious thing in the world. 'And I will play no part in this.'

'Actually, I meant here on this planet, which is a lot more meaningful than some qualification. I'm a big believer in destiny you see. So if you are gonna help, then it was always gonna be that way. Now, to those who want to show Professor Thistle what you're really made of ...' She reflected for a moment to be sure she was confident about her decision and then looked around the room at the silent observers and said, 'Let's do this.'

☐

~ CHAPTER SEVENTEEN ~

This ain't no movie

Pedestrian wasn't ever a word Alexandra would have used to describe herself, but while Courtney was across the Atlantic, acquainting herself with her new friends and talking about the rather monumental and exciting idea of how she was going to steal a world famous professor's notes to help her figure out how to go back in time, in contrast that was exactly what Alexandra had unintentionally become after accepting Courtney's offer.

There she was, sat on a sofa, sinking back into the soft plush cushions with her legs extended out in front of her on a giant fluffy bean bag whilst enjoying her fourth glass of red wine that evening. Her eyes looked a little red as a result, causing her to feel a little reflective about her situation. 'Thank you, Courtney ... and thank you God, if you are really out there,' she said poignantly.

As well as her apparent home comforts, her appearance had also improved somewhat. Her hair had grown, and she looked like she was taking pride in her appearance again. She was even wearing an elegant silk nightgown and pink fluffy slippers.

The whole scene was representative of someone who had been given a second chance in life and was clearly enjoying every second of it. When Alexandra accidentally bumped into Courtney three months ago, her life changed forever. She realised that making friends with people based on truth as opposed to lies, actually meant something. She had concluded that Courtney must be making waves on her journey to discover the answers she was desperate for, because relaxing with a glass of wine in blissful comfort, certainly didn't 'suck'.

She began to reminisce what Courtney had said to her as they sat together over coffee in McDonalds. 'I'm going away for three years to study in Los Angeles,' said Courtney. 'But before I go I want to buy back the house I used to live in with my mum. Problem is, I won't be around, and the only way I can do it is if someone could house sit while I'm away. I can't leave it empty for that length of time. So if I'm gonna end up with homeless squatters,' she said with a grin. 'I may as well have one I know and can trust. I don't want to come back to a wreck, so while I'm gone you'd have to treat it like it's your own. You can stay there rent free and I'll pay you a caretaker's wage to make sure it stays in good nick. Then, when I'm ready, I'll come back and find out what exactly happened in that house when I was five. You don't believe all that stuff anyway, so you'll be fine, right?'

How amazing life was, Alexandra thought to herself. One minute I'm on the street, begging for change and dodging men's advances, thinking that's the extent of my life. Next thing, I'm sitting down in a nice house, sipping wine and waiting for *The X Factor* to start. You just never know what's coming around the corner. You just have to take everything as it comes, knowing that when you're at your lowest, it can only get better. 'Things ... can only get better,' she sang at the top of her voice.

She raised her arms up in celebration, one of which was holding the glass of red wine, and as she belted out the lyrics of the song all the joyful swaying caused her to spill the crimson party juice all down the front of her nightdress. 'Oh crap, that's not better. That's cold and wet.'

A little frazzled, she stood up, placed her glass on to the wooden coffee table in front of her and started to pull her nightdress off. As she lifted it up and struggled to get it over her head, she stopped in the most compromising position, realising that the blinds on the garden window were still open. She quickly fumbled it back down. 'Oh no you don't, mister neighbour dude, you can trick me into stripping ... I mean, you *can't* trick me,' she said slurring her words. There were no nearby houses, but common sense was not currently her best skill.

She walked wonkily up the stairs, while complaining about the coldness of the wine as she tried to pull the silk nightgown away from her skin.

The house was silent but for a few creaks on the loose floorboards each time she placed a foot on a step. At the top of the stairs, only two doors led off the landing. She reached out to one of the door knobs, but as she was about to push the door open, her heart skipped a beat as she heard a bubbling noise coming from downstairs, similar to the sound a kettle makes when it boils and is about to click off. 'I didn't put the kettle on, did I?'

She quickly dismissed it, assuming it must be the alcohol in her bloodstream playing tricks on her mind. She twisted the door knob and pushed the bedroom door open.

Inside was a small room with two canvas wardrobes against the right hand wall and a small window at the end, but no bed. As she was the only one occupying the house, she had decided to use the room as a walk-in wardrobe. Over in the corner was a small TV that she would use to pass the time during her lengthy sessions as she decided what she should wear for the day. She didn't have much of a social life so it was mainly dress up sessions, almost as if she was a real life 'Bratz' doll.

She finally managed to pull her nightdress over her head and threw it down on the floor. As she stood there naked, she reached for a silk dressing gown that hung from one of the wardrobes, but just as was about to place her hand on it, the lights went out and the room went totally dark. 'Huh,' she gasped and quickly pulled the dressing gown towards her chest. The fear of someone being in the house quickly sobered her up, and her happy demeanour was replaced with fear and bafflement.

All of a sudden, the lights came back on. She turned to face the window and carefully pulled the curtain to one side to see if there was anything unusual outside. Through the small opening, she saw that the gravel road was calm and quiet but the woods in the distance looked menacing under the moonlight and made her feel uncomfortable.

Seconds later, the lights went out again, leaving her stood in the darkness once more. A loud bang echoed from downstairs. She quickly fumbled about in desperation, trying to put her dressing gown on as quickly as possible. The light flickered on and off at a pace that would be impossible for a human finger to achieve, causing a flip book effect as she went from naked to covered. She couldn't help but think that something inhuman must be causing them to flicker as she stood frozen, panicking about what it could possibly be. However, her disbelief in those sorts of notions also made her unable to erase the most realistic scenario from her mind; someone entering the room and attacking her in the dark.

Suddenly, the lights stopped flickering and remained on. She stood in silence wondering if anything else was going to happen. Her eyes then widened in panic as she remembered something – something that immediately sent shivers down her spine. She slowly walked back to the door, but as she did, she simultaneously heard a crackling noise come from the small TV in the corner of the room. She twisted her neck and saw sparks fly out from the back. 'No way.' She turned back and quickly ran to the door, grabbed the handle and pulled it open. The crackling from the T.V. grew louder. She stepped into the hallway, pulled the door shut and held onto it tight with her face and body pressed up against it. Just as she was about to breathe a sigh of relief that she was out of the room, there was an excruciatingly large bang. The TV exploded, shattering it into pieces. Shrapnel and glass instantly flew all over the room from the intensity of the blast. She pulled the door even tighter, as she heard the debris repeatedly slamming against the wood on the other side. With tremendous force, a large shard of sharp metal pierced through the wooden door and stabbed her in the chest.

Meanwhile, at the very same time back in Los Angeles, Nathan, Ellie, Becky and Courtney were all standing by the bank of the creek.

Nathan whispered, 'Are you sure these boats are safe?' He then cautiously placed a foot inside a small motorboat. 'I don't feel comfortable being on one of these in the dark.'

Nathan, Becky, Ellie and Courtney had managed to separate one of the hire boats from the rest that had been tied together for the night.

Ellie, Becky and Courtney were already on board, sitting timidly on two wooden benches that stretched across their dubiously borrowed mode of transport.

During the day, the boats were hired out to tourists wanting to take short trips up and down the creek. However tonight, Courtney and the others had a different use planned.

To operate the electric motor on the boat, they would need a special key, which at that time of night was locked inside the ticket sales booth. So instead, they had decided it would be better to use the oars.

As it was dark, they could not see much beneath the gloomy waters below. Becky was clinging onto a small torch but it only illuminated a short distance in front of them.

Nathan then said, 'So what are we actually looking for?' He was still feeling confused about what they were doing in a boat on the creek, at eleven thirty at night and in complete darkness.

'This is ridiculous,' replied Courtney, looking around and analysing the seriousness of the situation. 'I think I may have got a bit carried away with the adventure side of things. Maybe we should just go back to the house and forget I ever said anything.'

The others stared at her in silence for a second or two.

Nathan was agitated by her sudden mood change and snapped, 'What? We've just stolen a boat in the middle of the night, because of something you said, and now you're telling us you're full of baloney?'

'No, no, don't get me wrong. I still stick by everything I said. I'm just not sure that we'll find some great breakthrough in the professor's office that will send us hurtling through time just yet. Otherwise wouldn't you think he would already have done it by now?'

The others stared at her with a slight realisation on their faces that she could have a point.

'I mean, whatever will happen, will happen, but this ain't no movie. Things still have to follow certain logic, don't they?'

Ellie looked at Becky who looked back at her; both had puzzled expressions on their faces. Becky then turned to everyone and said, 'I say we still go, just for the hell of it. I mean, why not? We're already on the boat.'

'If Becky's up for it, then I'm certainly not gonna back down,' said Ellie excitedly. 'I'm not sure what happened to this girl since you've arrived, Court – I can call you Court right? – but I have to say ... I like it.'

∞

Back in England, Alexandra loosened her grip on the door as she felt blood dripping onto her hand. She looked down and saw the large pointed piece of metal protruding from the door. She then noticed a blood stained tear in her nightgown and pulled it open to see a deep gash in the side of her chest. Luckily she was standing against the door slightly side on so the wound was only superficial. She quickly jumped back before something else came through and caused more serious damage. As she stood there in the hallway, contemplating death, she scrunched up her face and for a moment wished she was back with her mum and dad. Even if she was the unfortunate result of a prostitute and her client, that life suddenly became very appealing compared to death. She was reminded once again of Courtney's prediction that life will always suck.

Suddenly, the noises from inside the room stopped. She stood there for a moment; extremely nervous and still shaken, then stepped slowly forward and edged the door open.

Inside, she saw the remains of the TV. Glass was spread all over the floor so as she was barefooted, she couldn't walk back inside. Her heart felt like a train speeding through an isolated station, beating so fast she became light headed trying to get her head around what could logically have caused all the devastation to have happened. Very quickly, she recognized that if she had remained in the room any longer, she would most certainly be dead right now and so began to palpitate heavily at the realisation.

Then she remembered what she was about to do just before the T.V. exploded and closed the door once again. She looked down toward the bottom, and Etched into the wood of the door with what looked like the precision of a child, was the word 'Courtney'. The room she had just been in and was nearly killed by, was the same room where Courtney had spent her childhood and witnessed her first chilling encounter with the 'evil spirit'.

Back on the boat, a text message alert sounded from someone's mobile phone. Courtney recognised the tone and grabbed her cell out of her jean pocket.

In amazement Nathan said, 'Who the hell is texting you at this time? Nobody knows we're here.' A look of fear appeared on his face. 'Oh God – maybe it's Wazer back at the house warning us that somebody's found out and reported us to the authorities and–'

'It's alright, it's not Wazer. It's from a friend of mine in England. She's house sitting for me. Wait, let me just read it.' Cradling the phone in her hand, Courtney looked at the screen which read:

> Court, come home
> immediately.
> Something terrible is
> happening in this
> house. I'm lucky to
> be alive. Call me.
> Alex.

'Oh crap.'

'What is it? They're coming for us, aren't they?'

'No, Nathan,' barked Ellie, who had just pushed the boat out into the creek and was already rowing. 'She just said it's from her friend in England, you idiot.'

Then with a genuinely concerned tone Becky said, 'What's the problem, Courtney? Is everything ok?'

'This is very bad.' In that instant, she suddenly had a light bulb moment as she thought about what it could mean if Alexandra had actually seen something back at her house close to what she had spent her life trying to convince people of. Whispering to herself she said, 'Could this be a sign?'

Alexandra's heart still hadn't pulled into the station and was continuing to beat rapidly as she stood staring at Courtney's name on the door, while at the same time recollecting everything her friend had ever told her about that bedroom. 'I believe you now,' she said nervously.

She looked up as she heard a loud bubbling noise coming from the loft and a very similar crackling to the one seconds earlier that culminated in her near death experience with the TV. This time the crackling was coming from the living room. She looked up at the loft hatch, eyes wide in anticipation of what could possibly happen next.

As she stared at the hatch, a droplet of water fell from the ceiling and onto her hand, causing her to jump from the boiling heat. Another drop then landed on her scalp. The dripping became more frequent and she flinched as droplets repeatedly burnt her head, body and arms.

The loft hatch was seeping and in no time turned into pouring water. At the same time, the crackling from the TV in the living room grew louder. As she stood in the hallway feeling petrified and trapped, she wondered if these were now her last moments. Parts of the ceiling collapsed and boiling water was pouring down onto the carpet. Then there was another bang, but that time it caused the whole house to shake violently. 'What the hell was that?'

After a couple of seconds, the shaking stopped and all went strangely calm. She looked up, realising she needed to move before everything collapsed right on top of her.

She quickly ran down the stairs, stepping barefoot on the boiling hot water that was gushing down the steps. As she reached halfway, she looked over at the large flat screen TV and saw smoke and sparks coming from the back. A loud crash suddenly came from upstairs. The whole ceiling had collapsed and at that exact moment, the TV exploded. 'Nooo ...'

As the water swept down the stairs, it pulled Alexandra's feet from under her, causing her to slip and fall hard onto the steps. She screamed in pain as her back crunched on one step after another. 'Please, enough already,' she cried in agony but although painful, it was actually a blessing in disguise as at that precise moment, the debris from the TV flew straight over her head and hit the wall beside her, breaking its impact and leaving it to drop a little more gently on top of her. Just a split second earlier and some would have most certainly embedded dangerously into her skull.

The rest of the debris hit the side of the stairs making a barrage of noise against the wood panelling, like heavy rain hitting the roof of a tent.

'Aaarrrrggghhh.'

Chaos had erupted all around her. She had small cuts on her face from the falling glass and her skin was also burning through her clothes. She was desperately looking for an end to the nightmare.

On the boat, Nathan was also a little worried and said, 'What's going on? Why do you look so worried?' He was now sat at the back with his arms crossed, still sulking about constantly being the butt of Ellie's jibes.

'Don't worry, it's just a bit of a problem at home but there's not really much I can do about it now anyway. I'll deal with it later. Let's just carry on. Like you say, we're here now, and I s'pose it's kind of exciting. If we find nothing of interest, it will at least be a funny story we can tell our kids.' She smiled unconvincingly and chuckled nervously at her own comment.

Ellie continued to row the boat down the creek whilst Becky shone the torch ahead.

Courtney could not help but be distracted by her text message but also felt it would be unwelcome, as well as ungrateful, if she were to ask the others to turn back now. 'Actually, I might just see if I can get through on my phone ... make sure it's nothing serious.' She was attempting to lessen the impact in case she had to cancel their adventure. She dialled Alexandra's number and turned her head away from everyone so that she could talk on her phone quietly in the background.

The others continued to whisper amongst themselves.

'So,' said Nathan. 'Are we still going to break into campus and into the professor's office just for the hell of it?' Really, he knew the answer but felt like he just had to ask anyway.

'Uh huh,' responded Ellie with a smile. 'Cool huh?'

'Oh, that's just great.'

'You could always swim back to the house. That's if you can swim,' said Ellie still mocking him. Her face then adopted a deadly serious expression. 'You can swim can't you, because I'm not rescuing you if this boat capsizes?'

'Why on earth would it capsize?'

'Because I may start doing this ...' she put her hands on either side of the boat and purposely and mischievously rocked it from side to side in the water.

∞

As Alexandra contemplated what she should do to get safely out of the horror that was unfolding, her mobile phone started to ring. She lay on the stairs defeated but mustered enough energy to take the phone from her nightgown pocket. She answered it and began to scream down the phone at a ferocious speed. 'Courtney, you need to come home. This house ... this house is possessed. You were right ... No, no ... nobody's glowing. There's some sort of bad energy in the house though. It's caused everything to explode and nearly killed me. I don't know what to do.' At that moment, the house shook once again. 'Oh my God, I think it's a poltergeist. The whole house is moving again.'

At the back of the boat, Courtney, who had been listening to Alexandra rant on the other end of the phone, lost her balance from Ellie's irresponsible behaviour. To prevent from falling in the water, Courtney put both hands down to grab onto the side of the boat, but as the hand with the phone tried to hold on, she lost her grip and the phone instantly dropped into the water. She had no choice but to watch as it hit the side of the boat, before bouncing overboard and into the murky Creek. She tried to grab it at the last second but Ellie was still rocking the boat too hard for her to risk letting go of the sides. 'Ellie,' she screamed. 'My phone is in the water.'

'Both T.V.'s have exploded ...,' continued Alexandra. '... and they weren't even turned on. The water tank in the loft started boiling and leaking and–' In the middle of her rant, the phone went dead. 'Courtney? Courtney? Nooooo. Now the phone is gonna explode. Arrgghh.' In anger and fear, she threw the phone straight across the room, got up and ran into the hallway towards the kitchen. However, before she could get there, she stepped into a huge hole in the concrete floor and fell flat on her face, grazing her cheeks. As she raised her head she noticed the front door was off its hinges and that she was actually lying on it. Was someone else in there? She got up and entered the kitchen where the kettle was still boiling and began to spin around in despair, looking at everything electrical that could cause her harm. Crying from the shock of consecutive anomalies that had occurred, she totally lost her cool and screamed with her arms flailing wildly, 'Leave me alone. What is it you want from me? You've got the wrong girl. I promise you ... I'm not

Courtney.'

∞

Ellie had finally stopped rocking the boat and they were all looking over the side for Courtney's mobile phone. It was too dark to see anything so Courtney grabbed the torch from Becky and pointed it into the water but all they could see were bubbles where it had sunk.

'Well done,' said Nathan.

'Sorry. It's just ... well, he was annoying me and ...' Ellie cut herself off mid-sentence and sighed. 'I suppose I'll get you a new one.' She knew it was her fault but was not relishing the idea of having to cough up for a replacement.

'There's not a lot we can do about it right now I suppose, so let's just keep going. But please, if we don't want to get caught, we have to take this a bit more seriously,' said Courtney firmly, shining the torch into Ellie's face.

'Ok, ok, I said I'm sorry, didn't I?'

Courtney waved the reply away, thinking again about Alexandra. 'This is starting to feel more and more like fate by the second.'

Interested in her analysis Becky said, 'How do you mean?'

'Something strange is happening at my house back in England. The same house where I witnessed the spirit when I was five, but what she is saying doesn't fit with any of my experiences.'

'Why not?'

'She's talking about some huge energy causing strange things to happen. Thing is, I've lived in that house most of my life, and I never witnessed anything like that. So whatever is causing the disturbance has only just arrived. Now she's either in the middle of some huge unprecedented electrical storm which we don't really get over in England, or something else is happening that's not quite so easily explained. What is making me wonder though is that energy is what's needed to even entertain an idea of travelling through time, and what makes it more interesting is that we are all on a boat, heading towards the office of the foremost

115

professor on time travel. Could that really be just a coincidence?'

Everyone was silent as they all looked at each other and pondered.

'You mean, you think we can harness the energy of bad spirits and use it to travel through time?'

Courtney looked at Nathan for a second, then to the others who all seemed to be waiting for an answer to his question.

'Maybe ... I'm not sure. I don't really know anything for definite yet. Anyway, why are you looking to me for all the answers? You're all supposed to be budding scientists too.'

All of a sudden the boat collided with something, bringing their discussion to an abrupt end. They piled forward and fell onto one another. As they lifted their heads to see what could have caused the crash, they were surprised to see nothing in front of them, nothing visible anyway. However, they could now see the large section of the Creek and the school in the distance beyond.

'Well,' remarked Ellie. 'It seems something doesn't want us to go any farther, so I guess that can only mean ... we're here.'

~ CHAPTER EIGHTEEN ~

It's not the fish I'm worried about

Nathan was not someone that would normally jump into a practical challenge head on; he was more of a theorist who preferred someone else to do the dirty work but something about Courtney and her inspiring ways was bringing out the tiger in him. Realising he was the only man on the boat, he moved carefully up to the front to take a look at whatever had blocked their path. He was relieved to find that the boat had actually collided with the very real barrier that purposely sectioned off the LosTech campus from the rest of the creek.

A row of wooden stumps that jutted out from the water made up the obstacle and stretched from one bank all the way over to the other. On each side, high iron fencing completed the barricade with the sole purpose of keeping the actual grounds of the school from intruders.

Nathan looked at the others and said, 'What do we do now? The only way onto campus from here is to somehow get into that Creek and row on up to the banks, but how the hell do we get over these to do that?'

'Whoa, look at the school building in the moonlight,' said Courtney, who was looking out from their stationary position in the river and out across the large pear shaped Creek ahead of them.

The main school building's Art deco style mixed with all the modern glass was quite a sight in the moonlit darkness, and they could all sense the eerie vibe the view ahead of them had created.

Cutting into the silence Courtney said, 'How deep is it

here? Anyone know? Ellie, stick the oar down and see if you can touch the bottom with it.'

Ellie leaned over the side of the boat and poked the oar into the water. 'Why exactly am I doing this? You're not going to make some wisecrack about me sticking my oar in, are you?'

'Tempting though it is, sadly no. I just thought if we can stand up, maybe we can all get out and lift the boat over.'

'Are you crazy? We'd never lift this boat,' exclaimed Nathan.

'No, it's shallow, look,' said Ellie, as she banged the oar against the bottom of the river. 'She could actually be on to something.'

'These wooden stumps aren't very high,' said Courtney. 'They're just here to stop boats drifting in. If we all get out, I reckon we could lift it and drag it over. Don't you think guys?' She looked toward both Ellie and Becky for assurance and then in turn they both looked out across the Creek.

All Courtney could think about as she gazed over at the school building was what Professor Thistle had told her earlier about the murdered family. She did not really fancy the idea of swimming all the way across, not knowing what might be lurking beneath them. Even the thought of briefly getting in to hoist the boat over filled her with dread. She didn't want to mention it to the others though, just in case the thought had not crossed their minds.

'Well,' said Ellie. 'I guess we don't have many other options other than to swim ... or go back. So I say we swim. Nathan, you're the guy. You go first and make sure it's safe – and also not too cold.'

Nathan looked over the side of the boat into the dark water and instantly forgot he was meant to be brave. He mumbled, 'That's just great. Why do I have to be the only guy?' Like a child about to flick their bogey down the side of the sofa, he slyly dipped his hand into the water to check the temperature so nobody could question his chivalry.

'Look out for the dead family,' said Ellie as she clocked what he was doing.

He immediately wrenched his hand back out in a panic.

'Ellie,' snapped Courtney.

'What? Well, they're obviously still in there somewhere, aren't they? I'm just being real.'

'Well sometimes, we don't necessarily have to be so ... real.'

'Alright, alright, enough, I'll do it,' he said frantically in a moment of unrecognisable bravado.

In shock Courtney said, 'Really ... wow, why?'

He took a deep breath to compose himself and said calmly and proudly, 'I guess I am the man of the boat.' He rationalised in his head that the characters from his favourite movies would not back down from a challenge, so neither would he.

'Wow ... I'm going to call it the 'Courtney effect' from now on. It seems to be hitting everyone like a hammer to the head lately,' said Ellie. 'Who will succumb to your power next?'

'Shut up and leave her alone,' said Nathan. 'Now listen, if I get in there, you better all follow straight after.'

'Of course we will, brave warrior,' said Ellie. 'We didn't come just for the ride and to watch you take a swim. It's just that we need a masculine, hero type guy to make sure all is safe before we get our delicate bodies wet.' She gestured sexily at her curves, turned and gave a cheeky smile and a wink of encouragement to Becky. 'Anyway, look. I told you, it's shallow.' She banged the oar once again onto the ground beneath the water.

Nathan stood up in preparation to jump over the side of the boat. All the others looked at each other nervously.

During the day, that sort of thing would not be a problem, but the darkness that enveloped them and blanketed the water made it another proposition altogether.

In a moment of tremendous bravery, Nathan leapt off the side of the boat and into the water; perhaps with a little more gusto than was probably needed. He did it as a sign to the others that he was the man, but the move was also synonymous with the behaviour of someone caught under the spell of a crush. With three ladies in the boat, a small infatuation was likely to be the best explanation. As his feet touched the water, the others gasped. A second later, he was gone. He disappeared underneath the water. The girls looked at each other in shock and for a moment, all was silent before everyone burst into a simultaneous panic.

'You said it was shallow,' screamed Becky.

'It was. You saw me bang the floor.' Ellie had lost her initial bluster and found it had been replaced with dread.

'You must have been banging a rock you idiot,' screeched Becky.

Moments later, there was a thud underneath the boat and the three girls screamed in unison.

'He's stuck underneath,' yelled Courtney.

'The reeds must have gotten him,' said Ellie, still in a panic. She felt very guilty that Nathan had jumped into the Creek on her assertion that the water was shallow.

'We have to move the boat,' said Courtney. 'Quickly, everyone jump out, but grab onto one of the stumps for support, or we'll all end up being dragged under.'

Spurred on by Courtney's authoritative tone, they immediately stood up. As they balanced themselves in their unstable mode of transport, there was a slight hesitation from everyone, but any doubt was quickly scared out of them as they heard another thud beneath the boat. They stumbled about trying to keep balance as the boat swayed in the water. Ellie screamed as the momentum practically forced her forward, leaving her no choice but to jump. 'Ohhhhhhhh craaap.'

A split second later, with the boat swishing dangerously around in the creek from the momentum of Ellie's fall, Courtney and Becky were forced to follow and landed in the water with a smack. Each of them quickly scrambled towards a stump. Courtney grabbed the one nearest to the boat and used her legs to kick it away in order to free Nathan. They waited in silence for a few seconds. It was too dark to think about diving down to find him.

Then, with a huge gasp and a splash, Nathan suddenly

emerged from the water gasping for air. 'Help me, help me,' he called out in desperation, while choking with water like he was auditioning for a part in a Titanic sequel.

Hanging on to a stump with one hand, Ellie used her other to reach out and grab Nathan, pulling him towards her. Fearing he'd disappear once again underneath the depths of the Creek, he grabbed onto her so tight she felt as if her blood vessels were going to burst. The four of them each clung to a wooden stump like their life depended on it; which it quite possibly did.

The darkness of the water began to provoke their imagination as they all wondered what was beneath their feet. The boat had now drifted away from them and back down the Creek. In her panic, the force of Courtney's kick had stranded them.

Courtney looked at Nathan who was looking a little perturbed and said, 'Are you ok?'

'I'm fine, no thanks to her,' he said, gesturing to Ellie with his chin.

'It's not my fault there was a huge rock under us. It gave me a false reading of the water depth.'

They all stared at her.

'I hope you're not implying I did it on purpose? I'm a scientist not an oceanographer,' she screamed. 'Anyway, we're even now. I just saved your arse.'

In an attempt to calm everyone down Becky said, 'Guys, none of that really matters now does it? What do we do now? That's the question. Either way we have to swim. We've got no way of getting the boat over these stumps if we can't even stand in the water. So we either swim to the boat and go home or swim across the Creek to the banks of the school.'

'Things keep touching my feet, and it's freaking me out,' said Ellie. 'What kind of fish are there in this Creek anyway? They better not be pike.'

'It's not the fish I'm worried about,' said Becky, nervously.

'C'mon let's just do it,' asserted a brave Nathan, still trying to prove that he was macho. 'We're in the water now and we've come this far,'

He took his shoes off and placed them on top of the wooden stump he was clinging on to and then began to swim in the direction of the school. 'We may as well just go for it,' he shouted back.

The others looked at each other in surprise. Ellie shrugged her shoulders, took her shoes off and also began to swim after him. After a moment of being left by themselves, Courtney and Becky did the same and followed, all leaving behind a row of shoes atop individual wooden stumps. During the day, it would not have been too far to the banks, probably the length of an Olympic swimming pool, but at night it felt like the edge of the Creek was not getting any closer.

As they felt their muscles weaken from every stroke they made, each one of them started to panic within. They couldn't help but think they may have made a big mistake and that they were going to all end up at the bottom of the Creek alongside the murdered family. However, they pushed on relentlessly, motivated by the thought that the others were probably fine and that they would look weak and stupid if one of them began to scream.

That motivation was quickly wearing away though as they felt themselves being pulled down by the weight of their clothes. Each time a weed stroked their bare feet, it gave them a small burst of energy and they pushed harder and faster in sheer panic at the thought of what else could be touching them. Thankfully, the edge of the Creek was finally getting closer.

All of a sudden, Nathan shouted, 'They're dragging me down.' He felt something particularly large wrap around his ankle. He was convinced in the lack of light that somebody had grabbed his foot from underneath him. He kicked his legs frantically in the water to get free whilst screaming at the top of his voice in the most girlie way imaginable. Though each time he opened his mouth, he swallowed a mouthful of the Creek and choked violently at the thought of swallowing water that was contaminated with dead skin and blood. In a frightened panic, he began to ferociously swim to the edge.

With every kick of his feet he felt like a hand had grabbed his ankle and was pulling him under. In his head he could see the image of a dead carcass with its eyes wide and tongue hanging out, reaching for his leg with its flaky, loose-skinned hand.

The others panicked at his reaction and started to swim at super speed, not knowing what was actually happening to him. This indirectly helped them to make the last few hundred feet and before they knew it, all four of them were scrambling out of the Creek and slowly hauling themselves up onto the side of the sodden bank.

They wrenched themselves on to their stomachs while dragging with them slushy mud and weeds. Nathan had thankfully escaped whatever had hold of his feet and then they finally managed to get themselves on to relatively dry land. They slowly rose and stood next to each other on the water's edge, dripping wet and staring at the school building under the glow of the large, nearly full moon.

Moments earlier, Professor Thistle had just finished yet another late night of research in the school lab and was packing up his things in his office to head on home.

As he turned toward the window to grab his jacket from a chair, he noticed four figures slowly emerging from the Creek. He watched as they stood, all glistening in the moonlight. The identities of Courtney, Ellie, Nathan and Becky could not be made out from that distance. All he could see were what could easily be mistaken for a husband, a wife and two children.

For a brief moment he panicked at the possibility that he was seeing the ghosts of the deceased family, bringing into question his own beliefs on the universe and more importantly, making him look like a fool to all his students. 'Impossible.' He closed his eyes in the hope that it was the late hour causing his mind to play tricks on him.

'Oh my God, the professor's light is still on,' exclaimed

Nathan in the loudest whisper you've ever heard.

They all gasped in unison before instantly diving to the floor to avoid being spotted.

Professor Thistle slowly opened his eyes to see if the ghostly figures were still there. They were not. 'You're a stupid, crazy old man.' He grabbed his jacket, then his bag and finally, he picked up a large red notebook. The notebook was very nondescript with no design markings on the outside but what the pages contained on the inside was in definite contrast. Scruffy and packed full of wonderful pencil doodling and different coloured pen markings, it was a life's work and contained all his most current and important findings. He used the notebook for all his latest thoughts and workings-out before having to reluctantly but eventually store them on his computer. His rationalisation was that if it had no markings, it could be left with all the other books in his office without drawing attention to itself; a sort of homemade security that he felt was safer than leaving it on a hard drive to be stolen or destroyed by time itself. After all, he knew his compilation could possibly be the most sought after piece of science literature in the world, and ironically he didn't feel comfortable leaving its security down to technology.

With that in mind, he finally moved towards the door, but before leaving, he placed the red notebook safely in amongst the abundance of books on one of his many, well stocked bookshelves, then stood back and watched as even to him the red needle disappeared and was swallowed up by the giant haystack of books.

~ CHAPTER NINETEEN ~

It's time to really get this adventure started

Courtney, Ellie, Nathan and Becky had been lying flat on the prickly, damp grass on the banks of the Creek for ten minutes, making sure that whoever was at the window had well and truly gone. With mud beneath them and after having swum across the huge body of water, they felt like crack commandos on an elite mission, and perhaps in a way they were. It was a feeling that motivated them to keep as still as possible.

'That was him by the window, wasn't it? I bet he saw us,' said Nathan, sounding worried. 'What are we going to do?'

'Don't panic,' responded Ellie calmly. 'We'll just wait here for a few more minutes. I'm sure he's left by now, and if anyone does start to come this way, we'll just slide back into the water.'

They waited in silence for the next few minutes until Nathan decided to break the peace by probing Courtney a little. 'So this problem at your place,' he whispered. 'Do you really think it's somehow connected with what we're doing? Because if we are to believe that time travel will one day be possible, it would be a safe assumption to believe that if we *are* on a journey that will lead to one of us travelling in time, then we may have already been there and left clues for our past selves.'

'Nathan, you are priceless – actually scrap that, I'm too nice. You're an idiot.'

'Ellie, he's right,' said Courtney in defence. 'Theoretically it's possible, but the only way that would be the case is if fate said we were meant to discover time travel. In that way, the clues would just be pointers sending us in the right direction as opposed to things that are changing the past, because I don't believe the past is changeable. That's why I think we are ok to look for clues, but we'd be wrong to assume the past is changing because of anything we are doing.'

'It does seem like a huge coincidence,' said Becky.

'Let's deal with our present predicament first though,' replied Courtney. 'But yeah, it does seem intriguing that's for sure. First thing I'll do next, assuming we get out of here, is fly straight home to find out what's been happening and to discover the true history of that house. One way or another, I'm gonna find out who would feel the need to come back from the past and haunt me. It just seems really off.'

To any normal set of teens and twenty-something adults, the type of conversation they were having would have seemed ridiculous and perhaps a little nerdy, but because it was all these teens had ever thought about, they saw it as relatively normal; as if they were asking for something as rudimentary as driving directions. In class however, they had so far never been totally focused on the subject; perhaps only around seventy percent. Because after being given the driving route to take, they would always still be somewhat confused and unsure about where it was they needed to go. Their big problem was that all their ideas and theories had only ever been discussed in the classroom; a safe clinical environment. There were no field trips or practical assessments when it came to time travel, but Courtney was giving them their first glimmer of hope in finding out if what they had been studying for years was fact, or fiction. As they were lying on the grass, scared and damp, they realised they were on their way to fulfilling that last remaining thirty percent.

Ellie stood up with determination. 'Right ... let's go. As much as this is all really interesting, I think he must've gone now, and we've got stuff to be getting busy with.'

The rest of them followed her lead, stood up and started to walk towards the building. They reached the back door and waited while Becky craftily entered the combination on the keypad beside it. Consequently there was a click and the door opened slightly. She nudged it open a tiny fraction farther, and a bright wedge of light streamed through the gap. For a moment she hesitated and then she peered inside, looked back at the others and smiled. 'The lights are on but nobody's home.'

They hurried into a corridor and followed it round to the main atrium at the centre of the building before turning left down another corridor to the rear. A sign on a large wooden door read, 'Professor Pinakin Thistle, President, LosTech.' Courtney recognised it from earlier and so edged it open to be faced with the long empty waiting room she had been in previously. Again the light was on. She waved the others through and they all walked down to the end of the room where they waited for Becky to work her magic with the combination keypad again.

They scurried into the dark and ominous headquarters of the organisation. The only light was the pale blue reflection of the moon that was shining through the huge windows. All was totally silent as they looked around in awe at what they had just achieved. Ellie then reached to turn the light on.

'No,' said Nathan in a heightened whisper. 'We can't turn the lights on. Someone might see.'

'The lights are on in the hallways.'

'But that's the hallways, not the professor's office – his personal, private, locked office,' he insisted.

'How the hell are we supposed to find anything then?' She didn't like being told what to do a single bit and most certainly not by Nathan of all people.

'We'll just keep this door open slightly,' he said. 'The light out there was left on for some reason, so we can't be blamed for it.'

Becky looked around the room as if she was scanning the area but then realised something and said, 'Courtney, what are we actually looking for anyway?'

'I guess we just need to see if he has any documentation that points toward any kind of new research. Stuff he may

127

not want to share yet in his classes or even to the world because it's untested or so new.' What she said sounded a little like she was almost trying to create what it was she wanted to find in her head, in the hope that it might just appear somehow through positive thoughts. 'Nathan, you keep watch by the door and holler if you see something.'

He muttered to himself and said, 'Of course, what else would I be here for?'

The three girls searched around the office but struggled to find anything of much interest. All they came across were standard office items and tons of useless books on the shelves and floor.

Courtney searched the desk drawers, but as she did, she suddenly got the feeling that what they were doing was wrong. Yet although she had not been brought up to rummage through other people's property, strangely, she could not stop herself either as her obsession to find the answers she wanted was so embedded in her head; consuming her whole being and driving her to cross boundaries she had dared not to explore before.

As the girls continued searching, Nathan remained on guard by the door, peeking through the gap to make sure there was no sign of movement outside. As boredom struck, his mind started to lose focus on what he was supposed to be doing and instead, he glanced over the book titles on the shelves next to him. What stuck out was the fact that the books were all in alphabetical order; much like a library. *Makes sense with this many books.* As he looked at the vast array on the shelves, he wondered if they would be better off in height order instead. *At least they would look neat. That red one with the ceramic ornament in front of it is so tall it should be at the end of the shelf.*

The ornament he'd seen was the only one on the shelves and was conveniently placed in front of the book he was staring at. What was stranger and really quite a coincidence though, even if Nathan was not aware of it, was that the ornament in question seemed to be an exact copy of Courtney's figurine of Jesus that was smashed by the spirit when she was five. Nathan didn't think twice about it though because he was unaware exactly what Courtney's lost item actually was as she hadn't told anyone.

Then he saw something that he did find particularly odd. As he scanned the shelves, he realised that the red book behind the ornament was the only book that wasn't a professionally published one. What is a notebook doing up on these shelves? Nathan wondered. He reached forward to grab it, but just as he was about to place his fingers on it, a noise from outside reverberated.

Becky whispered, 'What was that?' She then hit her head as she stood up too quickly from under the desk.

Courtney and Ellie also stopped what they were doing and froze in unison.

Nathan stopped reaching for the book, looked toward Becky and wondered why she was under Professor Thistle's desk. 'What are you doing?'

'What? I saw it in a film. Sometimes there are hidden compartments under desks,' she remarked with an innocent tone and expression on her face.

Courtney didn't have time to chit chat and said firmly, 'What did you hear?'

'I thought I heard a car door.'

'What? Ellie, check the window,' ordered Courtney.

Ellie went over to the furthest window and squashed her face against it so that she could just see the corner of the car park over to the left. Startled, she jumped back from the window. 'It's the professor – he's coming back.'

'He must've forgotten something,' said Becky, who was close to tears after suddenly realising the implications of their actions. 'What do we do?'

They stared at each other, each hoping that somebody else had an idea.

'He's not in the building yet,' said Courtney. 'Everybody ... out.'

The three girls hurriedly ran towards Nathan, who quickly opened the door for them to let them through. They passed him in a flash, straight past the bookshelf that had an apparent exact copy of Courtney's figurine. Just as he was about to follow, he stopped. He could not shake away the feeling that the red book looked out of place on the shelf.

Becky, Ellie and Courtney, all ran down the long waiting room outside Professor Thistle's office. Courtney noticed that Nathan was not following behind and so skidded to a stop. 'Nathan, what are you doing?'

At the other end of the waiting room, the door handle turned. Becky also skidded to a halt and Ellie slammed straight into her.

'Huhhh,' squealed Ellie in a whisper, as she watched the door handle as it slowly turned.

Becky spun around to Courtney and Nathan and whispered urgently, 'Guys hide – now.'

Nathan was about to move, but in a random moment of audacity he grabbed the red book off the shelf and quickly left the office. In a split second they all dived under the benches that lined the wall. The door at the opposite end began to open just as the door to the professor's office slowly closed. They squeezed in tight under the benches and tried to stop breathing. The door edged open and Professor Thistle stepped in just as his office door at the other end had clicked shut.

Nathan, who was clasping the red book for dear life, suddenly noticed the floor was wet due to their damp clothes. 'Huh,' he whimpered in shock.

Courtney kicked him to be quiet. Nathan's foot, which sported a smelly soaking wet sock, was centimetres away from Courtney's face. From her facial reaction it may as well have been alive and about to slowly glide its tongue up her face in a sordid manner. He fidgeted his toes and it edged nearer to her mouth. She grimaced but could not move as Professor Thistle took a couple of steps forward. They froze like statues under the benches.

Professor Thistle paused for a moment as if he had heard something.

The gang continued to hold their breath. Their faces became red and they all started silently praying in the hope that he would not stay for long.

Professor Thistle listened in silence. He then reached over to the wall, flicked the light switch off and left the room.

After a few moments of silence to make sure he had gone, they all let out a huge release of breath, particularly Courtney who immediately pushed Nathan's foot away from her face and exhaled in huge relief at no longer being in close proximity to him and his pungent wet feet. One by one they rolled out from under their hiding place and lay flat on their backs in massive gratitude.

'Well that was a hell of an anti-climax,' said Ellie with a smile. 'He just forgot to turn the damn light out.'

'I never want to be put in that position again,' said Courtney who then looked straight at Nathan with her eyes wide. 'And I mean ... literally.'

Nathan looked at her totally oblivious to what she was talking about.

'Alright c'mon,' said Courtney. 'Let's just go home now guys. This was a stupid idea.' She couldn't help but think she had made a terrible mistake breaking and entering into the school on her first day. Her heart was still beating like a steel drum after coming so close to capture and seemingly all for nothing.

They all got up from the floor, except Nathan who remained there, facing the ceiling and holding the red book open and out in front of him. He had a contented and smug look on his face as he snapped it shut and brought it close to his chest. The others all stopped in reaction to the loud bang and turned to see him lying on the floor. 'Not so fast, guys.'

They stared at him with pale frightened faces, waiting for a response.

'He thought he could hide it by making it nondescript, no markings, and no reason for anyone to touch it, but you see in doing so, it stuck out like a sore thumb.'

They all had no idea what he was talking about and so Ellie said, 'What are you babbling on about, Rambo?'

'Rambo indeed, or perhaps even Sherlock,' he responded proudly as he raised his eyebrows with confidence before quickly realising Sherlock was not as attractive to females. 'Or maybe the body of Rambo and the mind of Sherlock, but that's not what's important because you'll be pleased to know that I may have found what we came here for.' He held the red book out in front of him and in a manner only comparable with a T.V. talent show voice-over he said, 'Ladies and Gentlemen, the moment has arrived. Now ... I think it's time to really get this adventure started.'

~ CHAPTER TWENTY ~

The girl I used to call a witch

The jumbo jet's wheels screeched on the wet runway at London's Heathrow airport. As often happens in London, the rain had been falling through the night and into the morning, though from the clear blue sky it looked like a warm sunny day was due. Plenty of rain mixed with occasional hot days was a typical English summer; very different from where the aeroplane had just flown from.

Inside the cabin of the huge aircraft, Courtney sat alone by a window. Two days had passed since she and the others had broken into Professor Pik Thistle's office and stolen his journal. With no news of a break in, it looked as though they had gotten away with their social discrepancy, although Courtney knew it was not conclusive as the school was closed over the weekend. She had managed to catch a flight on Sunday night in the hope that she could assess the damage at home and if there was really nothing unusual, be back at LosTech by Wednesday; Thursday at the latest.

Arrival time was 7:20A.M. Monday morning and as the jumbo jet taxied to the arrival gate, Courtney closed Professor Thistle's red journal that she had been reading with great concentration throughout the flight and placed it on her lap. Her expression exhibited some confusion, as well as a slight sense of regret and her demeanour was undeniably tired as she waited for the seatbelt sign to go out.

For much of the journey, aside from a couple of hours in an uncomfortable position trying to sleep, she had scoured Professor Thistle's journal from front to back looking for a breakthrough. What was in the journal did appear to be Professor Thistle's latest calculations and thoughts on time travel. However, she could not make any sense of them or find anything useful she could use to help in her quest.

Reality had hit home and she wondered whether they would have been better off returning the notes before anyone found out they were missing. *Can I really find the answer to time travel in an old man's notebook?*

As the aeroplane finally came to a halt, Courtney quickly unbuckled herself and grabbed her bag from the overhead compartment so she could be one of the first to exit the aircraft. As soon as she entered the airport terminal, she quickly grabbed a phone out of her pocket and switched it on. Although, it wasn't hers; Ellie had lent her phone to Courtney, under slight duress, in replacement of the one that was now surely at the bottom of the Creek. As she walked towards passport control, multiple text alerts sounded, and she looked at the screen to find two new text messages. The first read:

Hey it's me. I'll be
waiting in arrivals.
I hope you get this
message, coz the
number you gave seems
to be American. Alex
(";)

Courtney smiled, before opening the second message which read:

Court, got a call from
a friend. The word is
out that there was a
break in. It doesn't
make sense as it's not
even Monday yet. Best
hurry back. It may look

like you ran. Becky.

'Oh great,' she said with a sigh and a shake of the head. *There wasn't even anything useful in the bloody book.* It didn't make sense. *Why would Nathan find it? There must be a reason. He couldn't have just happened across the one book the professor seemed to be hiding all for nothing.*

On her long flight over, she had developed some massive doubts about everything and thought that maybe her life was destined to 'suck' after all. *How could I, a mixed race girl from an average working class family who saw ghosts and had grandiose ideas about travelling back in time, even think about becoming a great scientist?* She bowed her head with indignation as she continued to walk through passport control, then customs and finally out into the arrivals hall.

'Courtney,' shouted an excited female from behind the barriers.

She looked up from her despondent state and saw Alexandra waving and smiling. Nobody could have guessed that the girl who bullied her in primary school would now be the only person waiting to welcome her at the airport, ecstatic to see her. For a brief moment, she felt better about herself and smiled at Alexandra.

'You do not know how pleased I am to see you,' exclaimed Alexandra.

'Yeah, it's good to see you too.'

'What's that?' Alexandra pointed at Professor Thistle's journal that was in her hand. 'Homework already?'

She remained silent for a moment. 'This? Let's just say, unless I figure out what's in this book, my big American adventure could be very short-lived.' Her initial smile disappeared and she adopted a dejected and miserable look instead.

'What the hell are you talking about? Why do you keep hiding books from me?'

'Never mind, don't listen to me. Let's just get back to the house so we can get everything fixed. Did you call an

135

electrician?'

'Why would I call an electrician? What use would an electrician be against...? Oh, I get it. You think I'm crazy?' Alexandra snapped her fingers and jerked her head from left to right. 'You think a year on the streets has turned me into a nutcase who believes in poltergeists, is that it?' She felt a little hurt and humiliated by Courtney's reaction.

'No, Alex I—'

'Well that's just a little ironic coming from the girl I used to call a witch for exactly the same thing.'

'But that's just it ... it's not the same.'

Alexandra stared at her, a little confused.

'Let's not argue,' said Courtney. 'Let's just get back there and decide what it is and whether to start panicking. Has anything else happened while I was on my way?'

'Are you crazy? You think I stayed another night in there? I ran straight out and booked myself into a Travelodge. I didn't even look back.'

Courtney looked at Alexandra and sympathetically remembered the fear she felt as a kid when she first witnessed a ghost herself. 'I guess it's time we went and had a look then. I just hope for your sake that there's something left of my house because insurance is still on my to-do list.' She gestured to the exit doors. 'So ... shall we?'

~ CHAPTER TWENTY ONE ~

That girl was here for a reason

'Now, explain to me how you know exactly what has gone missing, yet you had nothing to do with it,' said Professor Thistle with an agitated tone as he stood staring dominantly out of his office window.

'Sir, please, I swear. I didn't have anything to do with it,' exclaimed Wazer who was standing behind him. 'I told them it was a stupid idea and that she was crazy, but they wouldn't listen. All I want is to become a great scientist like you.' He was trying to convince the professor that he was on his side but was having trouble hiding his fear as he stood in front of the professor's desk.

After being left behind and made to look stupid in front of Courtney, he decided to go straight to the school as soon as the weekend was over and tell Professor Thistle who was responsible for the break in; even though there was no evidence that pointed to them, and Professor Thistle had not yet discovered that something was even missing. His intention was purely selfish, wanting to put himself in favour with the man who would give him the grades to graduate with distinction. He thought it might perhaps gain him a little respect as well as stop him being the butt of everyone's 'fat' jokes forevermore.

'I don't suppose I really need to ask this question,' said Professor Thistle. 'But in the unlikely event that I am wrong, enlighten me. Who exactly are 'they' and 'she' in this story?'

Wazer looked down at the floor due to the authoritative tone that Professor Thistle had remonstrated. He remained still, using his last remaining ounce of loyalty to decide if he had made the right decision in betraying his friends.

'If you're standing there trying to decide if you've made the right decision about betraying your friends, don't. By the pure nature of you coming here, I now know exactly who was responsible and fear not, they will be severely reprimanded. Your only hope of remaining in this school is to show me you have the courage and conviction to follow through with your actions.' Professor Thistle's voice had become very loud and firm, so to stem his anger a bit he tried using a gentler and more restrained tone. 'Now ... who was it, boy?'

Wazer immediately jolted his head up and like a barrage of hailstones trying to escape their cloud prisons in the sky; he spat out his words at a fierce speed. 'It was the new girl, Courtney Sir, and all the others in the house – Ellie, Nathan and Becky. She said she had the code or something, so they hatched a plan and crossed the Creek. I swear I had nothing to do with it. I just want to help you, Sir. Help justice be served and stop anyone else from-.'

'Why?'

'Sir?'

'Why did they take it?'

'Well, at the end of the day when all is said and done, it's a case by where–'

'Get on with it.'

'Sorry – she said that she needed to find a way of going back.'

'Back?' Professor Thistle suddenly became very interested in what Wazer was about to say.

'Something about a spirit that was evil. It took something from her. I don't know it didn't make much sense.' Wazer spoke with a slight trepidation, knowing Professor Thistle did not like any talk of ghosts and spirits. 'What was in the book anyway, Sir?'

Professor Thistle stared straight at him, not really having listened to his request for information about the book as he was more interested in what Courtney could possibly be up to. *What's all this talk of evil spirits and going back? Could Courtney possibly be entertaining the idea of actually travelling through time on some bizarre personal quest?*

Wazer stood in silence, unsure why Professor Thistle himself had gone silent. 'Err ... that's if you don't mind me asking, Sir ... you know, about your book.' He was treading carefully, making sure not to annoy the professor further.

Professor Thistle's concentration reverted back to Wazer. As he spoke, he not only tried to explain the reality to him but was also working it all out in his own head too. 'My boy, this world is full of strange and wondrous things. All kinds of amazing and unexplainable events happen around us every day. I'm on a mission to find a way to make one of the biggest wonders of the universe a reality – time travel. That book they stole holds all my current research, particularly pertaining to gravitational waves and worm holes.'

'Oh,' said Wazer, not really knowing what he was talking about, but he pretended to so he would appear to be on the same level and wavelength.

'However, I assure you, there is nothing in that book that would even come close to giving anyone the capability of travelling through time just yet.'

'Oh, right,' beamed Wazer, as he realised what Professor Thistle was now saying.

'So your friends are either really stupid to think they could achieve this by stealing my journal, or they're smarter than you think and there's something a lot more interesting at play here. Maybe they know something I don't. Which would you say it is?'

Wazer suddenly felt confident in giving his opinion to the professor. He stood up straight with an air of confidence, convinced he had the right answer to the question and said, 'Oh, they're not very smart, especially the girl. I mean, firstly she's English,' he said with an all-knowing and cocky expression. He was making a sorry attempt to bring humour to their meeting. 'And secondly, she hasn't even spent a single day studying here under your good self. No, I'm confident it was the first inkling you had, Sir. They're definitely stupid.'

Professor Thistle squinted in disparity before grabbing a newspaper off his desk. He held it out in front of him. On the front cover was a CCTV image of four figures standing in the distance by the school Creek with the headline:

RIVAL SCHOOL PRANK ... OR THE FAMILY THAT SANK?

In frustration he threw the newspaper firmly at Wazer, but his reflexes were not great so looking flustered he just stood there allowing the newspaper to just drop to the floor. With a delayed reaction he quickly scrambled to pick up the school tabloid to look at the front page. 'Oh my God,' he said in reaction to what he saw. 'Could it really be them?'

'That's exactly who it is.'

'So they really are at the bottom of the Creek and the house really is possessed by that family? And I've been living with them all along?'

'Oh dear God.' The professor raised his head to the ceiling in utter dismay at Wazer's complete lack of comprehension. 'I mean it's them ... your friends, you idiot.'

Wazer dropped his panicked expression and replaced it with a look of bewilderment, like the dodo would have before causing its own extinction.

'My boy, it turns out that they are not the stupid ones. In fact, far from it, and this young Courtney is definitely the instigator.'

'How do you mean?' Although Wazer was very good academically he struggled with conversation, particularly with Professor Thistle and was not quite getting his comparison in intelligence between the others and himself.

'Within just one day of arriving, she manages to get hold of the code for this door, source vital local knowledge from me in our meeting as well as somehow manage to find the only book of any real importance to me in a room crammed to the brim with books. More than that, she did it knowing that I can hardly report a burglary when no forced entry can be detected and the only thing missing is an old man's notebook.' Professor Thistle took his first breath. 'Best of all, she hatched a plan to come via the Creek because she knows that many in this town will be gullible enough to believe the stories about the dead family at the bottom of it. She cleverly leaves you behind so that only four of them will emerge from the Creek in full view of the campus CCTV cameras. Cameras that she knew would be there to take the all important hazy snapshot image.' He grabbed the newspaper from Wazer and held it up in front of him again. 'Four figures mysteriously stood by the edge of the Creek in the middle of the night. Four figures that match the description of said family. Four figures that are now spread all over the local newspaper diverting any attention away from talk of a break in. And where is she now? As soon as she got what she came for, she flies back to London. Oh no, she is certainly not stupid and I clearly underestimated her.' Professor Thistle was extremely frustrated and the lines between his eyes had become pronounced and scrunched up due to his built-up angst.

'Er, I'm not quite sure that's how it went,' mumbled Wazer a little sheepishly. He realised that the balance of intelligence had shifted slightly. He knew that the events were a little more accidental but did not want to correct the professor for fear of being reprimanded.

'You want to help?' Professor Thistle phrased it as a question, but they both knew it was more of a statement as what he really meant, was Wazer would help.

Wazer stared at Professor Thistle and nodded.

Professor Thistle threw the newspaper onto his desk. 'Find out who she really is and why she stole my journal. There has to be a reason that I'm not seeing and you're going to find out what it is. Understand?'

'But–'

'You will not tell them I know it was them in the images or them that broke in. You will carry on as if nothing has changed. That girl was here for a reason, and I want to know what the reason was. Do that for me and I'll make sure you do alright here.'

'Yes Professor, I won't let you down,' said Wazer proudly, as he stared at him to make sure he had finished speaking.

'You can go now.'

He turned and shuffled quickly to the exit, but just as he placed his hand on the door knob, he stopped and turned back. 'If ... sorry *when*, I get the information you want, what's going to happen to them?' For a split second there was a glimmer of compassion in his voice.

Professor Thistle, who was now sitting at his desk, looked up at Wazer and stared at him with serious intent in his eyes. 'They will of course no longer be allowed to study at my school. They'll be expelled.'

Wazer looked down at the floor. Deep inside he was still not convinced he was doing the right thing.

'You have a problem with that? You think students that break into my office and steal my property should be dealt with differently?'

'No sir, not at all. That's exactly what they deserve,' replied Wazer. He knew that he would be stupid to disagree with him, although he was still only half convinced about what he had agreed to. 'I'll let you know when Courtney returns.'

Once outside the professor's office, he thought about the conversation and what he now had to do if he was to maintain his own place within the school. Actions that he knew would be extremely detrimental to the others.

On the other side of the door, Professor Thistle reached out to grab his coffee mug but accidentally knocked it over and spilt the contents all over his desk. Thankfully, there was not much to be damaged apart from the newspaper which bore most of the brunt of the spillage. 'Damn it.' He quickly grabbed the paper, removed the front page and put the remainder of the paper on the dry side of the desk. For a moment, he held the stained front cover featuring Courtney and her friends, out in front of him. You could no longer clearly see the date and the coffee had given it a vaguely antique look. He couldn't quite put his finger on it, but the coffee-stained image suddenly seemed important. He carefully folded the article and placed it in his jacket pocket, if not for anything else other than to use as an example to his students of how the human quest for knowledge of the unknown can turn the most innocent of things into something a little more spirited. 'Maybe Miss U.K. has something to contribute after all,' he said with a condescending grin. 'But rest assured little lady, one way or another I'm going to get my book back, and then I'll make sure you pay for ever daring to cross me.'

~ CHAPTER TWENTY TWO ~

The world of horror

The London Underground network was packed tight with early morning commuters who were all marching collectively like busy worker ants to serve their queen. Courtney and Alexandra were squeezed in amongst the hordes of daily commuters who all seemed to have completely lost their everyday usual manners the second they boarded the train; pushing and shoving their way on at each station, desperate to not get left behind. Courtney and Alexandra's destination was a long journey from Heathrow airport, practically the whole length of the line, and as they passed through the busy centre of London the crowds began to ease slightly, so Courtney proceeded to tell Alexandra all that had happened to her on her first day in the United States of America.

As Alexandra listened, she found it hilarious that Courtney had turned into just what everyone suspected she herself would turn into; a rebellious troublemaker.

'For good reason, I'll have you know. Sometimes you have to look at everyone's actions including those in charge, before you can call someone the guilty party.'

'Of course you do,' said Alexandra, mocking her. 'Because everyone in the whole world is out to get you, aren't they?'

'It's just like the whole system. You know it's corrupt, don't you?' Courtney was finding it hard speaking over the noise of the train which seemed to have gotten louder the deeper it went.

'Well, I know it's old and really could do with some air conditioning, but corrupt?'

'I meant governments, you div, not the tube system. All they do is steal from us twenty four hours a day and control what we do. Although, maybe that's more connected to the tube than we realise, because if they didn't force everyone on to the trains by making it so hard to drive in the city, maybe we wouldn't risk getting elbowed in the face every time we get on here. '

Alexandra was struggling to hear over the rattling train carriage. 'What?'

'You either just accept it and let everyone walk all over you, or you can ...' Courtney looked at Alexandra and realised that not only was she shouting loudly over the noise of the train about a very important topic that deserved more focused attention but that she was saying it to someone who probably wouldn't understand even if it was being said in a more appropriate environment anyway.

'What you saying?'

Courtney shook her head as if to say never mind.

They finally arrived at Tottenham Hale station in North London, jumped off the tube and transferred to an overground train that would take them from the busy urban city to Courtney's house in the quiet, quaint and beautiful rolling hills of Hertfordshire; the first county north of London and many years ago the home of England's aristocracy.

Courtney had not actually been back there since she was taken into care. The sale was completed only a few days before she left for America and she wanted Alexandra (at least for the first few years) to feel like it kind of belonged to her. However, the combination of her experience there as well as Alexandra's recent incident was making her feel a little anxious about seeing it again.

At long last the train pulled up at the station and they disembarked on to the platform. The sun was shining extremely bright, making a big change from the usual unpredictability of the British summer. Heat one day and pouring rain the next was the usual pattern, but for a change it was so hot that the heat was actually visible as it shimmered off the tarmac. It was a glorious English summer's day, probably one of the last before autumn sets in. However, as they walked up the station steps and onto the road, it was noticeable that both girls were not in awe of the unusual weather but were quiet in anticipation of seeing the house again.

They climbed the tall station steps and walked through an old rusty iron swing gate just off the road at the top, the type which is common in the English countryside for stopping bicycles entering and racing along the footpaths. The path led to a long river that ran parallel with the railway track; a short cut that Courtney had always used as a child whenever she took the train. The river was narrow and wound its way through the trees and past the backs of the quaint riverside houses that lined the route.

'It's like I can't get away from rivers. I wonder who's lying at the bottom of this one,' remarked Courtney.

'Don't say that. I used to swim in this during the summer when I was a kid.'

'Well I hate to break it to you, but this river dates back hundreds of years. There's probably a ton of people in there from way back.'

Alexandra walked to the edge and peered into the water. She grimaced but was immediately distracted by a distant scream.

Down the river, a teenager had just jumped from a bridge into the cool water below.

'I remember when I used to do that, but thanks to you, I'm now thinking never again. You know I'm so glad I know you. I mean, who else would be able to introduce me to the world of horror like you can?'

Courtney laughed out loud at Alexandra's attempt at humour.

They arrived at another swing gate which led to a main road. They quickly crossed and then entered a gate on the other side which opened into a large field that graded steeply upwards, leading into a wood of mature trees at the top.

Courtney's house was situated totally alone, somewhere

on the summit of the hill. Originally it was built as the servant's residence for a large estate; once home to one of the noble residents of the area. The main house had burnt down many years ago and the small Victorian servant's cottage was sold off privately. Courtney once asked her mum if Mr Rochester and Jane Eyre used to live there, but in her naivety of British literature she would say that if they did it was way before they moved there as she and Cliff bought it from a Mr and Mrs Plunkett.

As the two girls walked up the steep hill towards the trees, Courtney told Alexandra all about the building's unique history, much to Alexandra's dismay.

'Why on earth didn't you tell me this before I agreed to move in?'

Courtney chuckled, 'Why? What difference would it have made?'

'People burning alive and you wonder why you saw ghosts as a kid. No wonder the house is possessed. I'm not going back there now.' Alexandra immediately came to a halt by the entrance of the wooded section.

'What are you going on about? It's not haunted by a bunch of angry burnt servants and farmers.' She laughed at her own comment and then continued to walk towards the woods.

Just as Courtney disappeared into the trees, Alexandra shouted, 'Oh really, and what makes you so sure huh?'

'Because there was nobody there,' she yelled out as she re-emerged at the opening of the wooded area. 'It was abandoned for years. A bunch of kids were messing around one day and set fire to it, so it can't be haunted by any previous residents of that house, or unfortunately Mr Rochester's crazy wife.'

'Who is Mr Rochester, and what about the servants that lived in your house? What happened to them?'

'It's Victorian, built over one hundred years ago. How many Victorian houses are there in England and how many people do you think died in them over the years? Are you suggesting they're all possessed? Anyway, I don't think that a

147

haunting is limited to people that died in the place that's haunted. That's just a common mistake that people make. I reckon its people who are haunted, as that's the only theory that explains how the spirit knew exactly how to get into my head as well as the fact that I saw it again at the school.'

'Our school – you saw it at our school? You never told me that,' said Alexandra with a shocked expression.

'That's why I really don't think that what you experienced was a ghost. It's me that's haunted; not the house.'

Alexandra looked at Courtney with an uneasy expression on her face, a look that suggested she was not completely buying Courtney's explanation. 'So how do you explain what happened to me in the exact same house ... and in the exact same room?'

'That's what we are going to go and find out, but we can't do that standing around here. Are you coming or what?'

Alexandra remained still for a second as she contemplated what she had said. After a moment of thinking about the consequences of being left alone in the woods, she shuffled hesitantly towards Courtney, the trees and the house.

~ CHAPTER TWENTY THREE ~

What the hell is that?

Even though beams of light were penetrating through the gaps in the tops of the trees, with the leaves in full blossom it was still quite dark inside the wood. Having walked through the trees hundreds of times Courtney was quite used to the effect though and often thought how miserable you'd have to be not to find it beautiful, but as Courtney and Alexandra were just nearing the break in the trees where they would come out the other side and into the open, a similar lighting effect seemed to come from directly in front of them. Courtney stopped and turned to see what direction the beams of light above her were shining in and was totally bemused when she saw that the sun was above and directly behind them, but as she turned and looked back towards the house, unmistakeable beams of light were shooting straight at them and into their chests. She reached out and grabbed Alexandra's hand. Alexandra smiled at the sudden moment of tenderness from her friend, but then Courtney stopped walking, squeezed Alexandra's hand tight and looked into her eyes. 'If my house has burnt to the ground, you're in big trouble.'

Alexandra dropped her smile and raised one eyebrow at her.

Courtney was half serious, knowing that she had just spent a lot of money purchasing the house, but as Alexandra stared back at her, Courtney realised she needed to lighten the mood a little. 'Don't panic, it was probably the dodgy Victorian wiring, and I'm guessing you left your hair curlers in too long.'

Alexandra raised her other eyebrow.

They stepped forward and emerged into the open. The tiny, quaint Victorian brick cottage came into view, still in one piece, but now with a strange addition to its beauty.

They both froze, as they could not believe what they were seeing in front of them. The whole building emanated a strange yet beautiful white glow and shone so bright you'd be forgiven for thinking it was heaven's gate itself. Despite the hot sunny day, the distinct bright glow could still be seen very clearly, but for some reason neither of them thought it looked dangerous. In fact, after the initial shock, the first thought that ran through their minds was how beautiful it was. They both briefly considered the fact that maybe they had died and gone to heaven.

Still holding hands, they glanced at each other in awe of the spectacle that had unveiled itself in front of their eyes. Courtney looked back at the house. 'Well that's certain to put the value up.'

Alexandra snorted unattractively at the joke; a reaction brought on by a combination of fear and joy. 'A real diamond in the rough.'

'Do you have the keys?'

'Er, you won't need keys.'

'Ok,' said Courtney apprehensively. 'Well let's go and see why my house is shining above all the rest then shall we?'

They walked towards the house, squeezing each other's hands even more tightly than before. As they neared the front door the light engulfed them and Courtney cautiously reached out for the doorknob. As she clasped her hand around it, she noticed that not only was the door off its hinges, but it was barely in one piece. She looked at Alexandra who gave her a wry smile before gently giving it a push. They watched it first begin to creak as it moved slowly downwards, until very quickly it came crashing down into the hallway with an almighty thud.

'That's just great,' said Courtney with a hint of agitated sarcasm.

They stepped in over the door and were immediately struck by the smell of wet carpet. Broken glass was scattered across the floor together with bits of debris that had been carried by the water which had flowed down from the tank.

Courtney looked up and noticed that the glass was the remains of the light bulb that was previously screwed to the ceiling. 'What the hell happened here?'

'I have no idea, but rest assured, it gets worse.'

As they moved further inside, their feet crunched on the shattered glass.

'Whoa,' said Alexandra, as she put her arm out to block Courtney. 'Mind the hole.'

Courtney looked down and saw the huge indentation in the floor. She then looked at her friend and gave her a suspicious look. They continued in further to look around the kitchen, living room and finally the bedrooms. The first thing they were thankful for was that the only current strange activity was the beautiful glow outside. Inside however, it was like the aftermath of something quite catastrophic. What very quickly became obvious to Courtney was that anything that was electrical had been destroyed, and although what had happened in the house seemed clearly unusual, she was concerned by the amount of damage and what it would cost to get it fixed. The place was a total mess.

They spent the next hour checking everything electrical and discovered that the only things that had not been destroyed were a table lamp and the microwave. *An odd pair. What's their unifying element that left them untouched?* Then Courtney noticed something about the two surviving objects.

'They were the only two that were not plugged into the mains electricity when the phenomenon happened,' she said excitedly.

The lamp was a spare one that was not being used and the microwave had been unplugged when Alexandra needed to use the socket for the toaster on the morning of the event; evident, as it was still plugged in.

They stood in the kitchen both trying to work out in their own individual ways what it could all mean. Alexandra picked up the surviving lamp to see if it would still work, but as she grabbed hold of it, and before she could plug it in, she accidentally pushed the switch to on. She froze and looked at Courtney in shock as the bulb miraculously illuminated. She quickly put the lamp down on the work surface and backed away with her eyes wide. 'What just happened?'

Courtney was a little intrigued, but surprisingly not scared. 'I don't know.' She couldn't help but think how unlike her first encounter with the spirit it all was, but she could not quite put her finger on why. Perhaps it was the fact that it was daytime, or maybe it was because she was a lot older now. She reached forward, flicked the switch and the light went out. In case it was just a fluke she flicked it again and was astonished to witness that once more it came back on.

'I don't like this,' said Alexandra fearfully putting the lamp back on the counter top. 'Let's just get out of here.'

'No wait.' She walked over to the microwave, set the timer to twenty seconds and placed her finger gently on the start button. Before pushing it, she turned and looked at Alexandra, grabbed the power cord and held the end with the plug high in the air. Alexandra stared at her with a worried expression and raised her hands to her face. She turned back to the microwave and pressed the start button. To their amazement, the light inside came on, the motor started and the glass turntable turned. 'This is unbelievable. Do you know what this means?'

Alexandra looked at her blankly before speaking. 'I'm gonna go with ... no. I have no idea what it means, but what I do know is that I don't like it.'

'Don't you see?'

Alexandra looked bewildered.

'Whatever is causing this must logically be in this house. How it got here, I've no idea, but the effects seem clear. It's some form of major – and I mean major – energy source, and it's overloaded anything that was plugged into the electricity supply. The two items that weren't, have survived. Not only that, they work without electricity. Now without real facts and knowledge I guess it could be anything, and the obvious assumption would be a ghost, but something's telling me it's not that. It just doesn't seem ghostly to me, but it definitely has something to do with energy.'

'Ok,' replied Alexandra. She was beginning to relax due to Courtney's confidence that it was not some sort of poltergeist.

'Did you check the cellar? I think that's where the fuse box is.'

'I didn't even know there was a cellar.'

'Let's go check it out, so we can make sure nothing else will explode in our faces.'

They made their way to the cellar door, which Alexandra had previously mistaken for a cupboard under the stairs. Courtney opened the door and flicked the light switch, but of course it wasn't working.

Alexandra took her mobile phone out and used the camera's video light to help her go down the creaky stairs.

Courtney remained at the top for a second and watched as Alexandra struggled with the minimal light. 'Could you not have just grabbed the lamp? Would that not have been easier?' she said very matter of fact.

'Whatever. I'm down now. Anyway that lamp's spooky. C'mon, don't leave me on my own.'

Courtney shook her head and followed behind. They carefully edged their way around the walls of the cellar until they found the fuse box. Courtney reached up and flicked the large red switch, turning off the electricity in the whole house. She then noticed some replacement light bulbs beside her on a shelf. She picked one up and looked at it as if she had just come up with an idea.

'Are you holding that as some kind of symbol that you have an idea, or does your idea actually involve a light bulb?'

Courtney smiled. 'Actually, both ... now shine the light toward the ceiling. I wanna try something.'

Alexandra scanned the ceiling with her phone, small sections at a time.

'Stop,' said Courtney. 'Keep it shining there while I put this in.' She had spotted the light fitting on one side of the

153

ceiling and went over to put the new bulb in. As she approached, the shattered glass from the previous bulb crunched under her feet. She reached up, stretched onto her tip toes and unscrewed the tiny remainder of the broken bulb before fixing the new one in to replace it. 'There, now go flick the switch by the stairs.'

Alexandra sighed and using the light from her phone, walked back over to the stairs and flicked on the light switch. To Courtney's amazement, the cellar immediately lit up; even though the trip switch on the main fuse box was still off. They could now see the whole space and everything in it. They stood facing each other on opposite sides of the room, but their relief at being able to see stopped as their eyes were drawn to something peculiar situated between the two of them.

Directly in the centre of the room was a large, round, reddish coloured rock about the size of a bowling ball but with a rough surface. Although it was unlike any rock either of them had ever seen before, what was most peculiar was the large indentation in the concrete floor where it was positioned. It was as if its weight had pushed down on the ground and created a huge crater with further massive cracks stretching out from the source. The rock wasn't totally round though. On the side was a large indentation, as if a piece had previously been broken away from it.

'What the hell is that?'

Courtney couldn't answer; all she could do was look at it in awe. 'Honestly, I have no idea, but one thing I do know is that it clearly didn't fall out of the sky or I'd have a whacking great big hole in my roof. So I for one would like to know what the hell that thing is ... but more importantly ... how the hell did it get in my basement?'

~ CHAPTER TWENTY FOUR ~

The Dyson Sphere

Exciting times were ahead and both Courtney and Alexandra knew it. Just what the future had in store for them was as yet unclear, but it was abundantly obvious to both of them that whatever the bizarre object that had miraculously appeared in the cellar was, it would most definitely change everything for them. They both stared at the visiting anomaly, each wondering what you should do when faced with such a seemingly unnatural phenomena. Courtney looked quizzically at Alexandra and then broke the silence. 'Is there anything you'd like to tell me?'

Alexandra looked away from the rock for the first time since she set eyes on it and looked up at her with a blank and unreadable expression.

'Well?'

'You think I put that there?'

'Did you?'

'No,' exclaimed Alexandra in a huff.

Courtney stared at her for a brief moment in silence. 'Of course you didn't. What am I thinking? Don't listen to me.'

'Oh, I see. So now I'm not smart enough to have put it there, is that it?'

'I was actually thinking not strong enough.'

'Right yeah, exactly.' She then burst into a mode of excitement and amazement as the impossibility of the situation hit her. 'Exactly ... I mean, surely nothing that small could be that heavy right?' Alexandra walked towards the rock for a closer inspection.

'Going by the damage to the floor, it looks like it was dropped. But how could that be?' She reached out her hand to touch it. As her fingertips made contact with the surface, she instantly retracted her whole arm back in shock because of the incredible heat she felt. She extended her foot out, placed her boot on to the side and began to push it as hard as she could. 'Come here and help me push.'

They sat on the floor next to each other. Alexandra also placed her feet on the side of the rock, and then they both pushed with their combined strength. Their feet began to burn as the rubber on their soles started to melt, but their efforts were useless as they finally collapsed back, exhausted after having not moved it an inch. In frustration, Courtney picked up a hammer that was on the ground next to her and furiously threw it at the rock.

As the hammer made contact, the most extraordinary thing happened. Sparks flew from the rock's surface and a loud bang immediately followed the impact. Multicoloured gases emanated from it and paint pots and various tools leapt off shelves towards the rock. They stared at each other, eyes wide.

Then something amazing dawned on Courtney. 'No ... way,' she said really slowly and then quickly jumped up and ran to the stairs. However, as she put her foot on the first step she suddenly stopped, turned and ran back to Alexandra. She quickly snatched the phone out of her hand. 'I need the Internet.'

'What is that?'

She paused and looked at Alexandra. 'The ... source of all information, the global gateway, the oracle of-'

'No, you div – that.' She gestured at the rock.

'Oh right,' she said giggling. 'Well I'm not sure, but I've just got some form of inkling that ... it's a Dyson Sphere.'

'A Dyson what?'

'Let me just make sure though.' Courtney typed 'Dyson Sphere' into the search engine on the phone. Tons of results appeared and she clicked on the first one. She read with excitement. 'Oh my God, oh my God ... I think it really is one.' She looked up at Alexandra. 'I read about it when I was researching time travel years ago. It's a theory first developed and written about in 1959 by a physicist and mathematician called Freeman Dyson. It's about a type of technology that was later named the 'Dyson Sphere'.'

'Freeman Dyson ... never heard of him.' Alexandra suddenly became very nervous. 'You think he's the guy that's been haunting us?'

'No, no, no. He came up with this theory about a sphere, a sphere that we would one day use for all of our energy needs.'

Alexandra looked totally bemused but knowing Courtney for so long it was a feeling she was used to, so she just went with it.

Courtney took a deep breath and in her excitement, tried to plainly explain it to Alexandra. However, she could not quite contain her mood and it all came out at the speed of a train. 'Ok, so basically he concluded that such a sphere would be a system of orbiting solar powered satellites which are meant to completely encompass a star and capture most or all of its energy output. He speculated that such structures would be the logical consequence of the long-term survival and escalating energy needs of any technological civilisation. He also went on to say that if the human civilisation was to survive long enough, there would come a time when it would require the total energy output of the sun due to our expected advancements in technology. So he proposed a system of orbiting structures designed to intercept and collect all the energy produced by the sun. It's supposed to be impossible in our lifetime but in theory very possible at some point in the future. Some said it would be a man-made device that would collect the energy, but another theory was that the best kind of object to use as an orbiting satellite would be a genuine one, rather than a manufactured one.'

'Okey ... dokey,' said Alexandra dubiously. She did not understand what was being said to her at all. 'I see you've learnt a new language while you've been away called Blah Blah Blah. So how about you tell me in English what the hell you're going on about? All I got was something about a vacuum cleaner guy and satellite T.V.'

'No not the Hoover guy and not that kind of satellite. A natural piece of matter that orbits a planet is called a satellite. Didn't you learn anything while we were at school? The moon is a satellite. They come in all kinds of sizes. A small rock could be a satellite.' She gestured at the rock in the middle of the room with her hand in a frantic manner as if to say, what do you think that is? 'I mean what else could it be? It makes sense.'

'Yeah,' said Alexandra slowly, stretching the word out for maximum confused effect. 'No it doesn't.'

'Alright look ...' Courtney thought about how else she may be able to explain it. 'Right, just imagine ...'

'Wait, wait, wait,' said Alexandra. She tilted her head to the ceiling and placed her fingers on her forehead.

'What are you doing?'

'Imagining,' she said with a magical tone.

'And people wonder why England is no longer a superpower. So imagine a really, really large solar-powered light from the garden. Now imagine you could take that light and place it really close to the sun without destroying it.'

'Ok.'

'The sun is the biggest source of energy we know of, so powerful that it can power a solar light in a garden millions of miles away. Imagi- ... no, think what you could do if you could get really close to the sun and put thousands of those lights all the way around it, encompassing it like a ball, or sphere. Just imagine how much free energy they could absorb. I think that ...' she said pointing at the rock, '... is one of those 'solar lights', in a manner of speaking.'

'Plus, what we understand about energy tells us that the more you can cram into an object, the denser it becomes, therefore the heavier it gets. Look at the energy that this thing must possess to have made the house glow and enable us to use electricity without even using electricity.' Courtney was now bursting with almost as much energy as the rock seemed to contain. Anyone listening would be able to tell that she

158

was definitely in her element as she beamed radiantly at her new found discovery.

'That's why we can't move it.' She slowly walked away from Alexandra as she thought about everything. 'However ...,' she said spinning around to face Alexandra again. '... there are only two theories on how this could be possible. One is that an alien race far more advanced than us would have the technology to do it. Two, is that we the human race would achieve it at some point in the future but not for hundreds or more likely thousands of years.'

Alexandra stood scratching her head in response to all the information, and although she could now grasp a little of what Courtney had said, the word alien had flagged up on her 'ridiculousness' radar. 'Aliens?'

'No, no, I don't think it was aliens.'

'Thank God for that. So it came from the future?' asked Alexandra as if she had just worked out the answer to a pub quiz, even though it was Courtney's only other explanation.

'Maybe.' With a much bigger capability of believing in extraordinary things than most, that didn't stop Courtney from being a little unsure of what she had said, even though Alexandra had the impression she did. She was very much thinking and working it all out as she spoke.

'I think I get the logic of what you're saying, but even if it is the case, what do we do with it?'

Courtney stood silent for a second as she pondered what to do next. 'Energy, space, stars, physics. Hmmm, what happens to stars when they die?' She then looked straight into Alexandra's eyes with a realisation. 'We blow it up.

'What?'

'Yes, hopefully, we'll release its energy and then we'll really see what this thing is capable of.'

'Even with my limited knowledge, that doesn't seem wise – and anyway, we can't even move it, so how do you suggest we blow it up?'

'Well it looks like a piece has come away before, so maybe it's not as solid as it appears. We'll chip away a little piece and ...' she stopped mid-sentence and thought about what they could use to overload it enough to explode it. 'Something with that much energy might explode if it were heated,' she paused for a second and then blurted out, 'The microwave, we'll break off a small piece and stick it in the microwave until it pops. Remember, that thing is what's powering the microwave in the first place so it should just keep heating until one of them explodes. There must be a clue in this somewhere that will tell us where it came from and why it's here.'

With a hammer, a chisel and a large degree of cautiousness, they proceeded to bash away at the rock, trying to break a piece off that they could use. They covered their faces with their jackets to stop the fumes from getting up their noses and they began to sweat profusely from the heat it was giving off.

After twenty or so whacks of the hammer, a lose piece the size of a plum came away with a loud bang and shot across the room, hitting the paint cans that were stacked and spilling the contents all over the floor. Both girls ran over, and using Courtney's jacket to protect them from the heat, they picked up the tiny piece of rock and took it upstairs. They struggled to get it into the kitchen, as even though it was small, it still weighed a considerable amount.

Courtney grabbed the microwave and lugged it through the house and into the garden. She then came back inside the kitchen to rejoin Alexandra. They both then stumbled out of the back door with the rock. Fortunately, there were no neighbours around as the sight of them struggling to carry a tiny little rock down the garden would have looked hilarious and raised some eyebrows of anyone watching.

'We'll go down to that clearing in the grass,' said Courtney. 'That's where we used to put the bonfire on Guy Fawkes Night when I was a kid. The grass never grew back. I reckon that should be far enough away from the house.'

Without warning, as they lugged it down the garden, sweating from the strain, Alexandra's grip gave way and the rock dropped to the ground. Although it was very small, it created a large dent in the mud.

'Ok, go get the microwave, this should be far enough,' said Courtney.

Alexandra ran over and grabbed the microwave. They both lifted the rock and placed it inside. The glass turntable instantly smashed from the weight.

'Put it on for the longest time it can go to and when you press start, we'll both run.' Courtney spoke with a serious intent as she could sense she was on the verge of some kind of momentous discovery.

'What do you think will happen? Do you think it'll be like some sort of huge fireworks display?'

'I really have no idea, but whatever happens, it should be fun.'

Alexandra pressed the start button and as the motor started to whirr, they turned and ran as fast as they could back towards the house. They were not more than a hundred feet away when the microwave began to crackle with sparks and then very quickly it exploded with a gigantic bang.

Clouds of different coloured smoke burst into the air. Shards of glass and metal flew at ferocious speeds from the force of the explosion. Courtney and Alexandra screamed, cowered and held their hands over their heads as they continued to run as fast as they could before anything would have the chance to hit them.

A massive Shockwave seconds later threw them violently forward and high into the air. They were tossed like dolls across the garden before gravity pulled them back down with force, causing them to land with a huge thud, face-first in the dirt. All around went totally and eerily silent as everything became still and lifeless, including the two bodies that now lay motionless on the grass.

~ CHAPTER TWENTY FIVE ~

The absolute unknown

Courtney and Alexandra had been motionless lying in a crumpled heap on the grass and dirt for the past twenty minutes. Their faces were bloody, soiled and bruised and their arms and legs had harsh bleeding grazes in various places.

An erratic fruit fly descended gently from above, landing delicately on one of Courtney's eyelids. Wandering around aimlessly, not realising what it had landed on, it inadvertently sent tingling sensations to Courtney's brain; thankfully waking her up. As it fluttered away into the gentle wind Courtney's eyes twitched slightly and then she groggily opened them to see nothing but the blue sky above and the sun shining down on her. She had always believed that the sun was merely an illusion of beauty and happiness, when in actual fact; it was an intense searing fire that contained a future misery bigger than any the tiny human brain could comprehend. As she felt the heat burning into her grazed face, she rolled onto her front and slowly pushed herself up, groaning from the pain she felt all over her body. 'Ouch. That really didn't go as planned.' She pulled herself onto her bottom to see what had happened behind them. To her astonishment, it was still happening and as she looked on, all she could think was that they were sure to die. She nudged Alexandra but she didn't move, so she placed a blade of grass under her nostrils to see if she was still breathing. As she watched the grass flicker from the air coming out her nose she breathed a massive sigh of relief herself. After thinking about what to do for a moment she placed her fingers over her nose and began to squeeze Alexandra's nostrils until she was forced to wake up from lack of oxygen. Not wanting to reveal her chosen method of resuscitation, she quickly let go as Alexandra began to cough and groan.

Alexandra similarly struggled to get up and also slowly turned in pain to see what had happened. She was just as taken aback by what she saw as everything around them seemed to be moving in slow motion. Courtney wondered if her mind was playing tricks due to an aftershock from the makeshift experiment. *But how could it be if we're both seeing it?* 'You are seeing this right?'

'Uh huh.'

They were sure it was that moment just before you die when everything is said to move in slow motion. Yet just as they were contemplating the prospect of no longer being alive, Courtney noticed something very peculiar as a large piece of very sharp metal began to move through the air, straight towards her face; it was travelling in slow motion. As it came closer, she realised it was not a dream. *She* was still moving in real time and it was only the piece of shattered microwave that was in slow motion, getting slower and slower the closer it came, until finally it stopped just a few inches from her face. Alexandra was also experiencing much the same thing, but with a jagged piece of rock instead.

Then, all of a sudden, as quick as the microwave and the rock had exploded, the phenomenon imploded. Everything that was thrown from the explosion was immediately sucked back in. As all the debris reached the area in the grass where the microwave had been placed, a hole began to emerge in the ground with no solid surface beyond, just a bottomless gravitational whirlpool that was sucking everything it had thrown out straight into the void of darkness. The hole wasn't huge; probably about the size of a manhole cover and as soon as everything had disappeared into the black hole there was total silence.

Courtney suddenly had a random thought. She picked up a rock and threw it out in front of her. Before it could reach the hole it slowed down in midair and began to hover as if it had been stopped by a magnet with opposing polarity. When it was about a metre above the hole, it stretched into an oblong shape, and then in a flash, it disappeared into the void like a lone stray sock zipping up the tube of a vacuum cleaner.

'Wow,' said Alexandra, in awe of the events that had just occurred.

They looked at each other and quickly shifted backwards on their bottoms so as not to be pulled in. They sat in silence for a few moments and just stared, afraid to even move.

'We must have been thrown just outside its perimeter,' said Courtney.

Then to their surprise, something even more remarkable happened. The rock that Courtney had thrown in flew back out in slow motion before landing in real time right next to her hand. It was still in one piece with no damage, but what she found weirdest of all, and what she was racking her brain trying to work out was that nothing else that went in, like parts of the microwave or even the original rock, came back out. 'Did you see what just happened?'

For once, Alexandra was on the same page and realised that the only way the rock could have come back was if it had chosen to; as if it had been singled out by something, or even someone. She looked into Courtney's eyes and smiled. 'Oh – my – God, you've so just figured out how to time travel haven't you? There's someone on the other side, isn't there?'

'I seem to remember you saying that exact same thing about three years ago. Only this time, you don't sound as utterly ridiculous as you did back then.'

'Utterly ridiculous? I'll deal with that comment when you get back but right now, luckily for you, we don't have time. What are you waiting for?'

'It's not as simple as that.'

'Why not? People always over-complicate things. What have you got to lose?'

'Well, put very simply ... my life. Isn't that enough? That thing in front of us appears to be some sort of black hole or maybe even a worm hole. Don't ask me the details of how it really happened, because the science that exists today dictates that it's not possible to just create one. Nobody knows where they lead and nobody has ever been inside one. Plus most worryingly, the common thought is that if we were to enter one, we would be killed instantly.'

'Oh, well in that case, perhaps it's best not to then,' said Alexandra calmly before changing her tone completely. 'Are you crazy? You've waited your whole life for this. That thing in the cellar got here somehow and though I'm not the ripest fruit, I do know it didn't fall from the sky.'

Courtney contemplated very hard what her friend had said, as for the first time she was really making a good case and even made Courtney look like the one that needed help.

'That stone just came back didn't it? So there must be a way for you to get back as well. If not, well at least you'll be known as the first ever to enter a black hole, right? Surely you didn't expect to travel through time without taking some risks?'

Her comments struck a chord and Courtney realised that if the plan were to work, it would certainly mark her name down in history, as well as get up a certain professor's nose. Yet neither of those were enough to eliminate her fear. 'I just don't think I've got the guts to do it. I don't think I could do a bungee jump or leap from a plane, and I don't even have enough guts to ask a boy out and you want me to leap into that ... the absolute unknown? At least Marty McFly had a Delorean. I mean what if it's suicide?' She looked over at the anomaly and became deeply and genuinely concerned.

'That's just words separated by a technicality. It's only suicide if you know you're gonna die. You're not sure, so it can't be,' said Alexandra with a smile. 'Possibly a reckless accident, but definitely not suicide.'

'Oh great, that makes me feel a whole lot better.'

Alexandra grabbed her firmly by the arms. 'This is your moment girl, so you need to seize this day and not let go. Just like the time you stood up in front of the whole school and showed them all, including me, who you really are and changing everyone's mind about you forever. You meant what you said that day. I know, because I felt it, and this may be your one and only shot to do what you convinced all of us you were destined to do. If you don't take this chance, then someone else will and you'll be left in their shadow.'

Courtney shed a single tear at the depth of Alexandra's comments.

'Every great pioneer in history had to take a leap of faith at some point girl. Your dreams will stay in the darkness unless you open your eyes and let them escape into reality, but even then, to make them tangible you have to dare to leap where others have only fallen before you. Holy crap I'm good. Now it's your turn honey.'

Courtney giggled and wiped her tear with her sleeve. 'What do you know about pioneers?'

'I know right. I can't have created that. I probably heard someone on telly say it ... but damn you, I'm trying to be inspirational here, don't ruin the moment.' Alexandra smiled. 'Now, there are many things I'd like to change in my life. So please, if not for yourself, do it for me and go find out if it's possible.'

Courtney looked at her and at that moment, she made a decision. Her heart raced at triple speed, and her head span just thinking about it all. She jumped up and went inside the house with a huge surge of adrenalin. Alexandra followed behind wondering what she was doing.

She grabbed a pen and paper and wrote down Becky's contact details in America. 'Call this number and let her and the others in Creekside House know what has happened. They deserve to be a part of this as they did risk everything on a belief that I may actually be onto something special.'

They went back to the garden and Courtney grabbed Alexandra. She hugged and squeezed her as if it was the last she would see of her. 'Now listen, the most important thing is that nobody else, other than who I've told you about, knows about this. At least not till I come back, but if I don't return ...' She thought for a second about what she was going to say next to make sure it was the right thing. 'I suppose you should contact Professor Pik Thistle at LosTech as well. He should get a shot at analysing this thing.' Courtney had figured that although some of his methods had seemed dubious, if someone had spent their whole life working extremely hard on something like he obviously had, then they should get a chance to investigate the ultimate prize.

'Ok, are you doing this or what?'

'I know, I know. I'm talking a lot because I don't want to think about it. In a second I'm just going to do it; without thinking; probably mid-sentence while I'm expl–' Suddenly Courtney broke off and ran as fast as she could towards the hole, screaming as she went.

'Don't forget to send me a postcard,' shouted Alexandra. 'Oh, and if there are any hot guys, give them my number ... unless they're like a caveman or something.'

Courtney closed her eyes as she reached the point in the garden just in front of the phenomenon. She leapt into the air as high as she could reach and just like the feedback from a microphone dropped too close to a P.A. system, she screamed in the highest pith she could muster. All the school athletics classes she had endured were finally for something real.

Alexandra watched as the same magician like effects started to happen to her friend that she had witnessed happen to the remains of the microwave and the rock. Courtney moved incredibly slowly towards the hole and then froze in midair, suspended in a gravity defying state, metres above the hole. Her body seemed to stretch and elongate as if she was standing in a floating hall of mirrors. Her mouth was still wide open, but the sound of her screaming had stopped the moment she came in contact with the perimeter. Then in a flash, she was gone; unflatteringly sucked inside the foreboding unknown vortex below her.

~ CHAPTER TWENTY SIX ~

Frozen in time

Alexandra was sitting in front of a computer screen in a late night internet café trying to call Becky's Skype account but was getting very frustrated by the lack of signal she seemed to be getting, especially as she was paying for it. Then when it briefly would ring, nobody answered. 'Would you just pick up? Are you deaf?' Adrenalin was still pumping through every blood vessel in her body. Her heart was truly aching from the tremendous excitement and anxiety she was experiencing because of the unbelievable events she had just witnessed. Deep down, she wanted to tell the whole world what had happened, but thankfully the café was empty due to the late hour. She knew though that it would be too premature and could potentially put Courtney at risk, as well as get herself branded as crazy. Still, she was quite content knowing that she was a part of history in the making. That fact at least gave her a sense of pride and recognition on a level she had not felt for a very long time, if ever.

At Creekside House, Becky had a strained and frustrated expression on her face as she stood facing Nathan, Ellie and Wazer, who were all seated opposite her. 'Ok, it's what happens when ... er ... stuff, comes out of your mouth,' she said as she tried to describe a word.

'Spitting,' said Ellie with some excitement.

Becky's focus changed as she heard something in another room. She looked up inquisitively.

168

'Hurling,' said Nathan, trying to edge himself into the game of Articulate they were playing.

'Everyone quiet,' said Becky.

'Sleeping,' said Nathan, thinking she was still playing the game.

'I meant, shut up.'

'Annoying,' said Wazer quizzically.

'No, you're annoying. I'm not playing, you idiot. Just shut up. Is that my computer ringing?'

'It's likely to be mine,' said Ellie very matter of fact. 'I shouldn't have to remind you that I really am quite popular. Don't worry though you all carry on playing your geeky little game.' She stood up and walked to the door. 'Oh and articulate this.' She placed her hand on her forehead, shaping her fingers in the form of the letter 'L', before leaving the room.

∞

'At last,' said Alexandra, who had been nervously biting her nails whilst looking into the webcam that was positioned on top of the monitor. 'I was about to think nobody was home. Quickly, get the rest of your gang to listen up. I've got a message from Courtney. We can't waste any more time.'

∞

'You guys get in here – now,' shouted Ellie, in an unintentional impersonation of her favourite movie actor, Al Pacino.

In a beat, everyone came running into Becky's bedroom like a herd of Wildebeests stampeding through the Serengeti to join Ellie at the computer.

'Definition of loser,' said Becky, staring at Ellie. 'Someone who answers other people's calls to make themselves look popular.'

'Whatever, just listen. It's about Courtney,' she snapped back.

All their expressions changed upon hearing Courtney's name and they all crowded around the monitor to see

Alexandra's webcam image beaming from the screen.

'You guys don't know me and you'll probably think I'm crazy, but you will not believe what just happened to Courtney and she's told me to get in touch to tell you all. But listen, whatever I tell you, you must promise never to tell a single soul, yeah?'

They looked at each other in bemusement, partly because they had never seen Alexandra before and partly because of Alexandra's strong London accent.

'Go on then, quit the dramatics,' said Ellie. 'We're dying of anticipation 'ere gov'nor.'

'Is she ok?'

'Oh just ignore her, she hasn't had her medication yet,' replied Becky with a sly grin in Ellie's direction.

'Right ... well I don't know how to begin without sounding doolally. Do you know what I mean?'

'What about just laying out the facts in a logical and systematic way? That usually works for me,' said Becky.

'Yeah but I don't do logical, or systematic.' Alexandra took a deep breath and prepared to tell them the news. She knew she had to get it all out in the best possible way or they would dismiss her as a loon, which she knew would let Courtney down. She also knew that she did not have Courtney's ability to articulate her thoughts in such a passionate way. However as she sat there in front of the camera and after everything she had witnessed, she knew that right then and there was the time to try. 'She did it, she actually did it. Actually ... we did it,' she stammered proudly, remembering how inspirational she was.

The gang stared intently at her image on the screen.

'We have ventured into the unknown, just like Courtney dreamt of all these years.'

Nathan was getting a little impatient and said, 'Meaning what? Where the hell is she?'

'Where? I think you mean – oh God, I've always wanted to say this – I think you mean, *when* is she?' She struggled to contain her excitement as she spoke, but was also trying not to be too loud so as not to be heard by the owner of the café.

The gang looked around at each other in disbelief. The comment struck a particular note with Wazer who moved slightly back from the group to get his mobile phone out. He switched it to 'sound recorder' and pressed the record button before discreetly moving closer to the computer again.

'Courtney has vanished into this unbelievable black hole type thing, created by the explosion of a rock that was popped into the microwave.' The more Alexandra spoke, the more she regained her composure and momentum. 'And the microwave weren't even plugged in.'

Her colloquial use of the word 'weren't' raised a few smiles.

'It was solely being powered by this rock from ... well, God knows where. In fact, maybe literally, God only knows where.' She smiled at the realisation that her explanation was going rather well.

However, on the other side of the screen Wazer was not so convinced and whispered, 'Is she insane?'

Becky nudged him with her elbow, signalling for him to shut up. She caught him in the ribs and he nearly dropped the device that was recording everything Alexandra had said. He was very flustered and sweaty, but the others were oblivious, as they had been too busy focusing on the bizarre comments that the strange girl from England had been saying.

'The most important thing to consider is this,' said Alexandra. 'I think Courtney has found a way ... to time travel.' She exhaled. 'There, that's it, I've said it.' She was relieved to have finally put Courtney's message across to the group.

Total silence filled Becky's room as if everyone had been frozen in time. The only person not focused on the screen was Wazer. He had used the moment to slip his phone quietly into his back pocket. He proceeded to act as sympathetic and excited as the rest of the group.

Nathan then said, 'So what does she want us to do? Why are you telling us? How do we know you're not yanking our chain?

Becky quickly followed with, 'And do you know where

she's gone? And how it works?'

Then to finish the questions Wazer said, 'Back to Nathan's point, how do we know this is even true? Can you prove it?' He was trying not to let his ulterior motive sound too obvious.

'Ok, ok, slow down, too many questions. I have no idea where she's gone. I don't even know if she's still alive. I just know that I saw her disappear into a strange hole in the ground created by this huge explosion of something she called a Dyson something or other.'

In stunned realisation Becky said, 'Sphere?'

'That's the one. Anyway, just before she jumped in, she threw a stone and seconds later it came back. We presumed somebody must have thrown it back. Listen, I'm no scientist. Hell, I'm not even a school graduate, but I know what I saw and she wanted me to tell you guys to help make sure nobody else finds out and enters the hole themselves. At least, not until she comes back and proves it's safe.'

With an ulterior motive Wazer said, 'You mean the hole is still there?'

'Oh yeah, it's still here alright. So what do you say, can you get the next flight out?'

The group discussed the news excitedly, at the same time anxious about what they should do. Most of the talking was being done by Ellie, Becky and Nathan as Wazer quietly stepped out of the room. The rest continued to act like they had just won the lottery because each of them knew that it was the biggest thing they would probably witness and be a part of in their whole lifetime, or even their children or their children's children's lifetime. Could it really be true, they were all thinking? Had Courtney, the girl who hadn't even studied a single day at the world's foremost school on theoretical physics and modern studies of space and time, actually have found a way of travelling through time? They decided there was only one real way to find out.

'But we don't have the money,' said Ellie. 'How will we get there? I don't think there are student concessions from LA to London.'

'Maybe I can speak to my dad, tell him it's a field trip or something,' said Becky, a little cautiously, not wanting to totally volunteer her wealthy father for everyone's ticket.

'Courtney said she would help too,' said Alexandra. 'She said it was the least she could do after you guys put your faith in her like you did.'

'Yeah, that's fair. I did nearly die,' said Nathan, in a very sure of himself manner.

Ellie turned to him and scowled. 'What are you talking about, you freak?'

'Er, hello? I was nearly pulled under by some kind of un-rested soul. It had my leg.'

'It was weeds, you Nancy.'

'You were pretty quick to get to shore once I was under attack.'

Ellie shook her head and raised her eyes to the ceiling dismissively.

Nathan turned back to the computer screen. 'Well anyway, I really think that the last thing Courtney will be concerned about is money.'

∞

Out in the hallway, Wazer had sneakily taken his phone out of his pocket. He pressed play on the 'sound recorder' programme and listened to a short spurt of the conversation that had just occurred. He then pressed stop, lifted his head and smiled to himself with a sly look on his face. He then whispered with authority, 'Your time is up Courtney. It's now time to cement Zak Wazerton's place in the annals of history.' He then scurried down the hallway with his hackles up, like a mischievous hyena about to try and steal his place at the top of the hyena hierarchy.

173

~ CHAPTER TWENTY SEVEN ~

What the hell took you so long?

With the exception of a few raised land masses which were poking out like giant hippopotamus humps as far as the eye could see, there was nothing on the landscape but water. A huge expanse of violent ocean had swelled up from the effects of a storm that was incomparable to anything Courtney had previously witnessed in her life. Water fell from the sky with an unwavering ferocity.

Drenched and helpless atop one of the few humps, she looked totally lost as she stood, desperately cowering from the bombardment of rain, struggling to see further than a few hundred feet in front of her due to the intensity of the downpour. Never in her whole life, had she seen or even heard of such heavy rain. She tried to look up but was blasted in the face by what felt like hail, and the ground she was standing on was sodden.

The particular land mass she had found herself atop was about the size of a football pitch but it was totally bare and covered in nothing but mud.

As she looked around, trying to fathom where she was through the blackness of the dirt and the rain that was hitting the ground, she could just make out what looked like the opening to the hole she had arrived through. *Is this even real? Am I crazy?* She had always hoped and longed to travel back to the past, but it did not seem like any time she recognised. She could only rationalise that she must be dreaming, but her thought and decision process was very much intact; something she never felt in control of in her dreams. It was a bizarre sensation as everything told her it was real, but thinking back about what she had just done and now looking at where she'd ended up, she began to have a panic attack thinking her life would never again go back to being normal. She felt stuck in a dream landscape as if she'd crossed a line and in opening her eyes as Alexandra had instructed, she had inadvertently closed them for good giving her no way of ever escaping or returning to normality.

Soaked and hurting from the bombardment of the rain, she knelt in the mud, and for the first time since she was a child she began to say a prayer. She asked for a sign, something to tell her what she should do. The more she spoke, the louder she became as she tried desperately to shout over the sound of the rain, until it was no longer a prayer she was spouting but more of an attack. 'Surely, I didn't just experience the most wonderful thing any human's ever seen to just sit in some mud in the middle of an ocean getting soaked and quite frankly, a little hurt by the pounding rain? I mean, c'mon.' She turned her head and looked up into the sky. 'My mum always believed you were out there, so why don't you show yourself now? I dare you. Tell me ... why am I here?'

As she finished her rant into the dark grey sky, she saw something emerge at great speed from the murky thick clouds above. Her view was obscured by the rain, but she was convinced she could see what it was; a young man. He wore strange attire that clashed with the weather she was experiencing. The only thing he had on was a very sleek pair of dark grey and black skin tight shorts, but if Courtney didn't know better she would have sworn they looked painted on. There was nothing else; no top, no shoes, no socks, but all over his body he had various colourful illustrations. Yet rather than random drawings of women, angels or eagles as she was used to seeing on men, his were very artistic and seemed to depict events in his life as well as facts about who he was. Courtney was instantly gobsmacked, not just because he'd appeared out of the sky but because he also looked like an amazing work of art. He appeared to be around twenty five years old with short, brown hair. There was something else Courtney noticed straight away too – he was also very good looking with a physique not dissimilar from that of an Olympic athlete.

After emerging from the clouds like some sort of God he stopped and hovered above her. He didn't seem to be affected by the rain at all and as he looked down she continued to stare back in shock at what appeared to be a flying man. 'Is that Jesus? Am I in heaven, is that it?'

A split second later, he grinned at her.

'I never remember Jesus looking quite like that in R.E. class though.'

The man descended to the ground and landed directly in front of her. He grabbed her by both arms and as he did the rain stopped, but only in the area where they were standing. Courtney noticed immediately that the downpour was continuing with the same ferocity elsewhere, but she could no longer feel it on her, even though she could clearly see it a few feet away. In fact, if anything it was now fiercer as it pelted down relentlessly around them. However, they remained totally protected from the effects, like they were covered by a giant invisible umbrella. Most noticeable though, was that the loud noise the rain had been making also stopped the second he had touched her.

She noticed that the man was very tall; around seven feet five inches but totally in proportion. 'I really am in heaven, aren't I?'

In a deep and powerful voice he said, 'What the hell took you so long?'

'Huh?'

'I've been waiting ages for you. They didn't say you took this long. They said you came straight after the stone ... see.' He pointed to a very detailed almost photo like illustration on his chest of a stone with a detailed description of events written all around it. As she looked closer she realised that the body art was not painted on, it was actually moving. It was subtle, but the stone was actually turning like a floating meteor in space.

Courtney stared at it and spotted some key words relating to her arrival inscribed on it, but as she stared the words started to blur before changing into different words. It was like after he spoke it was updated instantly.

She wondered why he was acting as if he knew her and why he would have details about her written all over his body. 'Wait, wait, what is going on here? Who wrote that? Why is it all moving, did you drug me? In fact, who the hell are you? And why are you not wearing anything in this disgusting weather? Actually having said that, I'm weirdly starting to get a bit warm myself ... Oh my God, is this hell?'

'We really don't have time for that, we just need to get you out of here before they realise you're here.'

'Whoa, wait just one minute, Mister Giant Flying Man. What the hell is going on? I wanna know where I am – or come to think of it *when* I am?

'When you are what?'

'No, no. When – am – I?'

'Why are you repeating yourself?'

Courtney closed her eyes and shook her head in frustration at his apparent lack of understanding. 'Ok first things first. Since when do people fly?'

'I don't have time to explain, I really don't. I promise you though; I will tell you everything very soon. Right now, you're going to have to trust me because if I don't get you out of here immediately ... they're going to kill you and trust me, I simply can't allow that to happen.

~ CHAPTER TWENTY EIGHT ~

None of this is real, is it?

Courtney was transfixed by the tall stranger she had recently met and for the first time understood where the word stranger came from because nothing about him, or the way in which he arrived, could be described with any other word but strange. Based on her assessment she was trying to decide what to do about the situation as quickly as she could, but the more she attempted to understand, the emptier her thoughts became. She muttered to herself and said, 'Go with the half naked man or die?' She then focused her attention back toward him. 'Ok, erm ... when you say kill, you mean in a good way right? Like, wow that kills, man. You know?'

He looked at her with a quizzical expression and then smiled at the attempted humour. 'No, sorry, I'm afraid it means like when you die, but I'm not going to let that happen. My name is Dulko, and I'm here to protect you, but I won't be able to unless we get going.'

'Ah that's your name,' she said pointing to the letters D.U.L.K.O. that were emblazoned down his left arm.

Suddenly, an alarm sounded in the invisible dome they were in and all around them turned red, then back to clear.

'Damn it, they're on their way. We need to go – now. Please, just grab on to my back and don't let go. You may find it easier the first time if you close your eyes.'

'What the hell was that and why can't I feel the rain any more?'

'You really need to stop asking questions, especially about the weather as that's the least of your worries. That was a warning. They're on their way. We need to leave before you get us both killed.'

'Ok,' she said. 'I'll come with you, but please can you at least tell me where and when we are?'

'Well you should know where we are, it's the when that you'll find more exciting.' He turned around and put his back to her. 'Now I'll try to explain everything, but you need to get on my back first.'

Tentatively, she climbed onto his back. They immediately lifted off the ground and flew straight up into the clouds. She found it hard to see anything above them due to the heavy rain, so she glanced down below her to where they had just been talking.

'From my understanding of history,' said Dulko over his shoulder, 'that piece of land we were on was the location of your childhood home. First it was nicknamed 'The House on the Hill', but later it was changed to 'Time Hill'. Throughout my lifetime though, it's looked just like that. There hasn't been a building there for about nine hundred years.'

Courtney's face froze and her heart skipped a beat at what he had just said. Her mind immediately went into overdrive on hearing she had arrived nine hundred years in the future. *What could this mean? If this is really true, it must mean I was right all along and if it is possible to come into the future, then surely the past must be accessible too.*

Rather than seeing that it was a momentous achievement to be the first to travel in time, she was more focused on what it could mean to her in the long term. She was seeing the prospect of being able to go back to find out why her life had turned out the way it had. That was before Dulko then threw something in that would drastically change her view on things, at least for her immediate future.

'You've just arrived in the year 3016, just as they said you would. To do what must be done by you, because that's what's written in history.'

She nearly let go in reaction to his statement, causing her to slip down Dulko's back a little, but she quickly grabbed him tighter so as not to fall to her death. 'And what would that be exactly?'

He stopped flying and spun around so quickly that she did not move. Holding her in his arms he said, 'Keep time moving.' He then spun back around and continued to soar through the air.

As she took in his words, she tried to rationalise what they could mean in her very logical head. They flew through the rain and clouds at great speed, with no apparent device helping them and completely protected from the usual effects of travelling at such pace. Amazingly, there was no hair blowing or g-force on the face and they weren't getting soaked by the rain either. She was also slightly uncomfortable, yet at the same time somewhat excited about holding on to the future man's bare and well toned body.

Just as she caught herself looking at his physique, they broke into the clouds. Then, like pulling the blinds up in a dark room to let the early morning sun in, they broke through the other side to be faced with the most amazing sight Courtney had ever seen. All around was a world full of bright sunshine, nothing but blue as far as the eye could see. Every massive cloud beneath them now looked like a gigantic woollen rug.

What really took her breath away though was the sight of a world like no other. She saw a whole city above the clouds. Thousands of people were flying through the sky, above and below the buildings, which themselves were also quite unique. Although they looked much the same as any infrastructure you may see in any community, past or present, with a mixture of older styles and sleeker more modern designs, these were all unexpectedly floating. Nothing seemed to hold them in the sky; nothing below and nothing above. They were just sitting in the air like helium balloons at a school fair but without the strings holding them down.

Something else also seemed slightly odd about them. She could not make it out, but from a distance, they did not quite look real; a little like Dulko's shorts and body drawings but on a much bigger scale.

Suddenly, thoughts of the past vanished and her mind was

instead swamped with questions about the future and what part she was supposed to play in it.

Dulko continued on their journey and flew up and over the tops of the buildings and just as he was about to enter the flow of traffic, a large red cross made from light appeared in front of them. Dulko stopped.

'Why have we stopped?'

'I need permission to fly. Hold on.' He closed his eyes and the red cross vanished and was replaced with a green tick. They set off again across the top of the city, travelling so fast Courtney could not see what was below or around them.

'What is this thing we're in? We are *in* something, aren't we? You're not actually capable of flying?'

'No, you're right. It's basically an energy unit. It's how we live up here at these altitudes without being affected by the forces of nature and why most people wear very little. The technology is implanted into pregnant mothers so we are born with it. Unless you want to live on the surface, you have to have one or you would die. It controls everything and is connected directly to our brains for every purpose, from communication, to climate control, to traffic routes.'

'Where are you getting the energy from for this? You'd need something akin to the sun to power something like-' As Courtney neared the end of her sentence, she stopped herself, realising the sun was just what they must have been using. 'A Dyson Sphere,' she exclaimed.

'Exactly, very good. Now hold on tight, we need to drop out of the tracking system and change our route or they'll know exactly where to find us.'

They descended straight down, avoiding collisions by a whisker. Dulko very quickly came to a stop in what looked like a residential area, with buildings of different shapes, sizes and colours lined up and down the street. There was a collection of nearly every style of architecture since building began, from tall glass skyscrapers to individual English-style Victorian houses, some ancient Chinese pagoda-style residences and even an Egyptian pyramid. The whole place was a bizarre and eclectic mix of every type of living quarters, just floating in the sky. The closest thing Courtney had seen that even came close to the environment she was seeing was pictures and films of the strip in Las Vegas. People always wondered how they managed such an engineering feat in the middle of a desert, but it was clearly nothing compared to what she was witnessing in the sky right in front of her. She muttered to herself, 'How is this possible?'

'Ok, you can jump off but hold my hand and don't let go.'

She held his hand tight and looked down at the floor. She screamed at what she saw – or did not see. There was no floor beneath her even though her feet felt like they were touching something, and she certainly was not falling to her death.

'Ssshhh, please. Don't draw attention. You can walk as long as you hold on to me and stay in the unit. The great thing about this type of energy is that it can become solid. So every step you take is supported by a transparent layer of energy. C'mon, come with me.'

With a light hearted tone she said, 'You mean no need for shoes? That's not something I expected from the future. I always thought women would just get more and more shoes.' She loosened her laces and removed her boots. 'I am starting to feel pretty hot, but where will I put them?'

Dulko looked at her, smiled, grabbed her boots and threw them into the air.

She watched as they fell to the ocean below.

'You did not just throw away my D.M.s,' she said dogmatically.

'Shoes are just the beginning,' he said, not really understanding her attachment to them. 'Security is tight in these units. Nobody can get to you if you don't want them to. You could walk around naked and you'd be perfectly safe.'

Courtney stared at him with her eyes wide at his suggestion.

'I'm just making a point about safety, that's all.'

She accepted his faux pas with a grin and they walked as nonchalantly as possible down the groundless street. Others passed them by, totally oblivious to the fact that everyone was literally walking on air.

What Courtney noticed, aside from the fact that his comment about no clothes was not far from the truth, was that everyone was taller and bigger than she was used to. Evolution had continued to make the human race grow but not just intellectually.

People began to stare at Courtney as they noticed her oddities.

'I need to get you inside,' said Dulko. 'Before someone reports you. Not only are you quite short, and as much as I respect the whole wear-absolutely-everything look, you really have far too many clothes on to go unnoticed, as well as the fact that you look quite quaint wearing real ones.' He smiled at her timidly.

'Real ones?'

'Uh huh. What I said just now ... about clothes ... well we actually don't need them at all anymore. This is all just a projection that I can change to suit whatever mood or situation I'm in.'

She stared at him for a moment and then furrowed her brow as she looked him up and down. 'So just to clarify, what you're saying to me ... is that you're actually naked?'

He nodded.

'Ok, I'm getting that it's not just a guy thing here to ask a girl to strip, but I am new here so one thing at a time. I think my boots are enough to be getting on with. I mean, in theory someone could project onto them what I'm wearing now right?' There was something about her tone that had become very flirtatious. She had clearly become more at ease with the God like figure that had literally and figuratively swept her off her feet.

As she held his hand, she felt a strong sense of security and attraction. She had never really held a man's hand before, especially one that had written things about her all over his body. She didn't even get to hold her dad's hand as a child. Yet there she was in the future, holding a very good looking and very large man's hand. She definitely felt a certain liking toward him, initiated at first by the awe of his strong presence.

He turned down another street and after two hundred metres they approached a very authentic Western saloon bar. As Courtney got closer, she noticed that it looked a little like a computer game facade rather than a real building. She looked around, totally awestruck by the sights she was witnessing.

Dulko led her on towards another very peculiar sight at the other end. Directly in front of them was what appeared to be the Eiffel Tower? However, instead of being positioned in the middle of the Champ de Mars in Paris, it was right there, floating in midair; all three hundred and twenty four metres of it. As Dulko headed straight for the huge construction, Courtney looked at him, a little puzzled.

Before she knew it, they had walked straight underneath. Yet instead of getting the incredible view up inside the mammoth architectural wonder, it appeared that they had actually entered some kind of a living residence, though not in the traditional sense. They had walked straight through an invisible energy barrier that gave the illusion of the famous tower.

Once inside, Dulko let go of her hand. She gripped him tighter for fear of falling.

'You can let go now, we're safe,' he said, as he tried to disengage his hand from hers.

'None of this is real, is it?'

'Define real. I live here and it feels pretty real to me.'

Courtney looked below her and saw a floor for the first time. They were in a large square room, laid out in much the same way as any open plan modern living space. There was a bedroom, a living room, a kitchen and a bathroom but no walls; not even for the bathroom. So much light though, but strangely, no apparent light fixtures; the illumination was just there. 'No windows?'

'You want windows?' He concentrated and suddenly the floor and two of the walls disappeared. All the furniture in the room looked like it was floating and below Courtney were the swirling dark rain clouds. She could feel herself panicking within, as she could not seem to get herself orientated with standing on what looked like nothing.

'Don't worry; you're still standing on the same energy floor, except the fake visuals have now gone.'

Courtney could do nothing but just stand still for a moment, taking in the wonderful world she seemed to have entered; a real life wonderland. The 'Courtney effect' was certainly in full swing now. Even she couldn't ignore its power as she stood stunned, literally ... on top of the world.

~ CHAPTER TWENTY NINE ~

Time is mine

Courtney certainly had more about her than perhaps most would have initially thought. Yet that fact came as no surprise to Professor Thistle; after all, it was one of the reasons why he personally invited her across the Atlantic to study with him.

However, as he frantically paced up and down his living room, the fact that he knew that about her still didn't help him get his head around the idea that she could have created and then stepped into the world's first man-made black hole, and based on his studies of black holes and gravitational waves, if it were true and she was not dead he knew there was a definite possibility that she would have also travelled in some direction through time. Whatever it was she'd created, it was more likely to be some kind of worm hole.

Over the years, Professor Thistle had done a lot of research and investigations into the study of black holes, and though he still had relatively limited evidence due to the inaccessibility of a real one and the total absence and proof of worm holes, he had theorised and made popular the idea that they were connected to some form of time distortion; a shortcut across bent space-time.

He had listened over and over again to the recording that Wazer had sent him and could not get Alexandra's words out of his head. His mind was doing somersaults trying to rationalise it all, but the more he thought about the possibility of it being real, the angrier he became by the idea that Courtney could be somewhere in history being revered as the first to discover the very thing that he had devoted his whole life to, and all thanks to his work that she had stolen. He had convinced himself that in order for it to have happened, she must have found something in his journal; something that unlocked a pivotal element and enabled her to achieve what she could not have been able to on her own.

'I can't allow her to take away what is duly mine. If she has gone into the past, I would arguably already know. Or at the least, I wouldn't still have a complete memory of everything leading up to this point regarding time travel. Whatever she would have affected would in all probability, follow through to today in some form. So she must either be dead or perhaps ... in the future.' He continued to pace the length of his living room, wondering what he could do about the situation. He came to a stop by the bay fronted window. As he stared out, he noticed the reflection of something on the wall behind him. He turned to look, and hung on the wall was a picture frame his deceased mother had given him when he was somewhere around Courtney's age. Due to his clear love of all things to do with time, she had sourced all the best phrases on the subject and then had them inscribed on special parchment paper for his eighteenth birthday. He turned around and stared at some of the phrases, looking at them hard for some kind of inspiration.

Time to kill.

He froze for a moment as he stared at the set of words that were first on the list, and as inspiring as they may be to some, they didn't quite fit his current predicament. He shook his head and continued to read.

Time is of the essence.

As he read the second set he became instantly encouraged by the very old nostalgic memento from his mother and continued enthusiastically down the rest of the list.

Time waits for no one.

'It certainly doesn't,' he said, before glancing down at the final set of words; a quote from Robert Orben; the speech-writer for Gerald Ford; 38th president of the United States.

Time flies. It's up to you to be the navigator.

He took a deep breath upon reading the final quote and raised his chin with an inspired gesture. He then picked up a marker pen from his desk before marching back to the picture. He pulled the lid off the pen and scribbled something under the last line, speaking the words as he wrote. *'Time – is – mine, Prof. – Pinakin – Thistle.'* He stared at it proudly. *'There's* a quote for you mother. If history is going to recognise anyone, it's going to be me. Not some delinquent English child who feels it's ok to steal.'

He grabbed his jacket in a huff and stormed out of the room. In the hallway, he pulled his phone out and dialled Wazer's number, but it continuously rang until his voice message came on.

'Wazer, I'm going to the school to get Courtney's address. There's no way she's going to take this from me, not if I can help it anyway. I've worked too hard to let some brat take the credit. I need you to go online and book me a ticket to London. You also need to keep those thieving cronies distracted while I get to that hole and study it for myself. If she has gone somewhere and I can follow quickly enough behind, maybe it can still be my name that's written in history. I need to leave tonight, so get it sorted.'

By the time he had ended his message he'd reached the end of the pathway and arrived at his car; an old blue Mustang that seemed to be stuck in a bit of a time warp itself. He got in, slammed the door shut and sped off down the road in a rather dramatic attempt to somehow take back what he believed was his rightful destiny.

~ CHAPTER THIRTY ~

The dead seal

Ellie was just packing the last of her things into a small weekend bag, ready for the big trip. She stuffed as much in as she could, which turned out to be not much at all by the time she had squeezed in a number of jumpers; a slight overreaction to all the tales she'd heard about England's intermittent weather patterns. As she reached over her bed to grab her toiletries bag (the last item that needed to be placed inside with surgical precision) she caught one of the earphone wires she was using to listen to her music on the zip of the bag. One of the earpieces was yanked from her ear, and as the outside world became audible again, she heard the ringtone on someone's phone before it stopped abruptly mid ring. 'Whose cell was that just ringing? Wazer, wasn't that your ringtone?'

'Yeah, it's mine,' he called from downstairs.

'Get shot of whoever it is. We can't afford anyone finding out about this.'

'Don't worry, it rang off,' he said as he walked into the kitchen and picked his phone up off the table in one hand and the remnant of a cookie with the other. He looked at the screen of the phone which read: Missed call - The Prof – 08:45

He looked over his shoulder quickly to see if anyone else had seen him. Thankfully (just like Ellie) Nathan and Becky were busy upstairs finishing their last minute packing. Music was playing and he could hear giggling from the girls. 'Or is that Nathan, it's hard to tell the difference,' he said mocking him from a safe distance which made him feel safe in the assumption that he was all alone downstairs.

He put his phone to his ear and listened to the message. Whilst waiting for it to play, he couldn't help but wonder if everything was all really happening. Once the message started he heard a real sense of urgency in Professor Thistle's voice, something that Wazer had not experienced before and so scared him a little. At the same time he realised that it was he rather than somebody else that Professor Thistle had called for help; a fact that was giving him a slight superiority complex over the others in the house. As he stood by the huge kitchen window that looked out onto the completely overgrown backyard, he raised his chin in satisfaction and pride.

'Who was that?'

Wazer spun around in shock and saw Ellie who was standing in the kitchen doorway.

'Well?'

Wazer panicked as he wondered how long she had been there. Although he knew it would have been impossible for her to have heard what Professor Thistle had said on the phone, he was still alarmed by her sudden appearance, and so his head began to bead with sweat as he said, 'Phew, it's getting hot, huh?'

'If you weren't so fat, maybe you wouldn't sweat so much, which I'll be honest, would do my sense of smell wonders.'

'If you were as funny as you are stupid you would make a fortune and then maybe you wouldn't need to be here, annoying me. It's just a shame your jokes are about as funny as me.' His expression changed to doubt as he realised what he had just said.

'I see the point you're trying to make. I really do and you're right, you're not much of a joke teller. However, I do find myself laughing at you all the time. So I'm afraid, right there is where your statement just crumbles away. Kind of like those cookie crumbs around your filthy mouth.'

'No, you don't get it. I'm not funny, at all,' he said, whilst wiping off the remaining evidence of his gluttony.

'Oh my God, didn't this begin with you calling me stupid?'

His face was a picture of bewilderment as he tried to figure out how the tables had managed to turn on him yet again.

At that moment, Becky entered the room and walked over to the sink to get some aspirin for the plane journey.

'So c'mon, who was it? It's not like you have friends,' continued Ellie.

'What, somebody actually called him?' Becky used a hint of sarcasm as she searched through the medicine cupboard beside the sink.

'Yeah, I know, can you believe it?'

He began to sweat a lot more as he sensed his deception was about to catch up with him. He was never really good at lying as he was always far too transparent.

'Getting fed up with asking,' said Ellie one more time. 'Well?'

'It was nobody, it was just ... my mum.'

'Your mum? Now I know you're lying. Your mum likes you less than we do.'

'Hey, c'mon Ellie, that's maybe a little too far. He's not that bad. You're going to give the boy a complex.'

'No, I'm worse,' he quietly muttered to himself, as he thought about what he had planned. He hung his head down in guilt, but as he momentarily took his eyes off the girls, Ellie quickly approached and grabbed the phone out of his hand. 'Hey. I swear to God, give that back to me,' he screamed in panic.

'Ellie, give it to him. This isn't what we've become is it?' Becky felt a tinge of guilt due the way they had always treated Wazer.

Ellie raised the phone to her ear as if she was going to listen to the message, but Wazer knew he couldn't allow that to happen, and so he smashed his hand down on the kitchen table in defiance. 'I'm not messing,' he said loudly. His aggression was not too effective after his voice cracked into a high pitched tone from the pressure.

'Ooohh,' said Ellie in a similar but exaggerated high pitched tease. 'Come and get it then, big boy,' she said seductively as she circled the kitchen table.

Desperately gasping for air and with sweat pouring from his balding head, he started to chase her.

'You seriously need to lose weight,' laughed Ellie. 'I shouldn't have to keep reminding you, young man.' Instantly, her face lit up with excitement as she proceeded to sing the tune of YMCA with matching arm actions, 'Young man, you should really feel down. I said, young man, coz you're big, fat and round. Bom – bom – bom – bom – bom, I really want to know Y – YOU'RE SO FAT ...'

Wazer growled and moved in her direction. As he neared her she screamed in a playful girly way and jerked her body away from him. She then lowered the phone and pressed the number one button continuously, activating the voicemail that said, 'You have one, saved message. To listen to the message, press one.'

Wazer was becoming more furious and desperate as he circled the table trying to catch up with her.

To halt the proceedings, Becky suddenly jumped in front of Ellie. 'Ellie enough, it's not yours.'

Ellie stopped and stared at Becky. 'And?' She brought the mobile down again and pretended to press the number one button to listen to the message. As she did so, Wazer came up behind and not having enough time to stop his frantic stampede, he knocked straight into her.

They tumbled forward as Becky jumped out of the way. Wazer's phone flew out of Ellie's hand, and like a jungle tree that had just been felled, they both came crashing to the ground. Wazer landed directly on top of Ellie. The phone began to play the message from Professor Thistle as it flew through the air, but thankfully for Wazer nobody could hear it due to the commotion on the floor.

Ellie screamed in agony at the weight of Wazer on top of her. The phone hit the opposite wall, bounced off and skidded along the floor, before it stopped right next to the two of them. The battery cover came off but otherwise it was fine. They all heard a faint voice coming from its speaker. Professor Thistle's message was now in full swing.

Still lying on top of Ellie, Wazer quickly picked up the phone and smashed it straight into the ground, destroying it completely. 'Now look what you did,' he screamed in partly fake anger, as he rolled off Ellie in an exhausted state.

'Eeeww, you stink sooo bad,' said Ellie as she tried to stand up.

'You know Wazer, I think it was only the battery cover that came off,' said Becky.

Wazer struggled to his feet. He looked at Ellie and Becky with a serious expression. 'You'd like to think that, wouldn't you? Now, I've got things to do and I'd be delighted if I didn't see you for a long time. You've given me a very good reason not to come to England, and I can't afford it anyway.' He then stormed out of the kitchen.

'Wow, being smothered by the dead seal was well worth it if it meant keeping him from coming. Excellent result all round, I'd say.'

Becky shook her head disapprovingly and noticed that now the room had gone silent, she could hear something coming from the phone's speaker again. She glanced down and though the screen was smashed and the battery cover was off, it seemed to still work and so she picked it up.

'What, what is it?'

She put the phone to her ear. 'Sssshhh,' she said as she listened. 'It's still playing.' She lowered the phone down from her ear. 'Unbelievable. When you don't want your cell to break, it only has to fall off your lap and–'

'Alright I get it, it's stronger than your average phone, but who the hell is it?'

'Wait – it's asking if I want to replay the message.'

'So what are you waiting for? Oh, give it to me.' Ellie grabbed the phone from her and pressed the button to replay the message.

'Ellie,' exclaimed Becky, as she grabbed the phone back. 'It's not our message.' She put the phone back to her ear to end the call, but as she did she heard something that kept it glued there instead.

'... *keep those thieving cronies distracted while I get to that hole and study it for myself.*'

Becky looked at Ellie in shock as she continued to listen to Professor Thistle's voice.

'*If she has gone somewhere and I can follow quickly enough behind, maybe it can still be my name that's written in history. I need to leave tonight, so get it sorted.*'

Becky's face suddenly dropped and her eyes widened.

In excited desperation Ellie said, 'What is it?'

Becky looked straight at her and after a considered pause she said, 'You better get Nathan. It would appear we have a serious problem.'

~ CHAPTER THIRTY ONE ~

Collateral damage

Since 1946, when America provided for the recognition of the independence of the Republic of the Philippines as well as the relinquishment of American sovereignty over the Islands, a few influences of the occupation have remained; the abundance of large shopping malls, the frequency of fast food restaurants and even the American accent that has incorporated itself into the local dialect. However, perhaps the most noticeable is the reliance and love of motor cars and the resulting endless amounts of traffic it brings with it. One of the best places to see the original seeds of that influence was Los Angeles, the place where you can't travel far without realising that pedestrians have become an endangered species and that your life is shortened by the seventy two hours a year you spend in traffic queues.

'If time travel really does exist,' said Nathan who was sitting in one of those motor cars along with Ellie and Becky. 'I'm going to make it a point to come back to now and make sure this traffic somehow gets cleared, so that this cab can get to the airport and allow us to get to England before the professor does.'

They had been very slowly making their way through heavy traffic to L.A.X. airport, but the time had at least allowed Nathan to rack his brain as he tried to think of every scenario that he'd ever read about in literature, to establish how time travel could possibly work if it were indeed real, as well as trying to remember all the films he had seen just in case any of the ideas in them could help their situation.

'But if that were the case, I would already have done it and we would now be reaping the benefits. So maybe it is all just a crock of–'

'Thank you,' said Ellie, 'for your ingenious insight, yet again Nathan. I don't know what we would do without it.'

'You know,' remarked Becky after a moment's reflection. 'Why is it whenever we think about time travel, we focus on what we would come back and change? Why don't we just make sure we make the right decisions today? That way, we wouldn't have to come back and change anything. The future would then be the product of inspired and insightful actions. I mean, what if the past can never be changed? We must make sure we are always happy with the decisions we make right now, today; because they ultimately dictate our future.'

'That was a little bit deep,' whispered Ellie. 'So how does tying Wazer up and locking him in the cupboard rate on the scale of right and wrong decisions?' She was referring to the moment a few hours ago, when they found out Wazer was helping Professor Thistle. They had not intended to tie him up, but it all happened so quickly, and after they confronted him, they realised there was not much they could do to stop him. So in a frenzied fit of desperation, they pounced on him as he tried to leave, and he subsequently ended up with his hands and feet tied together with a pair of Ellie's tights before being dragged inside a cupboard.

'Maybe it wasn't the right decision, I don't know, but what I do know is that until we find out whether Courtney is even alive, we should do all we can to protect her. We need to do just as she asked, and Wazer was about to seriously get in the way of that. Perhaps he's just collateral damage.'

'It seems your idea doesn't work so well in the heat of the moment,' said Ellie with a smile on her face.

'I never said the right decision was always going to be an easy or pleasant one, did I? In the grand scheme, I hope it will still turn out to have been the correct choice.'

Ellie and Nathan stared at her with a dubious look in their eyes.

'Alright, when we get to the airport, we'll ring someone

and tell them to go to the house and let him out. Ok?'

At that moment, the cab started to move a little faster down the freeway.

'Holy baloney and macaroni,' yelled Nathan excitedly in the vein of a children's television presenter. 'I think I must've just changed the past.'

∞

While Courtney's gang of teenage helpers were on their way to the airport, Professor Thistle had repeatedly been trying to call Wazer on his cell phone. He was not too hot on using computers, so he was depending heavily on assistance from his new helper to get his flight booked. As the hours passed, he realised time was very quickly running out.

He contemplated going straight to the airport to see if he could grab a last minute seat on the next flight to London. After one last attempt of trying to call Wazer and still getting his voicemail, he grabbed his bag and jacket, jumped into his car and decided to act on his impulse.

As he arrived at L.A.X. Airport, he parked his car and made his way to the ticket desk, but as he walked into the terminal building, he was struck by a few moments of genuine doubt over his actions. As he stood in the long snake like queue for tickets, he wondered if Ellie, Nathan and Becky were also at the airport and whether they would have been bothered to even book a flight. 'Is this all one big practical joke at my expense,' he quietly asked himself.

He was thinking about the past and some students who had been known to conjure up a good enough illusion to make Professor Thistle think he had travelled through time. It was the annual practical joke, although none had ever succeeded.

'Perhaps until now,' he said cautiously and with slight trepidation. 'Have they changed tact and now want to get me to believe someone else has discovered time travel?'

People in the line looked at him suspiciously as he continued to mutter to himself.

A lady who was standing behind him noticed. 'You ok?'

Professor Thistle turned to her and continued to talk as if she knew what he was talking about. 'I could still go home and nobody would be any the wiser. Maybe I've pushed everyone too far and they're trying to get some payback. If you study time travel for a living, you open yourself up to ridicule you see.'

'Sure, I can definitely see how that could be a problem,' said the lady sarcastically.

Professor Thistle wasn't really focused on her and missed her sarcastic intention. He became noticeably angrier though the more he thought about it all. He stepped forward and edged his way closer to the ticket desk.

∞

In another section of the airport, Ellie, Nathan and Becky were standing in a separate queue for a different airline. They also had not booked and also hoped to get a last minute ticket.

Nathan looked particularly nervous as he fidgeted around while waiting for their turn. 'What are we going to do when we get there anyway? What if the professor gets there first?'

Becky looked at him. 'If this is all genuine and there really is a wormhole, all our lives will dramatically change forever. There's no doubt it'll be huge. We need to make sure that the right thing is done. So maybe we'll need to relocate whatever the device is that made it all possible and get it somewhere safe until we can decide what to do with it. More importantly however, we can hopefully figure out how to get Courtney back.'

'What if she's gone forever? If she has travelled in time, you would think we would already know somehow.'

'This isn't a movie Nathan,' said Ellie, with a frustrated tone. 'Things don't always have to run like they do in the movies.' She then changed her tone and smiled as she reflected on things. 'Anyway ... if anything, it would be a novel because I'd have to be much better written than a one-dimensional movie character.'

'There is no way anybody would put you in a book. You

can't even read. Think of the incongruity.'

'I swear,' said Ellie, 'and I say this out of love. You're such a loser, you're never gonna grab a feel of some boobs if you keep using words like incongruity with girls and pointing out ridiculous inconsistencies. I wouldn't be here if I couldn't read now would I?

In front of them and standing behind the ticket desk was a very attractive and well made up young blonde woman. She looked at them and said, 'How can I help you, guys?'

They stepped forward and slapped their passports down onto the counter.

'Well, our presence here is totally incongruous...,' said Ellie. She turned her head, raised her eyebrows at Nathan and then spun back around to the ticket clerk. '...but we need three tickets to London please.'

'Ma'am, I have no idea what you just said, but I did understand three tickets to London, so let me just take a look and see what there is.'

'That is a point well made and I will take note for the future. Won't I, Nathan? Note to self, apart from yours truly, attractive females don't understand long words.'

Nathan remained silent as the ticket clerk looked through the lists of available flights. There was no clever comeback that time, however much he wanted to retaliate. After a short wait, it seemed they were in luck.

'I can get you on the next flight at seventeen thirty five.'

Becky immediately interjected and said, 'There's nothing earlier? That's what, seven hours from now?' She did not relish the thought of spending all day at the airport, allowing Professor Thistle time to catch up.

'I'm afraid not. You could try another airline, but they also depart at roughly the same time.'

The three of them all looked at each knowing there was really no other choice.

With a defeated look, Becky turned back to the ticket clerk. 'Five thirty it is.'

'Seventeen forty sir,' said a ticket clerk at another desk, from the other airline.

'That's fine,' said Professor Thistle. At that moment his mobile phone finally began to ring. He fumbled around trying to answer it while purchasing his ticket at the same time. He managed to get it out and pressed the call button only to be bombarded with a rant, as Wazer hurriedly tried to explain how he had been tied up and locked in the cupboard after the others found out he was helping him. 'So they must be at the airport as well,' said Professor Thistle when he could finally get a word in. 'What exactly are they trying to achieve? They're in way over their heads.'

Wazer didn't have any answers for the professor, only to say that they did not seem to know themselves what they were doing, or going to do.

'Alright, Wazer my boy ... this is what I want you to do, so listen carefully. You're going to call the police department and tell them you were assaulted and tied up ... with a rope. Tell them you know who it was and that they are now at the airport trying to leave for London, tonight. Don't do it yet; wait four hours. Their flight won't be until this evening either. That should narrow their window for still making the flight even if they let them go for lack of evidence or something.' He spoke with a focused and slightly twisted determination in his eyes. 'Have you got that?'

Wazer was not convinced about doing something so drastic to them. Even though they had recently had their differences, he had lived with them for some time now and did think of them to some degree as friends. Then again, they did tie him up and lock me him in a cupboard. But then they did use Ellie's tights to do it and made sure they called someone to let him go. He felt like he was under a lot of pressure from the professor but also wanted to make sure he made the right choice. He went silent for a moment and then said, 'Don't worry, Sir, I'll do the right thing. Leave it to me.'

Professor Thistle pressed the end call button and then smiled deviously as he handed over his credit card to the ticket clerk and said, 'One ticket to London please.'

~ CHAPTER THIRTY TWO ~

It's a matter of life and death

Professor Pik Thistle had been keeping a secretive eye on Ellie, Nathan and Becky, who had positioned themselves in a seating area underneath one of the many departure monitors. He had selected the best spot for optimum efficiency; a sushi restaurant some distance away where he could see them at all times but where they would have little chance of spotting him in all the hustle and bustle.

Every time the airport security walked passed, his heart skipped a beat in anticipation of his plan with Wazer succeeding. However, as of yet they just continued to walk on by. Three hours passed and they were still in the lounge, looking incredibly bored. Professor Thistle was still watching from across the way, only pausing once to go to the toilet. He was extremely anxious about something that could imminently happen. Many cups of coffee had already been drunk, evident by the shakes he had from all the caffeine that was coursing through his blood. At least he knew there was no chance of falling asleep.

Ellie was slumped in her seat, watching yet more travellers as they passed her by. Becky and Nathan had fallen asleep from boredom a while ago, but Ellie had found that she couldn't relax knowing what they were about to do, so she took to doing the next best thing – people watching. She had mainly thought about spotting a hunk, but if she was really lucky, she thought she might just spot the professor.

As she sat and stared at the various different types of travellers in the airport, she realised quickly that she couldn't get her mind focused on hot men because so many other things were distracting her. Disappointing as it was she knew it may have been the focus she needed to get her mind back on Professor Thistle. She nudged Becky and Nathan awake. 'Hey, don't you think it's a bit odd that we haven't seen him? I mean, this is the only way anyone can get to London quickly, isn't it? So he should be here. But then if he is, aren't we going to turn up at the same time? We should've thought of a smarter way to get there before him, this is all starting to feel a bit wrong.'

Nathan yawned and said, 'So what are you saying?'

'I'm just saying it's not exactly highly covert is it? Sitting at the airport for hours waiting for him to just turn up and get on the same flight? Do you think he's going to be that stupid too?'

Becky and Nathan had a look of realisation as the logic of Ellie's comments struck home.

'We should have thought about this more – I should've thought about it more.'

They all went silent and looked at each other reflectively.

Four hours passed, then five. Professor Thistle became progressively more frustrated as he sat waiting for what felt like forever. He repeatedly called Wazer on his mobile phone but just kept getting his voicemail. Finally, the seven hour wait for their flight was almost up, but Ellie, Nathan and Becky were now all asleep in very uncomfortable positions, spread across a number of the lounge seats. They had been like that for the last couple of hours. Then the speaker system suddenly announced both parties' flights, informing passengers to make their way to the relevant gate for departure.

Ellie opened her eyes upon hearing the call. Professor Thistle looked on with an angry and slightly disturbed expression, as it seemed that Wazer had clearly chosen to let him down by putting his allegiance with his housemates. He took a deep breath, got up from his stool and walked straight over in their direction. He was fully aware that they could not possibly travel together and would have to do something drastic to stop that happening.

Ellie nudged the others. 'C'mon guys, we're leaving now. They want us at the gate.'

Relieved, they stood and stretched after the long uncomfortable wait.

'I promised myself I'd never wake up next to you,' said Ellie to Nathan a little groggily.

Nathan smiled at her with repressed contempt.

As she leant down to pick her rucksack up off the floor, Becky caught a glimpse of Professor Thistle in the corner of her eye, marching over towards them. She immediately jerked upward and froze on the spot. Her heart pounded faster because although she was well aware of what they were doing, the reality of seeing the professor coming towards her at the airport brought it all quickly home. 'Hey guys,' she said nervously.

Ellie and Nathan turned to see Professor Thistle who had stopped on the other side of the seating area. They all stood staring at each other not quite knowing what to do next.

All the jesting and sharp-tongued jibes that Ellie would normally use disappeared as she found herself speechless. Taking pot-shots from a safe distance was one thing but being faced with the ominous presence of the world renowned Professor Pik Thistle, was another. They all knew that they had each played a part in ransacking his office and stealing his book, and that fact made them all feel very stupid and scared.

'Maybe we should just apologise and see if we can just forget everything and go back to class tomorrow,' whispered Nathan awkwardly.

Suddenly, a male figure stood directly in front of them and blocked their view of the professor. 'Nathan Widdle, Ellie Ruby and Rebecca Humphrey?'

They looked up at the tall and broad shouldered L.A. policeman who towered in front of them. They nodded in unison, totally shocked and a little confused.

'You are under arrest on suspicion of abduction and kidnapping. You have the right to remain silent. Anything you say can and will be used against you in a court of law. You have the right to an attorney present during questioning. If you cannot afford an attorney, one will be appointed for you. Do you understand these rights?'

They stood there in utter disbelief. Was that really the way it was going to end? They all thought.

'No, no, you can't do this. You don't understand,' said Becky in desperation.

With a little more aggression the officer said, 'Do you understand these rights?'

Becky looked at him with a totally lost and defeated expression. 'Yes, but-'

'Put your hands behind your back,' he demanded.

Two other police officers appeared and grabbed Ellie and Nathan before all three were put in cuffs.

'You can't do this,' said Nathan. 'We need to be on our flight. It's a matter of life and death.' He unintentionally used one of his best movie lines to affect the situation, but it was let down by the panicked high pitched feminine voice that came out once again.

'I'm sure it is, Sir. It's always a matter of life and death and you can explain just how and why down at the station.'

'Oh God, my mum's going to kill me,' squealed Nathan, as he realised the magnitude of what was happening.

Everyone in the waiting area was staring at what had become a scene with most assuming they must be terrorists. Because of that there was a little bit of panic and commotion, allowing the professor to blend in with the crowd. The three prisoners were led through the departure lounge and the prying eyes of the baying crowd, but just before they disappeared, all three caught the eye of the professor. They stared at him knowing he must have had something to do with their embarrassing arrest. In subtle confirmation he stared back, grinned and then disappeared backwards into the throng of nervous passengers.

~ CHAPTER THIRTY THREE ~

Someone else is coming

Controlled chaos had erupted inside the airport terminal. Staff members were busy trying to calm passengers down by convincing them that the arrests had nothing to do with a terror plot. Ellie, Nathan and Becky knew though that the potential consequences of discovering time travel could have far bigger implications than any terrorist could hope to conjure.

Becky turned to the police officer next to her who was frog marching Ellie out of the terminal and said, 'We're allowed one phone call, right?'

'Yes, ma'am - one phone call.'

Ellie looked at Becky and knew exactly what she was thinking. They both realised Professor Thistle had arranged their convenient arrest with a little help from their earlier victim. When they tied Wazer up, they did not imagine it would get that serious, but the fact that it had and the fact that Professor Thistle felt his trip was important enough to keep them out of the way, meant the short term was no longer important. The long term ramifications of what Courtney had potentially discovered were far bigger than the imminent predicament of their arrest.

'We've messed up big time – we've got to warn her. I'll try Alexandra's cell,' said Becky.

'This is so bad,' said Ellie.

'I know,' replied Becky.

'I knew we should have used rope. My tights should only ever get ripped by–'

'Ellie.'

'I'll try the landline,' said Ellie sheepishly.

Nathan was following closely behind the two girls with his arresting officer in tow. 'I'm ringing my mum.'

The two girls figured he had not tuned in to their silent understanding of one another. They sighed and rolled their eyes back, wondering exactly what he thought his mum could do to help them.

After yet another long ride in a car, they were escorted inside the police station and after being processed, were given their one phone call. One by one they were led to the telephone and first to dial was Nathan who as promised, dialled for his mother. He pleaded with her not to be angry and to come and help them get out. He seemed to have a lot of faith that she could be of some kind of assistance.

Next up was Becky, who dialled Alexandra's mobile. She tried a few times, but it kept going straight to voicemail. In desperation she rang Wazer to try and convince him to do the right thing by dropping the charges. She thought that if he did, they could still make it to Britain in time.

Then it was Ellie's turn. She dialled Courtney's home number, hoping Alexandra would be there. She waited patiently for someone to answer, but nobody picked up. Instead it just rang until the answer machine kicked in. 'Alexandra, this is Courtney's friend, Ellie. We were on our way over to you, but we got in a spot of bother at the airport. I don't know that we'll make it now, but I need to warn you. Someone else is coming, and even if we do manage to get there, he'll definitely reach you first. You must not let him near the house or the hole, otherwise Courtney could be in even more danger. Keep him away at all costs; call the police if you have to. Just don't—' The answer machine beeped and cut her off mid-sentence. 'Oh God, I didn't tell her his name,' she mumbled to herself. She thought for a moment and then turned to the officer who was present in the room.

He was a tall and skinny man in his fifties who stank of smoke. His shirt was soaked with sweat, particularly under his armpits and all down his back. On his head he wore a very obvious, totally black hairpiece which seemed to be very unsuitable for his age.

'Hi,' said Ellie, in her most seductive voice. She flicked her hair to the side and pushed her chest out toward him.

The officer smiled in appreciation.

'I need to call back, you don't mind do you?'

He looked at her dubiously.

'I could make it worth your while,' she said raising her eyebrows suggestively.

He looked her up and down with a continuous smile on his face. He clearly found her very attractive, but then to Ellie's slight surprise, he chuckled to himself.

Unusual reaction but perhaps he was just happy to be acknowledged by someone in her league.

'Ma'am ...'

Her face lit up at the thought of him allowing her to have a second call.

'There are two things I'm certain about. You're as sexy as hell, and I'm stunningly unattractive. But I'm no idiot Ma'am.'

'Huh?'

'You can bet your backside that if I actually thought it would really benefit me, I'd give you that call in a flash. However, I'm well aware of my position on the food chain and how this conversation will conveniently disappear once you've had your call. If I did want a woman like you I'm well aware that I'd have to pay for it ... one way or another. So kindly deflate your chest and get your pretty backside back over here ... please.'

Ellie's sexual charm had unexpectedly failed her. All she could hope for now was that her voicemail message would be enough. If not, she knew that not only would the professor have won but more crucially, both Alexandra and Courtney could be in terrible danger.

~ CHAPTER THIRTY FOUR ~

Some kind of poltergeist

The flight from Los Angeles to London was ten hours, but to Professor Thistle it felt like a lifetime. All he could think about the whole way over was what kind of marvel could possibly be awaiting him on the other side of the Atlantic. If all was to be believed it could quite possibly be the greatest discovery mankind had ever made – or womankind, he kept reminding himself with heavy disdain.

The only interference in his meanderings was to repeatedly check his watch, willing the hands to move faster in the hope of making his journey pass by quicker. Like a child in the back seat of a car and with the aeroplane staff representing the parents, they could almost hear him constantly screaming, 'Are we there yet?' Or like a little boy waiting for the clock to reach the moment when he could finally open his Christmas gift after sneakily seeing what it was the night before. Time just could not pass quickly enough.

To help a little, he altered his watch to match London time; a trick that, like Courtney, he had learnt as a child to make the adjustment easier and alleviate the jet lag. He moved the hands forward eight hours, smiled and whispered, 'Maybe time travel's not so hard after all.'

He had been to London many times before for conferences and speaking tours, so once the aeroplane had finally landed he knew exactly where to go and so proceeded straight through customs to make his way to the taxi rank outside. He handed over Courtney's address (that he had hurriedly scribbled on a crumpled piece of paper) to one of the waiting cabbies outside. There was a long drive ahead to get to the destination, but the cab driver willingly took such a long fare as he coincidently just came from that direction.

Due to the eight hour time difference, it was just approaching midnight. The traffic on the road was pretty clear, allowing the cab driver the luxury of only having to deal with late night travellers who had also just left the airport, as opposed to the usual daytime traffic chaos of London and the surrounding motorways.

Professor Thistle had adopted a hat and scarf to shield him from the drop in temperature between the two countries. Even though it wasn't freezing, there was a distinct chill in the air compared to California, especially at that time of the morning. Being the only passenger in the cab he could have taken the front seat, but he decided to sit in the back to avoid at least a little of the usual driver-passenger banter that can plague those types of journeys. He sat in silence for most of the trip, trying hard to focus his thoughts in spite of the constant hum of the car radio. He rested his head on the car window and a cool damp sensation struck his senses. As he looked through the gentle raindrops that were cascading down the cold glass, he became instantly aware of the various English difference, and although all motorways generally look as bland and characterless as each other no matter the country you are in, he was still being affected by the initial thirty minute adjustment period you get when you have just come from an airport and set foot for the first time in a long while on foreign soil. Normally he would put the familiar feeling down to new destination wonderment, but there was an additional feeling tonight as he sensed something major coming his way.

Within forty minutes, they had reached the picturesque Hertfordshire countryside where Courtney's house was situated. The town was relatively small and made up of predominantly Victorian cottages, though over the years more modern and arguably less attractive apartment blocks had begun to crop up.

The whole ride there Professor Thistle had been heavily deliberating what he might encounter once he finally arrived at the house, and as he neared the bottom of the pebble street at long last, his mind was not only trying to figure that out, but it was still in overdrive from trying to figure out everything that had happened in the last few days. However, as the cab pulled up the hill towards the house that could hold all the answers, his immediate issue was that if the wormhole was indeed real, it was supposedly situated within Courtney's property and so he therefore knew that it really belonged to her. *But then she wasn't concerned about the law when she took my book, allowing her to create the hole in the first place.* There was some resentment in his thoughts. *Should I just march straight in, or should I try to be nice and explain who I am? It's not as if I'm evil or a criminal. I'm just a scientist looking to take my rightful place in history. There's nothing wrong with that. I just want to take back what is mine, that's all.* He was recollecting everything that had brought him to that moment in the first place. *Why shouldn't I? It should've been my discovery – and it still could be.*

The cab driver had been using the rear view mirror to repeatedly glance back at Professor Thistle as he continued with his internal rant. He let him go on for a while before he interjected and said, 'You alright there, Sir?' You got an allergy or something? Hay fever's pretty big around here. It's all the pollen see.'

'I'm fine,' he said after realising how stupid he must have looked getting carried away in his thoughts.

'Well anyway, we're here,' remarked the cab driver as the car slowly came to a stop on the noisy gravel path. 'Lovely house this is. Who lives here then ... your daughter?'

Professor Thistle looked out of his window as the cab came to a stop outside an old Victorian building. 'Something like that,' he said as he continued to look at the house in awe, knowing that he might actually be staring at something that could hold the answers to all the puzzles he had been researching his whole life.

'Nice lighting effects,' said the cab driver, referring to the glow that wrapped itself around the house. 'I'd like to know how your daughter did that. The missus would love it for Christmas. Oh ... unless of course it's some kind of ghost causing it,' he said jokingly.

Professor Thistle averted his gaze toward the driver and stared in silence with a totally dead-pan expression on his face.

'You do know this is a real haunted house, don't ya?'

'Excuse me?' He continued to stare with intrigue at the cabbie.

'Yeah, a little girl and her mum used to live here. Supposedly, the kid witnessed some kind of poltergeist.'

'Really?'

'I'm sure it's just rubbish ... I mean garbage ... or trash. You know, not true. It was years ago now. Anyway, that'll be eighty quid please mate.'

Professor Thistle paid the driver, grabbed his bag off the seat next to him and got out of the cab. As the car sped off back down the hill, Professor Thistle stood alone in the glow of the house. Total silence reigned all around him, and in the traditional sense of the word he could not see any lights that were switched on inside or outside the building. Wondering where the intriguing glow could be coming from, he cautiously looked all around for an explainable source, but as he turned away from the house towards the wooded area some metres behind him, he caught a glimpse of a mysterious figure in the trees.

In the darkness, all he could see was a silhouette that appeared to stare right back at him. The area was very dark and eerie, and after the ghost story he had just been told, even he was a little spooked. However, his rational and scientific mind was telling him that ghosts do not exist, and everything in the world has to have some kind of explanation.

He slowly began to walk over to the opening in the trees, but as soon as he did the figure vanished. Professor Thistle gulped but his inquisitive mind could not let it go and so he continued to walk towards the foliage until he too disappeared into the thick of the wood.

All around was totally silent and at that time of night the

area had a particularly spooky feel to it. The odd crack of twigs could be heard coming from within the trees as well as the rustling of leaves. A vague mist around the vicinity, accentuated by the glow of the house, was causing a creepy atmosphere to develop.

All of a sudden he stumbled back out from the trees, shook his head and brushed his clothes down from the cobwebs that were clinging to him. 'This is just ridiculous. I can't see a damn thing in there. I have to do what I came here for and remain focused.' He cautiously approached the front door of the house and took a deep breath as he prepared to witness whatever was awaiting him on the other side.

He knocked on the door using the large, distinctly English brass knocker and stood waiting for someone to let him inside. He noticed that the door frame had some large splits in it and the hinges holding it on to the frame looked brand new. Obviously something had happened there, but he quickly dismissed it as thoughts about what he was going to say went round and round in his head. He stiffened himself in preparation, ready to physically take control of whomever was going to answer the door ... but nobody came.

He knocked again, but then he started to think about the possibility of nobody being home or perhaps being asleep in bed. He thought about walking around to the rear to see if there was any way of breaking in, but as he was just about to move, he heard a voice on the other side of the door.

'Who are you? I've already called the police and they're waiting on the other end of the line.'

He was slightly taken aback by the talk of police. 'I'm ... a friend of Courtney's,' he promptly said.

'How do you know Courtney? What's your name?'

He froze for a moment and contemplated whether he should reveal his name or not. *Would she recognise it? Has Courtney said anything, or has the rest of the gang I left in the airport been released already and gotten in touch?* In the limited time he had, he decided that he did not really have a choice but to tell her his name, and if she did recognise it, he would just have to find another way to shut her up. 'I'm

Professor Pik Thistle from LosTech University in Los Angeles, California.' There was a moment's pause. He became increasingly agitated realising something must be wrong. 'I'm here for a very good reason and if you do not open this—'

Suddenly the front door burst open and Alexandra instantly leapt out. She grabbed his arm roughly and hurriedly dragged him inside the house. She slammed the door behind her and turned to face him. 'Oh my God, I'm so glad you're here. You have to help me.'

'Help you? Help you with what?'

'It's the hole. I don't know what to do. You have to do something. You're a professor, right? If you don't help, she could be stuck in there forever.'

'What exactly has happened? What's the problem?'

She paused, looked straight at him in panic and said, 'It's closing – do you understand? The hole ... is closing.

~ CHAPTER THIRTY FIVE ~

She's gone isn't she?

There are very few moments in anyone's life that are capable of bringing out true joy and unrestrained excitement, the sort of feeling we start to become incapable of as we grow into adulthood, but as Professor Thistle looked into Alexandra's eyes his face became representative of a windup toy at that moment just before it's released onto the surface to go hurtling around the room. He waited in anticipation as all the built up pressure from the springs in the mechanism were about to be set free. For a brief moment he was totally lost for words, though it was not in any concern for Courtney's well-being, but then all of a sudden it was as if the coil had been released and he shouted, 'Where is it - where's this hole?'

Alexandra was somewhat taken aback by his show of adulation but was so worked up herself she joined him and screamed, 'Its outside – come on, I'll show you.' Alexandra ran to the rear of the house. 'I've been going out of my mind.'

He followed her down the hallway towards the back door in the kitchen. He passed by the telephone on the hall table and noticed a little red light flashing on the display, indicating there was an unheard message. He glanced at it briefly but quickly dismissed it, as Alexandra was already in the garden waiting for him.

As he paced into the kitchen, his heart pounded in expectation because everything looked like it was going to be much easier than he had expected. He reached the back of the house and stepped outside to finally join Alexandra in the garden. As he emerged from the back door, he suddenly froze on the spot in wonder. He couldn't believe what he was seeing in front of both of them; something he'd waited his whole life to see but truthfully never thought he would.

Professor Thistle stood, completely mesmerised at what he could only describe as some form of cosmic vacuum. He'd never seen anything like it nor imagined he'd actually witness it in his lifetime. Different coloured lights and gasses were being thrown from the anomaly, and at the same time it was sucking the atmosphere into the black hole. The whole thing was a beautiful spectacle that stretched right the way up from the ground. If he didn't know better he would have assumed there must be a pot of gold somewhere nearby and a giant in the clouds at the other end.

'Truly amazing,' said Professor Thistle wide eyed and with his jaw hanging down.

The two of them suddenly felt a strong pull from the anomaly so had to grab onto the frame of the kitchen door to stop them from being sucked in.

'It wasn't doing this before. It's just been getting progressively smaller,' shouted Alexandra over the noise it was making. 'What's happening? What will happen to Courtney?'

Suddenly, as quick as it started it all stopped and there was total silence. They both fell to the ground from the release of the pull. For the first time since Courtney and Alexandra blew up the microwave, everything had returned to normality. Alexandra immediately got up and ran down the garden towards the hole.

Professor Thistle followed but found it hard to focus his mind while his eyes were almost falling out of his head in excitement.

Alexandra reached the end of the garden and stared at the ground where the bottomless vortex had previously been, but all she saw now was a very deep crater. She jumped in as she could see it was now just a big hole in the ground, but she needed to make sure all the same. The hole enveloped her all the way up to her neck. She landed with a thud and looked up at Professor Thistle with a blank and devastated expression on her face. 'She's gone isn't she? She's really gone.' Her eyes watered as she thought about the consequences of everything; after all, she knew it was her that convinced Courtney to jump in the first place.

Professor Thistle had all sorts of things running through his mind, but what was most pressing was that whatever he had just witnessed and whatever Courtney had apparently disappeared into was the thing he came all the way over to England to see. However, the most worrying thought was that it seemed to now be gone forever. For a moment, they mourned together; albeit a different loss.

I didn't just sit on a plane for ten hours for nothing, thought Professor Thistle. He turned to Alexandra and in desperation said, 'You need to show me how you did this. Show me what made this happen, and I can try to get Courtney back.' He knew that everything rested on creating another hole and to do so he would need to stay in favour with Alexandra; the only person left who had witnessed its creation. 'If you don't, Courtney may also be gone forever. It's imperative you immediately show me what made this possible before it's too late.'

She looked up at him from down inside the crater. She was in a temporary state of shock, trying to rationalise what had just happened as well as what he'd just said to her. After a couple of seconds of considered thought, she outstretched her arm and offered him her hand.

Professor Thistle reached forward and smiled at her apparent cooperation. He grabbed hold of her hand, looked into her eyes and said, 'Don't worry child, you can trust me. I will fix this ... once and for all.'

~ CHAPTER THIRTY SIX ~

Why time travel exists

'That is a very good question,' said Dulko. 'The simple answer is ... all our buildings are designed in much the same way as our PEUs.' He had been busy for the last hour trying to explain to Courtney the science behind his house as well as everything she had seen since she entered the city; including what enabled her to be standing on what looked like nothing.

She was very uneasy in her new environment and was too petrified to move a single muscle. So she just gritted her teeth, tentatively twisted her head to Dulko and gently said, 'And a PEU is?'

'Sorry – it's the Personal Energy Unit that we flew here in. Our cities are built using exactly the same technology. Once inside a building, our PEUs are deactivated and then the building's energy links in to our internal system. It works like a force field and acts as a solid barrier of energy that we can use to build anything. It's the one piece of technology that really saved us. It means we no longer need the planet's surface.'

'Yeah but ... how?'

'Well ... forgive me if this sounds insulting, but what's your knowledge of particle physics like?'

Courtney looked at him with a staid expression that Dulko found very hard to read.

'Am I preaching to the choir? That is the saying isn't it?'

'Yeah ... I mean no. I mean yes that's the saying, but I'm no expert on particles.' She was being unusually vague because she was trying to piece together what he had said with recent revelations from her own time and then she slowly said, 'You're not referring to the Higgs Boson particle are you?'

'Yes ... exactly. I wasn't sure because it was mostly developed way after your time.'

'The Higgs Boson is the reason everything has mass right? It's what causes all the other particles to stick together and become solid. But from my very limited understanding, it only has a lifespan of like a millionth of a millionth of a millionth of a millionth of a second or something. What's changed?'

'There's a lot of incredible science involved, but in simple terms our scientists figured out how to just keep constantly producing them artificially at a phenomenal rate by using power from the Dyson spheres and a super energy particle accelerator. As soon as they die, another instantly replaces it allowing all the protons, neutrons and electrons, that of course are present in all solid objects, to stop whizzing around and stick together. Then the particles are contained by an energy barrier that has totally wireless computer links to just about everything so that we can form whatever structure or object we want them to. This means we can not only travel anywhere with ease, secure inside our PEUS, but also build homes wherever we want, in any style and without the need for any traditional construction like in your day.'

'Wow. I don't really understand, but it makes total sense anyway.'

Dulko smiled. 'Hey, I'm the same and I'm certainly no scientist; I only know what I've been told. Trust me, it's basic info nowadays. So don't quote me; I may have even got it slightly wrong.'

The only traditionally built structures during that time were the huge concrete pylons that had been positioned around the world. They were responsible for transmitting the energy needed for all the technology to function. To make it easier for her, Dulko had already explained that those pylons were linked to each other a bit like mobile phone masts except on a much larger scale. They came up from the sea and stretched right up into the sky, stopping just below the start of the city and getting narrower the higher they went. Each structure had a base that was the size of an entire town and at their peak, they transmitted the power waves that enabled the world in the sky to operate including the PEUs. They had been embedded all over with rock particles that had previously been orbiting a star as part of a Dyson Sphere and were built in the oceans about one hundred miles apart.

'They look like they are literally bursting out from beneath the water. It's quite a sight to behold. It's all perfectly safe though, so you don't need to panic. I promise ... you can move. We've lived like this for a few hundred years now, combining particle physics with natural spacial phenomena. You see for the most part, the world below has become uninhabitable due to extreme temperatures that caused lots of rain and rising sea levels. There are still some remaining land masses which are habitable, like what was once Greenland and Iceland, but they are also the only ones where we can cultivate natural food. People have moved up into the sky so that we can have as much space as possible to grow the natural products down below because they are crucial for our survival.'

Something about what Dulko had said sounded a little scripted to Courtney, but everything was so overwhelming that she quickly put the thought to one side. Maybe it was just his way. 'This is absolutely unbelievable,' she said. 'I can't even comprehend what is happening right now. I'm ... just really ... I could literally pee myself with excitement.'

'Please don't — it's a nightmare trying to get stains out of this floor.'

Dulko's expression didn't change so she looked at him, wondering if he was actually serious. She then looked toward where the floor should have been for clarification, but of course, there was no floor.

'If you're wondering ... it was a joke. I'm just not too good with the delivery.'

She stared at him blankly for a second and then raised a nervous but friendly laugh, to which he smiled in acceptance of his clunky attempt to lighten the mood. She continued to chuckle at his humour, or lack of before finding a little confidence to test her footing on the transparent floor.

As she did, Dulko's smile disappeared and he became very serious. 'I'm afraid you don't have time to explore. There are a few things that need to be done and you're quite literally the only one who can do them.'

'If that's the case, would you mind if I use the toilet before I have an accident that'll short circuit this place? I don't like the idea of travelling hundreds of years into the future through a worm hole and then dying from my own wee.' She fell silent and hoped he would at least smile. As she stood waiting, she couldn't help but think that the whole situation felt like the first five minutes of a blind date.

Unfortunately, Dulko hadn't realised the etiquette and that he should have laughed at all her jokes, no matter how unfunny. Instead, he looked so nervous that he couldn't help but take anything she said seriously. 'Yes, I agree that would not be the way to go.'

She looked at him with a furrowed brow. 'I guess toilet humour is not too big up here,' she mumbled to herself.

'Oh and it wasn't a worm hole,' he said, desperately trying to make conversation. 'They don't exist.'

'What? Really? So how did I get here?'

He stared at her with a nondescript expression, but he was actually very taken in by her personality. Courtney didn't realise, but he was actually ecstatic inside. He was just too afraid to get too comfortable with her. He had never seen anyone quite like her before, physically as well as the fact that to him she was extremely famous, and he couldn't help but feel a little star struck; even if he was trying to hide it as best he could. She was nothing like what he had expected though. One thousand years was a long time and all records of what she looked like had been lost in time. As he continued to stare, he became lost in his own thoughts and totally forgot what she had asked him. So instead he just blurted out whatever he was thinking. 'You know we lost all record of what you looked like when the planet was flooded. The only record we have of you is your handwriting and thoughts from the Red Bible but I have to say, you are actually ... quite cute.' He smiled with a little nervous twitch.

'I'm sorry, what did you just say?'

'Er ... oh sorry not cute, I meant beautiful. You're beau–'

'No the other thing ... about a bible?'

'Oh ... well not long after you disappeared in time, they found your red notebook. It was genius. The stuff you were writing was way ahead of your time, and it's one of the reasons you're so revered today. It was preserved, and it's the only thing of yours to have survived until now. Religion pretty much disappeared when the destruction hit, but for some your book is probably the closest thing we now have.'

Courtney stared at him in shock. 'Oh God, what have I done? I should have brought it with me and then this couldn't have happened.'

'What do you mean? Brought what?'

'It's all a lie. I'm a fake. I don't deserve any recognition.'

'I don't understand. How can you be a fake?' Dulko suddenly became very concerned by the thought that he, along with everyone in history, could have made such a huge mistake.

She looked him apprehensively in the eyes before deciding to tell the truth. 'That ... wasn't my book. I erm ... stole it.' As she continued to stare, tears appeared in her eyes.

He looked right back at her trying to work out what it could mean. 'That's ... not going to go down well. What do you mean you stole it?'

'It wasn't intentional and I certainly didn't know this would happen. We could never have known. It's just an example of how a small decision can cause huge ripples and have massive consequences down the line.' As she finished her sentence, she became more and more upset.

'Now you listen to me – don't tell anyone else about this, do you understand? Nobody needs to know this. It doesn't really matter because what is still true is that you were the first to travel through time and that you can't change. So for the time being, you are just going to have to get over whatever guilt you may have because we still have crucial work to do.'

They were both silent for a moment. She wiped away her tears and came to the realisation that he was probably right. She knew it was too late to change what had already happened. Nothing however eased the guilt and regret she felt. However, in a world that is pre-destined, she thought that regret even seemed futile. 'So how do I use this toilet then? I mean, I know you guys walk around naked and stuff but surely you don't watch each other on the loo, do you?'

Dulko chuckled at the small return of her cheeky charm. 'It depends on who we are with and how well we know them I guess,' he said as he grinned at her. 'But I will grant you your privacy, as we've only just met.' He nodded toward the bathroom.

She turned to look and a pink wall appeared all around it. 'Wow, you have complete control of your house in your mind, that's wicked. I mean cool. Pink, though?'

They smiled at each other.

'There's nothing wrong with pink. But like I told you, the PEU's circuitry is implanted in us. It's part of us, part of our mind. Whatever we think is at our fingertips.'

'Except people, you can't control people.'

Dulko grinned.

'Well just don't think about the wall disappearing while I'm in there.'

They both spent the next hour getting to know each other, with Courtney explaining how she had struggled to relieve herself without falling into the giant toilets that they seemed to need. She told him how she felt like Jack who had just climbed the beanstalk, with everything around her being some degree larger than she was used to. Dulko went on to explain some of the advances they had made in the future. From the most obvious world above the sky to 'Toothpaste capsules that you put in your mouth and bite, causing a mini explosion in your mouth and eradicating within seconds any plaque and food left in there; leaving your teeth clean, fresh and white.'

'You sound like a toothpaste commercial. You know you could make a lot of money with those pearly whites back in my time.'

'It's tempting as I could do with the money but sadly, impossible.'

Courtney stared at him. She couldn't help but think that although she enjoyed the company and the lesson on the future, maybe it was time she found out why she was there. 'Seriously though, what is this problem that I need to fix?'

'Ok, listen closely.' He stood up and a see through digital presentation board appeared in front of them. He used his finger to draw diagrams and dates in order to explain everything. 'As history tells it, around one thousand years ago you discovered a massive energy source in something called ... a cellar? You quickly discovered how to harness this energy to form the world's first man made loophole which as history tells us, you jumped right into. Or perhaps not right into,' he said, as he looked at her with a playful expression. He was referring to her slightly delayed arrival earlier.

Courtney raised her eyes to the ceiling, indicating innocently that she did not know what he was talking about.

'Anyway, it transported you through time until you ended up here.' He pointed at that date on the board. 'In the year 3016.'

'I still can't get over that.'

He looked at her sharply, gently scolding her for interrupting.

'Sorry. I'm listening. So I jumped into a loophole in the system–'

'No, no. You actually jumped into a loophole. I don't mean metaphorically, I mean literally. Not to be confused with a wormhole, but a loophole.'

Courtney raised one eyebrow in confusion.

'I'll explain that in a minute. The point is that now you've arrived, people will try to kill you.' He drew a cross through his stick figure of Courtney.

'But why?'

'To stop you jumping back one thousand years, which

history again tells us you go on to do. You go back to a few days before you created the loophole - to leave for yourself to find - the energy rock that enabled you to initiate the first jump through time – thus completing the time loop. It's all supposed to happen. It's pre-destined. I'm here to make sure nobody gets in your way.' There were now lines everywhere, criss-crossing each other all over the board making it very hard for Courtney to keep up.

'Wait a minute – I'm a part of history? I'm why time travel exists?'

He raised his eyebrows making an expression that confirmed what she had said.

'Whoa, that is seriously mega, but who exactly would get in my way?'

He looked at her with eyes wide; a sort of 'deer in headlights' look and said, 'Well ... anyone. I mean, there are some strange people out there. The future hasn't changed that much.'

'But if it's all predestined, how could they get in my way?'

'We're not really sure, but we'd rather not find out. It's safer if things just stay the way they are supposed to, and helping you do that is all part of it.'

'What do you mean, we? Are you working for someone?'

'No,' he immediately snapped back. 'I meant *I*. It was just a figure of speech.'

She looked into his eyes and recognised the honesty shining out like a flare above the ocean in the midnight sky. She put her suspicions down to her own insecurities and the fact that she was in a world she knew nothing about. 'Ok, let's get back to the time travel. What you're saying is that it exists because I basically took technology that you created back to my own time, to then use it to come forward and steal all over again?'

'Exactly, but don't get me wrong. The world still regards you as the pioneer and genius responsible for placing our technology with your research and experiments.' He was trying to make her understand that she needed to keep quiet about the book. 'You formed the world's first man made loophole, without which we simply wouldn't be time travelling today, as well as many other things. You see most importantly, we couldn't have developed the technology without you taking it back, giving your scientists the foundations to develop it into what we have today.'

Courtney couldn't believe what she was hearing. It scared her a lot, but at the same time she felt a huge surge of adrenaline pump through her blood vessels as she also knew that what she was being told was completely unprecedented.

Then Dulko hammered in the final blow and said, 'In short if you hadn't taken it back or more to the point if you don't take it back, everything I and everyone else from this time takes for granted will just vanish ... it will all be gone ... forever.'

~ CHAPTER THIRTY SEVEN ~

The beginning of time

A bombshell had been dropped and the shrapnel had well and truly hit its target. As Courtney stood in shell-shock, she stared at Dulko, stunned by all the information that was now embedded in her skull. 'I stole a book, and I put a rock in a microwave – it's hardly genius, is it?'

With a furrowed brow Dulko said, 'You put a rock in a what?'

'And what about Professor Thistle? This is his thing, not mine. I'm only here to re-establish a connection with my dad, not to change the world, or not ... to change the world. Oh, I'm getting really confused.'

'Who is Professor Thistle? Is he your father?'

'Oh God no. Wow, he is gonna be so pissed nobody knows who he is. What about these people who want to kill me? Who are they and why will it help them to have me dead?'

Dulko poured a glass of juice into a giant-sized mug. He offered it to Courtney and she gripped the very large handle with one hand whilst placing the other underneath for support.

'In this age, travel to the future has been banned,' said Dulko. 'The government has restricted time travel to visits to the past only, mainly for educational and recreational visits. You can basically observe the past, but that's it. Some believe it's a conspiracy. They say it's to stop people becoming obsessed with their own future, which would ultimately lead to the planet's detriment. However, some say it's because the government has been to the future, and it's a future where things are very bad, so they want to control public hysteria. Insiders say they are keeping it from us to stop a rebellion.'

'Ok, but I still don't see how it would help if I was dead.'

'Most people do want you to take the rock back, but once you have, they're going to kill you to stop any risk of you causing further complications. You see, they need time travel to exist, because throughout the ages, technology has been passed around like candy. Einstein, Da Vinci, even the seed for the invention of the wheel was given to the Sumerians, but worst of all was Gates.'

'Bill Gates?'

'The wheel changed everything but very slowly. There were no huge leaps or advances after its invention because it was just a simple change that helped us get things from A to B quicker and easier, but the computer ... well that changed everything far too quickly. That's why we are where we are now. Why do you think the computer age advanced so quickly in such a short space of time? Too much was released too fast. In just fifty years, your time achieved more relatively speaking, than the human race achieved in two thousand years. Why? Because of us – people from the future who think they know better than the people before them. What isn't a fact though, at least not yet anyway, is that you have to die.'

'Whoa, that's crazy. You're telling me that Microsoft was a product of time travel? I always thought that guy was too smart for his own good, but you're saying we're years ahead of ourselves artificially? If that's true, someone needs to go back and stop whoever is passing down all the technology.'

'That's exactly the sort of thinking that determined why they want you dead. Remember what I told you, your book has become a sort of new bible. There are some dangerous people who don't want you around to escalate the following it has. Religion clashes too much with their ethos, as well as the fact it goes too far back. Like I told you, the wheel was given to the Sumerians by someone who lived just five hundred years ago, not seven thousand years ago, and it wasn't all done by just one person. Then there's the fact that people can't actually change the past anyway.'

'Come again.'

'Which bit?'

'Break this down for me. How exactly do you travel to specific times anyway? I mean, I just jumped into a hole without a clue where it would go. I actually thought I was gonna die, yet here I am. Also, what do you mean people can't change the past? You just said everything in history exists because of people changing everything.'

'No, they haven't changed anything; it's the way it's always been. That's the problem.'

Courtney suddenly realised in that moment that all her theories and predictions on time and space could very well have been accurate. If the past, present and future were all running concurrently, then how could you possibly change anything? Could a young girl from a small town in Hertfordshire, England, really have got it so right? Presumptuously, she couldn't help but think that it perhaps should've been her notes that became the new bible.

'Let me explain a bit about time travel. Wait; did I really just say that to Courtney Nivots?'

'Yeah yeah, alright, just get on with it,' she said a little embarrassed.

'Sorry. Well basically, the size of rock you use determines how far forward you travel. So the one you exploded brought you here, but one of different dimensions would have taken you to another time altogether. In essence, you're exploding the equivalent of a small star, so as real stars in the universe are dying all the time and are all different sizes, we can use them to travel even farther forward by calculating the size of the rock or star to the exact millimetre.

'On the edge of space, circulating around the Earth right now are hundreds of these loopholes I mentioned. They've been pulled there artificially by placing large enough objects in front of them and using their natural gravitational pull to lure them closer and closer until they orbit the Earth. They have become the portals that we use and are the only way of travelling to the past. The holes are so large and contain so much energy that they eventually fold back in on themselves. At first you go forward, but eventually it takes you so far forward you come full circle and start to come from the beginning of time again, making time endless. Much like the Earth when they discovered it was round with no edge, no barrier and no wall,' he said in a very matter of fact manner.

'You go back by going forward? That's just crazy. And by crazy, I mean wicked.'

With a little uncertainty he asked, 'Crazy and wicked are good?'

'Absolutely, now tell me more.'

'We discovered that time is basically ever expanding, just like the universe. So if you travel forward in time at a certain speed, you will never hit a barrier where time ends, you'll just keep going. However, if you travel faster than time itself, you will catch up with it and start to come back on yourself, which would eventually bring you to the beginning of time. So if you continue to travel forward, you're taken into what would be your past. In a similar way, to if you started walking around planet Earth; you would never fall off or hit a barrier. You would simply come back to where you started.

'Think of it like this. Imagine the Universe and time are balls, and just like the Universe, they are constantly getting bigger every second. If you were inside that ball walking around the surface along the bottom but you were walking slower than the speed at which the ball is expanding, you would always be walking along the bottom. You would never reach the curve that will take you up and around to the top. However, if you could walk faster than the ball is expanding, then eventually, you would hit the curve, walk upside down along the top of the ball, come down the other side and end up eventually back where you started. This is why you can only travel forward in time, but if you go fast enough you can still visit the past by doing a full circle.'

'Amazing, truly amazing ... I am stunned. But why don't these loopholes kill us as soon as we enter them?'

'That's a very good question that nobody has the full

answer to just yet. My theory is that time wants us to travel. It's as simple as that. There are reasons and explanations that we probably aren't even aware of yet or can even comprehend, but somehow ... I think its helping us.'

'It? Time is an 'it'?'

'Maybe, I don't know. Certainly when I was a child, that's what I used to imagine; that it was helping me fulfil my dreams.'

'Mr Time,' she whispered.

'Pardon?'

'Oh nothing, go on.'

'Anyway, that's not important. The fact is, we are able to travel through time and these portals are used to travel back to revisit history for tourism or educational purposes.'

'So why is there no record from the past of time travellers ever being seen?'

'Because as soon as people cross the point where time starts again from the beginning, we drop out-of-sync with everything and become invisible. We can't be seen, can't be heard and can't touch anything, making it impossible for anyone to change the past. Almost like a communication device that's not tuned correctly.

'However, that only applies to organic matter. There is an exception where material things, solid matter or devices are concerned. They can be left in the past to influence it. They just exist wherever they are, whenever they are. Don't ask me why, but I guess there is just no paradox when an object meets another object.'

Courtney thought for a moment. 'So I get back to my time through the same loophole? Kind of doing it in reverse?'

He smiled at her with a glint in his eye. 'Correct. If you use the same loophole you originally used, it will place you back exactly at the moment you left to go forward, putting you back in sync with your own time.'

'What if I use a different loophole?'

'Well first, you'll end up at a slightly different time, but it won't matter. Time won't let you exist in the same moment as another you. In other words you can't go back in time and talk to yourself. You'll stay invisible until the you from the past leaves to come into the future as you originally did.'

She listened intently to every single word that had come out of his mouth. What she just heard was not only massively life-changing and history-defining for the whole planet, it was also the single most amazing piece of information she had ever been privy to. Even though it was such a huge thing that she was listening to, it was also the most personal; like her childhood dreams were being realised right in front of her. Just as she was basking in all the wonderful, new and exciting information, every wall in the room flashed green. 'What's going on, have they found us?'

'No, no, don't panic. It's just somebody trying to contact me. Hang on.' He remained seated and looked into the air. A second later, he was connected to the call via his mind. 'Hello? Just one second.' He turned to face Courtney, who had her mouth open at the sight of him talking on his 'mind phone'. 'Sorry, I need to take this, I'll just step outside.' He got up, walked through the wall and disappeared outside.

Courtney was left on her own, sat on Dulko's floating sofa in his floating house, looking out through his huge clear wall at an uninterrupted futuristic yet breathtakingly open view that stretched for miles. She sat there in silence, too scared to even attempt to walk across the living room floor.

Dulko floated above the house, suspended in his PEU. He spoke with the voice of Eramask (a female with a stern and authoritative tone) through the Energy Communication System, or the ECS for short. To the outside eye, he looked as though he was talking to himself. Elements of the future were not so different after all. 'What the hell are you doing calling me while I'm still talking with her? I'm still trying to gain her trust.'

'Time is short, Mr Dulko. Have you found anything that could discredit her?'

He remained silent for a moment, thinking about Courtney's revelation regarding the book. 'No, not yet, but you won't need it. Trust me; she's going to help us. I've told her you're going to kill her. But don't panic; it's all part of getting her to trust me. She has to trust me to do what we ask, and I think I just about have her exactly where we want her.'

'I hope that's true for your sake. We spent a long time selecting the right person for this task – a very long time. It would be catastrophic for us all if you turned out to be the wrong choice, Mr Dulko.'

'I promise you, I'm not. Just let me get back to her before she gets suspicious, which will make my job even harder.'

'For all our sakes, I'm glad you understand the importance of what you have been selected for. You have twenty four hours, Mr Dulko. Do not fail.'

'I promise you, I won't. Just make sure you take care of the professor and I'll do my job.'

The line went silent for a few seconds.

'Twenty four hours, Mr Dulko. Your presence and all our futures up here rest on it.'

The communication ceased and he remained for a while in the air above his house. He then took a very deep breath, lowered back down to the floating street and just before re-entering and with a little melancholy he said, 'One may smile, and smile, and be a villain.'

~ CHAPTER THIRTY EIGHT ~

It's a good job you're ok

Courtney found herself somewhat more relaxed now that she had been in the future for a few hours. What seemed so unreal to begin with now felt a little more tangible and less like she'd taken some kind of hallucinogenic. Time had slightly eased the uncertainties she had on arrival, and she used that tiny piece of confidence as she waited for Dulko to return. Being very careful she tentatively had a look around his home. After a moment or two of subtly sniffing around with her eyes, she just couldn't help herself and began to really investigate his living quarters with full gusto. She didn't want to get caught snooping, so she had to be quite quick, but she just as quickly realised that there was not many clues about anyway; nothing that gave any details about who he was. There were no photos, no personal items or even any magazines giving away clues as to what he liked to do in his spare time. The whole place was incredibly sparse and she couldn't help but wonder if it was something she should be concerned about or if it was just a relevant style choice in that time, especially given their technology. She scrunched her face up and muttered, 'So ... who are you really?'

Just as she finished her sentence Dulko re-entered his house. There was no great warning as he silently floated back in, so upon seeing him she quickly jolted to a neutral position as if she had been caught shoplifting. To cover up her guilt she quickly asked, 'How do you do anything in here?' 'You know, for fun. This place is so empty. What about music or movies?'

233

Dulko looked at her with a slightly sombre expression; no doubt a result of his conversation outside, as it didn't seem he was too concerned with Courtney's prying. He lifted his head toward the clear wall that she was facing and closed his eyes for a second.

Immediately, a dramatic movie that was set during the time when most of the planet was submerged under water, played on all four walls, as well as the floor and ceiling. The entire room had become a movie and Courtney was sitting like a tennis umpire, directly in the middle of it all. Seemingly floating above the action that was all around her, she could no longer see any hint that she was just in a room. She watched as torrential rain and huge waves swallowed famous landscapes that she recognised from her time. She was literally sitting dead centre in an amazing 4D world; the likes of which she had never seen before. The sound blasted out of the walls all around her but with no sign of any speakers anywhere. It just emanated as if the action was really happening right in front of her. 'I feel like Ebenezer Scrooge. Are you sure you're not the ghost of Christmas past,' she yelled above the noise. She soared through the waves and destruction dodging obstacles with acute precision. 'Whoa. Ok, ok, I'm starting to feel sick. I get it. Turn it off, please. I'm not quite ready for that level of realism. I still even find documentaries hard to watch.'

The movie stopped and the images immediately went back to being walls. Courtney hadn't moved an inch. 'This is reality TV with a capital 'R'. How is that done?'

'It's footage from the past edited together into a movie. It's one of the many benefits of time travel. If you can't afford the very expensive trip back in time, you can watch it in a movie instead.' Dulko spoke with a blank and not very impressed look on his face. He was clearly still distracted by the previous communication. 'We need to go now though. Someone's been tracking us.'

Her cheery mood dropped and became a slightly concerned one instead. 'What do we do?'

'I'll need to get you equipped with your own PEU. It

involves a small surgical procedure but don't worry, it's nothing intrusive like in your day. I've seen historic documents of the way they used to actually stick metal contraptions inside your body.'

'You mean surgical instruments?'

'I mean the metal objects they used to use to cut your body open with. I don't think giving them a name takes away how gruesome they are. Anyway, I have a friend who used to work for the government; he can sort yours out, nice and cleanly, and with the additional capability of space support.'

She looked at him in wonder with eyes wide as she slowly mouthed 'Space support.'

'It will allow you to breath in space. The loophole you'll need to enter to take you back to a point before you left is above the atmosphere. It's usually only available for the very rich as a way of getting them to the surface when they go on their privileged group tours of history. Also, many years ago, before crime pretty much ceased up here, there used to be a special unit of the police force that used a robot interface on their limbs, called PAL – Power Assisted Limbs. I'll also have him equip you with this to give you added strength. You'll need it to carry the rock into space where you'll enter the loophole. It will take you back in time to the exact moment that you need to be. Then, as I've explained, you'll become invisible; enabling you to leave the rock in the cellar and putting in motion the events that lead you right back here with me.'

All through his speech, Courtney looked at him with a perplexed look on her face. 'I'm glad it's so simple. If it was in any way complicated, I don't know what I'd do,' she said with only a hint of sarcasm.

Dulko wondered if he had done the right thing in deceiving her. He actually really liked Courtney and contrary to what he had told Eramask, he was having a few doubts about what they were up to. However, with a hefty reward on offer for his services, he knew that jeopardising the mission now was too risky for all who were involved.

'So I suppose I'm going to know you for the rest of

eternity, as we go round in circles doing this an infinite amount of times. Well all I can say is, it's a good job you're ok.'

Dulko remained silent, a prisoner in his own guilt.

Courtney however was clearly feeling quite perky and said, 'So what are we waiting for? As has been said once before in history, apparently by a now very famous female time traveller ... let's do this.'

He stared at her and felt a genuine warmth and vulnerability that almost made him tell her everything right there on the spot. From a young age he had been fascinated by the origins of time travel and had built up lots of adoration for the historical figure that was Courtney Nivots. He could never quite believe that he had been born during the time when she was due to visit and always promised himself that he would do whatever it took to meet her once she arrived.

However, he knew there was a darker side to his present; a side nobody wanted to shout about, where everything still revolved around money as it had throughout time. Yet the worst part of it all was that you needed money to live in the relative comfort and safety of the sky. Anyone that could not afford it was left to survive on the harsh terrain of the Earth's surface and work to maintain the people above them. Most died young from the sweltering conditions and varying forms of mutated diseases, as well as the fact that food and natural resources were sparse. The government said there were simply too many people to accommodate and not enough money.

The planet had turned into a structure that had only one government ruling all, with no official religion and only two societies; the aptly named 'Gods', and the 'Earth Dwellers', one maintaining the other. The sole responsibility of the Earth Dwellers was harvesting food and controlling waste, as well as any other manual and dirty jobs that society needed doing, while the Gods lived in comparative utopia. The Earth Dwellers were the worker bees and the Gods were the queens. One lived in hope of attaining the other's status, whilst the other lived in fear of being reprimanded and banished to live out life at ground level.

Dulko was actually an Earth Dweller by birth and knew that if he had remained down there, he would never have got the chance to be considered as 'Guardian to the Visitor'. When he was selected to be her guardian, it came with a promise of money and the security of becoming a God if their instructions were followed implicitly.

They had chosen Dulko due to his classic good looks and charm, something that research had told them young girls from Courtney's time were more likely to respond to. It was now a rarity in men, simply because there was a distinct lack of men altogether.

The female gene had become the dominant one and there was now only one man for every hundred women; a result of science replacing men's main attributes. Many believed that the male species had two main purposes. The first was to procreate and populate the planet, but that had been replaced by childbirth technology that no longer required men. The second was to go out and hunt for food, but that attribute had not been needed for many thousands of years.

So as much as women used to enjoy the companionship of men, the need for them slowly disappeared and the human race evolved accordingly. With the world needing fewer men for the survival of the human race, nature had stopped them being made quite as often.

Yet every now and again, someone very unique was born – a smart, strong and handsome male like Dulko. This made him very special – but only as long as Courtney was around.

Dulko had well and truly dug himself into a giant hole, but in his opinion, it was a hole worth occupying to get the opportunity of meeting a very special young lady whom he truly revered.

After a long pause reflecting on everything, he looked up at her, smiled and said, 'Yes ... let's do this.'

~ CHAPTER THIRTY NINE ~

Gods of the sky

A day had passed since Courtney had agreed to Dulko's incredible plan. Of course that was just Courtney's perception of it, as everything in her world seemed pretty incredible right now. In that time, they had been extremely busy getting everything prepared for what she would have to do in order to succeed. Dulko had taken her to a secret location on the planet's surface, telling her that he had been made aware of the place by a mysterious female within Eramask's team who seemed to want to help in causing Eramask some added trouble. He said she only communicated via PAL, so he had never actually met with whoever it was, but she seemed to want to make sure Courtney was fitted with the technology Dulko had mentioned she would need for her monumental task. The procedure was straightforward, to the point where Courtney barely even knew anything had been implanted. Everything went exactly the way Dulko had said it would, with no problems and no pain, giving her very few reasons to distrust anything he said.

The longer the two of them spent together, the closer they were becoming. Time had brought them together in such a manner that it would be hard to deny their destinies were meant to intertwine, like a rare and beautiful total-solar-eclipse. Yet time was also the thing that would appear to ironically want to keep them apart, with their destinies seemingly pointing to the fact that they couldn't ultimately exist for very long in the same moment just as the moon would always eventually pass by its very occasional life partner. Courtney felt that Dulko was quite possibly the nicest man she had ever met, someone who truly appreciated everything she had to say and certainly wasn't scared nor threatened by her intelligence.

In some ways, she knew that he was not as smart as her, but being from her future, and having over one thousand years of knowledge at his disposal she couldn't help but think that she may have found her perfect match.

For the first time, Courtney had experienced what it felt like to have a man really care for her and treat her with total respect. The first time she didn't have to hide anything about her past or what her beliefs were. The first time she could just simply be Courtney. However, she was finding it hard to understand why any creator would put that one person she could actually relate to, over a thousand years in her future. She looked over to Dulko who was now sat on a seat fashioned out of an old park bench with oil barrels placed inside where the seat would normally be. Courtney was lying on a hammock made from plastic sheets used previously for D.I.Y. and construction, feeling utterly exhausted and trying to get some rest after all she had been through; knowing what she had to come.

'The plan is set for when it turns dark,' whispered Dulko. 'Two hours after sunset. There will be a flying ban in force once the sun goes down to stop any midair collisions occurring. For an inexperienced flyer it'll be easier to sneak you up into space to enter the loophole then, as the traffic flow will be substantially less. All I have to do is shut down the central tracking systems so nobody knows you're up there.'

Courtney believed him, as she simply had no reason not to. However, Dulko knew full well there was no such ban and that the advanced tracking technology meant that as long as the PEUs were set to follow a pre-registered course, it would be virtually impossible to crash. Courtney had witnessed that fact when she first arrived, but as everything she had experienced was so overwhelming, it had slipped her mind. Dulko looked at her as she took in what he had said, but she stared back at him blankly with no response. She could barely keep her eyes open after all the day had beset upon her, and she struggled to keep listening to his endless technical talk until eventually her eyes permanently closed up shop for the night; just like the moment when a puppy has been hyperactive all day and she finally slumps down to rest but resists desperately in fear it may miss out on something exciting. As she lay there peacefully asleep, Dulko continued to watch her, silently taking in all her energy and beauty. Now she was asleep he could reflect on how guilty he felt about everything. He knew that the government had actually put in force a local area flying ban at the specific time he'd told Courtney to fly, allowing her to follow through with her mission smoothly and without any interruptions.

The people of the sky city had been aware of Courtney's arrival for hundreds of years and had been taught as children that her actions were what the world depended on for survival. Unwittingly, the whole world was actually in on the deception.

Up in the sky, people were at home or at work, thinking about what the next few days had in store for them and ultimately whether they would even exist in a few days' time. Most were petrified. They had waited a long time for the day to come, and if all the theories were wrong and the future was not pre-destined, they knew they would really need Courtney to succeed. So as the monumental evening arrived, they sat at home on tenterhooks, wondering whether the years of government planning were going to save them, allowing them to carry on with their comfortable, safe and normal lives. Satellites had been set up to track her every move and her progress would be watched by millions around the world in the comfort of their Personal Energy Residences, or PERs. It was twenty four hour news coverage on a whole other level, and Courtney was totally oblivious to it all.

Down on the surface it was very different, as stories of

government deception were prevalent. The Earth Dwellers were resentful at the way the rich were allowed to live in comparative luxury and were convinced that the government was doing very little to make it any different.

The people felt they had just been left to suffer on little or no land. Most of the only liveable terrain was used to harvest food, predominantly for the Gods. So they were forced to live on muddy raised terrain where nothing much grew and the only food they had were minimal supplies that the authorities dropped out of the sky in little packages at periodic intervals.

The weather made the land below practically uninhabitable as it was too fierce to build any kind of society on. They merely existed like enslaved zombies as opposed to living any kind of decent life. Most were convinced that there must be another option; something that would help the whole planet survive, not just the self-appointed Gods in the sky.

However as much as they prayed and wondered, most knew there was nothing they could actually do. All they were left with was the hope that some other genuine God would eventually change something; something that would make their pitiful existences count for something once again ... something really worth living for.

~ CHAPTER FORTY ~

Thuntenn

Somewhere in an uninhabited section on the outskirts of the sky city, a huge contrast to the despair down below was taking place. Quite possibly the largest and most loved sporting event of the time was being contested; Thuntenn.

Thuntenn was the juxtaposition of finding fun in the very thing that had long ago caused all the misery on the planet's surface. A game played literally on top of swirling dark thunderclouds; clouds that had become a permanent fixture in the sky ever since the Earth's temperatures had changed for the worse.

Around the world, there were a number of relatively permanent rain clouds the size of an entire city which were constantly bursting full of electrical storms, causing huge lightning bolts to occur. Eruptions of thunder followed each other with a regular aggression and the electrical charges came so frequently that it was impossible to tell when the thunder and lightning would strike again – they just knew it would, and very soon.

The trick everyone learnt from their ancestor's childhood of counting how many miles away the storm was by how many seconds the thunder followed the lightning was impossible as well as totally unnecessary. The venues were chosen for their specific attributes of being directly in the centre of the storms.

A huge and joyful crowd of thousands were all standing (yet floating) in their individual PEUs around a huge circular section of the cloud, cheering every hard-earned point. A number of the PEUs were darkly tinted as a privacy measure for VIP guests, but no matter whom you were, everyone found the whole thing exhilarating. Thuntenn was the ultimate game; a test of acute agility, as well as the added unpredictability of the lightning bolts.

Two female players were hovering millimetres above the rain cloud on either side of the circle, trying to collide with the lightning bolts whilst at the same time hitting, with incredible force, an artificially created ball of energy across the circle. Both players were using racquets that strongly resembled the historic game of tennis – only they were bigger, much bigger.

In one of the tinted PEUs at the very back of the crowd was Eramask, standing six foot five inches tall. Her face was harsh and gaunt, and she sported a short, cropped brown hairstyle; certainly not traditionally attractive. Although she wore a dress, she also didn't look particularly feminine. She was very skinny and her dress was long, tight and black; a colour she was convinced reminded everyone that she was a government official. The length and fit also suggested that she was very much in control – almost like a strict headmistress, choosing to wear the outfit as a sign of her authority, rather than walk around wearing next to nothing like most other members of the population. In her modern society, it was not unusual for women to hold such high positions, as they now outnumbered men quite significantly. On her feet, she wore matching killer high heels, convinced that if she towered above others, it would help accentuate her position of power; giving her a distinct superiority complex whenever she was looking down on those she was dealing with. There was also a rush of energy and a strong sense of self-worth, like a drug that kept her needing to be more and more in control; a feeling that was multiplied threefold because stood next to her was a very special visitor from the past who was utilizing the same PEU; Professor Pik Thistle.

After his initial shock at having seen the vortex in Courtney's garden, he convinced Alexandra that he was there to rescue Courtney. With her help, they quickly created another hole that he immediately jumped in to, with the hope of following Courtney to wherever she may have gone.

For many years, the government in the future had examined the past diligently and so knew Professor Thistle had followed Courtney very soon after she had jumped into the first hole. So as soon as he arrived, they brought him up into the sky and begun their manipulation by taking him to the best loved sporting event of the time.

They had concluded that if the past was at all changeable, it must start from the moment Professor Thistle arrived, by getting him on their side. However, they had a cunning plan that they believed would work for them either way.

Some years ago, a special unit of the government was set up to take care of future events; in particular, Courtney and Professor Thistle's arrival. The government needed to make sure that things went exactly how they wanted them to.

Eramask was placed in control of the special operation with anyone or anything available at her disposal. On succeeding her objective, she and anyone else involved were assured permanent residence above the clouds for the rest of eternity – however long that may be.

As Professor Thistle stood next to the towering leader, taking in the peculiarities of the match, it was obvious he was having trouble with the rules that were being explained to him. At the same time, he was also trying to understand how they were even floating above the clouds in the first place.

'If the ball of energy hits a lightning bolt ...,' explained Eramask. '... it is destroyed, and the player who struck it loses a point. Each player has one hundred points to start with, and the first to lose all their points loses the match. If a player is struck by lightning, they get an energy boost and can fly high above the arena to receive a free smash of the ball, straight down towards the other player. If the receiving player can keep it in play, they can carry on and try to win the point. It's all about anticipation.'

'That's wonderful, really wonderful, and scientifically it's ridiculously intriguing. However, I know I'm not here to become an aficionado of ...'

'Thuntenn,' said Eramask, showing a vague hint of a smile. The fact that her face looked like she had bitten a lemon, gave a small clue that smiling was not something she was accustomed to.

'Thuntenn?'

'Yes, I believe it derives from a historic game that's no longer played, called tennis. Maybe you've heard of it. I suppose the Thun is short for thunder. Do you know, I never really thought about it until now?' She looked at him, a little surprised that his arrival had forced her to learn something new.

'It's fascinating, it really is, and I'm glad I've helped widen your understanding of the past. Quite honestly though, I'm just a little perturbed about being here in the middle of some kind of female growth experiment, watching a game that involves being struck by lightning, whilst floating in midair with two hundred thousand other freakishly large women surrounding me. So could you please let me know what it is you want with me, because I'm quite sure I didn't come one thousand years into the future to watch sports?'

'You certainly didn't. I just thought it may help ease you into everything. But you seem like a straightforward man, so I'll get straight to the point. You came to help us, and in doing so ... we may just be able to help you.'

'Help you do what exactly?'

'Save us, Professor Thistle. That is, if you still really want to cement your place in history.'

His eyes widened as he listened to what sounded like a direct attempt at appealing to his deep-seated aspirations.

At that moment, the crowd cheered in response to a particularly long rally in the match below.

'We need you to make sure history follows its rightful path and help make sure time travel lives forever. Our society and all future societies depend on it. If you can help us do this, we can make sure you also get what you want.'

'And I suppose you know what that is?'

'How does your name recorded in history, as the first man

to travel through time sound? Not to mention being known as the one who saved us all?'

He took in a deep breath as he contemplated her very appealing proposition.

'I know all about you,' said Eramask. 'What you want and what you missed out on. But that's only after extensive research. That girl, on the other hand ... people can barely speak a sentence without her name being mentioned. Maybe it's time you changed that.'

Suddenly an energy ball from the match smashed into their PEU, causing a huge cheer from the thousands watching. For a moment though, Eramask's tinted PEU became transparent due to the electricity of the ball, allowing a brief glimpse inside.

'We need to go,' said Eramask. She feared the crowd may have noticed Professor Thistle, as there were not many who were capable of growing a beard in that time. She needed to keep a relative calm in order for the upcoming events to run smoothly. 'Hold on, I'm going to show you something amazing.'

'And what would that be, another one of your great sporting events?'

She grabbed hold of him tightly, looked down into his eyes and said, 'No, no more sports ... just the real reason why you're here.'

~ CHAPTER FORTY ONE ~

Putting your name in the history books

Just as the sun was setting across the sky, Eramask and Professor Thistle came to a stop high above the floating metropolis, high enough so that they could see for miles. The red from the sun had created a beautifully coloured landscape that majestically blended with many different brightly coloured energy residences below. Dark purplish and black rain clouds swirled dramatically underneath; a magnificent sight and one that could capture anybody's heart and imagination, whatever time you were from.

'You certainly never get a view like this from Sears Tower. It's ... unbelievable,' said Professor Thistle with genuine sentiment.

'Yes it is, Mr Thistle. This is our world, our home. It's all we know. As you can imagine we've come to love it, and we'd like to keep it that way. We couldn't begin to tell you what the people would do if anything were to get in the way of what they have built for themselves over hundreds of years.'

'You mean what you've built? Which brings me to how you all ended up in the clouds in the first place? What exactly did you do?' He was working on the assumption that governments never change no matter what timeframe you are in.

'This all started a very long time ago I assure you; way before I was ever here. Mistakes were made in the past, but it's right now that counts, that's important. Everything we've done was with the people in mind, always with the people in mind. There would be no need for anyone to be here to look after them and build this better world if the people themselves weren't here. Would there?'

Professor Thistle remained silent for a moment as he tried to comprehend what he considered to be a slightly twisted logic. 'I'm still missing what this has got to do with me.'

'I'm going to level with you, Mr Thistle. You've come from our past so we know all about you. You may not be recognised by the masses, but we've built up a profile on you, and we know why you do what you do.'

'I want my place in the history books, right?' He smiled and looked directly at Eramask. 'So tell me ... how exactly can I achieve that?'

'We've been to the future, Mr Thistle. It's one where people are not so happy. It would seem technology only takes us so far before it comes back and bites us. Being up here instead of on the planet's surface was just the beginning of that.

'We're not here through choice are we? Nobody chooses to be born during a particular time. But as this is the time my people were placed in, we've made it comfortable. We've adapted. If we were to tell everyone, or let them see the future for themselves, everything you see below you would end. The world would go into panic. The only way we can maintain this level of comfort is with the age-old remedy – money. Oh, as well as keeping an element of power and fear of course.'

'Right ... so how exactly do you generate this money?'

'Time travel to the past. It's a commodity, like oil was for so long in your day. When all the oil finally ran out, we needed something else. I'm sure you understand that in order for governments to work, we will always need something that the public need. Tourists pay huge amounts of money to see how their history unfolded. See things as they happened, when they happened; they just can't resist it. But we cannot change the past; it's just physically not possible. Therefore, our futures will come, no matter what.

'That's why you and Courtney are so important. You were there at the beginning. You are the one window that did change the world forever, because you were the first.'

Professor Thistle's heart was palpitating at the scale of what was being said to him.

'We need to make sure time travel always exists, or we will all *cease* to exist a hell of a lot sooner than we are supposed to.'

'I'm failing to see what I can do if it's already happened?'

'That's just it, it hasn't. Very soon, Courtney is going to take back to your time the key to time travel's future, but there is no real reason we can find to say that it has to be her. It's just how it is, or was.'

'Of course,' said Professor Thistle in realisation. 'The meteor rock – that's the key isn't it? She took it back and placed it in her cellar, didn't she?'

'Not yet she hasn't, so it could still be you. It doesn't matter who it is as long as it happens. What's to stop you taking her place and putting your name in the history books?'

'Why would you want to change history like that? How would that benefit the world? What would you gain out of it? If Courtney's going to do it anyway, then–'

Eramask looked directly into his eyes with a serious determination before cutting him off mid-sentence. 'Quite simply, two chances at success. We'll give you everything you need to take her place and then it's up to you to get there first. What we have learned about you and your character is that you'll do anything to erase her name from the history databases. We were right in that appraisal ... weren't we, Mr Thistle?'

He contemplated what had been said, but it was so much to take in, he couldn't help but wonder what the future he was standing in would look like, if neither of them had ever come there. Would it mean time travel wouldn't exist at all? What else has time travel done to us? Professor Thistle wondered.

'Do you really want her to take all the credit, a girl with no real qualifications? This world reveres her, hailing her Red Bible as some kind of new order – a religion of sorts. She needs to be stopped or people will go back to the days of killing each other for what they believe in. That kind of existence is no good for anyone.'

Professor Thistle was about to say that he in fact was responsible for the red book but he stopped after hearing the resentment in Eramask's voice. 'So who are you, the Roman empire?'

Eramask scowled at his comment which appeared to strike a nerve. 'I know who you are. You're a nobody and you always will be unless you do something about it. It took a lot of digging for us to find any mention of you in history. Is that really what you want your life to be?'

'You're pitting me against her, to discredit her and ensure your immediate survival?'

'Is there something wrong with wanting to survive? What do you care anyway? As long as you get your name embedded in the minds of all future generations to come you'll be happy. You'll be long dead before all of this transpires and isn't that why you're really here anyway?'

Professor Thistle thought hard for a moment.

'The clock is ticking. The window of opportunity is closing. We don't have long to put the plan in place.'

'Where is Courtney now?'

'We'll get to that. First, I need your answer. Will you help us?'

In that moment, every thought and every dream Professor Thistle had ever had on what his life would and could become, as well as the newly added quote that he had scribbled on his framed parchment paper, flashed through his mind. He looked at Eramask and with a determined expression said, 'Show me what you want me to do. You're right – it's about time I fixed this mess.'

~ CHAPTER FORTY TWO ~

Our Future

Vertigo was not really a condition that Courtney had ever had to deal with before. She wasn't under the impression she suffered from it, but she never really had any experiences with any great degrees of height before where it would become evident. There were a few ladders and the odd tree in the woods, but as she floated high above the Earth and the clouds, closer to the stars and farther away from the planet's surface than she ever thought it was possible to be, she wondered if vertigo was even a worthy enough word to describe what she was feeling. Whatever it was, it had temporarily frozen her to the spot.

Everywhere was dark in the night sky and the dead silence was ironically deafening, or perhaps it was just a natural inbuilt tinnitus that she never even knew she had, made apparent by a peace so fierce that it may even have been the minute workings of her own brain that she could hear.

Courtney's PEU had been specifically programmed so that she did not have to worry about doing anything herself. She'd been told that it would automatically take her to the loophole that she would need to enter, as she did not want to risk entering the wrong hole by using her own inexperienced intuition. However, what panicked her most was the thought of having to make her own way from outer space all the way to her house in Hertfordshire once she reached the other side. So as she floated high above the world, she waited for the sign, holding in her arms the rock that she had last seen on the floor in the cellar of her house. After the struggle she had with Alexandra when they tried to move it, she couldn't believe how easy it now was to carry; a result of being implanted with the PAL system.

PAL consisted of small round discs under the skin of each of the user's joints that connect to the axons and receive messages from the motor neurons in the spinal cord via the brain. The discs intercept these messages whenever the user goes to move muscles in their body. They instantaneously send a message back to the brain, telling it to use all the stored energy that was previously reserved for life threatening situations; moments that were occasionally seen in history and regarded as miracles. Like when mothers rescue their trapped children from upturned cars by lifting the seemingly impossible weight and flipping it over with ease. The brain then sends back another message by shooting out impulses from the motor neurons down to the muscles telling them to react appropriately and giving the user incredible strength. With all of it being done in a split second the user would become almost super human. They had been placed on the underside of each of Courtney's wrists, the elbows and the backs of her knees as well as one under each foot. She remembered seeing something like it before back in her time, albeit a primitive version; a natural adaptation and evolution of the full robot body suit that was first developed in the year 2005 by Japanese scientists.

'The evolvement of time really is the true miracle. It seems we really can achieve anything, if we are given enough time to do so,' said Courtney in reflection.

While she was waiting for Dulko to send her into space, she thought about testing the system a little. She attempted to move around by using her mind, just as she had seen Dulko do before when she first arrived. *Go up two feet at two miles an hour.* Yet nothing happened. 'Oh ... Go.' Still nothing happened. 'Oh, of course, it has to read my thoughts.' *Go.* She then proceeded to move straight upwards, the exact distance and speed she had thought about. Smiling to herself she started to feel a bit more comfortable with her surroundings. Although she appeared to be floating, she felt like she was standing on solid ground, so she stamped her feet gently to test it further and then a bit harder, as she began to play around a little. *Move left five feet at ten miles per hour. Go.* She quickly swished left the second her thought was read. 'Whooo,' she yelled. Her heart was beating fast from the adrenaline that was pumping through her veins.

Every time she had experienced something wonderful in the last few days, she did not think it could be surpassed. Yet floating high above everything, learning how to fly, truly topped it all. The tears of joy in her eyes were proof of that.

Drop down five miles at one hundred miles an hour. Go, she screamed in her head excitedly, getting a little bit carried away. In a split second she had dropped down at a tremendous speed, and the reality of what was happening suddenly hit her like a clear glass door that you don't expect to be there. 'Aaaaarrrgggghhhhhhh,' she cried out, but sure enough, she came to a complete stop after five miles.

Unbeknownst to her, the rest of the world was watching on and laughing together at her playfulness and naivety, caused by the lack of experience with their technology. She'd been told that her thoughts need not be so literal and that soon the technology would merge completely with her mind allowing her to control it seamlessly, but that wasn't helping her in these initial moments and with absolutely no idea she was being observed and with abundant joy she said, 'Wowwww! Oh my, that was sooo cool. This even beats the Vortex ride at the town fair.'

At that moment, a voice began to transmit through the PEU's communication interface. 'Courtney?'

'Dulko?'

'What are you doing? You're not ready for that, you need to be careful.'

'Oh my God, this is amazing though. I can't believe what is happening here. Oh man, I so wish my family could be here to witness what I'm doing. This is just so wonderful.'

A silence between the two permeated the airwaves before Dulko plucked up enough courage to speak. 'I know I'm not family, but *I* am here, and I think you're doing a wonderful job. As long as you don't lose concentration again and start darting around the sky like a balloon with a hole.'

She smiled and thought for a moment. 'I know you're here, and honestly, I wouldn't be able to do any of this without you. You've been great. It's just ... my father died when I was born, and from the age of five my mum wrote me off because I used to see ghosts. Then she died in a car accident still thinking I was a nut. So I just wish ... I just wish that they could've been here to see this. I know they would have been so proud and maybe ... just maybe, I would have had an easier and happier childhood and my mum wouldn't have died with the thought that her only daughter was a loon.' Her voice broke slightly with the sentiment.

Dulko listened intently, knowing that he'd heard real emotion in her voice and couldn't help but wonder if there was anything he could do to help her; to help alleviate some of her pain.

After hundreds of years of being a figure in history that he idolised, she had now become a lot more tangible to him. If only her mother had believed her. Maybe then, her pain would leave her.

'Oh God, listen to me,' said Courtney, as she wiped away a tear. 'I can't believe what I'm saying. Don't listen to anything I say, ok' She raised her chin in a gesture of confidence, trying to mask her emotion. 'Right, are we doing this thing?'

'We're just about ready to go, but ... I just want you to-if I could think of any way of erasing your pain, I would do it for you in a second. That ... I promise you.'

'I told you, don't listen to me. I'm just being ridiculous, but thank you anyway, that's kind of sweet.'

Around the world, onlookers could feel the obvious connection between them with many shedding tears in response to something most had not seen between a man and a woman throughout their entire lives.

'Courtney, we're nearly set to go. I think it's all clear up there now. Just bear with me for one second while I get clarification from my sources.'

'Ok, I'm not going anywhere.'

Dulko was sitting on his sofa, in his house some three thousand feet below Courtney. The back and side walls were grey, but the front wall had Courtney's every movement covered. Every possible angle of her was plastered in separate boxes across the entire wall and was split into ten different sections. He looked at the screens and 'sound muted' appeared over every image of Courtney. The box directly in the middle was then replaced with an image of Eramask.

'Everything is set, you may proceed Mr Dulko.'

'Why do you look so worried? What's happened?'

'Nothing's happened and nothing will, as long as you do what you're paid for and get her moving.'

'What about the professor?'

'The professor is not your concern.'

'What exactly do you have planned? If you are putting Courtney in any danger, I swear I'll pull the plug on this.'

'Mr Dulko, you seem to forget what's at stake here. If you do anything to put this moment at risk, none of us will exist tomorrow. This really isn't the time for negotiation. We are seconds away from what we've waited all our lifetimes for. Do you really want to be held responsible for the destruction of the planet? Let alone your family's immediate happiness and freedom?'

He sensed her panic and felt a surge of confidence run through him. He quickly realised that if there was ever a time to get answers to questions that usually would not be entertained, it was now, when everything was at stake. Nonchalantly he asked, 'Why aren't we allowed to see our future?'

'I just told you, this isn't the time, Mr–'

'On the contrary, this is exactly the time,' he yelled back. 'What is the real reason? Why?'

Eramask became silent as she realised the seriousness of his intention.

'I am ten seconds away from telling Courtney to abandon the mission and you better believe she'll listen to me. If you want this to go to plan, you'll tell me what I want to know.'

After another few seconds of contemplation, Eramask calmly said, 'We're all dead.' She then became louder and angrier the more she revealed. 'Ok? Everybody's dead. But there is nothing we can do. Trust me, we've tried and thought about everything. We need her to do this so that we can look after everyone, at least for the time we have left. What do you expect us to do? Announce to everyone that their children have no future? We're out of options. When the ice caps melted, that was your God telling us to get off his planet. Well guess what, we did, but it seems not far enough and soon he will take his ultimate revenge for killing his paradise, by taking away our world completely.'

Dulko was stunned at the revelation and could barely think what to say in response, so he did the only thing he could think of and cut Eramask off his screen. All he could see in front of him was Courtney who was patiently and innocently waiting for her next set of instructions. However Dulko knew that he now had a very important decision to make – and fast.

~ CHAPTER FORTY THREE ~

The road to hell

Courtney could do nothing but wait as she floated high above the Earth. Dulko on the other hand was in a state of panic. He and everyone else living down on the surface had suspected something about the motives of the government regarding their policy on travelling to the future for a long time. The only ones oblivious were those up in the sky. They were happy to continue without asking any difficult questions, so long as they were made to feel safe and comfortable.

He had to make a quick decision though. A lot was at stake and his communication alarm was going crazy. He squeezed his eyes tight and reconnected with Eramask. 'You did this, didn't you? You did this to us. Thousands of years of government after government, thinking only of yourselves, your jobs and whatever else made your lives convenient even if it was at the expense of the less privileged. And now it's too late to put it right. You failed the human race with your arrogance and deception and now you want to place the blame on a God that you destroyed.'

'We all played our part, Mr Dulko and here you are, playing yours. This is what needs to be done right now. This is what's best for everyone.'

They both went silent as Dulko thought about that exact point; what is best for everyone?

'I'll make sure some more funds go down to the surface. I promise; I'll make it my personal project. But please, just tell Courtney to go – now. We have very little time left.'

Dulko thought about what she had said and realised that the least he could do was secure some kind of better future for the deprived society where he was raised. As much as he hated the reality, he realised there was very little that could be done about it, and he knew that as much as he despised her, Eramask was right. He needed to do what he could for the people that were still alive. 'Fine, I'll do it. Yet again I'll have to put my faith in the government, even when I know you're screwing us. You have an amazing knack of destroying us and then standing up as the only hope of any help or survival. What other choice do I have? But know this, there are many people dying down there and it's your conscience that you'll have to wrestle with if you break your word.'

'Mr Dulko, please. We don't have time for sentimentality. Let Courtney know that the path is clear and that nobody is going to get in her way.'

Eramask's image disappeared from the screen and was replaced with Courtney again. Dulko sat and stared at all the screens for a moment while he pondered everything that had happened as well as taking a moment to admire Courtney herself. 'So beautiful,' he whispered.

'Dulko, is that you?'

He had spoken without thinking and was stunned at the possibility of Courtney having heard him. 'Oh, er ... the sky. It's a beautiful night, isn't it?'

'I guess, but isn't every night the same when you're above the clouds?'

'Yeah, of course it is, it just looks especially stunning tonight for some reason. Anyway it's time to go, so get set and I'll see you when you get back. And good luck, though I know you'll do great because you were born for this. Now remember, you'll be on your own once you get to the other side. I can no longer communicate with you until you get back.'

'Understood.'

'Oh and Courtney?'

'Yeah?'

'Don't hang about. Do what you have to do and then get

straight back.'

'Ok, no dilly-dallying.'

'No diddly-whatlying?'

'Never mind,' she chuckled, mocking his attempt to copy her. 'I'll see you when I get back.'

All of a sudden, she shot up high into the sky like a bullet, edging closer to the stars. Within seconds, she had broken through into orbit and was immediately blown away by the sheer fact that she was now in outer space. 'Holy Mary, mother of ... Jesus Christ ... this is unbelievable.'

Panicked by her tone Dulko said, 'What's wrong, what happened?'

'Check me out baby, I'm in space,' she laughed. 'I'm actually in outer space.'

'Oh right, yeah. How is it?'

'Simply put, it's ... life changing. I wish you were here with me to see it. Now this really is beautiful.'

The vastness and silence filled her whole being with inner peace, giving her a strong spiritual connection that she hadn't felt in a while; forced upon her by witnessing the magnificence of the environment that surrounded her. She moved upwards automatically due to the pre-entered coordinates and was faced with an unbelievable and unique view of space. Far more colourful than she had ever imagined it could be.

Ahead of her, more colours came into view, except these ones were artificial. Lighting the blackness in front of her she could see millions of multi-coloured light beacons that were laying out what looked like various different pathways. 'Whoa.' *Those must be pathways to different holes leading to different times.* She felt her whole body tingle with anticipation as she wondered which one could take her back to when she was five.

The PEU took her past pathway after pathway, lined on either side with thousands of light beacons the size and shape of beach balls; each one a different colour; presumably to differentiate one path from another. She imagined what an amazing sight it must be up there during the day when the place was open for business and full of traffic. 'Heathrow really has expanded.'

Finally, she slowed down as she arrived at the route she was to take, a route that was marked in red. 'Ooh, that's the danger colour where I come from. You're sure this isn't the road to hell? I'd much rather go down a pink one.'

'I thought you didn't like pink?'

Dulko's voice was like a comfort blanket; the only thing she recognised in the vastness of space. Unfortunately, she knew she would soon lose even that to time as she ventured forward into the unknown. For now though, his voice was all she could trust. 'I don't like pink bathrooms ... but pink destinies? Not so bad at all,' said Courtney.

'Perhaps another time.' He closed his eyes, feeling guilty about his frivolous conversation while being bogged down with everything he knew. However, he was aware the world was listening along with the ones in control and so had to keep the conversation at a certain level. Perhaps she was right though - perhaps it was the road to hell.

As Dulko was pondering just how long the world had left before everyone on it would be wiped out, Courtney shot down the red-lit pathway towards the loophole that awaited her at the end, and was becoming increasingly nervous as she twisted and turned down the clearly marked route. Usually, it would be ships carrying anything from one hundred to one thousand 'Time Tourists' through the portals, so it was very wide, making Courtney look like a pin prick.

'Courtney, you're approaching the hole,' said Dulko. 'You have thirty seconds.'

Her heart raced as she neared her destination. She squeezed the rock tight and a piece broke off in her hand, crumbling from her strength. Rather than let it go, she managed to slip it into her pocket just as everything suddenly became very slow.

'Five seconds.'

She remembered the feeling from when she first jumped into the hole back at the house. Just for a second, she seemed to come to a complete stop. From the distance, she looked as if she was elongating like a piece of melted plastic, until finally she was gone.

She didn't experience slow motion or anything else until she entered the blackness. Something wonderful happened inside though. She wasn't just a person travelling through a portal, her whole body felt like it had become one with the space around her, as if she was the blackness and the blackness was part of her. She felt in complete control of the journey, almost as if she had become the loophole.

She saw a light far ahead of her in the distance; a tiny bright white light. As she stared ahead, she recognised the light from all the movies she'd seen and for a second wondered if she was about to pass through to heaven. Although strangely, she felt as though she was not even moving – just floating, and yet the light was nearing her at a tremendous speed. She couldn't turn around and go back; a massive contradiction to the control she felt, but one that all the same felt so right. As if there was nowhere to go back to; as if the only option in existence was forward.

Only one question for her remained. Am I really going to achieve my lifelong ambition of travelling into the past? She looked at the white light as it encompassed her and said, 'I guess only Mr Time can tell,' and with that she was gone.

~ CHAPTER FORTY FOUR ~

Oh my God, that's me

'Thank you Courtney ... and thank you God, if you're really out there,' said Alexandra. She was sitting alone on the luxurious sofa with her legs extended out in front of her, on a large fluffy bean bag.

Outside the living room window staring in, was Courtney. She had successfully managed to come through the other side of the loophole and made her way down to the surface and to her relief, her PEU was still working. Before she left, Dulko had explained that the PEU worked much like a solar battery and as the circuitry is part of the human body, the battery was in essence, her. In his time, where the technology existed to power the PEU, it constantly drew on external energy, but in her time, it reverted to stored energy. He had warned her that it would only last for a short time before it would run out and cause the PEU to fail. He wasn't sure how long, could be a few days, could be a few weeks, but nobody had dared to stay outside their time too long to find out, as once it did happen, you would never be able to return. Although she knew all those facts, there was still a part of her that was ecstatic to be stood safely on the ground she was most familiar with.

A huge sense of relief dawned on her at seeing the Earth as it was supposed to be, according to her perspective anyway. As technologically wonderful as the future was, she could not help but think that her own time was a far better way to live, but the generations before her would probably have said the same thing.

She had been watching Alexandra getting progressively

drunk in her house for the last thirty minutes, smiling to herself at her friend's increasingly intoxicated antics but not having actually been inside yet. Knowing how she'd previously helped Alexandra overcome the darkest moment of her life so far, she sighed from the realisation that those moments in everyone's lives when they are struggling with something that will affect their existence dramatically are miniscule compared to the weight and ultimate ramifications of the task that was firmly in Courtney's hands right now. The rock had been placed some distance away from the house so she could take a look around, as she wanted to take in what it was like being in the past before being forced to get started with what she was there to do.

Her mind was spinning in astonishment by the idea that at that very moment, Ellie, Nathan, Becky, and even more amazingly, herself, were at Creekside House, getting themselves ready to make the journey by boat to Professor Thistle's office.

Many things ran through her mind about what she could do and change if only she were able to totally sit in sync with that time. However, there was just one thing she was capable of achieving and it was that mission that had resulted in her being stood outside her own house about to save the world ... or so she thought anyway.

While she stood and watched Alexandra, she began to have some random ideas. 'What would happen if I took the rock right now and threw it into the sea? What if I never put it in the cellar? Surely, everything would change? But change how, if the future has already happened? Which I know it has because I've just come from there.' She debated all sorts of scenarios in her head, but just kept getting more and more confused the more she analysed it.

In the end, she realised that too much was at stake to attempt any sort of experiment that would deter her from what she was there to do. 'I've got to do this,' she whispered.

Just then, she heard singing from inside the house.

'Things ... can only get better!'

Courtney looked on and giggled at Alexandra's playful but

tipsy antics. 'You go, girl.'

Alexandra then spilt her wine all down her front, causing Courtney's mood to immediately change.

'Oi, mind the sofa. Oh my God, you're such an idiot Courtney. What the hell am I talking about? This house has got a lot more coming to it than a little bit of wine on the sofa, and I'm the one who's gonna cause it. I don't believe it. Maybe I can leave it in the garden instead. But then if nothing happens to the house, Alex won't call me. Damn it, arrgghh, so annoying.'

She was torn between saving the world and keeping her house tidy; not an easy decision for anyone. 'What am I like? Let's just get this done.' She turned away from the house and went to get the rock.

At that very moment, Alexandra began to head upstairs to get changed.

What Courtney had not realised was that everything she had just thought about, whether she was in any doubt or not, had led her down a path that fitted exactly with what had already happened. Nothing had gotten in her way to stop her from doing what she knew had already been done before. Past, present and future did appear to be pre-destined.

Running back to the path, she grabbed the rock and hurried to the front door. When she tried to grab hold of the handle, her hand passed right through it. 'Oh my God.' She hadn't yet got used to or even quite realised that she was not only invisible, but she could pass through solid structures. Although she knew it in the back of her mind, it felt very different experiencing it for real.

Now with the intention of passing straight through the door, she took a deep breath and walked towards it again. However, as soon as she reached it, she was stopped in her tracks as the rock collided with the door. Although *she* was not solid, the rock was. 'Now what?'

All of a sudden, screaming could be heard coming from behind the window upstairs. The close proximity of the rock seemed to instigate the string of catastrophic events that happened to Alexandra.

'How did I get in? Think, how did I get in? I know I must have somehow, or I wouldn't even be here in the first place.' There was a large explosion from upstairs and more screaming echoed through the walls. Courtney became very disturbed at hearing Alexandra in so much stress and couldn't help but feel terrible about it all. 'I'm so sorry, but everything will be ok. I promise.' Tears of guilt appeared in her eyes. 'Think, think, THINK.' Her mood was now desperate as she began to panic.

Then everything became relatively silent for a brief moment. The screaming stopped, but Courtney was still outside, and she knew that she quickly needed to get inside before Alexandra came back down or she would see the rock float through midair. 'Not something Alex had said happened, although it's possible,' she said. 'Wait ... the door – of course, the front door was off its hinges. Without these robot interfaces on my limbs, I wouldn't even be able to carry the rock, so think of the destruction it could cause. That's why the door was off its hinges,' she said in realisation as a smile emerged on her tensed lips.

She took a few steps back in preparation, and with a mighty heave, threw the rock straight at the top of the door. An almighty loud bang echoed through the house as it hit the solid oak, pushing it off of its hinges and smashing it beyond repair as it landed flat on the hallway floor.

She ran inside, picked up the rock which had left a huge dent in the door, as well as a whacking great big hole in the floor and quickly made her way to the cellar. When she got there, the cellar door was also closed, but it was on a push-click system. So holding the rock out in front of her, she gently pushed the door with it until it clicked open.

The kettle in the kitchen was bubbling and the TV in the living room was crackling loudly. Then there were more screams from Alexandra and a massive thud on the stairs. Immediately looking to her right, she saw water pouring down into the hallway. Then with a huge bang, the TV in the living room exploded and Alexandra screamed hysterically. Courtney winced upon hearing the escalated distress from her friend.

She looked at the rock and disapprovingly shook her head, almost as if it was alive and she was mentally telling it off. Alexandra's feet then appeared at the bottom of the stairs and Courtney froze, unable to move from the shock of it all but was almost immediately broken out of it by the ring of a cell phone.

'Courtney, you need to come home, this house is possessed. You were right ...'

'Oh my God, that's me she's talking to,' she whispered in shock. 'I've got to get out of here.' She ran down the steps to the cellar and dropped the rock onto the floor. There was a slight tremor in the rest of the house, as the impact produced a crater beneath the rock along with a huge plume of dust. She ran straight back up the steps and back into the hallway, where she saw Alexandra throw her phone across the room after having just told the Courtney on the row boat in Los Angeles that the house had moved again. Looking at the door to the cellar she realised that as she had nothing to touch the cellar door with, she couldn't close it. *But any second now, Alexandra would come running around the corner and see the door open.* 'That can't happen; she doesn't even know there is a cellar.'

Suddenly, she remembered the piece of rock that came off in her hand and that she had put in her pocket earlier. So she took it out and carefully used it to close the door.

Just as the door closed, Alexandra ran into the hallway. With no time to move, Courtney froze as her friend came straight towards her. A second before they were about to collide, Courtney raised up her arms to block her path. 'Mind the—'

It was too late; Alexandra passed straight through her. Subsequently, she stepped into the hole in the ground and fell flat on her face. Getting up and dusting herself off, she continued into the kitchen. Courtney took a deep breath and walked slowly behind, watching Alexandra as she spun around in distress.

'Leave me alone. What is it you want from me? You've got the wrong girl. I promise you ... I'm not Courtney.'

screamed Alexandra, as she collapsed onto the floor and cried.

Courtney looked on with guilty sadness, realising that she was to blame for Alexandra's distress, but ironically she also felt a huge sense of relief. Unfortunately, even though she felt on top of the world, she was unaware that what she had just achieved was in direct opposition to everything that she stood for and believed in. 'Don't worry, you've played your part just as you were supposed to. Everything's gonna be fine now. And don't worry, you're definitely not me,' she said with a smile. 'It's time for me to go. I still have to save Jesus, but I promise I'll see you soon. In fact, I'm sure we'll do this all over again. Because of you, I go on to become the first to travel through time, meet a great guy, which I know you'll be happy with, but most amazingly, go on to save the world ... apparently.'

~ CHAPTER FORTY FIVE ~

I have everything under control

'Courtney, you're approaching the hole,' yelled Dulko. 'You have thirty seconds.' He and the rest of the world were sat comfortably watching on as Courtney suddenly became very slow at the perimeter of the loophole. While hours would pass for Courtney on the other side as she negotiated placing the rock in her cellar, everyone on Dulko's side of time would only have to wait a matter of milliseconds to see her almost instantaneously return. Dulko was taking deep breaths of anticipation and was feeling very mixed emotions about watching Courtney do something that the world had waited hundreds of years to witness. He was concerned for her safety of course, but he knew that the technology had been tried and tested many times before, so it was her mental and emotional well being that was most concerning him as well as the fact that he was feeling extremely tense from the possibility of Courtney finding out he deceived her. The full aftermath of his actions was just around the corner; literally seconds away.

Not too far from Dulko inside a huge domed structure and high above the clouds, a major political gathering had commenced. Officials inside were also preparing themselves for the momentous occasion.

Strongly resembling The White House in Washington D.C., the building was positioned above the residential sections of the city overseeing everything that happened down below; the most recognisable image of power had lasted through the ages to become the definitive symbol of the world's ruler. Just like the original, a totally white appearance decorated the current incarnation but with one main difference to the former; no windows. Like most buildings of that time, even though they were designed to resemble past structures, windows were the one element they decided not to recreate. Of course they were not needed, but there was a feeling that even having fake windows gave others the belief that it was ok to snoop into other's affairs.

Eramask stood inside the large domed section, amongst hundreds of other government officials from different sections of the world. They had gathered to be near the location of the historic event that was taking place as well as to watch and make sure their much deliberated plan would ensue without complication. They were all standing in the round, staring in silence at the projected image of space in the middle of the vast circular room. As Courtney entered the loophole there were gasps from various sections of the dome. They now had only seconds before she would return.

'It seems everything is going to plan,' remarked Eramask to a lady called Emerikar who was standing next to her. 'It seems our years of worry were unnecessary after all.'

Emerikar was a lot older than Eramask and by her demeanour; she was clearly of a higher status in the system too. An immovable stony look on her face gave the distinct impression that she had never experienced any other type of expression, certainly none with a more upward persuasion. With Eramask wearing similar clothing, together they could easily be mistaken for mother and daughter.

However, the reality was very different. Emerikar was the appointed leader of the planet and whom Eramask had styled herself heavily on, in the hope that one day she would emulate her elevated position in the world.

'Your career may still have a future after all, but I suggest you wait for her return before you begin your celebrations,' said Emerikar sternly.

The respect only went one way.

Eramask stared at her before surreptitiously facing forward from the embarrassment of being scolded by her peer.

As quick as she disappeared, Courtney was suddenly back; spat from the hole like a discarded melon seed. Immediately coming to a stop she took a deep breath. The second she reappeared, millions of people around the planet cheered in relative unison. Had it worked? They were all asking.

Chaos erupted inside the government dome. Everyone was talking; buzzing like worker bees in their hive, whilst the queen was getting ready to make her next strategic command. The racket inside was deafening as they noisily deliberated what may have just happened on the other side, hundreds of years in the past.

Then Dulko's voice echoed around the dome and everyone quickly fell silent after a multitude of shushes. Nobody was immune to the tension that had built up inside.

'Courtney? Can you hear me?'

She raised her head and smiled. 'I can hear you.'

'Ask her if she did it,' called out a random voice inside the dome.

Dulko tentatively said, 'Were you successful? Did you manage to do - I mean, how long have you been gone?'

Eramask and Emerikar's eyes widened as they held their breath in anticipation of her answer. The dome was totally silent along with the rest of the world, as they waited with baited breath for her response

Courtney opened her mouth and was about to speak, when out of nowhere, an unidentified object shot up into space at the speed of a bullet and stopped directly next to her. She turned and in complete shock and disbelief said, 'You?' Hovering next to her and the object of her astonishment was none other than Professor Pik Thistle.

He grabbed her arm and even though Courtney was equipped with the PAL interfaces, as much as she tried, she could not seem to shake him off.

'What are you doing? How did you ...?'

Inside the dome, pandemonium erupted amongst all the officials as though a dangerous predator had suddenly attacked their hive and stole their precious honey.

Emerikar screamed, 'What's the meaning of this? Who is that man, and what does he think he's doing?'

Dulko also watched on in just as much disbelief as everyone else.

Everything happened very quickly and within a second of Professor Thistle grabbing Courtney, he had pulled her down out of space and back into the Earth's atmosphere; travelling at the same speed at which he had arrived.

Everybody from all over the globe watched in astonishment. They were not used to seeing someone travel so fast because everyone's routes were always pre-programmed and speed limits were set. However, Professor Thistle had timed his interruption very well, knowing that the skies would be totally clear due to Courtney's mission.

Residents at home were in tears after being put on the edge of their seats by the events that had unfolded and that had been made worse by not actually getting an answer from Courtney.

Without a word from Professor Thistle, he and Courtney shot head first straight downward; plummeting at tremendous speed through the thick rain clouds. Once they had broken through to the other side, they entered the ferocious rain that was pummelling the sea below and became a white blur that blasted its way through the torrent towards the swirling dangerous looking ocean below.

Dulko watched on, completely unaware that anything like that was going to happen. 'Where are they going?'

The whole world went silent as they edged closer to the devastating sea swirls. Everybody inside the Dome was speechless and it remained that way for a whole minute until finally, the quiet was dramatically broken by Emerikar. 'What the hell just happened? Who the hell does he think he is? If I find out who allowed this to happen, I will bring a reign of terror upon them so fierce it will ...' She was so perturbed by the events she couldn't even find the words to finish her sentence just letting out a grunt of frustration instead.

Eramask was writhing about next to her, not saying a word.

With a new motivation Emerikar turned to Eramask and screamed, 'I want to know what that girl was about to say. Do you hear me?'

'Don't worry ma'am, I have everything under control,' fired back Eramask with confidence. However, there was something about Eramask's body language that slightly suggested she was not quite as in control as she was making out.

Then, with a huge splash, the stakes changed as Professor Thistle and Courtney hit the water causing a huge temporary crater in the already turbulent ocean before being swallowed up by the abundance of froth, foam and unwavering spray caused by the huge waves of destruction. Not a place any sane person would normally want to go, but nonetheless Professor Thistle's intention seemed unwavering, as finally … they disappeared from sight.

~ CHAPTER FORTY SIX ~

You're really beginning to freak me out

Nothing could have prepared Courtney for the things she had recently experienced and surviving a collision into the open waters at such velocity would normally not only be amazing, but with her understanding of how the world works, also impossible. However, impossible was a word that was becoming extinct the longer she stayed in the future, as surviving the impact was not only possible, but they were travelling so fast that Courtney didn't even know where they were or what surrounded them, as they dived deeper and deeper into the dangerous waters.

Just like outside on the surface, their PEUs were watertight and held their own oxygen, but for the first time, the profile of the energy unit was now visible as the water rose over the outer shell; like a war submarine descending from the surface. Although unlike a submarine, the outer hull was not visible. All that could be seen was the outline the water produced around the invisible energy barrier that surrounded them, giving the illusion that the outer walls were made of water.

Courtney felt different sensations as they travelled from outer space to the ocean below, but at the speed Professor Thistle was maintaining she couldn't see anything. Unfortunately for her, what actually surrounded them was absolutely stunning; a wonderfully colourful ocean full of all kinds of new and wonderful life forms. There were newly evolved sea creatures of varying shapes and sizes and amazing underwater plant life on a massive scale. Evolution had secretly been working away beneath the surface of the water and had created something entirely new and spectacular.

As they sped through the strangely supple and rubber like branches of huge hybrid underwater trees, it became increasingly darker the deeper they sank into the abyss. Although Courtney could not see what was happening, she sensed the darkness as it began to creep up on her, until eventually everything was totally black. She had trouble telling if her eyes were open or closed because the darkness was unlike anything she had experienced before and it was causing her senses to become extremely disoriented.

They neared the bottom and levelled out before continuing at the same speed along the seabed. They traversed east along what used to be the original City of London, skirting around old ruins of buildings that had been underwater now for hundreds of years which Courtney would have never seen before as they came many years after her lifetime, as well as many which were still there from the city she knew so well: the Olympic Stadium, Big Ben and even a huge Tesco Extra Superstore.

However, none of those wonderful sights were visible to her and she had no control over where they were going or at what speed. Everything was in the hands of Professor Thistle, whom she was waiting patiently to shout at once he finally decided to come to a stop. Anything she said now would clearly be fruitless as she realised that he was obviously taking her somewhere intentional. So she just closed her eyes and waited for the ride to end.

Within ten minutes, they had already reached the former west coast of England and continued into what used to be called the Atlantic Ocean. They descended again deeper into the ocean mass until they were thousands of metres down.

They had travelled for a good hour and all around them was totally dark. One thing Courtney knew without a doubt was that wherever they were, it was quite some distance from where they had begun. Clearly Professor Thistle was on a set course to somewhere specific and as far away from the sky city as possible.

Eventually, they slowed to a stop and Professor Thistle brought them both upright. Courtney still couldn't see a thing in the darkness so had no idea where she was. All she could do was remain still and wait to find out the answer.

Then she felt the professor let go, leaving her standing alone in the middle of the dark and deep ocean, totally helpless and blinded by the complete absence of even the faintest light. She knew she could literally be anywhere. It was so dark, the location or terrain of where she was standing was impossible to determine. She panicked about being literally, as well as metaphorically, kept alone in the dark as Professor Thistle was still yet to say a word to her. Her heart pumped so fast she could actually feel it palpitating inside of her. She had a deep worry about where she was and what was going to happen next. 'Please, Professor, let me go,' she said with a vulnerable and nervous tone.

When he didn't respond, she looked around in the hope that her eyes would acclimatise and something would become visible. 'I don't like this, you're scaring me. Please, where are we? What do you want? Are you helping the government? Is that it? We don't have to be enemies you know. Look ...' She thought for a second before taking on a more sincere tone. 'I know all about your daughter and I'm really very sorry. But please, this isn't the way to get her back. I've lost family too, but I don't go around kidnapping people. Professor? Please, you're really beginning to freak me out now.'

All of a sudden there was light all around her. For the first time, she could see where she was though it took a while for her eyes to adjust after being in the dark for so long.

As she became aware of things, she slowly realised where she was and couldn't quite believe what she saw, as it appeared as though she was standing in what used to be Professor Thistle's office at LosTech University. The whole place was now submerged along with most of the rest of the planet in the middle of the new worldwide ocean.

Energy light balls were floating all around lighting up the whole area. They gave the most surreal view of an incredible underwater world. However, as she stood taking it all in, she noticed a very large omission from the scene in front of her. She was totally alone and Professor Thistle was nowhere in sight.

All she could do was stare in awe at everything around her, partially fascinated, partially too scared to move and totally lost for words. Just a few days earlier, she had been stood in exactly the same position, as she struggled to stay awake from the heat and the jet lag whilst preparing herself for what she thought would be the biggest adventure of her life. How right she had been.

The office was surprisingly similar to how she last saw it, except now there was the addition of some large and strange looking fish of all different shapes and sizes swimming around her instead of confined in a small tank. Sand covered the ground and through the windows she could see coral and weeds. Strangely, there was not much inside the office. It seemed as though it had all been removed and definitely didn't look like it was *naturally* free of plant life.

Courtney couldn't help but think that what she was witnessing was what it must have been like to stumble across the lost city of Atlantis but more amazing to her was how she was able to talk and walk freely as if she wasn't even under water. 'This is crazy,' she said in astonishment as she reached out to touch a school of giant coloured fish that swam past. They shot away from her hand though and quickly swam underneath her. Strangely, they looked more like mini hippos than fish and were all different neon colours. She looked a little closer as they passed below and surprisingly discovered that she could actually see their internal organs inside their heads. They were totally see-through, similar to a glassfish, and as they swam, they appeared to be able to shift their eyes directly upwards to look through the top of their heads and straight at Courtney. They were a strange but beautiful sight and had tails like a whale's, but also seemed to have stumps underneath that looked like legs.

'Whoa, can you guys go on land as well as water? That must mean there's land close by.' As she turned to watch them swim away, she noticed the bookshelves still had books on them and so stared at the abundance of literature and wondered how there could still be books on shelves that were under thousands of metres of water and hundreds of years after they were first put there.

Just as she was pondering all the weirdness, Professor Thistle silently glided in through one of the huge arched windows which startled Courtney as she did not hear him lower himself down and stand right behind her.

'Miss Nivots ...,' he said in a commanding voice, causing Courtney to shriek in terror. With no discernible expression on his face he then said, 'Don't you think it's about time you put back the book you stole from me?'

~ CHAPTER FORTY SEVEN ~

There are some things you need to know

With guilt written all over her face, Courtney instantly swung around upon hearing Professor Thistle's voice behind her. For a second she stood frozen with her eyes wide. 'Sorry, I don't have it, I swear. It's back at my house though, so we can-'

'Calm down child, it was just a joke,' said Professor Thistle in a playful manner. He spoke with a slightly softer voice than Courtney was used to and there was something about his face that was not as sharp and stoic as when she first met him. 'I promise you I'm long over that; I now know it was merely a necessary step on your journey.'

'I'm sorry? Is this some kind of a trick? Why would you say that to me?'

Noticing something peculiar compared to when she last saw him, she began to spot some differences. Only having seen him a couple of times she couldn't claim to be an expert, but he seemed a tiny bit older with a few more lines on his face, and his beard was a lot fuller than she remembered as well, with the white stripe in the centre noticeably more prominent. *That's weird. He's only been here a few days.*

Unable to understand anything that was happening to her, she just stared blankly at him for a moment and then said, 'Where were you just now? Why do you look so old all of a sudden? I haven't been here for years and not realised, have I? Or have you taken us through another time distortion or something?'

'So many questions ... no, it's nothing like that. I had to

quickly go to the surface to make sure we weren't followed; pretty unlikely though, as hardly anyone is brave enough to venture into the oceans these days. There's a whole new world forming down here, and not all of it is pleasant. But I needed to check to be certain. This is far too important for silly mistakes. Oh, and my ageing ... unfortunately it's a natural affliction.'

Still confused she looked at him and said, 'How can that possibly be? Look, why am I here? Is this some sort of revenge? What's going on?'

'Revenge? Not at all. The reason I brought you here is because it's the only place I know they won't find us. There are some things I need to tell you and I need you to listen intently without interruption. There's too much at stake.'

'What are you talking about? What do you want from me?'

'I'm not here to hurt you; I'm here to save you ... and save us all.'

'I'm hearing that a lot lately and to be honest, it's getting on my nerves. I never once said I wanted to save the world.'

'You don't have to say it; I'm afraid it's just who you are.'

'No it's not,' she said sounding like a spoilt child. 'What do you know anyway? I mean, you've only been here like a day or something. What makes you think you're capable of saving anyone? And save us from what exactly?'

'From time travel. Mankind's biggest evil and I'm not ... you are.'

'What ... are you crazy? That's why I'm here, to make sure it continues.'

'Courtney, whatever you do, you cannot take that rock back. That's why I'm here, to stop you making the biggest mistake the human race ever made and in turn ... become the saviour.'

'You mean, so you can take it back instead and take all the credit? You're mankind's biggest evil.'

Professor Thistle shook his head and exhaled, showing his disappointment.

'Besides, it's too late. I've already done it. Time travel is safe and sound.'

On hearing that he had reached her too late, he dropped into his chair knowing that he had misjudged the window for stopping her. As he stretched his hands across his bald head in disbelief and despair, his face went visibly red and the veins on his temples began to throb.

Courtney couldn't understand what had made him so distressed, but she was a little frightened by his erratic behaviour. She felt like she had been told off for something, and for a moment, it was as though she was back in school. *Why would he be so distressed by the thought of me succeeding when he should be ecstatic about it? Something doesn't make sense. After devoting his whole life to time travel, could it really be that he was just so put out by not being the first to use it that he would go to these lengths?* Realising she may have affected his life in such a big way; she began to feel very scared of what he might do to her.

'Courtney, sit down.' He gestured to a chair on the other side of his desk.

Being sure to do whatever he told her, she quickly sat down.

'He's not your friend you know?'

'Who isn't?'

Professor Thistle lifted his head and looked into her eyes. 'Dulko ... he's not your friend.'

'What do you know about Dulko ... or anything for that matter? He's helped me more than you ever have ... or ever will.' Her natural personality was coming back as she stood up to him with a stoic defence.

'I very much doubt that child.'

'I know all about you. How you're only interested in your own legacy. Oh, and I'm not your child.' She didn't intend to say that, but she had become very defensive of Dulko; the man who had taken care of her since she had arrived in the future and whom she'd now come to trust.

'What? Who have you been talking to? Actually, it doesn't matter. None of that matters now. You have to believe and trust me. There is much more at stake here. I admit, I used to be focused on only one thing and I pretty much would have done anything to achieve it. There's no doubt, it did incense me that you made it first, so much so that if your friend Alexandra had gotten in my way instead of helping me ... well, without being graphic, let's just say I was ready to do whatever it took.'

On hearing his admission, Courtney took an uncomfortable gulp.

'It's hard for me to even admit that, because I know it could make you scared of me, but I'm not that man anymore. It was a temporary blip – you have to trust me. We need to work together to fix this. It's bigger than any resentment from me or from you. I've had a lot of time to analyse the situation and some things are not quite what they seem.'

She sat back in her chair and stared at him curiously. 'So enlighten me.'

'Just look at everything that he's done. You can work it out; you're a smart girl.'

She narrowed her eyes at him.

'If everyone was out to get you, why weren't they there when you arrived? Why has nobody chased you? How convenient he knew where to find you and nobody else did. They had hundreds of years to work it out. And who ends up finding you but a nice, clean-cut, good looking boy not far from your age and with a trusting face. You have to understand that's something that doesn't exist much in this time anymore.'

She pondered what he had said and it soon dawned on her that there was some sense in it. Yet at the same time, she couldn't work out how he could know so much in such a short space of time, therefore she couldn't think of him as trustworthy in any way, as it looked like he was just plucking his theories out of thin air. Something just didn't add up.

'It's not about the science of time travel, Courtney. It's about money and how to keep it rolling in. This government are just like any other government; one thousand years doesn't change anything. Time travel has become a commodity like everything else. They needed you to keep the circle complete or they'd lose their biggest source of income. Plus, think about it, if you've taken the actual key to what makes time travel possible back, think what else has been passed backward over the years. How much of what we have achieved have we actually achieved in our own time? You need to find out why time travel to the future is being controlled by the government. Why is nobody allowed to see it? Why just the past? My personal theory is that there *is* no future because we eventually wipe ourselves out and they don't want anyone to know. Perhaps it's too far down the line for them to care and they'd rather the money just kept rolling in for as long as it's possible. I don't know, but you need to speak to your boyfriend. I think he probably knows more about that side of it than he lets on.'

'Aha, now I know you're lying, because you couldn't possibly know all this. And by the way, he isn't my boyfriend.' Although the words came out of her mouth, she was not totally convinced by what she had said, as nothing really made much sense any more. 'And why does this office look just like it did a thousand years ago?'

'Well ... it's quite simple, Courtney. You see, this is my home now ... and I've actually been living here for the last two years.'

~ CHAPTER FORTY EIGHT ~

I'll find the truth, I promise you

Courtney jerked her head back in stunned disbelief at what she had just heard Professor Thistle say. 'I'm sorry, what? How could that be? I just saw you a few days ago and you knew nothing of this.'

'That's right, you did, but I haven't seen *you* for over two years. Ask your PEU to show you the history databases for that time.'

She stared at him and wondered what he was trying to prove.

'Go ahead, ask.'

Deciding to humour him she spoke in her head, asking for the databases. Like a hologram, a see-through screen of information immediately came up in front of her. The first thing that caught her eye was Google's trademark in the corner. *Amazing.* 'Wow, some things never change, do they?'

'Ask for results on time travel and loopholes relating to all news on that subject for up to ten years after the first event.'

Slowly, she was beginning to understand where he could be going with his instructions, but she still needed confirmation and so did as he requested. Front pages of newspapers from one thousand years ago appeared and they looked almost like they were actually there; letters and images floating in the water right in front of her. However, they were actually highly advanced computer images being transmitted via the Sole Information Network (or SIN for short) which was being fed into her system. Inquisitively, she looked at the articles that were dated some weeks after she had first vanished through the hole.

'Now narrow it down to information on Professor Pik Thistle.'

She looked at him suspiciously and he smiled at her.

'That's me.'

As she continued to do as he told her, all information other than news relating to Professor Thistle disappeared. Reading through it, she quickly realised that he may actually be speaking the truth. Right there in front of her, the information stated that soon after she and Professor Thistle had taken the first trips through the hole, the authorities discovered the rock in Courtney's cellar. For some reason they decided to spend years investigating its properties rather than send anyone else into another hole to follow. Something had scared them away from creating more loopholes and leaping in.

'Why Courtney, why the delay in going through another loophole?'

Looking up at him with a solemn expression she said, 'It says you never returned.'

'That's right. The hole you came here in was created by a rock of a certain size. By the time I got to it, it was closed. Holes of that size don't last long before they collapse. I had to create my own using another piece of the meteor, but it wasn't as big as yours. It brought me into the future, but two years earlier than you arrived. However, when I got here, the government knew I was coming; just like they knew you were. They tried to dupe me into thinking they were happy, genuine and contented by taking me to their most treasured sport, trying to draft me in to help them. Ironically though, I realised that this so called sport wouldn't even exist if it weren't for their inherent destructive mentality. They hoped I would have information on you they could use. But with everything I was witnessing, I began to realise that time travel was perhaps not the best discovery mankind had ever made; a very, very hard thing for me to come to terms with believe me.' Momentarily he paused as an uncontrollable sadness permeated his soul, as reflected in his eyes; almost as if he was mourning for someone he deeply cared about. 'They then did all they could to contain me so I couldn't spoil the plans they had in place for your arrival.

'However, there are a lot of discontented people on the surface that want change. With their help, I was able to escape and I've been hiding here ever since, waiting for you for the last two years. I've used the time to scour the ocean for bits and pieces that would make this place feel ... well, like it did about a week ago I suppose - like home.'

'Whoa ... every time I think I've seen or heard it all, I'm astounded by something else. So you've been living here for years, under the ocean like Spongebob Squarepants?'

'Yes, but what I don't even know and what is somewhat – wait, Spongebob ... I don't think so. I think ... Captain Nemo. Anyway, what is more disconcerting is why I don't show up in the news reports as having returned. Suggesting I will eventually either die here or live out the rest of my life in this man made travesty. Right now, I'd actually like nothing more than to get home. So from that I can only assume I must give up the ghost here. That being the case, I want to do anything I can to help. Simply put, I have nothing to lose anymore. I thought I was put on this earth to discover time travel, but it now seems it was to discover you.'

Courtney stared at him with a new found respect and admiration.

'One government, or more to the point one lady, cannot and should not rule the entire planet. It's a scary world when that's the case and to put something as powerful as time travel in their hands is simply downright dangerous and ultimately, it would seem, catastrophic. Dulko has been working for a government official called Eramask. She's the same lady who tried to recruit me and she has a pretty high opinion of her position in regards to the fate of this planet. However, she ultimately answers to the leader of the planet, a lady called Emerikar.'

'Whoa wait, you're telling me that Miss ... America rules the world?'

He smiled at her mispronunciation of the name but saw

the irony of her statement. 'Not quite. You see she doesn't go by the title 'Miss'.'

Courtney smiled at what he had inferred with his joke and deliberated on everything he had said. She was still not convinced that Dulko was part of a major plan to deceive her. She wanted to give him the benefit of doubt because she had never felt for a man the way she felt about him and amazingly in such a short space of time, but Professor Thistle's story seemed so convincing in all other areas. 'Supposing all this is true. I've already done what was asked of me. The rock is safely in place at my house. As proven by the fact that we are both still here talking to each other. So it looks like I've made the biggest mistake the human race ever made. So what would you suggest we do now?'

It was Professor Thistle's turn to think, and after some deliberation he said, 'I don't know, but we have to do something. I'll need more time to think of a new plan.'

'Perhaps it's just meant to be that way and there is nothing we can do. I mean whatever I do, whatever I say and whatever I think is being pre-empted by time anyway. We're not in charge, time is. So if what you're saying is true, then it would seem we're going to have to be the ones in control; that's if we're going to survive.'

'You're absolutely right,' he said with a glint in his eye. 'We need to find a way of getting around destiny. We have to believe that as much as it seems like our future is written, perhaps there is something in the small print that we can erase or perhaps rewrite slightly. You see destiny equals a lack of freedom. In reality, it's a prison where choice isn't even a luxury - its non-existent. Time is the governor; time is in control and to attain our freedom, like you said we need to take control by overthrowing the warden - destiny.

'Very profound.'

'Thank you.'

'But hang on a minute, if the hole I used to come here closed when you got to it, how the hell do I get home? What do the history books say about my return?'

'Don't worry about that, as the facts stand right now, you

do return. So let's just stick with that knowledge, and everything else should take care of itself.'

Courtney pursed her lips; not totally convinced, but for now she thought she would go with it. 'Ok look, thinking about it, the rock being taken back probably was the most obvious marker in time to try and change things. But what if it goes even further back than that? What if it all stems back to when I first saw the ghost in my bedroom?'

Professor Thistle thought about it for a moment but then shook his head in disapproval. 'There are two major problems with that theory. The first is that while I've been here, a major discovery has determined that ghosts don't exist, and in order for me to come to that conclusion, I found out the second problem which is that things don't always begin where you think they do. They often start somewhere in the middle of the story, and what you think is the beginning can often be the end.'

Courtney looked blankly at him and for the first time understood how she must have sounded when trying to explain the Dyson Sphere to Alexandra. 'What on earth are you going on about?'

'Remember that past, present and future, as you correctly theorised, are running concurrently. If one doesn't happen before the other as we've all been programmed to believe, then why would an ongoing event always have to start in the past?'

'That's a very interesting notion. I presume you can explain yourself.'

'Remember the murdered family at Creekside House?'

'Yeah ...'

'They never existed. It was all a very elaborate example of Chinese whispers and ... well, are you ready for this?'

Just like a little girl who was being offered candy she quickly nodded.

'It all began with you.'

'Me? But how could that happen? Surely it all started when the family was murdered?'

'Wrong, because I told you they didn't even exist and

nobody was murdered. But what's interesting is that I knew of the story before I even met you.'

As smart and as used to weird and wonderful things as she now was she was still struggling to get her mind around such bizarre realms of possibility. She looked at Professor Thistle with a slightly puzzled expression as for the first time she felt like a student in an actual lesson, learning something worthy of her intelligence.

'Quite simply,' said Professor Thistle, 'I brought the newspaper article with the CCTV image of you and your friends here to the future. While I was waiting for you to turn up, I took a sightseeing trip back to the year 1889. I wanted to find out more about the family to help me understand a little better where our fascination with ghosts comes from. I found out there has never been a family of that description living in that house and more importantly, nobody was ever murdered there either. But just before I came back, as I was struggling to understand everything, I decided to read the article again. But I must've dropped it at some point, because I couldn't find it anywhere.'

'And somebody picked it up,' said Courtney, as she started to understand the unfolding pattern of events. 'Then they read it and began the long-lived but totally untrue myth about a family slaughter in that house.'

'Exactly. The past is not behind us, it's just another moment in the ever expanding circle of time. So you see in your case I wouldn't be so sure that everything began when you think it did.'

'Well maybe it didn't, but we don't have much else to go on. We have to do something or we'll constantly be second guessing ourselves.'

'But Dear child, you seem to be forgetting what else that discovery means. Ghosts do not exist. I've proven that they are just stories made up to satisfy our need for there to be something beyond this life.'

Courtney looked hard into his eyes trying to process what he had said, as he seemed to be right about a lot of things so far. She then began to slowly shake her head from side to side. 'No, I'm sorry. I can't accept that. Your example is of a ghost that nobody ever actually saw; I saw one.'

Professor Thistle raised his eyebrows, doubting the reliability of her statement.

'I'm telling you I saw one,' she said. 'It not only stood right in front of me, it physically grabbed something and threw it at the wall. Explain that.'

'You were five. I really don't mean to be patronising, but can you really remember what happened? You're an emotionally scarred child, there's probably a very simple explanation.'

'Right, that's it.' She pointed her finger at Professor Thistle's face with an agitated expression. 'If one more person says I made it up, I swear I'll ... look, you need to understand I have to do this. I'm not crazy; I promise you, and I'm convinced that when I finally get back there, that episode is going to reveal some important truths that may hold the key to everything.'

His expression softened on hearing the honesty and conviction in her voice.

'Whether you believe me or not professor, I know something monumental happened to me and it's what brought me here. Trust in me, please. I'll find the truth, I promise you.'

At that moment, a silent alarm was activated inside Professor Thistle's PEU. Courtney recognised it as it flashed red like Dulko's had when he said the government were nearing them.

'We have to go somewhere else. C'mon, have you ever been to Hollywood? I'll take you there.'

Courtney was still focused on how familiar the sound was and said, 'What was that?' She thought about Dulko and why his system was alerted of the government's arrival if he was really working for the government. Things were not making total sense to her just yet, even if certain pieces had started to fall into place.

Professor Thistle walked over to the remains of a window and stared out into the darkness.

'That was an alarm wasn't it? What's the problem?'

'Yes it was. You've seen it before?'

'I have, but now I'm not sure if it was a warning at all.'

'Trust me, this one is and it's the reason nobody comes down here. The waters are occupied by some pretty large and very nasty sea creatures that have evolved in these enormous oceans. They're attracted to the light and this alarm warns me when they're on their way. Right now we are like a lighthouse in the middle of the ocean but instead of avoiding us, they are heading straight for us.'

'But I just saw some of them swim by, little multicoloured hippo type things. They looked amazing.'

'They were in here? You didn't touch them did you?'

'No, although I did try. Why?'

'In all honesty, if you had, you'd probably be dead. They are some of the most dangerous and violent creatures in the sea. They generate their own electricity and send thousands of volts shooting through your nervous system.'

'But they looked harmless. They just swished away when I went near them.'

'That's because they were babies and my alarm has gone off because their mother will likely be on her way. It's best if we just go somewhere else for now. Trust me; there are plenty of places to explore down here. Paris? Sydney? Rome? Take your pick.'

He seemed to know too much to have only just arrived, so Courtney felt she had no choice but to give him the benefit of the doubt. He had sold himself well and the next thing she needed to do was confront Dulko. She was starting to wonder who the bad guy really was. *Is Dulko working for the government but more importantly, could he really be that cold to just pretend to like me? Well ... I think now is the time I found out.*

~ CHAPTER FORTY NINE ~

I think they just want to go home

'Three hours – they've been down there for three hours,' said Eramask to a lady stood next to her called Randlech.

Randlech was Eramask's second in command, slightly shorter than her superior but she was much more curvaceous. Her shoulder length, dark brown and very thick hair, was accentuated by the large and beautiful curls that went right the way down to the tips. She was very pretty but didn't have a model's physique. In fact to modern day standards she actually verged on being overweight but still managed to maintain a very attractive demeanour nonetheless. She also had a much gentler tone to her voice.

They both walked down a long empty corridor that led from the observation dome to the rest of the government building. With no clouds across that particular section of the sky, they could see straight down onto the rough sea waters thousands of feet below.

'Ma'am, perhaps we should just let them return to their own time. The report has come back that nothing in the future has changed and we're still here, so she must have done what was asked of her.'

Eramask stopped walking and looked directly at Randlech. 'Your empathy is misguided. I strongly suggest you redirect it. I very much doubt that he is just taking her sightseeing around the ocean. We need to know exactly what he's up to. We cannot afford to wait until it's too late. We have two travellers from the past running loose in our time. We simply can't allow that to happen without total control over it.

Because even if she has succeeded, with him influencing her, who knows what she could undo.'

'So then where do you suppose they are, and how do we find them?'

Eramask looked down over the water with a concentrated expression. 'They're somewhere down there and when they finally come up for air we'll be ready and waiting. Now assemble the SS and place one thousand of them over every major city submerged under water. Once in place, get them analysing and scanning the area for any movement. Is that clear?'

The SS were the Security Service in the year 3016. Their PEUs were deep red all over so that nobody could see who or what was inside. Some on the surface often wondered if there was actually anyone inside at all, or if they were just empty floating red spheres in the sky. Nobody had ever managed to find out for sure though. They were mainly used to monitor the resident's movements on the surface. However, it wasn't for their protection but for those who controlled them.

The authorities above didn't care much about the surface dwellers and everyone down below knew it. The SS were there to stop any kind of revolt that could lead to the sabotage of the natural resources which were being grown below. Hardly any crops ever reached the people who actually cultivated and looked after them. So occasionally, the odd resident would become resentful and start to think about ways of destroying the crops.

The SS would usually hover from a distance like floating watchtowers. They were permanent fixtures over the skies of the remaining land masses and kept a watchful and sinister eye on the people below. Yet for the first time ever, they were not there, and everyone on the ground below was left wondering why. From the first time they were put there, they had never left the sky. Usually they would hover like giant red eyes but would never disappear completely.

Large crowds had gathered in their thousands to stare into the empty sky. People quickly began to talk as they wondered where they had all gone. Naturally suspicion grew and created unrest amongst the people below. Work on the surface had ceased as people slowly realised nobody was there to watch them. They knew something had happened, with most believing that perhaps their time had arrived and things could finally be about to change. Eramask's orders had been followed and the SS had been put in place across the ocean. No other security existed in the year 3016, as the punishment for any crime was to be banished to the surface to never return, resulting in crime predominantly ceasing to occur at all. However, the sight of thousands of red spheres positioned all over the surface of the ocean was a sign that someone was definitely about to change all that.

The SS waited patiently for something to happen, but another hour passed and there was still no sign of Courtney and Professor Thistle; just miles and miles of violent ocean that had not been explored for over six hundred years. Eramask knew that they could potentially be in any part of the world, or in any city for that matter.

Thousands of SS hovered in rows over the water, waiting for any movement that could be picked up by their sensors. As many of them as there were though, even Eramask couldn't ignore the fact that their numbers were nothing compared to the mass of ocean that was spread across the planet. It was also the main reason why she did not want to send them down to physically search just yet. Then there was also the problem of sea creatures (small and large) that would cause added danger to the units and would also be picked up by the sensors, thus confusing their search further.

Some three hours passed before the wait was finally over and the quiet was suddenly replaced with shock and chaos. Somewhere over what would have previously been Europe, shot a white blur out of the water at tremendous speed and headed straight up towards the sky city.

All security spheres were immediately notified and instantly mobilized towards the recorded coordinates of the blur.

In the observation dome, Eramask and Randlech were

standing alone, looking more worried than ever before. Live images of what had transpired were being transmitted all around them via thousands of satellites. The white blur appeared on a huge screen in front of them while the rest of the dome had a distinct red glow due to every other screen that displayed the SS which were travelling at high speeds in the direction of the blur. The masses of officials that would usually be in there were gone, leaving Eramask and Randlech alone in a dome that now resembled a giant planetarium.

'That's them,' said Eramask. She then began to speak her demands in her mind, communicating directly with the spheres. *Apprehend them before they reach a time portal. They must not be allowed to disappear. They must be stopped at once.*

'Ma'am, perhaps we should get Dulko in case we need him to talk to her. He seems to have a connection, don't you think?'

'Had a connection - he had a connection, but it's now been severed. We no longer need him and he won't be seeing her again. He's served his purpose, just like all the other men on this planet.'

'Ma'am look, they're heading for space. I think they just want to go home. Perhaps—'

'They're not going anywhere. I want to know exactly what they're plans are.'

The blur broke through the clouds, edging towards outer space. Thousands of SS followed behind with more and more joining them all the time.

Breaking into orbit, the blur entered outer space and in quite a bizarre manner began to dart around in all directions. The SS were allowed to easily catch up, turning the event into a futile game of cat and mouse as the blur seemed like it was deliberately playing with them.

All of a sudden, it shot straight back down towards the Earth's atmosphere and then stopped abruptly in the middle of the sky.

In seconds, hundreds of SS had surrounded the blur, creating the shape of a giant ball. Each sphere hovered directly next to one another until they had created a solid circle allowing no escape from inside. Hundreds more placed themselves on the outside, creating a second layer, then a third and a fourth.

A solid huge red ball made up of thousands of smaller ones was now floating in the sky, forming an amazing prison for whoever was within. Then, on the inside, the face of each of the small spheres projected a live section of different parts of Eramask's face which put together created one giant image.

Floating directly in the centre of the red prison with nowhere left to go was only one person - Professor Pinakin Thistle.

'It's been a long time Mr Thistle,' said Eramask gleefully. 'Did you really think you could hide forever?'

'It's Professor Thistle, and you're a fool if you really think you've just succeeded in anything.'

Eramask went silent for a moment as she quickly realised Courtney was not with him. 'What have you done with the girl? Where is she?'

'She's just sorting out some personal issues and then she'll be right back to fix yours for you.' He smiled. 'Isn't that nice of her?'

'What have you done?'

'Ma'am, perhaps we should–'

'Perhaps, you should stop saying 'perhaps',' snapped Eramask to Randlech, whose image could not be seen by Professor Thistle. Eramask was clearly now panicking as her voice quivered with disbelief and dread.

Professor Thistle interrupted and said, 'What's the matter? Afraid you're losing control?'

'Well I'm very much in control of you that's for sure, and I'm going to make sure you never return home. Do you understand me?' Eramask's tone was vindictive and spiteful as she screamed at him in frustration and her whole body was quivering at the thought of having failed her mission.

Professor Thistle's expression looked as though he expected it. 'I realised long ago that I wasn't the important one and strangely enough, that I was never going home. I'm aware that everything doesn't revolve around me. It's just a pity you haven't come to the same conclusion yet. You can do as you wish, but it won't stop the plan that's now in motion. Don't worry though; it's going to be better for everyone, including you.'

Eramask's face looked like it was going to explode with rage. She was like a spoilt child who was about to throw a tantrum because she could not get her own way in the school playground. She attempted to centre herself, knowing that she needed to retain control if she was still going to win. 'Just tell me where she is. We can still work this out.' She was trying to regain her composure as well as get his trust back.

'Honestly, I don't know, but because you've kept me talking for so long, I can tell you where she isn't. You see she went to see a friend, but after all this time you've wasted with me they'll be long gone by now.'

Eramask's eyes widened as she realised who she had gone to see and then said, 'Dulko.'

'Ma'am? Perha—' Randlech froze as she remembered she was not to say perhaps again. 'May-be ... we should have—'

'Shut up, shut up, shut – up,' screamed Eramask through gritted teeth as she tried to contain her anger in front of Professor Thistle, realising that Randlech had a good idea earlier when she said they should have talked to Dulko.

'You know, you'd probably do well to listen to your assistant more. She seems like a very wise young lady,' declared Professor Thistle in a very matter of fact manner.'

Randlech smiled at the professor's compliment. She had never experienced that from a man before, and it caused her to suddenly feel a warm glow inside. That was until Eramask turned to look at her, causing her to immediately drop the smile. She reacted like a student who had just been caught making faces behind the teacher's back.

'Bring him to me,' said Eramask. 'I want him to watch.'

With some concern Randlech said, 'Watch what?'

Eramask abruptly turned and looked at her. As she stared into her eyes, she began to smile with a hint of malevolence and said, 'Watch – her – die.'

~ CHAPTER FIFTY ~

Our worst nightmare

Dulko looked around and saw a world like nothing he'd seen before. Even though he was from the future, what he was witnessing was a totally new experience, and he couldn't quite believe he'd never had the privilege before now. However, he hadn't travelled into the past or farther into the future. Instead, and quite annoyingly, he'd always had the wonderful world that surrounded him right at his feet. Yet as much as he was in awe of his new surroundings, he needed to know something and with a little bit of wonder he said, 'Why have you brought me here?' He was standing directly next to Courtney in what appeared to be a giant shopping mall under the sea. 'And where exactly *is* here anyway?'

'We're in Manila ...,' said Courtney proudly, equally taking in the breathtaking sight of the aquatic mall. '... In the Philippines.'

'We're in the what?'

When Professor Thistle said she could visit anywhere, she instantly knew where she needed to go. 'The Pearl of the Orient, as it used to be called,' she said. 'It's where some of my ancestors are from. I always wanted to visit but my mum never got the chance to take me. She used to tell me stories of how everyone here was obsessed with shopping, or to be more precise, window shopping. That was the joke you see, most people were happy to just look and use places like this as an excuse to get away from the heat and into the air conditioning. So the government allowed the building of hundreds of malls. I mean, yeah, they received healthy commissions - if you know what I'm saying. But people were happy even with little or no money. I think your society could learn a little from them. We always seem to want more. Why couldn't we have just remained happy to just hold a photograph in our hands, or write someone a handwritten letter instead of sending a text? Anyway, I digress; this was one of the largest malls – The Mall of Asia. I so badly wanted to come here and see it for myself. Four hundred and ten thousand square metres of shops. Can you believe that? Talk about excess.'

All around them the water was bright, clear and calm, giving them an indication that they were not too far from the water's surface and that although still submerged, the weather patterns were a little more forgiving there. They were stood in what looked like a central junction in the middle of the mall, with avenues leading off in four directions, but instead of shoppers, it was now all the brightly coloured sea-life doing the window shopping instead.

Most things looked in surprisingly good condition; aside from the floor that was covered in sand and coral. Some stores were untouched while others had been totally demolished.

The water had originally poured into that part of the world with far less ferocity than it had elsewhere; still destroying a great deal but leaving a lot more intact or with minimal damage. Anything not secured down was long gone. Yet amazingly, a lot of things still remained.

'I just thought that this would be a quiet place for us to chat.'

'This building used to be a country?'

'Not quite,' said Courtney smiling. 'But what's funny is that it appears this place may have become the shopping centre for the whole country, before it was submerged. I had a look around and it seems over the years this mall was connected to every other mall from here to the city of Makati by suspended walkways, moving walkways and other malls in-between with everyone's homes sitting on top. So it would seem that at the very least the capital city of Manila became one giant shopping mall. Crazy, huh?'

Dulko was amazed at what he was seeing. He had never been under the sea before and certainly never been to the Philippines, but he was uncomfortable with the small talk, sensing that Courtney must now surely know something of his deception. 'Courtney, there's something I need to say to you.'

She stopped and looked at him, knowing the time had come to get serious. She felt her throat tighten a little and her mouth became dry. 'So much water and yet not a drop to drink,' she muttered to herself.

'Sorry?'

Looking up at him and into his eyes she said, 'It's all true, isn't it?'

He stared at the floor and then slowly lifted his head again to look straight into her eyes. Gently nodding his head he said, 'Yeah, it is ... but Courtney, please let me explain. I can't lie to you anymore. I need to tell you everything and I want to put it right, because what's transpired between us since you arrived, that's not a lie. I swear.'

'Well that's alright then,' she said resentfully. 'You like me loads and yet you're still able to lie to me. I should smash you right in the face with my power assisted limbs and crush your head between my hands so tight that your eyeballs pop out for all these fish to eat.' She spoke with a fierce aggression and speed but had used comical words to juxtapose her mood a little.

'You don't understand. All this started with good intentions and I believe it can still end that way if you give me the chance.'

She looked at him hard, then turned and walked over to a stone bench, sat down and put her head between her hands where she remained for a moment deep in thought.

Dulko quickly rushed over to her. 'It's no excuse, I know, but you need to know I was also duped and trapped. They used me too.'

'They used you,' she said indignantly. 'If you don't give

me something to cling to that will give me some kind of reassurance that you're not a total waste of space and within the next five seconds, I swear to God I'll–'

'Please let me explain. From what we understand of time, my future may already be written. It may already be set. But the thing is, I don't know what that future holds. I haven't seen it – nobody has - except maybe a select few. What I do know though, is how I'm feeling now, and I think from that I can probably tell what the future might hold for me ... and maybe even you. See, I don't feel evil. I don't feel like I want to hurt you ... truthfully. What I do feel ...' He paused for a moment as he carefully thought about his next few words.

Courtney looked up at him upon hearing a little sincerity in his voice and subsequently became a tiny bit interested in what he was about to say. However, she wanted to maintain a modicum of firmness and said, 'You do feel what?'

'I do feel, very strongly like I need – no, like I ... want to help you and make things right. So I can only assume that's exactly what I'm going to do. I did betray you initially, but it was all done so that I could meet you. Doing what I did was the only way and now that I have, I'm sorry, but I don't regret that decision or wish it were any different. Otherwise, I wouldn't be here with you right now accompanying you on your first trip to the Philippines.' He smiled, attempting to lighten the mood.

She looked back down at the floor to conceal a similar smirk.

'More importantly, I wouldn't be here offering to help you. Think about it. Everything happens for a reason ... that is what you believe isn't it?'

She immediately looked up at him. 'How did you know that?'

'It's crazy I know, and it doesn't all make sense but I have to believe that the reason I was sent to deceive you was to put myself in a position to help you, which we both need to trust will ultimately help us all.'

Courtney stood up on the bench to look into his eyes and see if she could read whether he was really being genuine.

'Courtney, there is one other thing I feel though,' he said as he came face to face with her.

Nervously she said, 'Oh yeah, and what would that be?'

'Are you sure you don't know? I mean, I think you know – that is, I hope you know.' He continued to smile coyly, trying to alleviate his embarrassment.

She laughed and playfully pushed him away. 'Oh my God, that was sooo corny.'

He immediately pulled her back to him as if they were both magnetised by something.

For the first time in Courtney's life, the feeling of a man's arms around her caused her heart to beat rapidly in excitement and anticipation. She was so close to him that she could actually feel his heart beating fast in the ripples of the water between them, and in that moment she realised that what he had said was truly heartfelt and totally genuine.

For Dulko, it was as though he had touched something that was so precious he was going to explode with gratitude at being allowed that close to such a delicate and unobtainable treasure. As well as being able to express his feelings to her without the added censorship he'd previously had to adhere to.

They gently and tentatively moved their heads towards each other until their lips were just about to meet.

Suddenly, hundreds of fish darted around them; clearly panicking about something.

Courtney jumped back in surprise just before they had a chance to touch lips. 'What the hell is going on?'

'Don't ask me, I've never been to the Philippines before.'

'Well neither have I; remember. Something's scared them though and I don't think it was the sight of us about to kiss, do you?'

He smiled and chuckled nervously, although more from her comment than the spooked fish.

'C'mon, let's walk.'

'Wait, look … they're coming from all directions and meeting here in the middle. Whatever's scared them is all around us. We're trapped. Where's the professor anyway?

Could he have something to do with it? What happened after you came down here with him?'

'The same as with you; the truth, and now I need to fix what I've started before it's too late. I just hope he didn't have an ulterior motive for helping me.'

'Courtney, there's something you should know. The future ... it doesn't exist. We're all dead. I swear I didn't know before but you taking the rock back has–'

'I know. That's what we need to fix. That's what *I* need to fix, but it means a lot that you told me.'

The fish swirled around more ferociously as more and more appeared, but it seemed that they were being scared into the middle atrium by something else.

'What do you mean ... fix?'

She looked at him, then at the sea life that was swirling around inside the mall. 'I told you that my ancestors were from this place right, but they're not just mine; they're yours too ... they're everyone's. We aren't supposed to be living in the sky. What happened to us?'

'Well ...'

'No, it's rhetorical. I've realised that we were never supposed to create the ability to time travel. I spent my whole life devoted to finding out how it could be done, just to satisfy a selfish notion that I could touch my father again, when I should have been figuring out how to stop it ever being invented in the first place.'

'How can that ever be possible?'

'Time travel exists because of time travel itself, but it couldn't come to be all on its own. It needed us to help it along. The problem was, because of our inherent need to discover, we became willing participants constantly searching for the road that would eventually lead us to it.

'Now, in order for us to stop it, we need to remove the interest, desire and drive that brought us towards it. So that it has nobody to help in its creation. It must be stopped at all costs.

'No country or leader or even religion is responsible for our ultimate downfall. It's time travel; an entity all of its own.

I never thought I'd say this, but its evil - pure evil and unless we stop it, we are all doomed. Don't you see ... time travel is the real bad guy here?'

'Are you serious? My whole existence is based on its existence. Everything I've ever done was instigated by wanting to meet you.'

'I know but at what cost? More than anyone I realise it makes great reading, great TV and it's fantastic fodder to get our brains working overtime, but ultimately the reality of something actually existing that can take us forward and backward in time has terrible, terrible ramifications for the human race. Far worse than any world war you could possibly imagine. Something that seemed fun is now our worst nightmare. You just said it yourself, we're all gonna die. So as I was the first to use it, it stands to reason that I am the one who can stop it.'

Dulko stood in shock at what he was hearing.

'Like you told me, everything has been given to us by our future selves. Time travel has advanced us beyond our years. We should be hundreds, if not thousands of years behind our current capabilities, and if we were, the planet would be in a better state right now. We've clearly invented very little within our own times. For all I know, everything I was ever taught in school about our history was in some way warped and not our history at all, but our future.'

The noise of the swarms of fish darting around began to get louder and louder and Courtney quickly found herself having to yell to be heard. 'With the technology we've been given, we've destroyed our planet because we weren't ready for it. We simply didn't understand the consequences. Our only hope of survival now is to somehow stop time travel ever being used or more to the point ... ever being created.'

'But how? How will we do it? I already messed up by getting you to take the rock back. Then again, maybe we wouldn't be here having this conversation if I hadn't, huh?' He smiled at his attempt to alleviate his guilt.

'Time is our enemy, it controls everything we do. Just like how you figured out how to outrun it when we travel back, we now need to figure out how to outsmart it too so we can undo the mistakes that have been made.'

Suddenly over Dulko's shoulder, down one of the avenues of shops, Courtney saw something appear. A bright red sphere stopped and froze on the spot.

'What the hell is that?'

Dulko slowly turned around and looked at the sphere. He recognised it instantly from his many years on the surface, but he had never seen them anywhere other than hovering over the skies, keeping order and watching everyone. He had also heard stories of people disappearing in the night if they had shown some form of disobedience. Everyone had realised only the hovering red eyes could have been responsible. They had become a symbol of fear and control and the sight of one here warned him that things were about to get very bad. Turning to Courtney and with a stern sense of urgency he said, 'That means we're out of time. We have to go. Whatever you were going to do, you have to do it now.'

~ CHAPTER FIFTY ONE ~

Chasing ghosts

Like the quiet before a storm, the Mall under the sea was unnervingly calm apart from the intimidating dread the lone red sphere had brought with it. After a brief moment of stillness it smoothly backed down the avenue and disappeared out of sight again.

'We don't have long,' said Dulko urgently. 'In about thirty seconds, this place will be swarming with those things. I don't know how they found you here but they have and now they're going to—'

'Come on,' said Courtney, grabbing his arm. 'I saw a sign for a movie theatre up on the second floor, we'll hide in there.'

They both shot upwards in line with a very rusty escalator before disappearing over a glass balcony. Dulko's fear was then realised as moments after they both vanished, hundreds of red spheres came storming into the central atrium like a surge of desperate shoppers, hungry to get inside for the start of the New Year sales.

∞

Inside the observation dome, Eramask and Randlech watched what was happening under the ocean through the eyes of the red spheres. Stood behind them was Professor Thistle in a contained unit that was surging with electrical energy.

'I want her alive. Escort her back here to me,' demanded Eramask.

Professor Thistle looked on quizzically and then asked, 'How did you find her?'

'Do you really think we'd let what happened with you happen again? We put trackers on her implants and you'll be glad to know that your interference and stupid games have made no difference,' she said with spite.

'Maybe she can help us figure it out,' said Randlech. 'Maybe there is a way for us to still survive.'

'You really should listen to her,' said Professor Thistle. 'You're just going to end up killing us all. I can see it in your eyes. It's a look that history has already seen many times before you came along.'

'You know nothing about me. I am here to protect you all, don't you see that?'

'All I see is a crazy and deluded woman; a sad reflection of what governments become if they're allowed too much power, although there's always someone who is destined to bring some form of order back. Courtney's going to stop it, she'll save us all. This isn't the way it's going to end, I promise you that.'

∞

Some of the chairs in the dark and dilapidated cinema were floating near the ceiling while others were still securely screwed to the ground. The only glimmer of light shining into the once magical place of fantasy and escapism was peering its way through a section of damaged ceiling, gently lighting up Courtney and Dulko who were sitting as quietly as possible hoping the red spheres would not find them while they finished their conversation.

Courtney softly leant over and whispered, 'What do you think was last shown here?'

'What do you mean? What is this place? What did people get up to in here?'

She looked at him and grinned. 'Never mind.'

'So what's the plan?'

'It's simple ... I think. I need to go back again. Except this time, I need to go farther. I need to go back to the day it all began – to when I was five.'

'What will that do?'

'Hopefully, it will stop me ever putting the idea in my head in the first place. Erase the interest.'

He looked at her in wonder.

'You see this?' Courtney held up her left hand and showed him the scar that stretched across her palm. 'I got this at my mum's funeral. I was chasing ghosts. How ridiculous, huh? How selfish.

'I spent my whole childhood chasing ghosts when I should have been enjoying the one parent I had left. Now she's gone too, and even when I should've been saying goodbye, I was busy looking for answers to things I had no control over. Perhaps if I'd just stopped and started being a kid, everybody I love would still be alive today. Time travel would cease to exist. We should have been happy to just wait patiently and see what the future would bring us. So easy to say in retrospect though, isn't it?'

'Yeah, it really is.' A tear appeared in Dulko's eyes, but he quickly wiped it away before taking her left hand and holding it in his. 'There are things I wish I could change but they're done now and I just have to live with them. Even if they did cause pain, I promise you, they were done out of love.'

'Maybe I can help. I need to go back and somehow try to communicate with my younger self. Perhaps I can stop her ever dreaming up the notion of travelling in time. If I'm successful, I'll never go down that path. I'll never write my piece on time travel. The professor will never read it. I'll never get invited to study at LosTech, and so I'll never find that rock in my cellar because I won't have put it there. My life and everyone else's won't exist in the same way if at all, because every piece of technology from the future that was passed down via time travel won't exist to get passed down. Right back as far as the Sumerians, up to my present and the boom of the computer age; the planet will go back to its natural state of evolution. We may have to go back to simpler times but at least the planet will be saved.' She thought for a second. 'It's sort of like Noah's Ark all over again, except this time we're going to reverse the flood.'

Still Dulko hadn't understood her analogy and consequently widened his eyes as he scratched his forehead. 'But where's the ark?'

'We're the ark. It's the result, not the method. It's about planet-wide cleansing.'

He looked at her with a determined acknowledgement. 'To cleanse the Earth of all its wickedness.' His tone then changed slightly. 'But we're not God.'

'No we're not but neither was Noah. He was just a messenger or perhaps just someone who wanted to do the right thing. Maybe that's the true meaning of God, doing the right thing for each other without worrying about what you'll get out of it.'

Dulko pursed his lips as if to say, you have a point.

'It's a lot to take in, I know ...' said Courtney. '... and maybe I'm overdoing it slightly. My mum would kill me if she knew I was speaking of myself in the same breath as anyone from the bible. But trust me, I've worked it out and everything hinges on that one crucial moment in my history.'

'There's one major problem. How will you communicate with yourself?'

'That's kinda what I was hoping you'd help me with as well as figuring out how to get me up into space without being seen.' She smiled at him with the biggest grin she could muster so he would hopefully find her hard to resist.

'I've only ever known of a few occasions where some tourists have become visible when they've travelled back, but we've no idea why or how to replicate it. Trust me; they've been trying to figure it out for years. Imagine the power they would hold if the past was changeable.'

'Well as much as I don't like saying it, we need to pray that it is, because it's our only chance.'

Dulko looked at her with some trepidation.

'I know ... it's not really a solid plan, is it? It sort of leaves the future of the world a little to chance, but it's the best I've got and at least if I know it's possible, then there's some hope; rather than just accepting defeat.'

'As far as getting you into space, you'll need to get past the SS.'

She looked at him in bemusement.

'The red ball you just saw, they're the security services - the SS. They're all linked to a particular power tower. I know because it sits just off the coast of my family home. If you can take that tower out, I would summarise that they should all fall to the ground, giving you free passage. I've just transmitted the coordinates to your PEU.'

'Ok then, time to roll. Oh wait – the professor. He'll have been caught. We need to help him.'

'No we don't.'

'What are you talking about?'

'If your plan works, nothing here will matter. He'll be fine. You only have to worry about one thing; how to convince yourself that you have no time for time.'

She looked at him and realised that he was right. With that in mind, she leaned over and kissed him passionately on the lips for the first and possibly also the last time. They squeezed each other tightly together, and Dulko placed his hand behind Courtney, cupping her head like a delicate rose. There was total silence all around, as they sat alone in the movie theatre, embracing each other under the water whilst the outline of their PEU's became visibly intertwined; like two love struck jellyfish in the ocean. They became still for a moment, resting their lips on each other's, before Courtney gently and tentatively backed her head away from his. Even though there kiss was consensual, and neither of them had pulled away from each other in opposition, they still felt a degree of awkwardness and embarrassment as they looked into each other's eyes. Yet at the same time, they felt the most contented they had felt in a long time, removing any urgency to do what they had agreed to. That feeling didn't have a chance to last long though, as all of a sudden five red spheres entered the movie theatre from behind them.

'Time to go,' said Courtney urgently. She leapt up and moved forward, through the water and towards the torn and dilapidated movie screen in front of them.

Dulko did not follow. Instead, he remained in his seat, deciding to stay where he was to take whatever fate had in store and giving Courtney a chance to escape whilst the SS were focused on him. As the five spheres surrounded his seat, he stared at them with all his twenty five years of fear and dread, but then as he turned and looked at Courtney, who had stopped to find out why he was not following her, he realised what needed to be done. Even if he would never see her again because of the results of her actions, he knew that the one moment he had with Courtney as he held her in his arms was equal in gravitas to a lifetime of moments anyone else would have. 'Go,' he mouthed calmly. He then smiled in acceptance and lowered his head as the SS slowly closed in on him.

~ CHAPTER FIFTY TWO ~

Back to where it all began

Courtney burst through the cinema screen and came out the other side into a dilapidated service hallway. The little light there was in there, she left back inside with Dulko. As she soared down the narrow space at high speed, she was only able to avoid the walls due to the rare moments of illumination caused by various electric fish that were swirling all around her and the odd piece of damage to the ceiling above her. Thundering back into the lobby of the cinema and then into the main atrium, she came over the glass balcony, stopped and looked straight down. All there was for her eyes to focus on below were hundreds of red spheres that immediately began to move at high speed towards her. Like valentine helium balloons after having their strings cut, they all rose together; except they weren't filled with messages of love.

Looking around and seeing there was no way out, she quickly realised that up was the only way to go, so she began to move just as a number of the SS appeared directly beneath her. Shooting straight upwards, she kept them on her tail as she neared the ceiling of the mall. With only moments before impact, she stuck her arms out ahead of her and closed her eyes.

'Arrrggghhh.'

Seconds later, she burst through the concrete ceiling; rocks and debris were flying everywhere. Yet they were drastically slowed down by the water, creating an amazing slow motion explosion. Instead of bursting through the rest of the roof, the SS followed her through the hole she had created. One after the other, they looked like Lotto balls being plucked for the draw. Once out into the open, they appeared to be everywhere and were coming at her from all directions simultaneously.

Reaching the surface of the water, she rocketed out into the air, her PEU flashed as if someone was trying to contact her. 'Hello,' she said cautiously.

'Courtney, you don't know me, but I'm here to help you,' asserted a gentle female voice.

'Whoever you are, I'm a tiny bit tied up right now.'

'I'm aware of that, but you need to know that those things chasing you don't have PAL – but you do. Someone's coming, I need to go. Please, you need to help stop this. We've been waiting a long time for you to come.'

The transmission ended. Courtney immediately stopped in midair and thought about what she'd just been told by the stranger. Then she turned to look downwards. Hundreds of SS were coming up below her and within seconds, two were by her side. Eramask's face appeared on both of them in a strange kind of facial stereo.

With a little trepidation Courtney said, 'Who are you?'

With malevolence and loathing Eramask responded and said, 'I'm the end of you.'

Courtney smiled. 'What the hell kind of cheesy arse movie did you get that line from?' She looked at the two spheres then down below at the ones that would imminently be all around her. She pondered what the mystery voice had said seconds ago and slowly pulled her arms in towards her chest whilst clenching her fists at the same time. With an almighty burst of energy, she pushed her arms outwards and smashed her fists straight into the face of Eramask using all the strength she had. The live image on them disappeared and the two spheres sizzled with an overload of electricity. Withdrawing her arms she then smashed them down on top of the spheres. The strength of her limbs sent them crashing downwards at incredible speeds, down towards the other spheres which were speeding upwards, creating a wonderful domino effect as they came crashing into one another. Stunned to see her actions had caused a massive midair collision, she used the temporary reprieve to catch some breath. *Whoa!* She never thought she'd actually be able to relate to a comic book character, but looking down at the devastation she had just caused, and with a cocky smirk she said in her best superhero impression, 'Well ... I think you'll find that's now the end of you.'

Her new superhero status gave her some much needed breathing space and so she remained still, trying to get her head around everything before setting off again across the ocean towards the almighty power tower that Dulko had given her coordinates to.

Something forced her decision to get moving a lot quicker than she would have liked though, as she noticed hundreds more SS following behind the fallen few. As she proceeded to move upwards to get away, she suddenly noticed them coming straight towards her from above as well, and so she had no choice but to put her head down and her arms out in preparation of the imminent impact. Within seconds, they were everywhere. Plummeting to the ocean in the hope of losing some, she managed to dodge lots of them as she flew downwards, whilst at the same time smashing through huge waves that burst out of the swirling ocean. Spheres that got too close, she whacked with her fist, batting them away as if she was in the middle of a game of *Super Mario*.

The area had become crowded with more and more spheres making it harder for Courtney to negotiate around them anymore.

'Oh for goodness sake, this is ridiculous.'

Then there was a moment of relief, as ahead of her she saw the huge tower she was looking for as it came up out of the ocean like a solid, frozen, white tidal wave.

Although situated far out in the middle of the ocean, the tower was so large it was just about visible to a large proportion of the surface dwellers. Some people on the ground noticed Courtney as she flew at great speed towards the tower with urgency. Word spread and more and more gathered to watch the unusual commotion. As she got close to the concrete structure, she suddenly changed trajectory and shot straight up into the sky. When she was high enough, she turned and descended at phenomenal speed, straight back down towards the tower.

Eramask was in a fit of panic and screamed, 'What is she doing? What is she doing?'

'She's doing what you should've done long ago,' said Professor Thistle with spite. 'Taking control.'

'Don't let her get near that tower,' she screamed at the top of her voice. Veins almost literally popped out of her neck and temples. 'Stop her at once, you hear me? Stop her.'

Courtney neared the structure from above and was only metres away from it, travelling at over one hundred miles per hour. At the same time, the spheres hurriedly gathered, one on top of the other, creating a solid wall in front of the tower.

The crowds on the ground had become vast. Thousands were watching on, as for the first time it looked like somebody was trying to help them make some changes. Many were wondering if it could finally be their long awaited salvation.

The spheres then did something very odd. Rather than going straight for Courtney, they began to imprison the structure instead. However, this time it was for their protection rather than somebody else's imprisonment. Almost like children protecting their mother, they flew in from all directions and created layer upon layer, until the entire tower was covered in red spheres.

'What are they doing,' said Courtney to herself inquisitively, as she began to slow down. 'Oh my God, they're getting scared,' she screamed in realisation. 'Ha, who's afraid now huh?' As she asked the question, huge powerful waves crashed up against the tower making the conditions very scary. Although she was in the safety of her PEU, she was well aware that she was not from that timeframe. Her subconscious suddenly made her very aware that she was miles out in the middle of a dangerous ocean with terrible weather conditions all around her. 'Oh crap. If this PEU fails for any reason I'm dead.'

Courtney knew there were very few options left. *If I fail here, I may well be stuck in this doomed future forever.* That was an option she refused to take. So she stuck her head down and sped up again with fierce determination. When she was only seconds away from hitting the spheres, she altered her course and dived straight down towards the violent waters below. Entering the water with a huge splash, she then disappeared underneath the ocean.

After a few seconds, a muted bang was heard and consequently the tower shook and dust and debris rained down. She then shot back out from under the water's surface and blasted high up into the sky again. Large numbers of spheres broke away from the makeshift defensive wall to give chase, but she had really got the hang of controlling her thoughts now and passed them with ease. She then plummeted back down and into the water for the second time.

Another muted bang and the tower shook again causing more dust and debris to hit the water like bullets from an AK47 rifle. Once again, she emerged from the water and looked at her target as it moved precariously. Immediately another humungous wave bombarded the structure and huge cracks subsequently appeared that travelled right up the tower to its tip.

'C'mon Mother Nature, do your thing ... or are you in cahoots with time?'

As she spoke it seemed she may have a friend out there as the huge waves in the water not only gave it a nudge to help topple it, but had forced the inner layers of SS straight into the concrete mass. In the distance she heard a unified cheer from the thousands who were watching and willing the powerful lone visitor to defeat their captors.

∞

'She's ruining everything,' screamed Eramask, as she turned and looked at Professor Thistle. 'It's time for her to die – and you're going to watch. She cannot be allowed to cause total disruption within our society. I'm sorry I didn't want to do this, but she's forced my hand.' She turned back to the monitors in the dome and transmitted instructions to the SS to end it.

'You can't do that,' said Professor Thistle as he helplessly stood in his crackling energy prison. 'That's murder.'

'And what will she be doing to this entire civilisation if she manages to succeed in changing the past? I think I would use a slightly more detrimental word ... genocide perhaps. Wouldn't you?'

'You think allowing the planet to be destroyed, thus killing everyone on it is a better option?'

'If that's what nature has in store for us then who am I to stand in its way? I'm not God Mr Thistle, and I don't claim to be either. Do you?'

Professor Thistle looked at Eramask and then back to Courtney on the screen where hundreds of SS spheres were closing in on her.

∞

The tower continued to slowly move as if it was crumbling from beneath, but Courtney thought she needed one, maybe two more goes at the base to make sure it would topple as amazingly, it was the size of a small town.

However, just as she was about to dive back down to pile through the spheres, she was taken aback by a bright round energy pulse that struck her PEU. The impact caused a huge electrical surge to shoot through her body, and for a brief second, she felt a tremendous pain in her brain.

In the time it took for her to regain composure, the spheres had created another wall directly below her, yet this time it wasn't for defence – they were preparing to attack.

'Oh God, that's not funny,' she said to herself. 'That really hurt.'

Just as she realised it wasn't a game and that she could actually die, hundreds more energy pulses were sent in her direction.

'Oh crap-a-doodle, this is actually quite serious. I'm so gonna die, I'm so gonna die,' she gasped in panic.

She launched herself at full speed into the sky, attempting to avoid death; a certainty if that many energy pulses were to hit her at the same time. She flew in a full circle before coming back on herself towards the bulk of SS that were protecting the tower. A number of them had also given chase and were coming up right behind the pulses. As the pulses neared her toes, she became more concerned than ever and quickly dived straight down to the wall of spheres, but at the last second, she turned and pulled back up into the sky.

The pulses behind couldn't change course in time as they were following her trajectory far too closely. Instead, they flew straight into their own defensive wall causing hundreds of SS to crash down into the sea below.

∞

The 'surface dwellers' went crazy with excitement and anticipation of what the wonderful turn of events could mean. Chants of 'FREEDOM' could be heard echoing through the wind.

∞

Courtney continued up into the sky. 'I really need to get out of here and find the loophole that can take me home before more SS decide to fry my brain.'

Thousands more SS soared up behind her, shooting pulses to stop her at all costs. The barrage was never-ending and her options seemed to have run out as they quickly gained on her. She struggled to focus as her mind had become tired from all the concentration. Pulses relentlessly and narrowly shot past her, and she did her very best to dodge them, but they were becoming all too frequent as they came up all around and were now very close to completely surrounding her. Feeling very vulnerable and terrified, she knew she had become a very small fish in a large ocean full of predators. With too many to take down with physical combat, she had run out of road and had nothing left in her defence. Nobody was left to help either, leaving only her own initiative to rely on.

She slowed down, allowing the remaining spheres to come up from below and totally envelop her. If she wanted to remain alive, she had no choice but to surrender. So reluctantly, she came to a complete stop and looked around, pondering what had become of her life. 'I've failed. I'm so sorry to everyone who ever trusted me. My instincts were obviously wrong. I can't change anything.' Tears appeared in her eyes as she looked at the spheres with horror and disappointment.

They surrounded her just like they had the professor earlier, and there was no escape. It was an impenetrable wall with layer upon layer piled deep. 'You win Eramask.' Courtney lowered her head and bitterly accepted defeat in preparation of whatever was about to befall her.

Eramask's face instantly appeared on the inside of the spheres. 'So … any last words, Miss Nivots?'

'You just don't stop with the cheesy lines, do you? But I suppose you're allowed a few when you're on the winning side. So you got me, now what?'

Eramask smiled from ear to ear. 'Now, it's time to–'

As Eramask was about to deliver Courtney's death sentence, a blessing from somewhere manifested itself out of the blue, stopping her mid-sentence. The outer cases of some spheres randomly started to disappear. As if by magic, Eramask's face cracked away, as one by one the outer shells vanished.

Eramask screamed to Randlech in despair. 'What's going on? 'Randlech, what's happening? Fix it. Do something – now.'

Courtney looked slightly bewildered as she watched the spheres disappear. 'The tower,' she whispered. 'It must be collapsing. Oh thank you God … whoever you are.'

∞

Down on the surface the tower was crumbling which had weakened its transmission strength due to the particles dispersing from each other. The pummelling from Courtney had been enough, even if it had taken longer than she would have liked. The crowds on the surface were cheering in unison, willing it to fall. With Courtney's pummelling as well as the energy and power from thousands of minds, the entire tower suddenly collapsed down into the ocean. With an almighty crash, the mass impacted heavily with the water causing huge waves to rise up on either side like a mini tsunami. After a few moments, the crowds that had gathered were hit with a torrential downpour. However, it was like tears of joy from the sky as they danced and splashed around in the resulting mud.

Hysteria had taken control as if they were in some kind of unified trance and they began the biggest celebration the surface had ever seen.

As the outer shells of the spheres disappeared, what was inside them also became visible - nothing. The rumours were true - there was nobody inside. They were indeed just empty eye balls of energy watching everyone and sending the information back to the security hub in the sky.

'Oh thank you, thank you thank you thank you,' said Courtney. She was extremely relieved as she didn't much like the idea of hundreds of helpless people plummeting to their death, even if they had tried to kill her. Suddenly she was all alone in the sky, at peace and one with the wind as she floated proud above her masterful, if somewhat delayed triumph. 'Oh yeah, it's back on baby,' she said gleefully with a nod of the head, having found her courage again.

Everything suddenly pointed to the fact that she was destined to meet her worse nightmare once again. She had defeated Eramask's army, but she knew that she now had a meeting with an unknown entity in the hope of possibly finding the answers to just about everything.

So she set course for space where she would locate and enter the hole that would take her back - back to where it all began.

~ CHAPTER FIFTY THREE ~

Cheeky monkey

For the first time since her extraordinary journey had begun, Courtney was now standing in a moment she had dreamt her whole life of returning to; a moment from her past that would go on to irrevocably shape and mould her future. Even though she had already travelled back once before, the moment was very different, as she was not only many years in the past, but she would also now come face to face with herself; something that her previous trip back of a few days would never be able to compare to. Seeing a moment from the past that she was a part of but had no real tangible memories of was completely surreal, as even the slight changes in fashion were clearly evident making her feel like a bit of an outsider looking in on a time that she'd normally only get a smidgen of what it would be like to exist in by watching a BBC documentary on 'how we used to live.' However, putting the nostalgia aside, she knew exactly what she had to do and knew that though it would not be easy, so much rested on her success, aware that if she could somehow communicate with her younger self, she could stop everything she had been through from ever happening. However, the possibility of changing the past went against everything she had ever believed in. Yet if, as she had always believed, none of it was possible and time couldn't be altered, everyone was ultimately doomed. As far as she was concerned, it was the biggest moment of her entire life; a moment when she would get the chance to try and save the world. Not something many eighteen year olds could say.

Yet something else concerned her more; something that was etched into her mind; an added motivation. As a side effect of saving the world from destruction at the hands of the human race, she knew that she would also get to finally see what really happened in her bedroom all those years ago. Who – or what had visited her and why?

She couldn't help but think it was incredibly ironic that an evil and angry spirit was the determining factor that led her on a path that would help her to try and save the world from its own evils, only to then lead her back to the same day to face the same spirit once more. Does it have a greater meaning? Courtney wondered. Was it really evil or did it somehow know that it would lead me here? Was it random chance, or was it just one really big dream that would very soon be over?

'Mummy,' said a very confident five year old Courtney in an assertive manner, unknowingly interrupting older Courtney's thoughts. She was sitting cross-legged on the floor with her arms out in front of her in a meditative pose. 'I'm being a monk,' she said placing her hands on her hips in annoyance.

Mazel who was sitting on a yoga mat next to her replied, 'Not a monkey?'

'No – a monk.'

'But you are a bit of a cheeky monkey.'

'I know I'm a cheeky monkey, but right now I'm being a monk. Ok?'

'You know that monks are bald?'

'Yeah, but–'

'Yeah, but no but.'

'Mum-myy-ya, stop annoying me.' She was becoming frustrated by her mum's attempts at humour. 'I'm going to show you what monks do when they pray. And I don't have to be bald ok.'

'I'll show *you* in a minute,' responded Mazel, still verbally playing with her daughter. Mazel found the serious conviction behind everything Courtney had said quite hilarious and had done since she was very small.

'Mummy.'

'Yes, I'm listening.'

'You're still laughing.'

'I'm not, honestly. Right, sorry. Go on, I'm listening now, cross my heart.' Pursing her lips together, she wanted to purposely show Courtney that she was trying very hard to stop smiling.

'Right, earlier ago, I saw someone doing it at school, but I decided to put my own words on top. So this is what you do if you want to be a monk.'

'Ok, and this all happened *earlier ago*,' said Mazel in jest.

'Yes, now you cross your legs like this; like when we do the yoga.'

Mazel wore leggings and a leotard, having just finished one of her weekly yoga workouts. Her legs were stretched out in front of her with her arms supporting her from behind; the total opposite to what Courtney had described.

'C'mon mummy, like this,' said Courtney, who was sitting with her legs in the correct meditative position.

'What, I have to do it too? I thought you were just showing me.'

'Oh just – do it. It lease I'm not asking you to do more yoga,' she said, raising her pitch at the end and opening her eyes wide, attempting to mimic the way adults talk.

'You mean, *at* least?'

'That's what I said; it lease.' Mazel chuckled at Courtney's naive mispronunciation of words. 'You're so funny.'

'Mummy ... you're funny,' replied Courtney, in a very matter of fact manner with her eyes wide.

'You're funny-err.' Mazel dropped the smile and replaced it with a competitive dead serious conviction.

'You're the funniest in the whole world. Anyway, just – stop distracting me, this is very important, the future of the world depends on it.

'Oh goodness, the future of the world ... ok I'm listening.'

'So ... you cross your legs, hold your hands out like this ... and then hum with your eyes closed. And mummy ... guess what?'

'What?'

Young Courtney's face lit up with excitement. 'Then, you ask for what you want in life and just like magic, it comes true.'

'Really?'

'Uh huh,' said Courtney. 'Like this.' She then began to speak in a monotonous tone with the last word of each sentence elongated, just how she had heard the monks chant on TV. 'We pray for there to be no more suffering in the worrrld. All diseases will disappear and there will be no more fightinnng.'

Looking at her, Mazel was genuinely a little taken aback by the depth of what her daughter was asking for.

'We pray that children in poor countries will have food to eat and clean water to drinnnk and that one day everyone on the planet will be equallll.'

Feeling very guilty, Mazel dropped her sarcasm for a moment as she realised her daughter was actually trying to say something serious and from her heart.

'We also pray that tomorrow mummy will buy minty ice cream with multi-coloured cones and maybe some Krispy Kreme doughnuts when she goes shoppinnng.' She slightly opened her right eye to sneakily glance at her mum's reaction and upon seeing her mums disapproving deadpan face; a smile began to creep in at the side of her mouth. On seeing the guilty smirk, Mazel immediately pounced onto Courtney like a lioness on a hunt, knocking them both on to their sides and then tickling her all over. Courtney burst into fits of giggles and could not control her laughter as mother and daughter rolled around on the floor in a genuine loving bond. Always able to find a special way of getting her mother to do things for her, Courtney had found that some form of manipulation was the best way to achieve the task and it was something she had mastered from early on; akin to the art form perfected by the greatest politicians of our time.

'I knew it was cheeky monkey really, you little monster face,' said Mazel as she continued to tickle in retaliation.

Young Courtney could barely get a word out through the

laughter, which after a while became silent due to the inability to suck any air in. It was a cross between the joy and pain that you get when you are a child and you cannot work out if you enjoy being tickled, or if you're actually going to die from lack of breath.

'Right my little choochiwooch. For that, you can go up and brush your teeth and then get to bed,' said Mazel, as she finally released Courtney from the loving ritual of torture.

'Doohhwww,' moaned Courtney, knowing her defiance would give Mazel permission to resume her punishment.

'Mummy, mummy, Ok - I'm going. Just stop tickling mee-ya.' Courtney's eyes had glossed over with the tears of joy from being tickled, and although she clearly enjoyed her little tussle with her mum, the joy was juxtaposed by the fact that she was severely struggling to regain some breath. One more tickle and she thought that could possibly be the end; she would not have enough air left to get through it.

Over in one corner of the room, older Courtney stood having just watched everything unfold. She had been there for a couple of hours taking it all in, knowing it may be the last time she would get to see her mother. Witnessing the great relationship she used to have with her before the incident was forcing her to once again see her mum in a positive light. Crying with joy at seeing her younger self have such fun, she watched on as mother and daughter developed a strong bond right in front of her eyes. Of course she remembered the day very well, but not because of the banter she had just been privy to as that had long since faded away and was replaced by the memories of the tumultuous events that followed. The fun she obviously had with her mother before being sent to bed that night had shamefully long been forgotten. Instead, the events which were due to unfold later that evening had erased any positive recollections completely from her thoughts, causing her to realise that it was definitely worth coming back if only for the few positive hours she had spent in her mother's company again. If I die now at least I die happy. She thought to herself upon witnessing and refreshing herself with the fond memories she was realising she should have kept close to her heart; the little fragments of bliss and the feeling of security and tender love between mother and child that so often gets lost to time as age creeps up from behind.

At that moment, five year old Courtney got up from the floor and went upstairs to brush her teeth. The time had arrived when little Courtney would finally be alone and older Courtney could get to work trying to communicate with her younger self before the arrival of the infamous and life-changing spirit.

The night was still relatively young, and older Courtney still had a few hours to wait until midnight; the moment her future changed forever, so she decided to stay with her mum and watch TV; something she hadn't done in many years and at least while her younger incarnation was getting ready for bed. The need to just be with her, even if only one of them was aware that they were actually together, meant a great deal.

In a strange place in her head, she sat on the sofa as close as she could to her mum, imagining she too knew she was there and that the only reason they were silent was because her mother's favourite TV show was on.

Occasionally, Courtney turned in response to something on the screen but then quickly realised *when* she was and that she could not be seen or heard. Feeling a mixture of emotions and ecstatic she had the opportunity to sit with her mum once more, she was also brought to tears by the frustration of not being able to let her know she was there.

Suddenly from upstairs a voice shouted down. 'Mum?'

Mazel responded and although she was now concentrated on the T.V. she said, 'Mmmmm?'

'Love you,' sparked little Courtney with a chirpy high pitched tone.

Mazel grinned and offered a little chuckle.

Older Courtney looked at her mum and gave her a melancholy smile. 'And I *still* love you,' she said quietly. There was sadness but more prominently a hint of regret in her assertion.

'I love you too, chooch. Hurry up though, I still need to

shower,' said Mazel to the younger incarnation upstairs without realising she had actually responded to not one but two daughters from two separate times. However, for one of them the sentiment resonated a lot deeper that time; the one whose tear had just dropped from her eye and landed on Mazel's hand.

Mazel panicked and waved her arms around in an exaggerated motion, attempting to flick away the spider or beetle that she thought may have landed on her. Courtney looked around but could not see anything on the floor or any flying insects in the air.

Mazel finally calmed down, looked at her hand and saw the wet droplet. Dismissing it, she wiped the tear away not realising that she had just made contact with an eighteen year old Courtney that she never got to see or meet.

A split second passed before Courtney realised that it must have been her tear that she had reacted to. *But that's impossible.* Then with some hope and anticipation she said, 'Did you just feel that? Mum – did you feel that?'

Mazel remained seated, totally unaware of older Courtney's presence next to her. Courtney shook her head over her mum's arm, desperately trying to make another tear drop. However, the more she tried the more her sadness was replaced by excitement combined with frustration which was causing her eyes to completely dry up. Squinting hard and making all kinds of strange faces, still nothing happened; the tears were gone. 'If part of me can touch something in the past by accident, then I should be able to concentrate and do it on purpose,' she said loudly but still to herself.

She stood up with a new found determination and hope, but there was also a little anger in amongst her feelings as she looked at the clock on the wall. 'I've got three hours to figure it out.'

Scurrying to the kitchen where she could be alone to concentrate, she tried hard to focus and formulate everything she knew. If she could work out how to touch stuff, then that would surely mean she could change things. But if she succeeds then surely that would mean other stuff could be changed which would mean futures are not as pre-destined as she always thought they were. 'Hmm,' she pondered.

With that in mind, she set to work, trying out all the things she could think of in the hope of being able to touch something.

Hour after hour passed and she was progressively becoming more tired and agitated at her failure to connect with anything. She repeatedly tried to grab things around her, thinking about different emotions and feelings in case one of them played a part, but she just kept passing right through them and it was taking its toll on her arms and her muscles that were now aching. Glancing over at the clock on the microwave she widened her eyes and said, 'Oh crap, it's nearly midnight. This is not good, this is not good. What am I gonna do?' In just ten more minutes, she knew that little Courtney's disposition would go from being playful, to a serious long-term devotion. 'I'm not gonna let this happen. I can't fail everyone now. I've gotta be here for a reason. Everything happens for a reason, right?'

In an anxious and agitated manner, she turned to leave the kitchen. Just as she did, Mazel entered holding an empty coffee cup and walked straight through her daughter. Courtney stood still as her chest thumped from the shock of coming that close to her mum again; almost like hugging someone in a dream until you awaken and realise that they are not really there. Reacting instantly, she raised her hands to her face. As she did, she felt something knock against her hand. A split second later, there was a smash and the cup that Mazel had been holding was on the floor in pieces.

'Ohhhhhwa,' said Mazel, frustrated by her apparent butterfingers. 'What is wrong with me?'

'No mum, it's not you. I think it was me again,' said Courtney as she walked in a reflective daze down the hall and up the stairs. 'What is going on, and how am I doing it? What's the connection? Please God, if you're really out there, tell me what to do.'

Arriving on the top landing, she grabbed hold of the handle on the door that led to her old bedroom and her heart skipped a beat as she took a deep breath and contemplated walking into a moment that she had thought and talked about for the last thirteen years.

Feeling her head spin from the magnitude of the situation as the blood rushed around her veins, all her nerve endings tingled as she prepared herself before finally taking a step forward to enter her old bedroom. As she took a look around inside, the most surreal moment occurred as she saw herself sat on her bed, dressed in her old red Chinese-style pyjamas. Taking a very deep breath, brought on by a massive apprehension and the biggest amount of nerves she had ever felt, she realised that all the resentment toward her mum; all the guilt and longing from losing the only connection she had with her dad; all the visits to the psychiatrist year on year; all the anxiety from being singled out as a freak and all the pressures of being responsible for saving the planet from the destructive effects of time travel – all came back to that moment.

Older Courtney now knew that everything that ever meant anything to her was about to be instigated by whatever was set to transpire over the course of the next ten minutes.

~ CHAPTER FIFTY FOUR ~

Mr Time 2

Little Courtney was sitting crossed legged on her bed, sketching on her white board. So far she had drawn clocks with earlier times and dates from the past as well as a hand drawn sketch of her dad and a large bowl of ice cream with the word 'Minty' written above it.

'I remember doing that,' whispered older Courtney, who was still in a state of disbelief from actually being in that moment once again. She whispered because although she was there to communicate with her younger self, the shock of actually being there still made her incredibly nervous. 'This - is really weird.'

A real sense of fear struck Older Courtney as she looked about her room mentally reliving her past memories; literally feeling like she had walked into a nightmare flashback in a video game. However, as she looked at the digital clock on top of the cabinet, she suddenly realised that the real nightmare was about to begin.

Slowly walking over to the corner of her room, the place where the spirit had first appeared, she called out and said, 'Are you here? Who are you? What did you come here for?'

Little Courtney was lying back on her bed staring at the stars and planets on her ceiling, and older Courtney's mind was now taken over by the years of longing to know why she had been visited all those years ago and why the spirit took her precious gift away.

Suddenly, all thoughts about saving the planet were gone. As the pivotal moment in her life approached again, she remembered the reason she was really there, and so she took a dangerous detour away from the professor's objective. 'I could still try to communicate with my younger self afterwards,' she said in a slightly unconvincing manner whilst trying to convince herself that the moment was now all about something else. 'The spirit; the poltergeist or whatever else it would prefer to be called.'

Her emotions became stronger by the second, and her heart palpitated at the thought of the spirit's imminent arrival. She turned and watched little Courtney stand up on her bed before stepping towards the clock.

Older Courtney gasped as she literally felt her heart in her mouth. Little Courtney jammed her finger into the clock and pushed the hands backward.

Older Courtney's face was red from apprehension and she shouted, 'C'mon, where are you? Show yourself, I know you're here. Why did you come? What did you want from me?'

Little Courtney looked up at the ceiling, lost her balance and fell back onto her bed. Older Courtney watched as she slowly opened her eyes and realised she had not travelled anywhere. Looking over at the clock, little Courtney saw the time was correct, rolled back over onto her back and giggled to herself. 'Ok, Mr Time, I may be too young for you right now, and you may have beaten me once again ...,' she said, just as older Courtney remembered saying thirteen years ago. '... but I promise I'll figure you out one day, my everlasting friend.'

Watching on, older Courtney knew the big moment was eerily close. Her breathing was fast and deep and she was swallowing repeatedly, trying to rid herself of the sandpaper-like sensation she felt in her throat as she continued to watch. After a short while little Courtney began to pray and older Courtney's memory was telling her that as soon as she finished praying, the spirit would appear. She didn't know what to expect but wished that something would happen between now and then that would finally allow her to communicate with it. Little did she know her wish was about to be granted.

Little Courtney reached over and picked up the Jesus figurine before closing her eyes. 'Saint Michael the Archangel, defend us in battle. Be our protection against the wickedness and snares of the devil. May God rebuke him, we humbly pray ...'

Older Courtney mouthed the words of the prayer as little Courtney spoke them. She hadn't spoken them for a very long time but remembered them as if they were said yesterday. 'O Prince of the heavenly host, by the power of God, thrust into hell Satan and all the evil spirits who wander through the world for ruin of souls. Amen.' Little Courtney opened her eyes and leant over to place the figurine back.

'No, keep it in your hands. Don't put it back or you'll lose it forever,' shouted older Courtney in a panic.

Her words were not heard and little Courtney's hand knocked against the side of the bed causing her to let go of the figurine. The precious item then fell towards the wooden floor for the second time in older Courtney's lifetime, but although she remembered the moment well, she instinctively and without thinking dived forward to catch the treasured item before it reached the floor.

Little Courtney's eyes widened in panic, but she was too scared to look over the edge of the bed to see what had happened. Instead she collapsed onto her mattress, huddled up and pulled the duvet closer to her.

Older Courtney caught the figurine in both hands just before it landed on the floor and quickly put it back on the side before she even had a chance to think about what she had done. It was an instinctive reaction and it all happened in a split second.

Little Courtney scrunched up her face waiting for the inevitable crash on the floor, but of course that moment never arrived and her pained expression turned into a look of confusion. She pulled the duvet closer to her and closed her eyes once more.

Older Courtney stood in shock as she realised that she had just touched something again. 'I just stopped it from breaking. Oh my God.' Her expression changed to determination. 'Ok then, so now it's time to stop you, whatever you are.' She turned toward little Courtney. 'Be brave,' she whispered and then turned to face the empty room. 'Show yourself, do you hear me? Show me who you are. I've waited thirteen years for this day, and I'm well and truly ready for you-'

'Angel of God, my guardian dear ...,' interrupted little Courtney. '... to whom God's love commits me here. Ever this day be at my side, to light and guard ...'

Older Courtney's mood had become quite frantic and she looked around the room and screamed, 'Where are you?'

'... to rule and guide, Amen.' Little Courtney reached up and flicked the switch on the lamp that was above her bed. The light went out and older Courtney stood frozen as she waited.

A split second later, little Courtney jumped up with the sharpest of movements and sat hunched in the top corner of her bed with a pale complexion and an expression that was nothing short of petrified as she breathed heavily whilst tears trickled down her face.

Older Courtney froze as she realised the moment had arrived. She turned to see the fearful look on little Courtney's face and the instant she saw her tears, all the memories from that night came rushing back. She remained still; partly from the shock but also from the apprehension of knowing that the spirit was now somewhere in the room with her.

'Mum,' pleaded little Courtney, but only a whispered cry came out of her mouth as fear had paralysed her voice.

Older Courtney then noticed that her little self was strangely now looking in her direction and suddenly remembered that the spirit did first appear by the window that she was standing right next to.

Tentatively and slowly she moved her head around. There was nothing to her left, so she turned her attention to the only place remaining; her right. Her eyes squinted in anticipation. Is this it, the moment I find out what everything means, she asked herself?

However, there was nothing to her right either. Unable to understand, she spun around in a full circle but still couldn't locate the spirit anywhere. 'Where are you?' She looked left; right; up; down; all over in quick, sharp and agitated movements. 'Why can't I see you?' She became more stressed by the second. She had waited a very long time for the big moment and it was not going the way she had always imagined it would.

Little Courtney was still repeating her silent call to her mum, but all of a sudden as older Courtney was herself panicking, she reacted with a stronger intensity. Her head jerked and pulled back and her eyes widened as if something had changed which indicated to older Courtney that the spirit was definitely in the room and history was repeating itself right in front of her eyes. Worst of all, there did not seem to be anything she could do. She could not communicate with her younger self and could not even see the thing that had changed her life so dramatically in the first place.

'Did I really make it all up? Are you just sat there pretending to see something?' She had a confused and slightly angry tone to her voice. 'No, I won't believe that. It must be something to do with the fact that I've come from the future,' she rationalised as she continued to look around the room. 'I must be on some kind of different frequency, similar to why little me can't see me. This really sucks. What am I supposed to *do* if I can't *do* anything?'

Her voice became high pitched as she tried to understand everything. 'Right,' she said with a new found determination. 'If I can't see you, then I've got nothing to be afraid of, and you can't get in my way. So let's see what you've got. If you can get to her, then so can I.'

Older Courtney walked around the room to see if she could build her skills at communicating. Already having touched something three times since she had arrived, she was thoroughly convinced that she was there for a reason and knew she could not just give up and go home now.

Jolting about the room and swooping her arms and body through anything in a desperate attempt to try and make contact with something, she became increasingly frustrated as she realised that she may never get to understand why things happened unless she could make contact. Quickly running out of time she realised she had to reassess why she was there.

Little Courtney was completely frozen, except for the tears that were rolling down her face. She tried to speak her prayers again, but hardly a sound came out of her mouth.

Older Courtney started to mull some things over and then came up with an idea. 'Simple, but possibly my only option left remaining. So ... there doesn't seem to be any way of talking with little self, but ... what went through my mind in the days and weeks that followed this event? The figurine ... it all comes back to saving the figurine of course.'

She realised that if she could somehow get hold of it again, she could stop it ever being destroyed. 'That has to be the best way of communicating indirectly with myself and in doing so; it will take all the power away from that thing. I've done it once, I'll do it again.' She knew that deep down it was her longing to keep some kind of connection to her father alive that drove her devotion and fixation toward time travel in the first place. So she rationalised that if the figurine was never destroyed, she probably would've been contented.

Walking over to the side of little Courtney's bed, she looked at her as she sat frantically repeating her prayers. 'Poor me,' she said with genuine sentiment. Tears poured down little Courtney's cheeks and older Courtney knew that she had very little time to accomplish anything. At that moment, little Courtney continued to follow her original path, as she suddenly pushed back against the wall and started shaking profusely.

'Its right here, isn't it? Don't worry, I'm gonna stop this. I promise. Your life will never be the same again.' She paused for a second and was then overcome with frustration, realising that the spirit must be right next to her and that she would never know who it was or why it came. 'What are you, why are you doing this? You stupid, irritating little piece of ... arrrgghhh.'

As she reached boiling point she began to cry as her emotions completely took over her. Then out of nowhere, she had a flash of memory that sparked a small glimmer of hope and possibility. 'It left the room,' she said as she turned to the window. 'I remember. Right about now, it left the room. Where did you go?' She walked over to the wall by the window, but as she did a tear of frustration fell from her face, and without her knowledge it impacted with the floor. Just as the tear reached the ground, she stepped on it and continued to walk towards the wall before passing straight through it.

On the other side, she saw the trees and the light from the moon shining down. There was nothing else - no spirit, nothing. 'I've had enough of this,' she said loudly. 'I'm running out of time. I don't care who you are anymore. I just need to fix this.' She then turned and walked back through the wall.

On re-entering the bedroom, little Courtney was still sat hunched in her bed. The time had come. She was probably less than a minute away from the figurine smashing into a million pieces. Quickly, she walked over to the chest of drawers and stared down at the figurine, trying desperately hard to focus all her energy on that one item.

Time had dramatically run away from her so in desperation, she tried to grab the figurine but her hands passed straight through it. The more she tried, the greater her frustration and disappointment became. Never in her whole life had she felt that much pressure; a feeling that was so heightened she began to feel dizzy from all the chemicals that rushed around her body. Angry at the thought of just being seconds away from being unable to change anything, she knew it was an impending catastrophe that would eventually and quite unbelievably lead to generations of misery after the discovery of time travel. 'It can't end like this,' she shouted out as she fought through her tears. 'It just can't. This isn't how it's supposed to be. Give me something,' she pleaded, as she looked up, appealing to a higher intelligence. 'Give me a way of communicating – please. I beg of you. Now is the time to prove you really exist.'

As older Courtney screamed, it seemed her prayers were answered. Little Courtney reached across her bed, put her hands on the rail and screamed in older Courtney's direction. 'Shut up, just shut up.' Her face was red from the amount of force she had put into her outburst.

Older Courtney realised she had just been told to be quiet and lifted her head. 'You can hear me?' A surge of the strongest emotion she had ever felt travelled from her head all the way to her toes as she turned (totally stunned) toward younger Courtney.

As she spun around, her arms swept across the dressing table and passed through everything until the pivotal split second moment that she came face to face with herself.

On seeing her own younger face staring straight back at her, she felt another even bigger surge of unbelievably strong emotion. For the first time ever it seemed someone from the future had made contact with someone in the past. Yet what heightened older Courtney's emotions beyond all realms of understanding was that the person she had made contact with - was none other than her own self; a shocking revelation she wasn't ready or prepared to accept.

In that instant, her palm somehow connected with something on the table. To both their horror, the Jesus figurine flew into the air and both their eyes widened as they watched it soar through the air.

Both their worst nightmares came true. The figurine hit the wall and smashed Jesus into a thousand pieces. In unison, the two counterparts let out a distressed yelp and older Courtney consequently turned and stared at little Courtney who stared straight back at her in shock and disbelief.

Suddenly, all the questions older Courtney had ever asked were answered right there and then upon the unveiling of the disturbing truth.

So she stood in shock at what had just been revealed to her by her own actions. Her whole life had been spent searching for answers, but she had been searching in all the wrong places and had always blamed others for things which were ultimately a result of something she was the architect of.

'It – was – me,' she said very slowly, as she looked at her younger, distraught self. 'It was you.' For the first time she stared directly into her own traumatised eyes.

People always say to look in the mirror before judging others; her younger counterpart was one mirror that had just truly unmasked everything.

Older Courtney could not get out of there quick enough, so she hurriedly left the room in disbelief and panic and went through the wall, down into the trees that faced her house and into the darkness. Nobody could actually see her but she just had an innate desire to get away from the house.

As she stood in the moonlit wooded area that looked down over the town, her legs involuntarily gave way as all the energy slipped from her being. She dropped her weary body down onto the muddy leafy ground. Her emotions were all over the place as she tried to understand what everything meant. 'How did this happen?' In astonishment she then spoke the words that would define her life. 'I'm the glow. I'm the ghost; the spirit. Why didn't I see it sooner? How could I have been so naive? Stupid, stupid, stupid, selfish little fool.' Guilt and blame were riding pretty high as she realised everything that had happened since she was five was indirectly down to her own doing. 'Can this really be true? Oh my God, ghosts are time travellers. Dulko did say it, 'Occasionally you can become visible when you travel back.' Unbelievable ... and every time someone has, they've been labelled a ghost; the walking dead from the past. When in actual fact they are very much alive and from the future. So the professor was right all along, it was just his hypothesis that was wrong – ghosts don't exist. Or they do but everyone's definition of them is completely inaccurate. But that means I was also right, everything *is* pre-destined. It was so simple. To stop everything, all I had to do was *not* come back. I couldn't even work that out. I never had to communicate with anyone. I never should have come here; it was just a selfish obsession. I'm so stupid.' She hit her own head at her self-appointed stupidity. 'And now it's too late. I can't even fix it. If I come back again, I'll just become a second spirit for myself to panic about. My one chance has gone, and to think I was actually holding my figurine in my hand. I had it. I was actually holding the whole reason the planet is in jeopardy.' She sat silent for a moment with no idea what it all meant and what her future would now hold.

Then her expression changed as a more selfish but wholly satisfying thought suddenly struck her. 'I've just got the answers I've spent my whole life searching for. Oh my god, there's no big conspiracy. Nobody wanted to take my dad away from me. It was all just one giant accident.' She smiled with joy for the first time since she had arrived. 'And as I was also right about the future, there was nothing I could do to stop it. I'm certainly not the only one in the world who has lost family, but at least I now have all the answers to my questions. My life has truly come full circle, and I can now start to live for whatever destiny has planned for me. For the first time everything makes sense. It may not be how I would have imagined it, but it all makes sense. What more could I ask for?' Feeling a strong sense of relief as if a very heavy weight had been lifted off her shoulders, she looked into the sky and took a gasp of air as if she had just reached the water's surface after being held down for a life threatening amount of time; something she had waited for since the whole unfortunate and terrifying event occurred in her bedroom. Liberated from the chains of her past she was now ready to embrace her future with contentment.

In reflection she remembered what Dr. Flux had said to her in their last meeting, *'Maybe you'll find out it was you who smashed it all along. Do you really want to put yourself through that? Think what it will do to your mother.'*

'How right but so wrong you were; it was absolutely all worth it.' She was complete now and nothing was going to change that. She looked up at the dark sky and called out. 'So Mr Time, it would appear that I couldn't quite figure you out after all. It seems you always had the upper hand. This time however, I think I can actually say ... I win ... my everlasting friend.'

~ CHAPTER FIFTY FIVE ~

Search and you shall find 2

'Ok, are you doing this or what?'

'I know, I know,' said past Courtney to Alexandra. 'I'm talking a lot because I don't want to think about it. In a second I'm just going to do it; without thinking; probably mid-sentence while I'm expl–' suddenly she broke off and ran as fast as she could towards the hole, screaming as she went.

Stood over in the trees at the side of the garden was present Courtney. She would remain a silent and invisible observer until that moment when her past self would disappear into the loophole allowing her to hopefully re-appear back in sync with her present. She had travelled back through a different loophole to the one that she had first entered, just as Professor Thistle had informed her to as the original one had collapsed shortly after she had first left. As she watched herself and Alexandra, she thought about the possibility of walking straight over there to stop her past self from leaving in the first place. If it were at all possible, she knew she could stop everything right there and then. However, as much as she really wanted to, there was absolutely nothing she could do due to not quite being in sync with her own time just yet. Even if she could, everything she now knew about her own life, which had made her the most contented she had ever been, would all go away. 'Everything happens for a reason,' she said reassuring herself that the end of the world was a very, very long time from now and was for someone else to worry about.

'Don't forget to send me a postcard,' Alexandra called. 'Oh, and if there are any hot guys, give them my number.'

Past Courtney closed her eyes as she reached the point in the garden that was just in front of the phenomenon before leaping into the air as high as she could reach, and screaming as loud as she could scream.

On hearing Alexandra's words, present Courtney was hit with her only moment of regret. 'I not only found a hot guy, but I think I may have stupidly fallen in love with him too.' At that moment, her past self stretched and slowed down around the perimeter of the hole. Then in a flash, she was gone; sucked into the vacuum. 'Whoa,' whispered present Courtney as she took a step backward in shock. Something then cracked under her foot, a sensation she hadn't felt for a while so she looked up to see if she had been heard by her friend.

Alexandra glanced toward the trees and Courtney shuffled backwards. Her friend shook her head and dismissed it as a rabbit or a squirrel. She then turned and walked back towards the house.

Courtney sighed with relief but at the same time was struck by the thought that she had possibly touched something from the present that she was trying to get back to. So she knelt down on the leafy ground to see if she had really made contact with a twig. *Have I actually returned?* Noticing a ladybird crawling across some leaves, she stuck her finger in front of it to see if she could touch it. As the ladybird reached her finger, it stopped and shuffled around, not sure where to go. 'Can you see my finger, little one?' She gently poked it and to her relief, it crawled up onto her hand. She stood up and stared at the insect as it explored its new surroundings. She had either just figured out too late how to touch things in the past, 'Or ... I'm back,' she said, smiling from ear to ear at the realisation.

The instant she realised she had returned to her own time, she desperately wanted to run to the house and tell Alexandra everything, but she remained in the trees for a moment and contemplated what would happen if she did. After what she had just witnessed when she was five, everything was telling her to leave well alone.

'What will be, will be and if I do anything to try and change things, it'll either make it worse or it it'll just stay exactly the same and change nothing. There isn't even any evidence that things can change at all, let alone for the better.'

Suddenly remembering that Professor Thistle was due to arrive at the house very soon to jump into another hole, she thought about what he had said to her when they were in his office under the sea. *It did incense me that you made it first. So much so that if your friend Alexandra had got in my way instead of helping me ... well, without being graphic, let's just say I was ready to do whatever it took.*

She panicked slightly but knew that if she told Alexandra anything now, there was a risk that events would play out differently when he arrived, and he might end up hurting her. She knew she wouldn't be able to forgive herself for that. No – she had to leave things as they were; at least until the professor had gone through the hole. 'Once he has gone, then I can show myself, because everything in the future that happened will then be safe.'

Hours passed by as she just continued to impatiently pace up and down amongst the trees, waiting for Professor Thistle's arrival. She was getting hungry and knowing her house was yards away with all the refreshments she needed was making her all the more tetchy.

Still, she knew she had no choice; all she could do was wait patiently for the right moment and so spent the next day camped out in the woods under a huge fallen tree that she had used as a secret playhouse when she was a child. She started to feel the effects of what living rough really meant though, as she had never actually spent an entire night there. No food, no money, no bed and nothing but leaves, mud and insects for friends; the closest she'd ever feel to Alexandra's previous existence on the streets.

The next night, as she sat going a little crazy from the solitude, she heard a car as it drove up the hill. Running to the edge of the woods, she watched as a minicab pulled up alongside the house. Inside, talking to the driver, she saw Professor Thistle. 'Wow, you look so young,' she said to herself in surprise.

Professor Thistle got out of the cab and the memory of how he had described his mood at that time made Courtney nervous. Unknowingly, she edged to a break in the trees and became visible.

Professor Thistle turned around to look at his surroundings, and at that moment he caught sight of her. He stared for a moment and then walked towards her. Panicked, she ran through the woods as fast as she could, away from the house. She had trouble picking her way past fallen trees and rocks as she only had the moon for light, but she knew the woods better than anyone and so it was no problem making sure the professor couldn't find her. But did he see her? The possibility of changing anything because of a stupid mistake panicked her as she thought about what the consequences could be if he had actually recognised her, even from a distance.

Stopping by an old rusty barbed wire fence, she waited for a while in the darkness. Suddenly, she was shaken from her daze by a huge noise that came from the direction of the house. Through the trees, she could see all kinds of different coloured lights as they exploded into the sky like a New Year celebration. 'The hole ... its collapsing.' As quick as she had run away, she ran back to the house, knowing that at any moment Professor Thistle would vanish into another hole. Once he was gone, she knew it was at last her cue to go home.

Maybe the nightmare was finally coming to a close. Any repercussions from failing what she was supposedly meant to achieve were thousands of years away. There was plenty of time to think about it if need be. Having run quite a distance in an attempt to get away from the professor, it took her a good fifteen minutes to find her way back to the house in the darkness.

By the time she got there, she knew that the professor had already figured out how to create another hole, because just as she arrived through the trees and onto her front driveway, she saw a huge explosion coming from behind the house.

She ran to her front door, opened it, entered the hallway and went through to the kitchen where she looked out of the window and was faced with the familiar sight of gases and colours emanating from a powerful phenomenon.

She had arrived just in time to witness the moment Professor Thistle jumped into the newly created loophole.

She saw Alexandra stood on the other side, watching as it started to collapse. The much smaller size of the professor's hole meant that it disappeared almost instantly. The house and garden were left in complete silence with mess and debris everywhere.

'Bon voyage,' whispered Courtney a little sadly.

Alexandra turned and walked towards the back door to come back inside the house. Not noticing Courtney as she wandered into the kitchen, she pulled a mug down from a cupboard and flicked the switch on a new kettle.

'Tea, please,' said Courtney.

Alexandra immediately jolted upright and spun around with a scream, almost breaking the windows with her high pitch. She placed her hands over her mouth in fright at the sight of Courtney. 'Oh my God, oh my God.' She ran over, jumped on her and squeezed her like an orange. 'What the hell,' she exclaimed, as she briefly let go of her for a second, before squeezing her again until she finally released her hold and stood staring in awe. 'You're alive and in one piece. I don't believe it. How are you? What happened? Didn't you go anywhere? How did you get back so quickly?' Everything was coming out in a frenzied manner as she prodded and poked her to make sure she had come back without any missing body parts.

'First of all, stop poking me; I'm really here I promise. But secondly, oh my God you won't believe where I've been. Now I'm back though, I'm back for good and I won't be going anywhere again.'

'Wow,' gasped Alexandra.

'Actually, I came back literally a second after I left

yesterday, but for your safety, I had to stay away until now.'

'Hang on – the professor; he's just gone off to try and find you and–'

'I know, I know. Don't panic, it's all fine, he's fine and he did find me. Or at least he was fine when he left here. I'm not actually sure he's ok now, or then … in the future I mean.'

Alexandra looked at her, and as usual was totally bemused by what Courtney had said.

'Oh never mind. Anyway, what I want to know is this. Why did you choose to help the professor when I told you to call Becky, Ellie and Nathan?'

Alexandra stared at her in silence, a little lost for words.

'It wasn't her fault,' said someone over by the back door with a familiar voice.

They both looked around to see who had spoken and to Courtney's surprise, Becky was standing in the doorway with Ellie and Nathan peering over her shoulders.

'She did call us,' said Becky. 'But the professor was hell bent on getting here first and had all of us arrested. Nathan's mum, who would you believe turned out to be a lawyer, got all the charges dropped. The cops let us go in time to catch the next flight.'

Courtney looked shocked at their experiences and with a surprised tone said, 'Arrested?'

'It's a long story,' said Ellie as the three of them walked into the kitchen. 'Suffice to say, you better take Wazer off your Christmas card list.'

'Anyway, we've finally made it,' said Nathan. 'But made it for what, I'm not sure. What on earth are you doing here, and where is this wormhole?'

Courtney and Alexandra looked at each other and smiled.

'Was this just one big prank? Are there cameras here from a TV show? Have we just been Punk'd or something?' Nathan was worried that nothing that they had been told was true, especially after calling on his mum's powers to get them there.

'Don't worry guys, it's all over,' said Courtney.

Courtney and Alexandra took them to the cellar and

explained everything that had happened. Alexandra also became a willing recipient of the story as Courtney told them everything she had experienced over the last week. They were stunned at the scale of it all and could not believe that they were part of something so monumental.

After Courtney had finished, Alexandra made a cup of tea for the two of them and three coffees for the Americans.

They sat down in Courtney's living room trying to digest some of what had been said. For a while they sat in complete silence until Ellie piped up in her usual quirky manner. 'So this fellow – on a scale of one to ten, how would you rate him?'

'Yet again, you don't fail to astound us,' said Nathan. 'Time travel; a murderous professor turned humanitarian; an evil government intent on destroying us all; super powers and people flying through the skies and living above the clouds ... and all you can think about is a man? Unbelievable.'

Everybody looked at Ellie who widened her eyes at them. 'All I'm saying is that he sounded like an important part of her journey.'

'Actually you're right, he was. He was amazing. I don't know if anyone could ever compare. I've never met anyone like him,' she said with a proud and dreamy, yet sadness filled tone.

'If he was as big as you said, how could anyone compare?' said Ellie with a cheeky grin.

'The question is,' said Becky, 'what do we do now? We can't just sit back and do nothing.'

'That's exactly what we do. I told you, there's nothing we can do. Just relax and be thankful you'll be able to live out the rest of your lives in relative safety and normality.'

'But what about our future relatives ... surely we have a duty to try and do something? After all, from what you've said, it's the people who ultimately destroy the planet.'

'It's just too big a message to get over to people. I mean who are we? Governments and political groups have been trying for years to get people to change, but when people get comfortable, change is the last thing they want. Governments know this and use it to make more money while pretending they want change. It will continue forever until we're all dead, and there's nothing we can do.

'The only hope was to stop time travel, but I failed. Time is in charge, not us. Time is the planet's true adversary. All that could save us now is if everyone started to think before they acted; but I don't see it happening. On the whole, the human race is just too selfish.'

'But we still have the source of time travel in the cellar,' said Alexandra. 'Surely we could do something ... couldn't we?'

At that moment, they all turned to the window as they heard vehicles pulling up on the gravel outside. Ellie jumped up to have a look out the window. 'Oh, cripes.'

They all looked at her and Becky said, 'What is it?'

'I would imagine ...' said Courtney. '... that the source Alexandra just mentioned is about to become the property of the governments I just mentioned. I told you, there's nothing we can do; it's just too big for us to even contemplate on. We simply can't change the past – or the future.'

'She's right,' said Ellie.

Everyone looked at Ellie wondering what reflections she could offer in support of Courtney.

'No, no ... I mean the vehicles. If they're not government, then you have a hell of a big delivery arriving by the number of cars, vans and trucks out there.'

'I did wonder how long a house could stay glowing without somebody noticing,' said Alexandra with a smile.

'They'll have been monitoring the energy that thing is spewing out ...,' pitched in Nathan, '... and wondering what on earth it is. No wonder they've come mob-handed.'

In the following hour, all hell broke loose as the house was taken over by officials from special units within the government. The whole place was cordoned off from below the hill and fences were erected around the perimeter, stopping anyone coming near.

'It's like something out of *The X Files*,' said Ellie.

Courtney had no idea what would become of her house

but after everything she had been through, she did not care much anymore, as long as she was compensated for any losses. The house had been nothing but trouble since the day she was born and she thought it was time for a fresh start.

Before she was removed from the house forever though, she wanted to make sure she took any precious items with her. Speedily she grabbed a suitcase and piled it full of anything that was valuable. For the most part, that meant sentimental value as opposed to monetary, and the suitcase was soon full of clothes; old family photos, jewellery and a few trinkets and ornaments she had inherited from her mother. Alexandra did the same before the whole gang were escorted down the hill and away from the house, where they were routinely tested for radiation and chemical exposure.

The mayhem had made the national news, but it seemed as though the government were keeping quiet about what was contained in the house. However, from the scale of the operation, it was clear to the world that it was something big.

People in the village below knew who owned the house and so Courtney's name was also all over the news. Locals who had witnessed strange lights and explosions were telling all sorts of stories about what they thought had happened.

The news channels were happy to hear all the conflicting stories until they had something official. Talk of real life ghosts, aliens and most absurdly, time travel filled the broadcasts, but the world was just waiting for the truth about what had happened at 'The House on the Hill'.

Courtney and the rest of the gang waited in one of the many Winnebagos that had been placed at the bottom of the hill to find out what was going to ultimately happen to them.

'It feels like we're America's most wanted,' said Ellie, as she poured herself another complimentary coffee.

'We'll be fine,' said Courtney who was sitting at the table with her suitcase open in front of her, looking through some old photographs. 'They're just trying to decide what to say to the world first. We're not terrorists. We've discovered time travel. It's gonna be huge. We're gonna be huge; trust me.'

'We're going to be so famous,' said Ellie gleefully as she

stretched the slats on the blinds open with two fingers and peered out. Ellie couldn't hide the fact that the sound of fame and fortune was very appealing. 'It's going crazy out there,' she said excitedly.

'Oh my God,' said Courtney with a flabbergasted expression as she sat and stared at one of her photos. 'There it is.'

Nathan, who was sitting opposite her asked, 'There what is?'

'The thing that started this whole conundrum in the first place – my Jesus figurine.' There was a melancholy tone in her voice as she stared at her most precious possession.

A tear appeared in her eye as thoughts of her father came flooding back. For the first time in her life the feeling of anger was replaced with satisfaction and contentment.

'Look.' She passed the photo across to Nathan with a smile. 'That must have been taken when I was around three or four.'

'Ah, don't you look cute,' he said, mocking her.

'I do as it happens, yes, but look beside me on the shelf.' She leant across the table and pointed at the photo with her finger. 'See that figure of Jesus and the little girl? If it wasn't for that, we very likely wouldn't all be sitting here right now.'

'That's weird,' said Nathan.

'Yeah I know,' said Courtney. 'Tell me about it. And it's even weirder to think that if Jesus was never born, none of this would have happened because there'd be no figurines of him. What a huge time ripple that is, huh?'

'No, you don't understand. I've seen it before.'

The others all looked around upon hearing what he had said.

'What are you talking about? That's impossible.' Courtney's expression of happiness suddenly changed.

'It's either impossible or the world's largest coincidence, but I saw that exact figurine in the professor's office.'

'That's ridiculous. Don't be stupid,' said Courtney.

'I'm serious. It was exactly the same. I wouldn't forget it because it was the only ornament on the shelf. It was next to the book the professor tried to hide.'

Everyone stared at each other as if they had all just seen a ghost. Ellie then whistled the theme tune to *The X Files*.

'There must have been loads of those produced in China,' said Becky, as she tried to make logical sense of it. 'It's got to be a coincidence, a large one granted but a coincidence nonetheless.'

'There's one other thing though ...' said Nathan.

Ellie looked at him with utter contempt and said sarcastically, 'Oh - what now, Mulder? Was it some kind of alien artefact?'

'When I lifted it out of the way to get the book, it had some kind of inscription on the bottom. I didn't bother reading it, but I saw some words ... what were they?' He squeezed his eyes with his hand, desperately trying to remember what he saw.

Courtney's eyes widened in anticipation as she stared at him in fear of what he may be about to say.

'I can't remember. Oh no wait, that's it ... yeah. It said something about searching for something.'

Courtney then blurted out and said, 'Search and you shall find?' Her heart was palpitating heavily in anticipation of the confirmation.

'Maybe ... no, I don't think so. Oh, I'm not sure. I didn't actually read it. I was too focused on the book at the time. I didn't think it was important then, did I.'

'This doesn't make any sense.' Courtney collapsed back onto her seat.

Then Alexandra pitched in and said, 'Oh my God, speaking of books ... did you get your book from the hallway table?'

'My book?' Courtney was still slightly distracted. 'No – but it doesn't matter anyway. As it turns out, it's actually the professor's book that's important. That's the one with the real science in it.'

Becky looked up, slightly concerned because of her involvement in stealing it. 'Why? What happens to it in the future?'

'They end up holding it in reverence as some kind of important book for mankind. To make matters worse, I apparently end up getting all the credit for it.'

'But that's impossible,' said Alexandra.

'No it's not. I told you, I've been there and seen it.'

'Court, I'm telling you. It can't be the professor's book. I was afraid to tell you, but just after you left I thought I'd better put the books somewhere safe, so I went to put them in the shed at the bottom of the garden. But as I was running I tripped and both of them fell in the pond. Yours was just at the edge, but the red one fell right in and because of the bushes it took me a while to get it out because I couldn't reach it. The red one was totally unreadable but yours survived ... kind of. I panicked and ran straight out to buy a new notepad and spent hours last night rewriting all your stuff in it before the original finally fell apart. I had to throw it away but I swear I managed to write everything in it down again.'

Courtney looked at her, totally stunned and at a loss for words. After a few moments she spoke, but instead of anger she used a curious tone and asked, 'What kind of notepad did you buy?'

'To be honest, it was the first one I found. Sorry, but I was in a hurry, so I didn't think about it too much. You could always get a better one. Oh no wait, you can't coz they've seized the house now, haven't they?'

'What colour was it?'

Alexandra looked at Courtney with a bemused look on her face. She thought that now was not really the time to be asking about her colour choice but nevertheless said, 'Red, I think. Why?'

~ CHAPTER FIFTY SIX ~

The Beginning

Courtney had really been on one hell of a ride, but as with all rides, they eventually slow down and come to a stop. However, when the park is about to close you occasionally get one more free go, and as she took in both what Nathan and Alexandra had just told her, she realised that she better hold on as the carriage was about to start moving once again. She collapsed back into her chair from the realisation that it must have been her work that the future held in such high esteem. All that time, she thought that she was some kind of fraud and that it was the professor who deserved all the credit. Yet she quickly realised that there must have been something in her doodlings that people in future years would grab hold of and look to as some kind of message. As much as she knew that her writings were nowhere near as scientific as Professor Thistle's, it began to make a little sense to her, as most of what she had written was about how the world would eventually suffer at the hands of humankind, as well as some of her best theories on time travel. Her writing didn't say anything that was particularly new, but she thought that the sentiment behind them combined with being the first to travel through time must have turned them into something profound.

At that moment, there was a knock on the door of the Winnebago and a short middle-aged man in a suit entered. 'Which one of you is Courtney?'

'That's her,' said Nathan, pointing.

Courtney turned to face the man and said, 'Why?'

'There's a man outside who says he's been searching for you for years. His name is Dave. Do you know him? He's quite insistent on seeing you.'

'Dave?'

'He says he's come on behalf of your mum. She's sent a message for you or something.'

The others looked at her wondering what was going on, especially Alexandra who was more than aware that Courtney's mother was long gone.

'Ohhh - Dave,' said Courtney, as if she remembered who he was. 'Of course – yes. Definitely, send him in.'

Alexandra was drinking her fifth miniature bottle of white wine that she had furtively taken from the complimentary drinks refrigerator and after the man had left she said, 'Do you really know who he is?'

'Haven't a clue,' replied Courtney. 'But with everything that's happened, anyone who mentions my mother, I'll make time for.'

The door to the Winnebago opened slowly and a tall, well-built man in his mid-forties entered. He had a lived-in face with quite a few wrinkles and plenty of greying hair.

'Who in the hell are you and what do you know about my mum?'

Closing the door he remained on the step, a little taken aback by the five sets of eyes that were burning a hole in him. 'My name is Dave. I used to be a fireman.'

'What do you want, a medal?' Alexandra seemed to be developing some sort of mood, as she continued to become tipsier by the second.

'I'll give him one,' said Ellie, with a twinkle in her eye.

Nathan looked at Ellie with yet another disappointed expression.

'A medal I mean, I'll give him a medal ... all firemen deserve a medal, right?'

'Not me,' whispered Dave solemnly.

'And my mum, how do you know her?'

He looked down at the floor uncomfortably. 'About three years ago, was the last time I was on duty. Ever since then

I've been wrestling with something. You see, it was the day I watched a young Filipino woman burn in front of my eyes. She was trapped inside her car after a horrific accident and all I could do was watch as the flames ate her up.'

The room fell silent for a moment while they took in what he had said. They all knew Courtney's mum had passed but didn't know the details.

Ellie looked at Courtney and said, 'You're half-Filipino aren't you?'

'I don't think I'll win any prizes for guessing that was my mum,' she whispered, without taking her eyes off Dave.

'Yeah, I believe it was,' he said apologetically. 'I'm so, so sorry. I couldn't get her out. I tried so hard. I swear on my life, but the flames were just too powerful and too quick.' His story affected the rest of the gang in the room, and they all began to feel very uncomfortable as they listened in on the details of how Courtney's mother passed.

'Is this all you came here for, to alleviate your guilt because you saw me on T.V.?'

'That's not it,' he firmly asserted. 'I did spend years living with the guilt, but I've just got my head around the fact that people do need me. Unfortunately, on occasion circumstances dictate that there will be nothing I, or anyone else can do - it's all in the hands of something bigger than any of us.'

'Amen to that,' said Courtney, realising the similarity in what he had said, to what she had just tried to tell the others. 'So why are you here then?'

He took a deep breath before he spoke and everyone could see he was clearly nervous. 'The thing is,' he said tentatively. 'Before she ... passed away, your mum told me something. It was a message she said I had to get to you. It didn't make any sense at the time and for years the thought of confronting you overpowered the urgency of the message, but ... I made a promise that I would find you.'

'Ok, now you're losing me. What on earth could she have told you that's so important?'

Due to the rising uncomfortable nature of the situation,

the others surreptitiously all glanced at each other.

'I've probably built this up too much now. It probably won't mean anything to you and I'll have caused unnecessary upset, but after seeing you on T.V. I couldn't help but think it may mean something.'

'What – did she say?'

'She told me, to tell you ...'

Everybody in the room was hanging on his every word and as a result the whole place was silent.

'Just before she crashed, she told me to tell you that she believed you and that she was so sorry for all the years she didn't. She said she saw something on the side of the road. She said ... it was glowing, and she couldn't take her eyes off it, causing her to crash. It took her by such surprise that she crashed into the lamp post.'

Courtney sat with her mouth open for the second time in ten minutes, gawping at the fireman because of everything he had just confessed. Bombshells were being thrown at her like tennis balls.

'I don't know if that means anything to you,' he said cautiously.

She collapsed down onto a chair in shock and stared at the table in front her with her jaw wide open. 'I don't believe this.'

'I wasn't sure if it would make any sense to you,' he said. 'But I just thought now was the time I should live up to my promise to your mum and by your reaction, maybe I should have come sooner. I'm so sorry.'

Becky looked over at Courtney and could see the concern on her face. 'Courtney ... are you ok? What does it mean?'

She raised her head and looked at everyone. 'Much, much more than you could possibly imagine.'

Alexandra pitched in, slightly slurring and said, 'It was a ghost wasn't it? Your mum saw a ghost and now you feel that all those years of you being treated like a freak could've been avoided if only she'd known sooner.'

'A week ago that's exactly what it would have meant, but no ... that's not it. Not quite,' said Courtney, with a furrowed brow, still trying to work everything out.

'Oh look, what a surprise. Alex gets it wrong again,' mumbled Alexandra, in a self deprecating way.

'There's one thing I forgot to tell you all about the future and ... about ghosts,' said Courtney.

Ellie excitedly pitched in and said, 'What, what is it?'

'Well let's just say ...' She turned to Ellie. '... if you are ever undressed and you think you see a ghost ... get dressed ... and quick, because they're not ghosts at all. They're ...' she paused as she looked around at everyone in the Winnebago.

Dave was now hanging on her every word.

'They're time travellers.'

Dave's face was a perfect picture of bewilderment. He did not realise quite what the message he'd been holding onto for all those years really contained. He couldn't help but wonder if Courtney had lost the plot a little from all the grief she'd obviously been through.

'Maybe I should go now, you lot seem to be a little ... bit ... well, I'm gonna leave you to-'

'Dave, you really don't realise what you've just done by bringing this message to me, do you? Look, I'm sorry I was so rude to you earlier. I'm sure you're a fantastic fireman, but with all due respect, that stuff really isn't important anymore.' She brimmed with a new found confidence, although it was mixed with a lot of anger as well.

Alexandra then said, 'Court, what does this mean? Spell it out for us thickos.'

'Well firstly, it means my mum was actually murdered.'

Everybody's eyes in the room widened as they took in the horrific comment.

'The glow she saw was a person. Somebody from the future was standing there at the side of the road, which caused her to crash. Don't you see? If ghosts are time travellers, then it was a real life living person that made a real choice to be there and caused her to crash, and it must be connected to the fact that I've just travelled to the future and pissed some people off. Whoever it was wasn't just stood there randomly. The technology in the future isn't just used to stand at the side of the Great Cambridge Road for no apparent reason. Now, she died before I even went to the future, so I understand it was probably always inevitable and I guess I have to think about the possibility it could even have been me going back to try and save her - perish the thought. But I'm still gonna find out who it was if it's the last thing I do. I may not be able to get my dad back, but it would appear that someone from the future wanted my mum dead as well, and I want to know why.'

The others all stared at her in amazement and shock, except Alexandra who for some reason seemed to be getting increasingly angry about something.

'It all makes sense,' exclaimed Nathan. 'You've actually solved the mystery – and answered the age old question of what ghosts really are. What an absolutely amazing revelation. It's just genius.'

'Well if you think that one's good, here's the kicker. You see strangely ... and more important than her being deliberately killed ...' she said, as she turned to Dave. '... is that my mum ... well that wasn't how she died.'

'What do you mean? She hit a lamppost outside the Crazy Horse kebab shop. Trust me; it's not a day I'd forget,' said Dave bluntly.

'Oh, I'm sure that's what you remember,' said Courtney, as she turned to the others. 'But guys ... the thing is, that's not what I remember. You see here's the thing. *Before* I left, she didn't crash into a lamp post. She crashed into a tree; a huge tree on the Great Cambridge Road. She hadn't even got to London yet. I must've *retained* the memory because it was still the case when I left. Somebody from the future did kill my mum ... but for some reason, they were slightly delayed in doing it, causing her to hit a lamppost outside some kebab shop. Now from everything I've learnt, that's impossible but it's happened nonetheless. This means the past can be changed ... and if that's the case ...'

They all looked at her blankly.

'... well don't you see? That means there is a way for us all to be saved.'

Everybody in the room smiled with excitement as they comprehended what the future could now hold except for Dave, who was still a little out of his depth and unsure if he had accidentally walked onto a movie set. 'It was definitely a lamppost,' he muttered to himself.

'But wait,' said Becky. 'What can you do if the government has commandeered your house and taken the device that makes it all possible? They'll never let us go near it again.'

Everybody's excitement was suddenly sucked away by Becky's vacuum of a statement.

Courtney looked around, noticed the change in mood and then smiled. They looked at her in anticipation. She reached into her pocket and pulled out the rock that she had broken away when she had crushed the sphere with her power assisted limbs; the very same rock that had helped her when she pushed the cellar door open. She held the rock high above her head in salute. 'This is the device; a piece of very special rock that after zapping in the microwave took me through time and initiated this whole adventure. This was solely responsible for me finding the answers to all my questions, even if Nathan has just made me realise that there are still a few yet to be answered. And you're right Becky – we can't allow our future to be destroyed, no matter how far away it is; I realise that now. We have an opportunity here guys. This rock will help steer our futures towards a hopeful and healthy planet everybody can be proud of.' She then threw the rock to Nathan, who immediately reacted to the unusually heavy weight. As she stood there and faced everyone, she realised that they had all become solely dependent on what came out of her mouth, causing her to suddenly feel a huge sense of responsibility.

The idea of her having written some kind of bible served to strengthen certain leadership qualities, giving her a new found focus. 'But first, we're going back to LosTech to get a look at that figurine. Something's telling me that it has a lot more to do with this situation than I first realised.'

As Courtney spoke to everyone, Becky began to ponder

everything deeply. Whilst in her thoughts, she began to look around and then something caught her eye. Noticing Courtney's Grand Central Station notebook, poking out of Courtney's bag, she discreetly pulled it free to find that it looked like it had been wet and that there were no pages inside. It also wasn't red as Alexandra had just said it now should be. She carefully and quietly opened it while Courtney was still speaking and on the only page left inside, she saw a handwritten note that made her eyes widen with confusion; the same note that Courtney had read in the playground three years earlier.

"DON'T TRUST ALEXANDRA."

Becky immediately looked at Alexandra who was next to her and quickly put the book back in Courtney's bag.

Meanwhile, Dave was still standing by the door with his mouth wide open. He hadn't been asked to leave and couldn't quite bring himself to. Although it all seemed crazy to him, he found it a bit like watching a death defying act; he knew he shouldn't watch, but couldn't stop himself.

Alexandra who had been seated silently for the last few minutes, turned to Becky without realising what she had just seen and whispered with a slur, 'It's all about Courtney, isn't it? Everything's always been about Courtney. Well what about me? Maybe I'm not going anywhere.'

Becky looked at her slightly confused but was now also a little concerned by her tone. 'What is the matter with you? You're drunk aren't you?'

'What-everrr.'

Becky dismissed her and then turned back to their self-appointed leader. 'So Courtney, you're saying ... this isn't the end?'

Courtney looked around at everyone in the room, and then with a forceful determination she looked straight at Becky and said, 'Oh I guarantee you, *this* - is just - the beginning ... or the middle ... or it could be the end. Oh whatever ... all I know people, is that this is *our* beginning, and the adventure starts - now.'

ABOUT THE AUTHOR

K.T. Jae is a graduate of the University of East Anglia and Mountview –Academy of Theatre Arts London. Qualifications include a BA (Hons) in Theatre Arts and a Mountview Diploma. K.T. has been writing in various forms since 1999, primarily concentrating on screenplays. Riddle of the Red Bible is K.T.'s first novel and fulfils a lifelong dream of creating a unique and exciting new angle on time travel. K.T. lives in Hertfordshire, England with a very patient partner, two daughters who are waiting to star in the movie and a rather large Rhodesian Ridgeback dog that would love me to stop writing, get my jacket on and do some exercise.

Printed in Great Britain
by Amazon.co.uk, Ltd.,
Marston Gate.